BLACK VALLEY

Also by Charlotte Williams

The House on the Cliff

CHARLOTTE WILLIAMS

BLACK VALLEY

MACMILLAN

First published 2014 by Macmillan
an imprint of Pan Macmillan, a division of Macmillan Publishers Limited
Pan Macmillan, 20 New Wharf Road, London N1 9RR
Basingstoke and Oxford
Associated companies throughout the world
www.panmacmillan.com

ISBN 978-1-4472-2356-6

A CIP catalogue record for this book is available from the British Library.

Typeset by Palimpsest Book Production Limited, Falkirk, Stirlingshire
Printed and bound by CPI Group (UK) Ltd, Croydon, CR0 4YY

Visit www.panmacmillan.com to read more about all our books
and to buy them. You will also find features, author interviews and
news of any author events, and you can sign up for e-newsletters
so that you're always first to hear about our new releases.

For John

ACKNOWLEDGEMENTS

I would like to thank Margaret Halton for her help, support, and guidance in getting this book into print. I am also extremely grateful to my editor Trisha Jackson for her skill and patience throughout the process. Thanks also to Katie James, Natasha Harding, and all at Macmillan who have worked on the book. And to my husband John Williams, as ever, for his continued support in every way.

PROLOGUE

Llandaff Green is a quiet place. There's a statue of a man in the middle of it, a cleric of some kind, frock-coated and gaitered, with a walking stick in one hand and a pile of papers in the other. He looks as if he's stopped on his way to work to check that all is as it should be in the diocese: in front of him, the crumbling remains of the old castle; to the left, the cathedral spire, poking up out of the hollow below, the crows flying around it; to the right, the road that leads down to the high street, into the bustle of town. He's a Victorian, this gentleman, and he looks out for the type of people he understands and recognizes: the dean, the canon, the chaplain, scurrying down the steps for matins or evensong; the organist arriving to rehearse the choir; the armies of elderly women who make tea, and bring flowers, and tidy and polish, and keep an eye on the visitors; and on Sundays, of course, the parade of portly burghers who arrive to celebrate the Eucharist, and their own good fortune, in this little corner of the city.

Then, of course, there are the heathen folk who have no cathedral business, making for the graveyard and the playing fields and the river that lie beyond it: the fishermen, the dog walkers, the teenage lovers. He keeps an eye on them, too, just in case there should be trouble. But in truth, very little of note has ever happened up here on the green, apart from that dreadful night during the war when a bomb blasted off the steeple and sent tombstones from the graveyard flying through the village. Order was quickly restored, of course, and since then the even tenor of life has gone quietly on, and in the view of the Venerable James Rice Buckley (1849–1924), it is likely, and highly desirable, that it should continue to do so in the future.

There are occasional newcomers, though, from time to time. They seem out of place, as if they have no business here, strangers from a foreign, modern world. Here's one of them now, driving in from the high street in his shiny silver car, slamming on the brakes, and parking slap in front of the green.

He gets out, this man, barely glancing up, and bangs the car door shut. He's got the hood up on his coat, and he's wearing a scarf over his mouth. He clicks some kind of contrivance. The car lights up and gives a shudder. He walks away quickly, a little too quickly, as if he doesn't want anyone to see him. Furtive. But there's no one here to see him, anyway. The green is deserted.

The Venerable watches him as he goes. He's walking towards the artist's house. She's a bit of a mystery, that one. Grew up there with her family. Nice man, the father, decent fellow. Dead now, and the rest of them moved away. Lives there all by herself, she does; never goes near the cathedral, even though it's just on the opposite side of the road. Lovely house, white, arched, elegant. Where the prebendary used to live. The rowan tree in the front garden is still there.

Lovers, probably. He's seen the artist many a time, crossing the road to go down to the high street. Small, pretty, fair-haired. Doesn't make the most of herself. Always shabbily dressed, in black, or brown, or grey. They don't look well matched, Young Lochinvar and the artist. She's too timid; he's got too much of a swagger. But you can never tell, can you?

Night begins to fall. To pass the time, the Venerable begins to recite the liturgy:

Almighty God, Father of our Lord Jesus Christ, maker of all things, judge of all men; we acknowledge and bewail our manifold sins and wickedness, which we, from time to time, most grievously have committed . . .

The spire of the cathedral glimmers in the twilight. The saints and the gargoyles commune, high up on their stairway to heaven.

. . . We do earnestly repent, and are heartily sorry for these our misdoings; the remembrance of them is grievous unto us; the burden of them is intolerable . . .

Hang on, here's the man again, coming out of the front door. He's carrying something, something flat and square, wrapped up in his scarf. He walks down the front path, past the rowan tree, and out into the street. He approaches the car, presses his gadget, and it shudders again, its lights flashing. He stops by the Venerable's feet, opens the car door, gets in, and deposits the intolerable burden, if that's what it is, on the floor under the front seat. Then he starts the engine, backs off, and drives away, with a squeal of tyres.

The crows fall silent. There's a rustling of trees in the graveyard. The tombstones huddle together, remembering their wartime night of horror. The gargoyles, high up above them on the flying buttresses, begin to chant. Their voices rise in unison. Malevolent. Blasphemous. The Venerable can do nothing to stop them. He can only listen and watch and wait.

Perhaps someone saw what happened. Someone next door, round the corner, in the high street. Perhaps someone will come.

But no one crosses the green.

MURDER IN LLANDAFF

Police were called to a house on Llandaff Green last night after a local woman, Ursula Powell, was found dead on the premises. Mrs Powell, whose family own a well-known Cardiff art gallery, is believed to have been killed during the course of an armed robbery at the house. The body was discovered by Mrs Powell's daughter, Elinor Powell, who had returned home from a shopping trip in the early evening. Police have launched a murder enquiry, and are currently appealing for witnesses who may have been in the area to come forward. PC Alun Evans commented: 'We believe Mrs Powell may have disturbed the thief, who acted in panic.'

Western Mail, Monday 14 October 2013

1

Jessica Mayhew was lying on the couch in her consulting room. She wasn't thinking about her next patient, who was due to come in at any moment. She wasn't examining her own internal conflicts. She wasn't clearing her mind, gazing up at the play of shadows on the ceiling, readying herself for what the day would bring: a steady procession of lost souls, some in states of emergency, others in the throes of anguish, yet others – the ones she found most exhausting, to be honest – simply playing for time, trotting through their sessions like sheep through a field, their passage marked only by a narrow path leading nowhere. No, Dr Jessica Mayhew, forty-three, psychotherapist, (ex-)wife of one, mother of two, was not thinking about any of this. She was not thinking at all. She was, in fact, fast asleep.

There was a knock at the door. Jessica woke with a start. For a moment, she wasn't quite sure what was happening.

She came to, and jumped up off the couch.

New client. Assessment. Name begins with an E. Jess glanced at her desk and saw, with relief, that she'd already set out her client's file. She grabbed it and walked towards the door, straightening her skirt and smoothing her hair as she went. She was wearing a forties-style tweed skirt and a cashmere cardigan, her hair up in a loose bun. There was a sour taste in her mouth, as if she'd just woken up in the morning after a night's sleep, yet she could only have drifted off for a few minutes. She'd have to be more careful in future. No more kipping on the couch, even for a second. There was too much going on in her life at the moment. She'd accumulated too much of a sleep deficit.

She hesitated a moment, then opened the door.

The woman who walked in was small. She had pale, luminous blonde hair like a child's, and an almost translucent quality to her complexion. Her frame was slight, her limbs delicate. She was striking, yet there was a timidity in the way she carried herself, as if her marbled beauty was a cross she had to bear, rather than a gift to be treasured.

'Hello.' Jess put out her hand and gave her a welcoming smile. 'I'm Jessica. Jessica Mayhew.'

The woman nodded, but she didn't shake hands, or smile back. There was a wary look in her eyes.

Jessica gestured at the hat stand, and the woman went over and took off her coat. It was a faded navy blue with a muted tartan lining. Rather worn, but stylish in its way.

When she'd finished, Jessica motioned her over to two armchairs by the fireplace that faced each other. Between them was a low coffee table with a box of tissues on it.

'Please. Do take a seat.'

The woman glanced questioningly over at the couch by the window.

'You're welcome to use the couch if you wish, when you come into therapy.' Jessica paused. 'But for an assessment, and in general, actually, I prefer to talk face to face.'

There was a short silence. Jess took in the woman's appearance. Underneath the mac, she was dressed rather scruffily, in a T-shirt, a thin grey sweater, black jeans and ancient plimsolls, worn with no socks. The muted tones of her clothing only served to accentuate the brightness of her eyes, which were wide, almond-shaped, and a clear, piercing blue. Her cheekbones were high, giving her features a Slavic look. From a distance, her small stature and diffident demeanour might have made her look girlish, but close up, it was obvious that she was well into her thirties. There were lines etched into her temples, running across her forehead, and beginning to drag at the corners of her mouth. She had the type of fair skin that age seems to mark more brutally than those with sallow complexions; or perhaps, Jess reflected, she simply seemed careworn, as if she hadn't slept well, not just the night before, but for a succession of nights in the recent past.

'Actually, I think I'll have to go on the couch. I need to be by the window, you see. I feel safer like that.'

Jess glanced at her notes. There wasn't much information there as yet. The woman's name was Elinor Powell. She'd been referred by her doctor for chronic claustrophobia following a traumatic family bereavement. Jess had tried to phone the doctor to get more details, but he'd always been busy when she'd rung. So that was all she knew so far.

Elinor crossed the room, opened the sash window a crack, and lay down on the couch. She gave a sigh of relief and settled herself.

Jess sat down on an armchair behind the couch. She was slightly put out by her new client. Already, despite her unassuming air, she'd got her own way: she was lying on the couch. As Freud had noted all those years ago, 'the neuroses', as he called them, are not just psychological aberrations; they always have a purpose, making demands that the bearer can't voice directly.

There was a silence. Jess didn't break it. She was curious to see which side of this woman's personality – the timid, or the forthright – would present itself first.

7

'It's getting out of hand,' Elinor began, staring up at the tree outside the window. 'I really can't go on like this. It started with tunnels and lifts, but then it was cars. Then buses and trains. It's got to the point now where I don't like being shut inside a building. I have to open all the windows, wherever I go. And I've taken to camping outside at night, in a yurt on the back lawn. I can't sleep otherwise.'

'That must be rather cold.'

'It is. But there's nothing I can do. If I'm indoors, anywhere, I feel trapped. And it seems to be getting worse.'

Jess hesitated, unsure of the situation. This was an assessment session, in which she normally felt free to intervene and give her opinion, but since her client was lying on the couch, it felt like a psychoanalytic one. She decided to go ahead all the same.

'Well, that's the problem with claustrophobia.' Jess took care to name the disorder clearly. 'It can be cumulative, you see. Avoiding things you're afraid of can increase your fear in the long term.'

Elinor didn't reply. Instead, she sat up. 'Do you mind if I open the window a bit more?'

Without waiting for a response, she reached up and opened the window as far as it would go. Then she lay back down on the couch again.

This is going to be a rough ride, thought Jess. Her new client had a disconcerting way of doing the opposite of what she'd just advised. All the same, she found herself intrigued.

'Could you tell me a little about how this started?' Jess shivered as a draught of cold air hit her. It was spring, but it still felt like winter. How anyone could sleep outside in this weather she couldn't imagine.

Elinor thought for a moment, gazing up at the branches on the tree. She seemed quite comfortable in the icy blast. Then she took a deep breath, and spoke.

'Four months ago, my mother was found dead in my house. Someone broke in and stole a valuable painting.' Her tone was abrupt, as if she was summoning a toughness she didn't possess. 'I was the person who found her. She'd been beaten about the head.'

Jessica was shocked, but she tried not to show it. There were housebreakers in Cardiff, like anywhere else, but it wasn't the sort of place where, in the normal run of things, people got murdered in the course of a robbery. She cast her mind back. She had a faint recollection of reading about the crime in the paper, or hearing of it on the news, but at the time she hadn't paid it much attention. Now she wished she had.

'The police don't know who did it. They've got no leads, and no witnesses have come forward.' Elinor turned her face to the wall. 'I'm sorry, I still find this difficult to talk about.'

'Of course.' Jessica did her best to reassure her. 'Please, don't feel you need to go into details at this stage.'

This was a tricky situation, Jess knew. According to the latest thinking on post-traumatic stress disorder, or PTSD as it's known in the trade, beginning any kind of counselling too soon after the event in question can be counterproductive, because the mind responds by 'splitting': that is, using the unconscious part to work through the horror, while the conscious part gets on with the business of living. Asking a client to recall the experience can disturb this delicate process. In terms of the current guidelines, Jessica was on safe ground, because according to Elinor, the event had occurred four months ago. But over the course of twenty years in practice, Jess had seen the guidelines change so often that these days she tended to rely on the unscientific factor of hunch. And her hunch told her that if her new client didn't want to talk about her mother's violent death with someone she didn't yet know or trust, she shouldn't be pushed into doing so.

'I felt pretty bad just after it happened,' Elinor went on, turning her head back. 'I had nightmares, flashbacks.' She paused. 'But I'm sleeping better now, and the flashbacks have gone. It's just the claustrophobia that's bothering me.'

Jess thought about taking her through a checklist of other PTSD symptoms – hypervigilance, difficulty concentrating, irritability – but decided against it. She didn't want to interrupt Elinor's flow.

'I still get anxious when I talk about what happened. And I still can't concentrate. I haven't got back to work yet. I'm a painter, you see. A fine artist, not a house painter. That's what I do for a living.' She paused again. 'Well, when I can make a living.' Her brow furrowed. 'Anyway, that's what I do.'

Jess was struck by the combination of directness and insecurity in her manner. She seemed quite sure of her status as a painter, a fine artist as she called it, yet not altogether convinced that anyone else would believe what she said.

'Elinor – d'you mind if I call you Elinor?'

'That's fine.'

'Well, it's very early days, isn't it?' Jess chose her words with care. 'Your . . . loss . . . was only a few months ago. It's hardly surprising that you should find it difficult to get back to work right away.'

'Yes, but I don't think it's that.' A sudden look of panic came into Elinor's eyes. 'It's a punishment, you see. I'm guilty, and this is my punishment.'

She came to a halt.

Silence fell. Jess knew Elinor would continue, so she didn't break it. And sure enough, after a while, Elinor resumed her story.

'It was my fault. I shouldn't have kept the painting in the studio. Everyone told me that.'

She passed a hand over her brow, and when she took it away, Jess saw that there were tears in her eyes.

'I live alone, you see. I'm single. My mother was just visiting. She had a key; she used to let herself in whenever she wanted.' She paused. 'She always told me the painting should be kept somewhere safe. This would never have happened if I'd listened to her.' Her voice was trembling. 'I feel terribly guilty about her death. I blame myself entirely.'

Jess decided against telling her that feelings of guilt are common among survivors of a tragedy. It was a truism, and besides, she couldn't assume that this woman had no reason to feel guilty about her mother. As yet she knew nothing of their relationship. So instead, she changed the subject.

'You say you find it hard to talk about your mother's death' – Jessica took care not to emphasize the word 'death', but she felt it should be used – 'and I fully respect that. But I'm just wondering if you're ready to come into therapy yet. As I said, it's very early days.'

'Well, I've got to do something. I can't carry on like this, can I?' Elinor's voice rose in anguish. 'I can't travel. I open windows wherever I go.' She furrowed her brow. 'D'you think you can help me?'

There was a pause.

'I don't know.' Jessica was honest in her reply. 'It's up to you, really. You see, the way I work, we'd have to discuss your mother's death. The circumstances surrounding it, your relationship with her, and so on. We would be looking for explanations for your claustrophobia there. But if you're not ready to delve deeper into that, there are other ways of helping you with your problem. Cognitive behavioural therapy, for example. CBT, as it's known. There's a method a colleague of mine uses that's been specially formulated to help people who've been exposed to traumatic events. I can refer you, if you like.'

'No thanks.' Elinor waved a dismissive hand. 'I've heard of CBT. I don't fancy it.'

'Oh?'

'Identifying your negative thoughts. Adjusting them. Making checklists. Writing out worksheets. It sounds tedious.'

Jess was amused. Although she respected her colleague, and knew many clients who had been helped greatly by CBT, she had to admit she felt rather the same. If one was honest, the type of therapy one practised, or chose to follow, was usually more a question of taste than a rational decision, whether or not one cared to admit it.

'But that approach can be very effective,' Jess said, in an effort to be fair. 'It's extremely practical. You'll develop ways of managing your fear, coping with everyday tasks, using various techniques—'

'I don't want that.' There was a note of irritation in Elinor's voice. 'I don't want to make checklists and be given homework to do. That's not the type of person I am.'

Jessica repressed a smile. She was beginning to warm to her new client. There was something endearingly direct about her.

'I suppose, being an artist, I'm more drawn to a Jungian view of the world,' Elinor went on. 'You know, dreams, archetypes, mythologies. That kind of thing. What about you?'

'Oh.' Jess thought for a moment. She didn't want to sound too theoretical, but there was no way round it. 'I'm what's called an existential psychotherapist.'

Elinor frowned, whether in concentration or irritation it was hard to say.

'It's actually quite simple,' Jess continued. 'We're rooted in Freudian theory, but we emphasize choice and freedom, rather than the idea that we're the victims of our past.'

'But I thought psychotherapy was all about the past. Delving into your childhood and so on.'

'It is, to some degree. Of course, the circumstances of our birth, and our upbringing, are vital to our understanding of ourselves. And, to a greater or lesser degree, we're limited by those circumstances. But every person has a set of choices as to how to respond to those limits.' She paused. She didn't want to come over as didactic. 'And if we're to live full, engaged lives, we have to acknowledge our freedom to make those choices, and act on them.'

Elinor looked puzzled. 'So how would this apply to my situation?'

'I don't really know what your situation is. Not yet, anyway.' Jess hesitated. 'But it's possible that your claustrophobia may be what we call a "call of conscience". It may be trying to tell you that there's something you need to address in your life.' She paused. 'You see, normally we tell a story about our lives, like the one you've just told me. But sometimes our bodies and our minds tell *us* a story, and we need to stop and listen.'

There was a long silence. Elinor looked pensive. Her eyes began to rove around the room. She seemed to be assessing it: the sash windows, the pale green velvet curtains either side of the bay, the antique wooden desk in the corner, the white-on-white Ben Nicholson-style relief on the wall. As the silence deepened, the consulting room seemed to take on a life of its own: peaceful, patient, expectant. The two of them, client and analyst, became aware of the low hum of traffic from the street, the faint rustle of the wind in the tree outside, the ticking of the clock on the mantelpiece. Secrets had been revealed here, maps redrawn, the compass realigned, new paths plotted. Jess was familiar with that history, that potency; she sensed it every time she walked into the room. For her new client, it was the first time.

'All right, then.' Elinor's voice finally broke the silence. 'When can I start?'

2

After Elinor Powell left, Jess didn't have time to think further about the case. Four more clients came in, all of them with pressing concerns: there was Harriet, a morbidly obese young woman with a complex set of emotional problems; Bryn, a man in his fifties who continued to rage against his widowed mother, on whom he was still entirely dependent; Maria, a single parent whose children were being taken into care as a result of her deepening depression; and Deri, a banker who had recently, and quite unexpectedly, lost his job in the City and returned home to Wales.

At the end of the final session, Jess hurriedly wrote up her notes, dealt with her emails, then headed for home, stopping on the way to pick up a trolleyful of shopping at the super-market. It was only on the short drive from there to her house on the outskirts of Cardiff that her mind began to stray back to her new client. All she knew so far was that Elinor's mother had died a violent death during a robbery at her house. That would be enough to tip anyone into phobia, she reflected. Moreover, the fact that the police hadn't found the perpetrator meant that Elinor would continue to be in a state of heightened emotion until exactly what happened became clear. It was odd, though, the way she'd behaved in the session, as if she constantly needed to assert herself in opposition to her new therapist. Maybe that was something to do with the mother; or perhaps a competitive sibling relationship . . .

It began to rain. She switched on the windscreen wipers, but they scratched ineffectually at the window. They needed changing, and she hadn't yet got around to it.

As she swung onto the main drag out of the city, peering through the smears on the glass, she thought of how Elinor had talked of her mother's death in terms of guilt and punishment. It was common enough, she knew, for clients to consider themselves responsible for events outside their control. The urge to blame themselves for anything and everything that went wrong was a kind of egomania she'd encountered many times with her clients, and she'd long ago realized that it was a perverse attempt to take control of the situation, to place themselves at the centre of the drama, rather than acknowledge that their role in what happened, good or bad, was often quite peripheral. Elinor had evidently fallen into that trap, judging by what she'd told her so far.

She left the city behind her, moving into a stretch of road where the trees clustered overhead. As she dipped down under them, she noticed that the leaves on the branches were beginning to unfurl; soon they would spread into a tunnel of green. The sight of them cheered her. She was always heartened by those first crumpled, sticky signs of spring. This year, after the long, hard winter, they'd been late, and she'd wondered if they'd come at all; but now, here they were, waiting to open out into a dappled canopy above her, something she could enjoy each time she took the road home.

She was tempted to look up the case on the Internet. After all, it was public knowledge now, having been reported in the local papers at the time. But, like a juror in a trial, she'd made it a strict rule not to conduct such searches, unless her clients specifically asked her to. It was up to them, she felt, to tell her their stories in their own way; knowing too much about their personal lives didn't help that process, since she'd be comparing what they said against her own supposedly more objective account, and forming her own opinions, which was not the point of the exercise. On the contrary, her job was to help her clients explore the internal contradictions within the stories they told about themselves, and let the truth emerge from that. Besides, there was a voyeuristic element to googling that she disliked; where her clients were concerned it felt intrusive, and nosy, and generally underhand.

She came out from under the branches and turned into the lane that led to her house, passing the church on her right. The ringing of the bells on a Sunday morning reassured her, too, although she never went to the services. As she parked the car outside the garage, she reflected that it was continuity she needed at the moment. She and Bob had lived apart for several months now; she needed to remain here in the house, with a settled routine, keep the job going, make sure the girls felt secure . . .

She got out of the car, went round to the boot, took out the shopping, and locked up. Then she walked up the drive to the front door and pressed the bell; one of the girls would answer it, she thought, so she wouldn't have to put the shopping down. There was no reply, so she pressed again. Again, no reply. Irritated, she balanced the shopping bag against the wall, on her knee, and fiddled with the key to get it into the lock. As she did, she saw the outline of her eldest daughter through the glass of the door, coming up the hall.

'Sorry, Mum.' Nella opened the door. 'I didn't hear you.'

Nella was looking particularly scruffy that day. She was wearing a loose sweatshirt, a pair of leggings and worn black ballet flats. Her hair was piled up on top of her head in a messy knot, and yesterday's mascara clung to the skin around her eyes, as if she'd just got out of bed and hadn't yet washed her face.

She kissed her mother on the cheek, took the shopping, and went off down to the kitchen. Jess took off her coat in the hall, then followed her. She noticed that the fabric of Nella's leggings was very thin, so much so that you could see the outline of her thong beneath them. I hope she hasn't been walking around the streets like that, she thought. She looks like a tramp. However, she kept her opinion to herself; Nella was seventeen now, and didn't take kindly to criticism of her appearance, to say the least.

'Where's your sister?' Jess asked, going over to the kettle, filling it, and putting it on to boil.

'Upstairs.' Nella started to unpack the shopping, found a packet of biscuits, and opened them. 'Doing her homework, I think.'

'How was your day?'

'Shit, as usual.' Nella took out a biscuit and munched it.

Jess busied herself with getting cups, teabags and milk from the fridge, and trying to hide her irritation.

'Tea?'

'OK.'

Jess made the tea, brought it over, and they sat down at the table together.

'Got any plans for this evening?'

'Gareth's coming over. Then we're going out to a gig in town.'

Gareth was Nella's boyfriend. The two of them played in a band together, and seemed to have forged a stable relationship. Jess was fond of him; he was open, kind and affectionate, and he seemed to adore her daughter, which had thoroughly endeared him to her.

'Have you handed that essay in yet?'

17

'No.' Nella gave a deep sigh. 'I need a break from it. I'm very stressed.'

Once more, Jess tried to hide her irritation, reminding herself that although Nella appeared to have been hanging around the house all day doing nothing, half dressed, she might indeed be stressed in some way.

'I can't bear going to college every day.' Nella sighed again. 'My heart's not in it. I just need to concentrate on my song-writing.'

They'd been through this before. After her GCSEs, Nella had wanted to leave school, get a job as a waitress, and work on her music. She'd been persuaded to stay on at sixth-form college but so far she'd hardly attended, and had been late with most of her assignments.

Jess gave a sigh of frustration. 'Nella, you're perfectly capable of getting three decent A levels, as well as writing a few songs. You're a clever girl. You just need to organize your time a bit better.'

'That's what Dad said.' Nella took a sip of tea and reached for another biscuit. Jess was relieved to hear that Bob was backing her up, but all the same, at the mention of his name her resolve weakened, and she took a biscuit too.

It had been three months since Bob had moved out of the family home. Nothing final, of course. They had simply decided that a trial separation was in order. It had been a long, hard struggle for both of them to make the decision. Over a year ago, Bob had told Jess that he'd had a one-night stand. She'd tried to be magnanimous about it, but she hadn't found herself able to forgive him. On top of that, he'd used some information about a client that she'd told him in private to further his own career. That had been the final straw, undermining her professional as well as her personal life. They'd carried on for a while, both doing their utmost to make amends, for the sake of the girls, but also because in many ways there was still a great deal of affection there. They had built a good partnership together over two decades, and it still caught Jess by surprise that they were now separated. She hadn't quite got used to it, and neither had he.

'Well, maybe Dad and you and I should get together and talk about all this,' Jess said, finishing her biscuit. 'But in the meantime, get that essay in. OK?'

'OK.' There was a pause. 'Do you want me to finish helping you unpack the shopping?'

Since the split, Nella had been much more helpful in the house. Indeed, she'd become quite protective of her mother. Jess was touched, but Nella's new-found solicitousness also made her feel guilty at times.

'No, you get on.' Jess got up and carried the cups over to the sink. 'See if you can get your work done by suppertime. You can go out after that. Tell Rose I'll be up in a minute.'

Jess tidied the kitchen, loading the dishwasher, cleaning the sink, and wiping the countertop. The girls were supposed to do it, but inevitably their efforts were somewhat erratic. When she'd finished, she went upstairs and looked in on Rose, who was lying curled up on her bed reading a book.

Unlike Nella, Rose hardly spent any time at all on the computer. She seemed to prefer reading to surfing the net, pen and paper to tapping on a keyboard, and visiting friends to social networking. She was eleven now, but she seemed younger. She'd grown her hair down to her shoulders, but continued to wear it held back in an Alice band, and her clothes were still neat, tidy and modest. True, she no longer wore sweaters with cuddly animal designs on the front, or socks with frills on the cuffs, but Jessica sensed that she would have liked to, had it been socially acceptable among her peers.

'How was your day?' Jessica came and sat down on the end of the bed.

Rose didn't reply.

Jess leaned forward and gently tapped her on the shoulder. Rose lifted her head, a distracted look on her face.

'How was school today?' Jess persevered.

'Fine.'

'Got much homework?'

'Just some reading.'

Jess glanced at the cover of the book. It was an old edition of I Capture the Castle that she'd had as a child.

'I've got to give a talk about my favourite novel in class tomorrow,' Rose explained.

'D'you want to try it out on me, once you've done it?'

'Maybe.' Rose put her nose back in her book.

Jess took the hint and got up. 'Supper in an hour or so. OK?'

Rose didn't reply, so Jess left her to it. Then she went into her room, got undressed and had a shower, hoping that the warm water would wash away her fatigue. It did, to a certain extent, though while she was soaping herself, she found herself mulling over Elinor's story again. What had Elinor's mother been doing at the house when the break-in happened? Would the theft of a painting like that really warrant murder – or had the thief killed her in a panic at being discovered? How had she been killed? And why hadn't the police come up with any leads, after four months? Were they just being incompetent, or could there perhaps be something that the family was hiding? Elinor hadn't insured the painting; nobody outside the family would have known it was there, would they?

She turned her face up to the shower head, letting the spray spill over it, before turning off the water. Then she stepped out of the shower, and began to dry herself. When she finished, she looked at herself in the mirror. She'd lost a bit of weight, especially around the waist and hips, she thought. All that lying awake at night and worrying, probably. She decided not to bother with underwear, pulling on a pair of loose patterned silk trousers and a baggy cashmere jumper, and went downstairs to cook supper.

It wasn't easy, these days, finding something that everyone in the family would eat. Rose had become a vegetarian, since she disapproved of killing animals. Nella was on a permanent diet, when she wasn't stuffing herself with chocolate biscuits. Jess herself was fairly flexible, although she tried to keep an eye on her weight. In the end, she decided to make roasted vegetables and couscous, sprinkled with grated cheese and pine nuts for protein. That, she hoped, would keep everyone happy.

She and the girls ate their supper in front of the television, watching an episode of *Downton Abbey* on catch-up. The girls adored it, and she quite enjoyed it too. She'd heard it was very successful abroad, and she could see why. The characters simply spoke the plot, and the dialogue was so straightforward that even someone with the most basic grasp of English could understand it. 'Darling, I'm divorcing you because you can't have children.' 'But that's not fair.' 'I know, I'm so sorry. But it has to be.' 'Well, then, I'll leave in the morning.' The terse dialogue meant that the story galloped on at a cracking pace. No waiting around for nuance or conjecture – it was full steam ahead all the way. Rather the way she felt her own life was going at the moment, to be honest.

That night, Rose crept into her bed. Jess woke, confused for a moment, feeling a warm body lying next to her.

'What is it, love?'

Rose was sniffling.

Jess put her arm out and touched her daughter's cheek. It was wet with tears.

'I miss Dad.'

'I know.' Jess drew her close. She wanted to say, Never mind, you can go and see him any time you want, but she knew that wouldn't help. Rose needed her sadness to be acknowledged, not brushed away.

'Do you think . . . do you think you and he . . .' Rose let her words trail off.

Jess sighed. 'Well, we're trying our best. But whatever happens, your dad will always be around. He loves you. You know that, don't you?'

Rose sniffed.

'We both love you. You're safe. OK?'

She sniffed again. 'Can I sleep in here for the night?'

Jess closed her eyes. She was exhausted. Recently, her nights had been disturbed by Nella's comings and goings, and now Rose had taken to waking her up, too.

'All right. Just for tonight.'

Rose turned over, and within minutes, Jess could hear the regular sound of her breathing as she fell asleep. She herself lay awake, wondering how much longer she could shoulder all this on her own. Maybe it would be easier to ask Bob to come back. It was the girls who mattered most, after all. Perhaps they could live together until both of the children left home, then look at the situation again. After all, they were still friends. And plenty of couples lived like that, didn't they, as friends, not lovers . . .

She heard footsteps outside, a low murmur of voices. Nella and Gareth. She checked the clock beside the bed. It was one a.m. She heard them let themselves in, and creep down the corridor to the kitchen. This was ridiculous. Nella had college tomorrow. She'd said she could go out, but not until the small hours.

She turned over, pulling the duvet up over her ears. Things were getting too lax in the house. Some male authority was needed.

She closed her eyes. An image came into her mind. A woman was groping her way along a dark cave, holding a golden thread. Ariadne, a voice told her. The minotaur. She felt exhaustion overcome her, and drifted off to sleep.

3

The following week, Elinor Powell began her course of therapy. Jess had suggested they meet once a week, but Elinor had been keen to come in more often. Jess had warned her that this might not necessarily speed up the process, but Elinor had been adamant, so in the end they'd settled on twice-weekly sessions, on a Tuesday and a Thursday.

On the Tuesday, Jess saw two patients, then went over the road and got herself a cup of coffee from the deli opposite her consulting room. When she came back, she logged on to the website of the *Journal of Phenomenological Psychotherapy*, looking for the most up-to-date papers on claustrophobia. She ran her eye over the latest explanations. One, rather obviously, that it arises when a person suffers a traumatic experience in an enclosed space, such as getting stuck in a lift, or being shut in a cupboard as a child. Two, rather intriguingly, that it's caused by individual differences in the perception of 'near space' – the space around oneself that a person considers to be a safe, no-go zone. Three, rather obscurely, that it's a vestigial evolutionary survival mechanism; four, rather familiarly, that it's connected to trauma during the process of birth; and five, rather alarmingly, that it's very often triggered by undergoing an MRI scan.

As she read, she wasn't looking for solutions – more for clues. Had Elinor perhaps discovered her mother's body in a small, cluttered room, triggering a connection between the traumatic experience and the place in which it occurred? Or could the claustrophobia have a more symbolic meaning, indicating that her mother had repeatedly invaded her privacy in some way, been clingy, suffocating, unable to let her daughter grow up and go out into the big, wild world?

There was a knock at the door.

For a moment, the image of the woman, the cave and the thread that Jess had seen the previous night just before she fell asleep came back into her mind. She'd learned, over the years, not to dismiss such passing thoughts. They were messages, codes, there to tell us something, as Freud had noted long ago.

Let Elinor feel her way back to safety, away from the minotaur, she told herself, rather than leading her down to it.

When Elinor came in, she looked dejected. She barely acknowledged Jess; simply gave her a quick nod as she took off her mac. She hung the mac on the hat stand near the door, then walked over to the couch. Jess had opened the window a crack – and turned the heating up slightly in the room – in readiness for her.

Jess went over and sat down in the chair behind the couch.

There was a silence. During it, Jess cleared her head of all her thoughts. Well, no, not cleared them exactly, but tried to watch them float by, without intervening, as the images passed: Rose, and her tears for her father; Nella, lying in bed with Gareth, missing her lessons; Bob, getting off a train somewhere, his mobile clamped to his ear; the windscreen wipers that needed changing. They all filed by, one by one, and she let them go. It wasn't hard to do; it was a pleasure, a joy even, to leave them all to their own devices while she got on with the job in hand, which was to attend to her client.

Elinor leaned over and opened the window a little wider. But not, Jess noticed, as wide as she had before. Then she lay down on the couch and gazed out at the tree outside. Eventually, she spoke.

'I did try to go down to the studio last night.'

'The studio?'

Jess pictured a room cluttered with painting paraphernalia. Elinor's private zone.

'It's separate from the house, at the end of the garden. That's where I found my mother's body that day,' Elinor went on. 'It was no good, though. I couldn't go in.'

She passed a hand across her forehead, then kneaded the skin over her temples. She had beautiful hands, Jess noticed, long and slim with tapering fingers. Artist's hands.

'I don't know what to do. Ever since . . .' Her voice trailed off. 'I just can't seem to get back on track.' She put her hand down from her face, and began to fidget with her scarf. 'I suppose I shouldn't try and work in the evening. It stops me sleeping.'

She paused, as if expecting advice, but Jess didn't voice an opinion.

'The thing is, I can't seem to find time during the day.' Elinor sighed. 'There are so many interruptions. Isobel comes round, always fussing about this or that, stuff to do with the estate – should she do up the house in Italy and rent it out or put it on the market straight away? Why can't I help with it all?'

Jess waited for Elinor to tell her who Isobel was, but she didn't. She seemed to assume that she already knew, which was a little odd.

'And then there's this bloody policewoman calling to ask me all sorts of stupid questions.' Elinor sighed again. 'I really wish she'd let it go, give us some peace.'

There was another silence. Jess waited for her to elaborate, but she didn't. Eventually, she prompted her.

'A policewoman, you say?'

'She's nice enough, I suppose, but she seems a bit dense. She doesn't seem to understand that the painting was worth an awful lot of money. It's not surprising that someone would . . . you know.' Elinor's voice trailed off for a moment, then resumed. 'But she can't see that. She obviously knows nothing about art whatsoever.'

There was a silence.

'I suppose she's just doing her job,' Elinor continued after a while. 'I mean, we all want to find the person who killed my mother.' She paused. 'But the way this woman goes on, you'd think it was one of us.'

Her words hung in the air.

'One of us?'

'Yes. Me. Or Isobel.' There it was again, that name without any explanation. 'Or Blake, her husband. It's a pretty small family, when you come down to it. And even smaller now, without Ma.' Elinor's voice trembled slightly.

She shifted her position on the couch, adjusting the cushion behind her head. Then she said, 'I suppose you want to know all about the details of the murder? And then go into all the problems of my childhood, my relationship with my mother, and all that?'

There was a slight hostility to her tone.

'I don't want anything, Elinor.' That wasn't quite true. Jess was inquisitive by nature, and her curiosity was more than piqued by this dramatic story of murder and robbery. She was also fascinated that the police had been continuing to ask questions, evidently not satisfied with the family's account of events. But through long experience, she'd learned to put such thoughts to one side, bracket them, for the time being. They got in the way of listening properly to her patient, which was the task at hand.

'It's for you to decide what you want to do here,' Jess continued. 'What kind of help you want.'

'I was hoping you might have some suggestions.' The hostility was still there.

'If I did, would you follow them?'

'Probably not.' A smile played briefly on Elinor's lips, but she repressed it.

Once again, silence fell.

'OK, then.' Elinor paused for a moment. 'This is what I want to talk about. I know it sounds awful, given that I've just lost my mother. But all I keep thinking about is that painting. It was a Gwen John, rather an important one, actually.'

Jess had seen Gwen John's work in the National Museum. She was the sister of Augustus John, who in his day had been much more famous. She painted quiet, rather disturbing portraits of unknown women sitting in darkened rooms with their hands neatly folded. They spoke of frustration, confinement, of a cloying, domestic sphere, yet there was an intensity to their muted tones that was, in its way, more powerful and seductive than her brother's flamboyant work.

'It hung in my bedroom as a child, mine and Isobel's, and I used to look at it when I woke up in the morning, before I got out of bed.'

Jess guessed that Isobel must be Elinor's sister.

'It was of a young girl standing by a wall, her shadow behind her. She was wearing a thin blue dress, and although you couldn't see the outline of her body beneath it, you could sense the structure of it, by the way the light fell on it. Yet it seemed to have been painted quickly, without lingering on the detail. I used to lie there in my warm bed, not wanting to get up, looking at the painting and wondering how she'd done it. It was very subtle, like all her work.'

Elinor shifted her head again. As she did, her shoulders seemed to relax.

'I suppose, looking back, it was a huge influence on me. Even

as a child, I think I must have been trying to paint like that.'
She paused. 'I've been trying ever since.'

There was a silence, but Jess didn't try to fill it.

'When I left home and went to art college,' Elinor went on,
'the painting stayed in the bedroom. I'd come back for the
holidays and wake up to it in the morning. It remained very
much part of my life. My father noticed how much I loved it,
so when I got my own studio, he insisted on giving it to me.'
Her voice softened. 'He was a very sweet man. Thoughtful.
Sensitive. He noticed what was going on with us kids. Every
detail. Not like . . .' She hesitated for a moment.

The mother, thought Jess. Not thoughtful. Not sensitive.
Intrusive, perhaps? Cloying?

'Well, anyway,' Elinor continued. 'To be honest, by that time
I didn't want it. But I didn't want to hurt his feelings, so I took
it.'

There was a pause.

'You say you loved the painting.' Jess repeated Elinor's words.
'Yet you didn't want to own it.'

This was another psychotherapeutic technique. Not simply
reflecting back, but pinpointing contradictions in the patient's
account.

Elinor nodded. 'It felt like too much of a responsibility. It's
worth quite a lot of money. And it wasn't just the practical side
of looking after it that bothered me,' she went on. 'It felt like
a responsibility in artistic terms, too. It seemed to limit me as a
painter. To set a goal that I could never turn away from.' A
look of sadness came over her face. 'In fact, I sometimes wonder
if it ruined my career. I went to Goldsmith's, you see, and during
the time I was there, that kind of meticulous style was completely unfashionable. It was all installations, warehouses, cows
sawed in half, conceptual stuff.' Her expression became more
composed. 'I did well on paper, of course; I got a first, because

there was no denying my work was good, but no one important came to my graduate show. No one was interested in collecting me.' She paused. 'I haven't done too badly, I suppose. I've made a career as a painter, which is more than most of my contemporaries did. But I'm not a hot artist, never will be.'

She pronounced the word 'hot' with distaste.

'And then, of course,' she went on, 'there was the family connection. I often wondered if I'd just joined the family firm, and had no original ideas of my own.'

She was beginning to unburden herself now. Jess had the impression that she had been mulling over these problems for a long time, never discussing them with anyone.

'You see, Gwen John is said to be a relative of mine. My great aunt, supposedly.'

'Supposedly?'

'Yes. Through my mother, Ursula. She claimed she was the illegitimate daughter of Augustus John, Gwen's brother. But it was never verified. He had rather a lot of illegitimate children, as it happened.'

'What was your father's view?' From time to time, despite her training, Jess let her curiosity get the better of her.

'My father died ten years ago. Cancer.' Elinor's tone was matter-of-fact, but Jess thought she detected a note of bravado in it, as if, after a whole decade, she had to marshal her best defences against her grief. 'He actually thought the story was a load of nonsense. My grandmother Ariadne was a very flighty woman. She'd had a brief affair with John, like so many others. My father believed that she'd exaggerated the importance of it.'

'Why would she do that?'

'Because John was so famous. And to annoy her husband, of course.' Elinor gave a wry smile. 'That was the kind of relationship my grandparents had. One that my mother repeated with my father, I might add.'

There was a pause. Parental conflict, thought Jess. The claustrophobia of an enduring but unhappy marriage, from which the child can never escape, carrying it internally into adulthood.

'But one way and another, the story became part of family history,' Elinor continued. 'And something of a curse, maybe, for us all. This tenuous connection to a painter whose work has influenced mine – for the worse, at least in commercial terms – and whose existence, in the end, seems to have caused the death of my mother.'

Silence fell. Jess had wondered when Elinor would begin to speak of her mother. The story of the painting was obviously important to her, but to some extent it was simply a preamble to discussing the traumatic event that had pitched her into claustrophobia. And, as so often happened in therapy sessions, she'd waited until the last minute to start talking about it.

Jess glanced at the clock. They were already over time.

'Elinor, I'm afraid we'll have to finish there for today.' Her voice was gentle. 'Perhaps we can talk some more about that in our next session.'

After Elinor left, Jess had another two patients to attend to, and then it was time for lunch. She and Bob had arranged to meet at the Welsh Assembly offices, where he worked, and to find somewhere to eat in the Bay. She was a little nervous about the encounter; she often spoke to him on the phone, or chatted briefly when he picked up Rose for the weekend, but they'd never actually gone out for a meal together since the split. She feared that perhaps this was an attempt on his part to woo her back; it was he who'd offered to take her out. He'd suggested a stylish brasserie in the vicinity; she'd countered by saying that she wouldn't have much time, and that perhaps they should grab a sandwich somewhere. He'd sounded disappointed, and in the end they'd agreed to take a stroll around the Bay and find somewhere on the day. On a Tuesday lunchtime, the restaurants and cafes on the waterside would hardly be packed to the gunwales.

Before she left her consulting rooms, she went to the loo, washed her hands, and combed her hair, checking her face in the mirror as she did so. She looked tired, she thought; there were bluish shadows under her eyes. To draw attention away from them, she took out a brightly coloured lipstick and applied it, rubbing the excess onto her cheeks. Immediately, she looked better; the slash of pinkish red suited her pale complexion and dark hair; it made her look sexy, but in a cheerful, rather than sultry, way. She stepped back from the mirror a little and adjusted her coat; it was a moss-green Harris tweed, with a nipped-in waist, a swing to the skirt, and a dark brown faux-fur collar. She always felt good in it; it was comfortable and snug, but with a touch of glamour, accentuating the curve of her waist. She wriggled her shoulders and hips, feeling the soft satin lining against them. Before Bob left, the coat had been getting a little tight for her. Now, with all this extra work and worry, she'd been eating less, and it was snug again, fitting just right.

She went downstairs, pausing to let the receptionist, Branwen, know her plans for the afternoon, then walked quickly to her car, parked a little way up the street. She got in, started the engine, and swung out into the traffic. The jams had disappeared now, and she had a fairly clear run down through the city centre to the Bay. Once she was there, she found a space at the back of the Assembly, parked the car, walked round to the front of the building, and went in.

Bob was waiting for her in the foyer, sitting reading the paper. That was a first. In the past, he'd always been in his office when she arrived, and she'd had to ask the receptionist to contact him, sometimes repeatedly, until he came down to meet her. Now the boot was on the other foot.

For a moment, before he noticed her, she watched him – dispassionately almost, as if she were meeting him on a first date. It was odd, she thought, how someone so familiar to her could, all of a sudden, seem like a stranger. Now in his fifties, he was still a good-looking man, she could see that; the type women found attractive. He had a full head of hair, greying now, but still wild and curly, as it had been when she'd first met him. His reading glasses, perched on his nose, seemed somehow to be foreign to him, as if he'd borrowed them for a moment, rather than depending on them daily to cope with his failing sight as he grew older. His shoulders were broad, and even though he was sitting down, you could see that he was a big, thickset man. In days gone by, whenever she'd seen him after a short parting, even after years of marriage, her heart had given a little jump of excitement. Today there was nothing; nothing but a kind of affectionate sadness for the memory of that feeling. She wondered if he felt the same.

'Jess.' He jumped up when he saw her, walked over to her, and enveloped her in a hug.

'Sorry I'm late.' She extricated herself as tactfully as she could.

'You're not. It's good to see you.'

The formal politeness of their greetings these days hurt her a little, but she tried not to show it.

They set out from the front of the Assembly, walking down the steps to the sea, and then on towards the far end of the Bay. It was a cold, grey day, and there weren't many people about.

'So, how are things?' Bob had pushed his specs up into his hair, and was narrowing his eyes against the bitter wind.

'Fine, really. Busy. You?'

'Not too bad. Hanging on in there.' He paused. Jess sensed there was something he wanted to tell her. Perhaps that was why he'd asked her to lunch.

They walked on in silence. Jess looked at the paving stones to the side of the walkway, where there were a series of carvings set into the stone like fossils: shapes of seaweed, starfish, wet sand, birds' footprints, mermaid's purses, shells. Sculpted into the stone, running along the top, was a wavy, indented line, like a trail – or perhaps it symbolized the water's edge.

'Shall we try the Norwegian Church?' she said. 'They've done it up.'

'If you want. But it's just soup and sandwiches, really. I wanted to treat you.'

'Thanks. That's sweet of you, Bob.' There it was again, that stiff politeness. 'Actually, I'd rather something . . . you know, informal.'

'Fine.' He looked a little downcast, but he didn't try to argue.

They walked on. Jess went back to following the trail marked out on the stones. Just as they came up to the little wooden church, it petered out. She'd never noticed that before. She wondered whether it had been the artist's intention for that to happen, or whether the council had just run out of money, decommissioning the sculpture at an arbitrary point. Whichever it was, it disturbed her slightly; something so familiar, that she'd assumed had a meaning, suddenly ending like that, for no good reason.

When they reached the Norwegian Church, they went inside and took a table by the window, with a view over the Bay. In the distance, you could see ships at sea, so far out that they barely appeared to move. The cafe was a cosy little place, the wooden walls festooned with twinkling lights, the windows slightly steamed up, a tempting smell of coffee in the air.

Jess ordered the fisherman's lunch – sweet herrings, mostly – while Bob decided on beef burger, salt potatoes and a couple of bottles of Hereford ale, one for each of them. Jess didn't resist. She rarely drank at lunchtime, but that afternoon she was due to go to the funeral of one of her ex-patients, and she felt she needed a spot of Dutch courage.

When the beers came, together with rosemary bread and olive oil, they made conversation for a while, dunking the bread in the oil, and then she said, 'So what is it you've got to tell me?'

'How d'you know I've got something to tell you?'

'You never normally take me out to lunch.'

He grinned. The beer was beginning to relax them both.

'I suppose you're right. But you know how it is. We're both busy . . .'

Jess nodded.

'Anyway . . . well, I was going to wait until later to tell you.'

'Later?'

'Over pudding, coffee.'

She laughed. 'You mean a bottle of wine later.'

Bob looked pained. 'I just wanted to enjoy being with you for a bit before I told you. Just in case you—'

'Oh go on, Bob, spit it out. Whatever it is.'

'OK.'

But then the food came, and they started to eat, aware that in a few moments the chance to savour their food might vanish, if things became awkward.

'I must say, you're looking really nice, Jess.' Bob swallowed a mouthful, leaned over, and poured Jess more beer. 'Is that a new dress?'

Jess had taken her coat off. Underneath she was wearing a fitted plum-coloured dress in fine wool, with a line of tiny silk-covered buttons at the bodice.

'I've had this for ages. Haven't you ever noticed it before?'

'Oh. I'm not sure.' He was flustered. 'Shall we get another beer?'

'No thanks. I don't want to be weaving up the aisle.'

Bob looked nonplussed for a moment. 'Oh God, yes. This

funeral. You poor thing.' He poured out the rest of the beer from his bottle and ordered another. As he did, his jacket fell open. Jess noticed that his belly was straining a little under the elegant cut of his shirt. He was gaining weight, and she was losing it. They were both struggling, she realized, with the separation and all it entailed. Both missing, if not each other, the security that had characterized their lives over the past two decades.

'Well, I suppose I should get this over.' He paused. 'The thing is, I've been seeing this woman.'

There was a silence. Of course Bob is seeing other women, Jess thought. We're separated. It was me who asked him to leave. Why wouldn't he be playing the field? He's an attractive man. But she still felt a stab of jealousy. And humiliation, because her tenderness towards him had been misdirected. He wasn't struggling with the separation at all. He'd gained weight because he was happy, contented. She'd been wrong about that.

'This woman?' She tried to keep her tone level, but there was a note of sarcasm in her voice.

'She's called Tegan. Tegan Davies. She's a newsreader on BBC Wales. You've probably seen her.'

'Maybe. What does she look like?' The question slipped out before Jess had a chance to stop herself.

'Well.' Bob looked uncomfortable. 'Blonde. Slim.'

'Attractive? Twenty-three?'

It was meant as a joke, referring back to their younger days when they were so politically correct, and they'd laughed over newspaper reports that began, 'Miss Jane Smith, blonde, attractive, twenty-three'. This time, though, it didn't come out as a joke, and she wished she hadn't said it.

Bob looked embarrassed. 'Well, she is a bit younger than me, actually.'

Jess said nothing, but continued to eat her rollmop. The fishy taste had begun to make her feel a little sick. She was glad she hadn't ordered anything heavier.

'Anyway,' he continued, swiftly moving on, 'she's asked me if she can meet the children. We've been seeing each other mostly at weekends . . .'

Jess put down her fork. She had a sudden vision of Bob's bijou residence in the Bay, an unmade bed, this Tegan woman wandering around in his shirt, all long tanned legs . . . She brushed it away.

'. . . And we thought it would be nice if Rose could stay overnight with us sometime, so we could do things together. Take her out for a pizza, over to Techniquest, that sort of thing.'

'Rose is too old for Techniquest.'

Techniquest was a sort of mini science museum in the Bay that the girls had loved when they were little. Bob didn't seem to realize that they'd grown up.

'Well, OK, maybe a boat trip.'

Jess knew Rose would love that. But she didn't say anything.

Jess picked up her fork and began to eat again. Bob's suggestion was not unreasonable, she knew. But it angered her. Why couldn't he screw his girlfriend during the week, and keep the weekends free for his daughter?

'It depends, really, on how serious you think this relationship is,' she said. 'I don't want Rose meeting every girlfriend you ever have.'

'Of course not.'

Did that mean that there were others?

'But Tegan is different.'

So there had been others.

'She really wants to be part of my life. And that includes my children.'

'And you? What do you really want?'

Bob stopped eating.

'You know my position, Jess. I never wanted us to separate.' He paused. Jess could see he was upset. 'I'm sorry I let you down, I really am. I've done everything I can to make amends. But since you won't – can't – forgive me, I've had to move on.'

The waitress came over with a bottle of beer. He took it from her and poured it out, offering Jess more, too. Although she'd previously declined, she nodded assent.

'I can't guarantee that Tegan and I will stay together, but I like her. She's a nice girl.' He checked himself. 'I mean, woman. I think Rose would like her. And Nella, too, if she'd countenance meeting her.'

'I think that's doubtful.'

Since Bob had moved out, Nella had become quite hostile to her father. She seemed to have decided that the rift was all his fault, despite Jess being scrupulously fair towards Bob in discussing it with her. She'd tried not to criticize Bob in the girls' presence; she knew only too well, from dealing with her clients, just how destructive it could be for children to witness continuous acrimony between their parents, and she was determined not to visit this particular misery on her own.

Bob took a sip of his beer. Rather more than a sip, in fact. More like a gulp.

'I can't see a problem with it, Jess. Can you?'

Jess gave a sigh. 'No. Not if it's a long-term relationship.' There was a slight tremble in her voice as she spoke. She'd got so used to Bob loving her, wanting her, and her pushing him away, that it was a shock to realize he'd given up and moved on to someone else. 'But please, be discreet. Don't throw the fact that you're sleeping with Tegan in Rose's face. She's at a very important point in her development. It could really upset her.'

'Of course. I'll—'

Jess interrupted him. 'I don't want to know about your

domestic arrangements. All I ask is that you make it easy for Rose. She loves you, you know.' Jess could feel the beer going to her head. 'She misses you.'

A look of anguish came over Bob's face. Jess realized, for the first time, that he missed Rose more than he missed her. She wondered whether he'd only wanted them to stay together so that he could be a father to Rose for a few more years before she grew up and left them, as Nella was close to doing. And she wondered whether, if she'd been a better mother, she would have let that happen.

'Right.' Bob picked up the menu. He never stayed sad for long. He was a doer, not a brooder. That was one of the things Jess had loved about him.

'How about a nice pud? Let's see . . . .'

Jess looked at her watch. 'I'll just have an espresso. And then I'll have to go.'

4

Frank O'Grady's funeral was a subdued affair. Frank was a former client of Jessica's, who had come to her for help with what he called his 'sex addiction', a condition that had come upon him late in life, after his diagnosis with advanced prostate cancer. He had been a difficult man: unfortunately, the sex addiction had extended to his relationship with his therapist, and he'd spent most of the sessions with Jess staring at her breasts, ogling her legs, and making lascivious remarks. She'd found the sessions most uncomfortable, and in the end had resorted to keeping a baggy cardigan in her consulting rooms, which she'd donned especially for his sessions. However, as his health deteriorated, she'd stopped wearing it, realizing that she had become the last person left in the world who would put up with his behaviour and try to understand him. A month ago, he'd gone into a hospice; she'd visited him there twice, and on each occasion, though he was painfully weak and thin, he'd found the strength to flirt with her, with a measure of affection, humour and respect. She'd responded similarly, no longer feeling the need to maintain her detachment, as she'd always had to do in the sessions; and he'd clearly taken comfort from her new-found warmth towards him. It had seemed like a small victory at the time, and she'd felt quite emotional when each of the visits was over; now that he was dead, she was glad she'd been patient with him, especially at the end.

The funeral was held at the Crem, as everyone in Cardiff called it. Jess had feared she might be the only person to attend; from what Frank had told her, she knew that he was on bad terms with his family, had few friends, and didn't get on with his neighbours. However, she needn't have worried; as it turned out, there was a respectable gathering of about twenty people. It was a short, simple service: a woman in her thirties, whom Jess took to be Frank's daughter, read the lesson; an older woman, who could have been his ex-wife, a carer or a neighbour, laid a small bunch of flowers on the coffin; a hymn was sung; prayers were said; and then it was all over.

Afterwards, the small crowd dispersed. There seemed to be no plans for a wake of any kind, and Jess knew no one there, so she, too, left discreetly. As she walked down the path to her car, she saw the hearse for the next cremation waiting, together with a knot of mourners, reminding her that Frank's body was one among many that would pass through that day. The words *sic transit gloria mundi* went through her head. There hadn't been much glory in Frank's life, she reflected, not towards the end of it, at any rate; but at least, she consoled herself, he'd had a decent burial, and a good turnout. The part of Cardiff where he'd lived was an old-fashioned place, in many ways; when someone died, whether or not he or she was well liked, the neighbours in the street turned out to the funeral, simply as a mark of respect for the passing of one of their number. Such rituals continued regardless of whether anyone believed in them or not; they were just what you did, without thinking, a common kindness extended to all.

As Jess got into her car and drove off, she felt suddenly exhausted. Frank had taken up fifty-five minutes of her day, once a week, almost every week, for the last two years. More if you counted the effort she'd put into reflecting on his problems, not to mention the wear and tear he'd inflicted on her own psyche with his relentless sexual harassment. Now he was gone. She wouldn't miss him; indeed, his passing was a positive relief. However, it left her with an uncomfortable feeling; trying as he had been, the fact that he was no longer alive and irritating the hell out of her made her feel flat, depressed almost. All that effort, to what end? Like the line imprinted in the paving stones outside the Norwegian Church, Frank's life had just stopped. The same with her marriage to Bob. The early days of passion, the arrival of children, the hard work, the gentle passage into familiarity and security and a sense of achievement . . . and then, quite suddenly, the drop into nothing.

She drove down the tree-lined path. It was raining, just spitting rather than a downpour, and the windscreen wipers were making their familiar scratching noise. She really should get them fixed, she told herself. It was the sort of thing Bob would have attended to in the past, and she hadn't quite acknowledged to herself that now it was up to her to do it.

She glanced at the clock on the dashboard. Her next session was coming up in half an hour. Perhaps she should have cancelled it, she thought, given herself a little time after the funeral.

A couple came up the road. They were young, in their twenties, and dressed in black. They were obviously late for the next funeral. As she passed, she saw that they were laughing. The woman was clumping along in a pair of ridiculously high heels, and the man had his arm around her, trying to help her run. Neither of them noticed her as she went by. There was an air about them that suggested a romance had just begun. Jess couldn't help smiling when she saw them. Life still went on, didn't it? Wearing stupid shoes, being late for appointments, falling in love . . .

Quite unexpectedly, she began to cry. She pulled over to the side of the road as soon as she could, scrabbled in her bag for a tissue, and sat sobbing at the wheel. It wasn't just about Frank, she knew, though that had been the trigger. It was about Rose missing her father, and Nella skipping school, and Bob seeing this new woman, and the lack of time she had to process all these changes in her life, what with the never-ending stream of clients passing through her consulting rooms. It was ridiculous, the schedule she was under; there wasn't even time to sit by the side of the road and shed a few tears after a funeral. The patients were beginning to feel like a burden; she was still receptive to their complex, volatile emotional demands, but the job was taking its toll, because she herself no longer had a husband whose role it was to attend to her needs. There was no one to share her worries with when she came home, whether about work, or the girls, or their finances, or where to go on holiday, or what colour to paint the bathroom. No one to laze around with on a Sunday morning, no one who told her she was beautiful, and wanted her, and made love to her, and . . .

She blew her nose and dried her eyes, chiding herself. Clearly, she was upset because Bob had lost interest in her, that was the truth of it. Seeing the giggling young lovers in the cemetery had sparked it off. She was behaving like a silly teenager, and like a teenager, she suspected she wasn't crying because she truly loved Bob, genuinely wanted him back; it was simply because he'd found someone else, and didn't want her any more.

She glanced at the clock on the dashboard again, realizing that she'd have to get a move on if she was to get back to her office in time for her next patient. But just then, her phone gave a cheery whistle. She glanced down at it. Text message. It was from Branwen, the receptionist, telling her that her next client had cancelled.

She felt a momentary sense of relief, followed by a pang of

concern about her client, Maria. She'd have to call later and find out if she was all right, perhaps rearrange the session. But for the moment, she had the luxury of an extra fifty minutes to kill.

She let in the clutch, and moved off into the traffic, heading towards the office. On the way, she decided to stop at Llandaff Cathedral. She wasn't religious, but sometimes she found that going into a church and simply sitting in a pew had a calming effect. It was something to do with the hush, the high ceilings, the stained windows, the air of otherworldliness that seemed both to focus her on, and lift her out of, her preoccupations. Also – and this was a motive she only dimly acknowledged to herself as she drove on towards the cathedral – it just so happened that Elinor's house was nearby, on Llandaff Green, and she was curious to take a look at the scene of the crime.

The traffic was heavy around the M4, but otherwise the drive through north Cardiff was reasonably clear. When she got to Llandaff, she parked the car next to the statue on the green. Before she got out, she looked up at it for a moment. She'd always liked this gaitered cleric with his pale green patina, who gazed out at the cathedral, surveying his little kingdom. He gave the village a peaceful, settled air, as if it was being overseen by some beneficent presence from more sedate, unhurried days gone by.

She got out of the car, and walked up to the high street, stopping to look at the flower shop on the way. On an impulse, she bought herself a bunch of snowdrops, for no other reason than that, after the sombre episode of the funeral, she felt she deserved a treat. Then she came back, slowing her pace, and took the road that ran alongside the cathedral.

Jess had mixed feelings about Llandaff village. It wasn't really separate from the city, but with its pretty shops and houses clustered on a hilltop around the twelfth-century cathedral, it had a distinct air of being a cut above. It was an expensive place to live, relative to the other neighbourhoods, housing well-heeled professionals, as well as a few of the local clergy attached to the cathedral. There was a private school nearby, which undertook the task of training choristers and future pillars of the establishment. All in all, one got the impression of a closed, rather old-fashioned microcosm, a world unto itself that was both attractive in its sedate Victorian values, and repellent in its sealed-off smugness.

When she saw Elinor's house, she couldn't help feeling envious: it was a white-fronted building with an elegant porch and arched windows overlooking an expansive front garden shaded by a large tree. There was a high, clipped hedge all the way around the garden, and a black iron gate leading into it. From where she stood, she could see that the stone path that led to the front door also ran round the sides of the house to the back, and that there was more garden behind the house.

She turned and crossed the road, walking down the steps to the cathedral. As she did, she saw a man come up to the gate of the house, open it, and go down the path. He was tall and broad-shouldered with dark hair. His collar was up, and he looked slightly surreptitious, as if he didn't want anyone to notice him. She only caught a glimpse of his face, but she saw that he wore a frown, as if concentrating on some serious purpose. He didn't notice her, intent as he was on his own business. She wondered who he was, and what he was doing. He didn't look as if he was on a social call; rather, he had the air of a man on a mission. She turned away, aware that she had no business to be snooping, and cross with herself that she hadn't understood her unconscious motive for coming here to the green.

She went on towards the cathedral, stopping for a moment to look up at the high steeple before she went down the steps to enter it. It always made her dizzy looking up at the weather-vane on the top, silhouetted against the sky. Today, there was a ladder attached to the side of the tiles – They must be repairing it, she thought – which added to the sense of vertigo. Crows flew in and out of the flying buttresses and in between the gargoyles at the top of the roof, cawing loudly as they went. She couldn't imagine climbing up there. Or rather, she could, and it made her feel sick to think of it.

She glanced back at Elinor's house. Only the top of the house was visible from where she stood. She saw a figure come to an upstairs window and close the curtain. She couldn't be sure who it was, but it looked, from a distance, like the man she'd just seen at the gate. She wondered what he was doing drawing the curtains – it wasn't dark yet. But she didn't want to pry, so she walked on.

She entered the doorway of the cathedral, nodded at the old lady sitting by the postcard shop, walked down the aisle, and took a seat near the altar. There was nothing going on at present, she was relieved to find. She gazed upwards at the Jacob Epstein, the strangely elongated figure of Christ with its placid visage, suspended over the massive concrete arch erected in the sixties as part of the restoration of the building after the war that, for all its majesty, reminded her of a motorway bridge. She couldn't get much sense of grace from either of them, so she closed her eyes.

There was no sound, except the soft echo of footfalls as a curate, or some such, moved around the choristers' pews, engaged in an arcane ritual of preparation for a service. For a moment, the world seemed to slow down.

She whispered a prayer, to a God she didn't believe in. She prayed that Bob would still remain close to the girls, would still be their father. She prayed that one day her sadness over the failure of her marriage would pass, that she would find someone else, or perhaps begin to savour life on her own, without the responsibility of a partner. She gave thanks that she still had her daughters to love, her patients to attend to, and good friends and family. That she was well established here, in this small, warm community. That she was important to people, and they were important to her. And she prayed that, for the time being at least, all this would be enough.

5

Jess was waiting for Elinor to arrive for her session. She was going over her notes, and looking over some further research she'd done on claustrophobia. It might be an idea, she thought as she read, for Elinor to have a further medical check-up: according to the latest neurological thinking, certain inner-ear infections and abnormalities in the nerve cells of the brain can result in the disorder, as in these instances sensory information may be misread, causing a panic response. That said, given that the claustrophobia had occurred since her mother's death, it seemed more likely that the disorder was purely neurotic, with no physiological cause. And it also seemed clear that, for the time being, it wasn't going to abate, since she was still under considerable emotional stress.

The door to the consulting room was open, and a few minutes past the appointed hour, Elinor walked in. She pushed the door to, but didn't close it completely. Then she took off her mac, hung it up, and walked over to the couch, acknowledging Jess with a brief nod. As before, the window was open a crack. Elinor leaned over and opened it wider. Much wider.

Bad sign, thought Jess, as she went over to the armchair behind the couch and sat down.

Elinor settled herself on the couch and closed her eyes. She looked tense, Jess thought. Her face was white and drawn, and there were pale blue rings under her eyes.

Silence fell. Jess shivered. She wished she'd worn a thicker sweater, or turned up the heating a bit more before the session.

She wondered what was going on in Elinor's mind. She sensed that there was something else troubling her besides her mother's death, something she had not yet mentioned. Yet she knew better than to press her. Whatever it was, it would emerge sooner or later, whether directly or in some more oblique way.

Elinor's eyes remained closed. Jess began to wonder, after a while, whether she'd fallen asleep. She'd had clients do that on the couch quite a few times, in the days when she was training. It was just another avoidance mechanism, along with all the others she'd learned to recognize.

As the minutes ticked by, she had the urge to tuck a blanket round Elinor's outstretched form. She looked so thin and white lying there under the window, with the cold air streaming in from outside, her hair so fair and fine on the dark green pillow, like a sick child. Poor thing, thought Jess. Her mother dead. Her father, too. Orphaned. Her sister married. Living all alone in that great big house, her family gone . . .

'You'd think they'd leave the relatives alone at a time like this.' Elinor's voice broke the silence at last. 'But they won't stop pestering us.'

Jess remembered the policewoman that Elinor had mentioned in the last session.

'She came round again yesterday, saying she wanted to go down and look at the studio. I let her in, but I stayed outside in the garden.' Elinor's voice quavered. She was near to tears. 'It made me so angry, having her snooping around looking through my things. It's been four months since it happened. Surely they could leave me alone now. I can't stand it any longer.'

Elinor began to sob.

Jess had an urge to reach forward and hug her, but she managed to maintain her professional composure. There was a box of tissues on a table beside the couch, so she leaned over and pushed it towards her.

Elinor sat up, took one, and dabbed at her eyes. Then she lay down again.

'The problem is,' she went on, the tears subsiding, 'I don't have an alibi. They've got me on CCTV when I was walking around Cardiff shopping, but there was no one else there when I found Ma.' She crumpled the tissue into a ball, kneading it in her fingers. 'Isobel hasn't got one either. She was in her house that day. She hadn't gone in to the gallery because she had a cold.'

'The gallery?'

'She runs the gallery now. The one my father used to own.' Once again, Elinor spoke as if Jess ought to know what she was talking about. 'The Frederick Powell Gallery. You must know it. It's the only decent contemporary art gallery in Cardiff. Or Wales, come to that.'

Jess murmured assent, in a noncommittal way.

'And then there's my brother-in-law, Blake.' For a moment, Elinor hesitated. 'He was apparently in London, in a meeting with Mia, his business partner. She runs a gallery in London, and he's an art consultant, advising rich people on how to spend their money. Hedge fund managers and suchlike.' Elinor's tone lost its forlorn quality. 'They'll take any old rubbish, as long as Blake talks them into it.' There was contempt in her voice as she spoke. 'Anyway, that's beside the point. Mia's backed him up, says they were at her flat, going through catalogues. But I must say, I don't altogether believe her. Or him.'

She stopped kneading the tissue and tucked it into her sleeve.

'He's a wheeler-dealer is Blake,' she went on. 'I think he

married Isobel to get his hands on the gallery. And on the Powell name.' She paused. 'I'm not saying he was directly responsible for Ma's death, of course – I don't think he'd go that far. But he knew where the Gwen John was kept. And he knew how much it was worth.'

Jess was taken aback. She wondered whether Elinor's distrust of Blake could be occasioned by jealousy of her sister. But perhaps that was the psychotherapist in her, always looking to the family dynamic for answers. Best not to jump to conclusions, she told herself, at this stage, anyway.

'To be honest, I feel bloody furious with my mother,' Elinor went on, abruptly changing the subject, which made Jess wonder whether her accusation against Blake had been serious. 'If she hadn't come round to see me that day, unannounced as usual, none of this would have happened.'

Jess pricked up her ears. This was what she'd been waiting for. At last, she hoped, Elinor was going to talk about the death of her mother.

Elinor tried to settle herself, wriggling her shoulders to get comfortable, but she seemed ill at ease.

'That afternoon, I'd gone to buy some ink pens in this nice little arts and crafts shop in the Arcades. Once I'd got in there, I spent hours looking at the different kinds of nibs, and so on. They have whole books of them, tiny little nibs with different shapes. Like a butterfly album.' She paused. 'I bought several tiny ones, just to see what I could do with them – I haven't used inks before – but actually, they weren't that good, as it turned out. They were so delicate, they kept bending out of shape when you pressed them on the paper, and splattering ink everywhere.' She looked thoughtful. 'Perhaps I was using them in the wrong way.'

Come on, thought Jess. That's enough about nibs. Get to the point.

'Anyway,' Elinor went on, realizing she was digressing, 'while I was out, my mother came round. She was over from Italy. They'd moved out there about ten years ago, when my father got ill and retired, leaving me to look after the house on Llandaff Green for them. I was short of money, you see, so they let me live there rent free. By that time, Isobel was married to Blake, and they had a big place in the Vale, so she was fine.' There was a note of bitterness in Elinor's tone. 'But when Pa died, Ma kept coming back. She normally stayed with Isobel and Blake when she was over, said she couldn't bear to be back in the old house, that it held too many memories for her. But in actual fact, she was always popping round for one reason or another, usually without warning. It was one of the things I found rather . . .' She hesitated. '. . . A little bit irritating about her. She was terribly lonely after my father died, though, so we tried to be patient with her. Isobel was better at it than I was.'

She came to a halt. There was a touch of resentment in her tone, but it passed as she continued.

'Ursula – my mother – had a set of keys to the house. She wasn't supposed to let herself in any time she felt like it, but she often did. Anyway, that day she came round, and when she found nobody there, she went down to the studio in the garden.' Elinor's brow furrowed. 'That was odd, I thought. She didn't usually go anywhere near the studio. She didn't like to see me working in all that clutter, she said.' She paused. 'It was a bit of a mess, I suppose. There wasn't much space in there. But it went deeper than that, I think.'

'Deeper?' Elinor didn't seem to need much prompting now, but occasionally Jess echoed a word, just to let her know she was following her story.

Elinor nodded. 'You see, she'd given up painting when she got married and had us. It was never quite clear why. I mean, obviously, when we were little, it wasn't easy to fit it in, but later, she had plenty of time. And Pa always encouraged her. But for some reason, she never took it up again. I think that made her restless and . . .' She hesitated again. 'A little bit jealous, perhaps. Of me.'

Elinor spoke the words tentatively, as if voicing something she'd known for a long time, but never expressed before.

'Anyway,' she went on, after a pause, 'for whatever reason, Ma went down to the studio. I don't know what she was doing, possibly looking for something, but when she got in, she found someone already there.'

Elinor spoke as if willing herself to continue.

'The man – I suppose it was a man – must have crept down the side path from the front of the house to the studio. It was locked, but he broke in.' A look of renewed anguish came over her face. 'I wish I hadn't kept that painting in there.'

'The Gwen John?'

Elinor nodded.

There was a silence.

'We don't know exactly what happened when she came in the door, but she must have disturbed him because he attacked her. Hit her with something big and heavy. The police didn't find a weapon. He must have taken it with him.' She paused, as if steeling herself to continue. 'Anyway, he beat her round the head, on the right-hand side.' Her tone became flat and unemotional. 'The autopsy said the impact to the head caused her brain to move inside the skull. A *coup-contrecoup* effect, they call it. She died of a massive brain haemorrhage.'

There was another silence, this time a longer one.

'When I arrived home and found her, it was a terrible shock, of course. I came into the house and went down to the studio. I wanted to try out my new nibs. I found the door unlocked, which I thought was strange. I turned the lights on and saw her there, lying on the floor. My first thought was that she'd had a heart attack. I rushed over to her, and then I saw the bruise on the right-hand side of her head. At first I didn't think it looked that bad, just a purple blotch on her temple. I thought perhaps she'd fallen over and banged it, that she was just concussed. Her skin was still warm to the touch. She was a terrible colour, though, very pale. Then I saw this clear liquid coming out of her nose and mouth. I pushed her hair back and saw it was coming out of her ears as well. That's when I knew something terrible had happened.'

Elinor shifted her head on the cushion, as if her neck was hurting her.

'I phoned the ambulance right away. I still didn't believe she was dead. While I waited, I did what I could. I laid a blanket over her, to try and keep her warm. I thought about pushing on her chest, you know, the Heimlich manoeuvre or whatever it's called, but I decided it was best not to move her. I wondered about mouth-to-mouth resuscitation, but I didn't have a clue how to do it. So I ended up just sitting beside her, holding her hand, as it grew colder and colder in mine.'

She came to a halt. Elinor let the silence surround them for a moment, as if to honour the gravity of what had happened.

'The paramedics examined her. They confirmed that she was dead.' Elinor's voice shook slightly as she said the word. 'They said I'd done all the right things, not moving her, keeping her warm. That I couldn't have resuscitated her, whatever I'd tried to do. That was important to me.'

Jess nodded silently. She'd heard that paramedics were now being given training as to how to deal with relatives when a death occurs. She was glad that, in this case, it had benefited Elinor.

Elinor took a deep breath, held it for a moment, then let it out again. She seemed more comfortable now, relieved that she'd got near the end of her story.

'After that,' she went on, 'everything started to happen at once. The studio seemed to be full of people. The police were called, and the coroner, and the undertaker, who took away the body. I was in a daze. The police started questioning me, asking if anything in the studio had been taken. It was only then that I realized the painting wasn't on the wall. I hadn't noticed it up to that point.' She paused. 'The funny thing was, although it had been my prize possession, I wasn't really bothered. I felt a sense of relief that it was gone, actually.' She hesitated for a moment. 'But then they asked me if anything else was missing, so I went over to my desk at the window, and saw that my paints and brushes had been meddled with. In particular, there was a phial of ochre that had been spilled. When I saw that, I suddenly felt absolutely furious. I couldn't understand it. My mother had just been murdered, and all I seemed to care about was the fact that someone had been mucking about with my paints.'

'That's quite a common reaction, you know.' Jess spoke quietly. 'It's a kind of displacement. When someone's had a shock they often find something insignificant to focus their emotion on.'

'But the feeling hasn't left me.' There was a note of anger in Elinor's voice. 'I'm terribly upset about what happened to my mother, of course, but sometimes I just feel fed up that my life has been disturbed. I've got this bloody claustrophobia to cope with now. I can't go into the studio. Or concentrate on my work.' She paused. 'And then, of course, I feel guilty about being so selfish.'

Jess chose her words with care, aware that she didn't want to offer meaningless reassurances.

'Well, your life has been disturbed. The shock does seem to have triggered this claustrophobia. You can't lead a normal life. You can't paint any more. It's not surprising you should feel frustrated about that.'

Elinor sighed. 'I suppose you're right. There are so many things to deal with now, it just seems never-ending. It took ages for them to release the body for the funeral, the inquest seemed to go on and on, and in the end they just told us what we knew already – that she'd been beaten about the head and had died as a result of brain injury. Then there was this police investigation, which hasn't yielded anything, either. And now there's a ton of legal stuff to sort out. I'm absolutely sick of the whole thing.'

Jess was concerned. Elinor seemed strangely detached – a coping mechanism, she knew, as was her anger at having her paints disturbed. But she also wondered whether there might perhaps be a grain of truth in the way Elinor had described herself, as selfish. That was what artists were like, she knew – she'd had quite a few of them in therapy. In general, she'd found them obsessed with themselves and their work, frustrated by intrusions of any kind – often to the point where they seemed unable to understand that anything else, including the death of a family member, could be more important. And she found herself questioning certain aspects of what Elinor had told her – if the police had no leads on the robbery, why did this police-woman keep turning up at the house? What was she after? And why had Elinor's mother gone down to the studio after letting herself in, thus disturbing the thief? Could she have been looking for something in there? Was it perhaps she who'd been looking through Elinor's paints?

Elinor fell silent, gazing out of the window. She seemed impervious to the cold, although by now Jess was having trouble stopping her teeth from chattering.

'Do you think perhaps we could close the window a little bit?' Jess formulated the question in the most tactful way she could think of.

Elinor sat up and, to Jess's surprise, shut the window completely. Then she lay down on the couch again.

'I'm glad I told you all that.' She sighed. 'I feel better now.'

So there it all was, thought Jess, just as she'd anticipated. The cramped, cluttered studio, where Elinor had experienced the horror of finding her mother's body, could well have triggered an association in her mind between an enclosed space and a terrifying event. Her anger at her mother's persistent meddling, which this time had led to tragedy, would have been another factor in the mix. Moreover, since she'd suggested that her relationship with her mother was a difficult one, she might perhaps be feeling a sense of profound relief, as well as shock and sadness, at her mother's death; her guilt about that, expressed as anger at herself for having failed to install a burglar alarm, might also have contributed to her neurosis. That much was clear.

However, there were many other parts of Elinor's psyche still to be explored – her relationship with her sister Isobel, her jealousy of Blake, and her rather paranoid accusation that he'd been behind the robbery.

'I think we'll have to stop there for today, Elinor.' Jess spoke in a low, gentle tone. 'Our time is up.'

6

Jessica was masochistically torturing herself. She was watching Tegan Davies presenting the news.

She'd tried to stop herself all week, but by Friday, her curiosity had got too much for her. The minute she'd come in from work, she'd switched on the television and watched the six o'clock news, which was something she very rarely did. Even more rare, she'd stayed watching until the announcement came on, 'and now for the news in *your* area'. Then Tegan had appeared, against a backdrop of the red-brick Pierhead building in the Bay, lit up at night. She was a pretty blonde, with regular features and a perfectly made-up face. Around her neck was a gold chain with a blue stone at the collarbone, matching the earrings that glinted under her coiffed hair.

Jess scrutinized her as she spoke, not hearing her words. Her clothes were odd, she thought: a cream jacket over a cream camisole. Like Lana Turner in *The Postman Always Rings Twice*, minus the turban. She studied her face; it was hard to tell what it was like under the make-up, but it seemed forgettable. Blue eyes, made larger by professionally applied shadow and mascara; a thin, rather insignificant nose; and fleshy lips, slathered in gloss. She looked down at her torso; it was difficult to see what her body was like under the modest blouse, but she appeared somewhat flat-chested . . .

'Mum?' Nella came into the sitting room.

Jessica picked up the remote control, pressed the button, and Tegan Davies disappeared.

'Come and talk to me for a minute.' Jess patted the sofa. 'How was your day?'

'Not too bad.' Nella didn't sit down. Instead, she hovered by the doorway, pulling at the hem of her T-shirt and standing on one leg, twisting the other round it.

'Did you manage to get in to college?'

Nella nodded. 'I was a bit late, though.'

Jessica was about to embark on her time-worn lecture about being punctual for lessons, but decided against it. Her daughter knew perfectly well what she was supposed to do; if she didn't keep up, she'd have to face the consequences, in the form of failing or retaking exams. Jess had explained that to her often enough. At nearly seventeen, she was too old to be treated like a child.

'Is Gareth coming over tonight?'

'No, we're going out.' Nella paused, as if there was something more she wanted to say, but had decided against it. She looked guilty about something, Jess thought. She wondered what it was.

'Well, text me if you stay at Gareth's, won't you.'

'Course.' Nella came over and planted a wet kiss on her mother's cheek. 'I may stay over at his place for the weekend, though.'

Jess couldn't help feeling disappointed. Nella could be moody, but more often these days she was a cheerful, affectionate presence around the house. When she wasn't there, Jess missed her, and she sensed that Rose missed her too, although she'd never have admitted to such a thing.

Nella went off to get ready. Just as she left the room, the phone rang. Jess picked it up.

'Hiya. How's things?'

It was her friend Mari.

'OK. Kind of.' Jess hesitated before continuing. Mari had been a pillar of strength during the split with Bob, but now that the drama was over, she tried not to offload on her every time they spoke. Besides, there was nothing particularly wrong at the moment.

'You don't sound very sure. What is it? Bob again?'

It was no good trying to hide her worries, Jess realized. Better to tell all, and then move on.

'Well, I had lunch with him in the week. He says he's seeing this woman' – Jess tried not to sound censorious as she said the word – 'and he wants her to meet the kids.'

'Who is she?'

'Tegan Davies. She's a newsreader.'

'Tegan? Never!' Mari had a weakness for gossip, but rarely of the malicious kind.

'So you know her, do you?'

'Not well. But I see her around quite a lot.' Unlike Jess, Mari was immensely sociable, and knew everyone in Cardiff's media and arts world.

'Well, I wouldn't worry about that, *cariad*,' Mari went on. 'I doubt it'll last.'

'Why d'you say that?'

'She's a nice girl, Tegan.' Jess remembered that Bob had said the same thing about her. It had struck her as odd at the time, faint praise from a man supposedly in love. 'But from what I hear, she's high maintenance. She'll start stamping her foot, and wanting it all her own way, and then Bob'll be off. You'll see.'

'I wouldn't be so sure.' Jess hesitated, knowing that she shouldn't pry. Then her curiosity got the better of her.

'How old would you say she is?'

'Late thirties, probably. But it's hard to tell. She's had a bit of work done – they all do.' Mari paused. 'Anyway, she hasn't got kids. So the old biological clock will be ticking pretty loud by now. And that'll scare Bob off, too.'

Mari had a cheerfully pragmatic view of life. An actress who was always in work, mostly in Welsh-language TV, she was thoroughly enjoying life as a single woman now that she was divorced and her children had grown up. She and Jess were like chalk and cheese – Mari flamboyant and impulsive, Jess reserved and reflective – but they were close, sharing a strong bond of affection and concern for each other.

The mere thought of Bob going on to have a new family with Tegan upset Jess, so she quickly changed the subject.

'How are things with you, then?'

'Pretty good. I've got a fabulous part in a new theatre production, *Sexual Perversity in Chicago*. I'm playing a bitter, twisted, man-hating bitch.' Mari spoke the words with relish. 'I'll tell you about it when I see you, but I'm in a bit of a rush now.' She paused. 'I was just ringing to ask if you want to go to a party with me at the museum tomorrow evening? It's a private view for this trendy new artist, Hefin Morris.'

'Oh yes?'

'He's a total mystery, apparently. Like Bansky. A bit of a firebrand. Doesn't want to be part of the whole art circus.' Mari warmed to her story. 'The rumour is, he's an ex-miner living somewhere up in the valleys, but no one knows where. He paints these massive canvasses showing the insides of abandoned mines. The terrible destruction wreaked by capitalism kind of thing.'

'Sounds a bit grim.'

'I know. But they're really pushing the boat out for this exhibition, I'm told. It's going to be a big event. Champagne, canapés, the works. *Le tout* Cardiff will be there. And it'll be full of incredibly pretentious people from this London art gallery where his work's being sold.'

'That's hardly a plus, is it?'

'Course it is. Listen to this.' She heard Mari scrabble for a piece of paper, and then she began to read. '"Hefin Morris explores the potential of peripherality, in a series of works that create tentative dialogues within an abstract, non-summative space, circumventing representation to question the notion of painting as a fully realized practice and reimagining it as a con-tinuous reconfiguration, enigmatically subverting the concept of political and artistic agency by distorting and mutating the idea of authorship and originality."' She paused. 'Come on, Jess, what's not to like?'

Jess laughed.

'But we might have to listen to hours of speeches like that.'

'No way. If it gets boring, we'll just skip off for a drink in town.'

Jess thought about it. Rose had arranged to go over to her friend's for a sleepover on Saturday night. She herself had made no plans, other than catching up on some reading.

'Why not?' she said, making up her mind. 'Though I might not stay for long.'

'Whatever you like.' Mari paused. 'Six thirty at the museum, then. I'll be in the lobby.'

'Fine. What should I wear, d'you think?'

'Something glam. Or arty. Whatever it is, don't look too matchy-matchy. Unless it's tops and bottoms in the same fabric.' She paused again. 'But then again, maybe not. It might look as if you're wearing pyjamas.'

'Right.' Jess was slightly nonplussed. Mari's rules about fashion violations never made any sense to her. 'Well, I'll do my best.'

'Till tomorrow, then, *cariad*. Ta-ra.'

Jess clicked the phone off, wondering whether she should have accepted Mari's invitation. She'd rather cherished the idea of an evening alone on the sofa with a book. Still, she thought, it was time she got out and about again, as a single woman. It would be a strange feeling, being on her own again in that kind of situation, without Bob at her side; but nothing ventured, nothing gained.

She got up off the sofa and went to find Rose.

She was in her bedroom, the door open to the landing. When Jess went in, she saw she'd laid out her clothes on the bed.

'Packing for your sleepover?' Jess came over and stood beside her.

'No.' Rose seemed preoccupied. 'More for the future.'

'The future?'

'When I go and stay with Dad.' She paused. 'And Tegan.'

Bob had picked Rose up from school earlier that day, taken her out to tea, and told her about Tegan. Jess had been surprised at how quickly he'd done it, but she could hardly complain, having given her permission for the visit to go ahead.

'I just want to make sure I've got everything I need.' Rose picked up a pink washbag covered in dancing hippos, and frowned at it.

'I'll buy you a new one.'

'Thanks. Now, which do you think, Mum?' She held up a pink cotton nightie. Then she gestured towards her favourite pyjamas, which featured a Moomin design on the front.

'I suppose the pyjamas would be warmer.'

'But the nightie's more . . .'

'Mmm.' Jess paused, realizing for the first time that Rose was thinking about what would impress Bob's new girlfriend. When she'd come home, she'd told Jess that Tegan was her favourite TV newsreader, and that she was excited to meet her.

'Well, wear whichever you feel more comfortable in.' Jess realized this was beside the point, but she couldn't think of anything else to say.

'And for the boat trip, I thought . . .' Rose reached over and picked up a woollen varsity jacket with the letter 'R' appliquéd on one side. 'With my denim shorts and black tights. And my Converse. Do you think?'

Jess nodded. 'Lovely, darling.' She paused. 'I'll plait your hair before you go, if you like.'

In the last few days, Rose had taken to wearing her hair in a French plait, which involved a complicated operation of plaiting plaits into other plaits, and necessitated Jess's help.

'No thanks. I think I'll wear it loose. But you could blow-dry it if you want.'

Jess pictured Tegan's shiny tresses, and realized that Rose was trying to emulate her look.

'Fine.' Jess changed the subject. 'Now, what shall we have for supper? Shall we cook something together? And then watch an episode of *Sabrina*, maybe?'

Sabrina the Teenage Witch was Rose's favourite old TV show. Bob had given her a boxed set for Christmas, and they still had quite a few episodes to get through.

'Maybe.' Rose went over to her wardrobe and began looking through it. 'I just want to sort this out first. It might take a while.'

She took out a pair of fur-lined boots with pompoms at the sides, and looked at them, furrowing her brow, evidently deep in thought.

Watching her, Jess felt a pang of sadness. Rose was growing up, she realized. She'd always liked to look neat, tidy and feminine, but up until now, she hadn't been particularly self-conscious about what she wore. Perhaps this had needed to happen, Jess reflected. Rose was rather young for her age, after all. But the change had been so sudden, and there was something a little sad about the fact that it had been prompted by news of her father's glamorous new girlfriend.

Jess went over and stood by the door. 'I'll do the supper, then. We'll eat in about half an hour. See you downstairs.'

7

When Jessica got to the museum on Saturday evening, she checked in her coat and bag, and then went to look for Mari. There was a crowd of people in the foyer. Drinks were being served from a temporary table set up near the entrance, so she went over and got herself a glass. She was expecting the usual acrid party fizz, but when she tasted it, she found it was subtle and delicious. She looked down at her glass, and saw an intricate trail of tiny bubbles rising from the bottom. Proper champagne. She took another sip, scanning the hall for her friend.

Mari was over by the staircase, standing in front of a statue of Perseus brandishing Medusa's snake-haired head, and talking to a good-looking man in an impeccably cut suit. She was wearing a figure-hugging burgundy dress that outlined her substantial curves, with a large rhinestone brooch clasped to her bosom. She looked extremely glamorous, and even though Jess couldn't see his face, it was clear that the man she was talking to thought so too. She was laughing a lot, throwing her head back, and he was leaning in close as she did.

She gave Mari a wave, and Mari waved back. She'd go over and talk to her later, she decided, give her some room for manoeuvre. In the meantime, she'd see if there was anyone else there she knew.

As she moved through the crowd, all twittering excitedly like sparrows in a tree, she began to feel slightly insecure. She'd spent a long time deciding what to wear for the party, and had finally settled on a little black dress and heels. She'd put up her hair in a simple French roll, added some clip-on earrings and a slick of bright red lipstick, and left it at that. She'd felt elegant yet understated when she left the house, but now, seeing the glitz and sparkle of the other women, she wondered whether her outfit was too plain.

She wished, for a moment, that she hadn't come. She was never at her best at parties. Couldn't do the banter, the small talk. And now she was starting to realize that since the split with Bob, she'd lost the taste for such social situations. Normally she would have enjoyed the buzz around her; but tonight, the sheer volume of chatter simply hurt her ears, and set her teeth on edge.

She looked around, hoping to find a friendly face. There was a knot of people standing over by the statue of the little drummer boy that graced the hallway. She peered at them, and as she looked closer, saw that Elinor was among them. She looked almost unrecognizable: elegantly turned out, and supremely confident in her bearing. She'd had her hair cut in a geometric bob, and was dressed in a quiet grey suit like a man's, with a cream silk shirt underneath, buttoned up to the neck. With her luminous blonde locks, high cheekbones and slanting blue eyes, her sober, serious look was more striking than the most bejew-elled woman there.

Next to her was a good-looking, broad-shouldered man with shiny dark hair, gelled into a playful, faintly ridiculous quiff at the front. He was suited and booted, but casually so, with a pink open-necked shirt and no tie. He looked familiar, though

Jess couldn't place him. She gazed at him, wondering where she'd seen him before. Then, with a shock, she realized who he was: the man who'd been walking up the path to Elinor's house the day she'd visited the cathedral. The man she'd seen at the window, drawing the curtains at dusk.

There was a tap on her shoulder, and she turned round.

Standing in front of her was another Elinor. The Elinor she knew. Diffident, otherworldly. Dressed in her ancient, faded clothes, her hair slightly dishevelled, a puzzled look on her face.

'Elinor. Hello. Oh.'

Elinor gave her a shy smile.

'Sorry, I'm a bit confused here.' Jess gestured at the woman in the circle of people by the statue. 'Who's that?'

'Isobel, of course. My sister.'

'You look so incredibly alike. D'you know, for a moment, I thought—'

'Well, of course we do.' There was a note of irritation in Elinor's voice. 'We're twins. I told you that, didn't I?'

'No.'

'I'm sure I did.'

Jess decided to let the matter pass. It was highly significant, of course, in terms of the therapy, that Elinor hadn't mentioned the existence of her twin, but this wasn't the place to discuss the matter.

'I'll introduce you later. Isobel would like to meet you. And Blake.' She lowered her voice. 'Remember, I told you about him?'

She gave Jess a meaningful look.

'Oh, right.' Jess was flustered. She glanced over at Blake, who was talking and smiling animatedly. He was definitely the man she'd seen visiting Elinor the day she'd stopped off at the cathedral. She'd watched him draw the curtains at the window upstairs, and had wondered if the two of them were having an affair.

'I didn't know you were an art buff.' Elinor was curious.

'I'm not. A friend invited me.'

'Well, I'm glad you're here.' Elinor adopted a conspiratorial tone. 'I hate these kind of events. I find them such an ordeal.' She paused. 'I had to be here, of course, to support Isobel and Blake. Hefin Morris is their new find.' She hesitated. 'D'you know his work?'

Jess shook her head.

'I think you'd like it.' She hesitated. 'We can go upstairs now, if you like, and have a look at the paintings. I can show you round, before everyone goes up.'

'I'd love to, but I'm meeting a friend.' Jess extricated herself as tactfully as she could. 'I think I'd better go and find her.'

Elinor nodded, but she looked disappointed.

'See you later, then.'

'OK. Later.'

Jess went off to look for Mari. She felt uncomfortable about bumping into Elinor. It really didn't do for her to be hobnobbing with a client outside the sessions. And it was entirely her fault that this had happened. She should have realized that Elinor and her family, as the owners of the Powell Gallery, would attend the opening of a major new exhibition at the museum. And that the artist they were showing might well be one of their protégés.

She spotted Mari heading for the drinks table. This time, she was alone.

'There you are. I wondered where you'd got to.' Mari gave her a hug.

Jess hugged her back. 'You seemed to be busy.'

'Mmm. I was.' Mari sighed. 'Lovely guy. Works for the Millenium Centre.' She sighed again. 'Married, unfortunately. No kids, though,' she added after a moment, brightening.

'He looked quite keen.'

'He was. But I can't go in for all that cloak and dagger stuff. Not at my age.' Mari put her head on one side, scrutinizing Jess's appearance. 'You know, that up-do really suits you. Very *continentale.*'

Jess rolled her eyes, but she was pleased at her friend's compliment. She often felt a little dowdy next to Mari, who was always the epitome of glamour, whatever the occasion.

Mari drained her glass. 'Let's go up and take a look at these paintings, shall we? Then we can sneak off. I don't want to get stuck listening to a load of speeches.'

They walked up the grand stone staircase, Mari teetering on her platforms, hanging on to the brass banister for safety. When they got to the upper floor, Jess lingered beside the cabinets displaying the old china. She'd always loved wandering around the museum. It was a fine early twentieth-century building, constructed as part of the capital's civic complex, with a graceful art deco interior. When the children had been little, Jess had often taken them there, to the natural history rooms to look at the filmed volcanic explosions and the woolly mammoths that bellowed and moved their heads mechanically. Since then, over the years, she'd dropped in occasionally to visit the collection bequeathed by the Davies sisters, two spinster daughters of a Victorian coal baron who'd spent their fortune on the groundbreaking art of their day. There were Turners, Corots, Millets, Rodins, Cézannes, and a fabulous array of Monets. Part of her felt she owned these paintings; whenever they were loaned out she missed them, and was glad when they returned. That was one advantage of living in a small capital city: you felt affectionate towards its treasures, rather than overwhelmed by them.

Once inside, Jess and Mari worked their way around the Morris exhibition. The paintings on show were striking, if not exactly to Jess's taste. They were extremely large, and very dark in colour, mostly brown and black with only a few specks of greenish grey, petrol blue and ochre. They were painted in oil, and covered in streaks of what looked like coal dust. Now and then, the streaks caught the light, showing a gleam of silver.

'These are awful,' whispered Mari. 'Don't you think?'

Jess gave a non-committal shrug. Mari was always too quick to form an opinion, in her view.

Mari went off and stood by the door, ready to make her getaway. Jess continued to walk slowly round the room, gazing at each painting, waiting to see what might happen. She knew from experience that there might be more here than met the eye; she'd often, in the past, gone to an exhibition and been unmoved, only to find herself thinking about the works later. She had a feeling these might have the same effect.

At the far end of the room was the largest canvas, spanning almost an entire wall. Beside it hung a nineteenth-century painting borrowed from the museum's collection. It was one that Jess knew well, a charming portrait of a goose girl by Jean-François Millet. The girl leaned on a stick, guarding her flock, the dawn light casting a soft glow over her, lending her the grave dignity of a biblical figure. At first, Jess wondered what she was doing next to the great black slab of the Morris painting. Then she looked closer at the girl's face, and noticed, for the first time, the look of exhausted dejection on it. Despite its fairy-tale setting, the painting was by no means romantic; the child – for she was not much more than a child – looked lonely and neglected; her shoes were too big for her, her clothes rough.

Jess took a step back, so that she could see the two paintings side by side: the Millet small, delicate, and vibrant with colour; the Morris huge, brutal, and coal-black. She thought she could see a connection. Perhaps Morris was implying that nothing much had changed over the centuries, that the miners who had dug the coal from the South Wales valleys were the direct descendants of Millet's peasants: poor, oppressed, exhausted, yet with a kind of ageless dignity in their toil. Jess peered into the gloom of the black hole, and wondered whether Morris was perhaps making a further point: that the last shred of dignity afforded the miners, of selling their labour to live, had been stripped away from them, leaving nothing behind but a great void, like the interior of the disused mines that still existed up in the valleys.

'What do you think?'

Jess gave a slight start as the man next to her spoke. He'd been standing beside her for a while, but she hadn't noticed.

She turned back to the painting. 'I'm not sure. Maybe it's to do with the mines closing down.' Jess paused. 'But I don't think I'd have got the point if it hadn't been for the goose girl.'

'Hmm.'

They both continued to look at the two paintings, side by side.

'I mean, you're never sure what you're seeing with this kind of painting.' Jess spoke quietly, as if to herself. 'You could just be reading things into it, couldn't you?'

'Isn't all art like that?'

Jess turned to look at the man. He was taller than her, but not much, with dark curly hair, brown eyes, and a day's stubble on his chin. He was dressed in a blue jacket, with a striped scarf around his neck.

Jess was slightly nonplussed. He looked like someone from the art world, clearly not just a gallery-goer like her. However, she persevered.

'I suppose so. But this contemporary stuff seems to be all about context, doesn't it? Commenting on what's gone before. Trying to do something different.'

She looked back at the painting.

'I'd say all important artists do that.' He followed her gaze. 'Millet was certainly commenting on the romanticism of his contemporaries when he started to paint common peasants, like this little girl. He was scorned at the time. Nobody wanted to see the reality of what was going on. Morris is the same, I think.'

He knew his subject, Jess thought. But he didn't seem to be a snob about it.

She turned and gave him a look as if to say, I'm not entirely convinced.

The man laughed.

'Are you . . . connected to this in any way?' She hazarded a guess.

'Kind of. I'm giving a speech tonight—'

There was a shout from the other corner of the room and the sound of people shushing. Jess turned to see Elinor and Blake walk in. Isobel was nowhere to be seen. They took their places beside a banner advertising the exhibition, with a microphone and lectern in front of it, surrounded by a crew of young women stylishly dressed in black.

'Ah. That's my cue.' The man smiled at her. 'See you later perhaps.'

'Ladies and gentlemen.' Blake stepped forward to the microphone and his voice rang out around the room. 'Tonight is a momentous occasion. We're here to celebrate the purchase by the National Museum of Wales of this painting' – here he waved a hand at the huge canvas at the end of the room – 'by the most talented Welsh artist of his generation, Hefin Morris.'

There was a small burst of applause. Jess noticed that Elinor, standing behind him, didn't join in.

'Now, as you know, Morris doesn't make public appearances, so he can't be with us tonight. But he's asked me to say a few words on his behalf. He is delighted that the National Museum has finally bought the magnificent *Heb Ditel Deuddeg ar Hugain*' – Blake didn't stumble over the words, but he had to concentrate – 'so that it can be seen by the people to whom it rightfully belongs: the ordinary people of Wales.'

A woman at the front of the crowd clapped enthusiastically. She was a beaky-nosed blonde, dressed in an electric-blue shift, with what looked like a bicycle chain around her neck. This must be Mia, Blake's business partner, Jess surmised; and she obviously admired him greatly, judging by the look of adoration on her face as he spoke.

Blake continued to talk about the painting now being owned by the 'ordinary people of Wales', very few of whom seemed to be present, and then turned to the man Jess had just been speaking to.

'I'd like to introduce Professor Jacob Dresler, one of our foremost critics and historians' – was there a slightly sardonic edge to his voice, or did Jess imagine it? – 'who has championed Morris's work from the start . . .'

Jess noticed Mari standing by the door, looking questioningly at her. She nodded her head over at Dresler to show that she wanted to stay. Mari gave her a knowing smile and retreated to the corridor.

Dresler took Blake's place in the centre of the small crowd. 'It's a great pleasure to be here tonight. And that's because, in my view, Hefin Morris is the most exciting painter working in Britain today. He's the Anselm Kiefer of the Welsh valleys, and like him, his work asks: what does the aftermath of destruction look like, *feel* like? What happens to a people when their entire history, knowledge, skills, culture disappear overnight?'

He seemed quietly assured as he spoke, his genuine, unhurried manner contrasting sharply with Blake's brittle enthusiasm.

'Morris was seventeen years old, just starting work as a miner, when the great strike began in 1985. The pit he worked in was closed for good two years later. As you can see from the paintings around you, he uses the metaphor of the mineshaft to tell the story of what happened to him, to his community, after that seminal moment in British history. Yet it's not just a metaphor; those abandoned shafts are, in reality, all that remains of a whole way of life.'

Dresler paused. He was an engaging speaker, Jess thought. Direct, to the point, and genuinely passionate about his subject.

'Hefin Morris was born in 1967 in Treorchy, the Rhondda Valley. He grew up . . .'

Jess listened, intrigued, as Dresler outlined Morris's career. He explained how the artist had begun to paint after being laid off, how he'd never been to art school, how he'd started to incorporate coal dust, iron ore, ochre, and various kinds of detritus in his work, how he'd eventually been spotted by a London dealer – here the woman wearing the bicycle chain smiled proudly – and finally, how he'd continued to maintain his anonymity throughout, as a measure of his disgust for the capitalist system in general, and the machinations of the art world in particular. Jess was sceptical about the last point – wasn't it more likely that Morris was simply trying to generate a mystique about himself by refusing to step out of the shadows? – but nevertheless, she found Dresler's account engaging. She also realized, as she watched him, that she was attracted to him. He was a good-looking man, like an older version of Blake, but with more genuine charisma; his dark eyes sparkled as he spoke, and there was a real passion in his voice and gestures. He was intelligent and decisive, both qualities she liked in a man; he held firm opinions, and he seemed to know what he was talking about. He'd be an interesting person to get to know, she thought – as a friend, of course. At first, anyway.

The speech came to a close. There was more clapping, and then people began to circulate again. Jess was surprised to find that, straight after he'd finished his speech, Dresler came over to her.

'Well done,' she said. 'That was great.'

'Thanks. I tried not to go on too long. After all, people are here to see the paintings.'

They looked around. Everyone in the room was talking to each other, clutching a glass. Not one single person was standing in front of a canvas.

There was an awkward pause, and then they both laughed.

'I'm going to have to leave in a minute,' Dresler said. 'They're dragging me off to a restaurant or something.'

Jess looked over at the doorway. Mari had reappeared, and was talking to a rowdy bunch of fellow thespians who were on their way out.

'I'll have to get going, too.'

Dresler reached into his jacket pocket, took out a card, and handed it to her. 'I'm coming back to Cardiff next week, to talk to the museum people. I wondered . . .' He hesitated, then made his decision. 'I wondered if you'd like to meet up at some point?'

'Oh.' Jess was surprised. She somehow hadn't realized until that moment that Dresler had been chatting her up. 'Well . . .' She hesitated, flustered by the unfamiliarity of the situation. 'That would be nice.' She took the card, glancing at it. It was printed on cream paper, with black lettering. Stylish, but simple.

'I'll be here from Monday to Wednesday.'

'Thanks.' She put the card in her bag.

Over his shoulder, she could see Mari looking at them with curiosity.

'Well, I must be off.' She paused. 'I'll see you next week, perhaps. I'm Jessica, by the way. Jessica Mayhew.'

'I'll look forward to hearing from you, Jessica.' He looked into her eyes. She held his gaze for a moment. 'Goodbye.'

'Bye.'

She turned and walked towards the door. Her heart was beating. She was surprised at her own boldness.

When she looked back, he smiled and held up a hand, and she responded to the gesture in kind. Then she went over to Mari.

'Out on the pull, I see,' Mari murmured as she joined the group of actors. 'Nice work, Jess. He looks pretty fit for a professor.'

'Oh shut up.' Jess felt herself blushing. 'It wasn't like that, anyway. We were just talking about the paintings.'

'Sure you were.' There was a smile playing on Mari's lips. 'Come on, let's go and get a drink somewhere, shall we?'

'I've just got to go and say goodbye to someone. I'll be back in a minute.'

Jess made for the group by the microphone, where Elinor and Blake were standing together, side by side, saying goodbye to people. Isobel hadn't reappeared. From time to time, Elinor leaned casually against Blake's shoulder, as if exhausted by the effort of socializing. Obviously, it had been a challenge, throwing this party so soon after Ursula's death, and they were both relieved now that the party was nearing its end. Yet there was a body language between the two of them, a casual familiarity with each other's touch, that belied what Elinor had said about him in the last session, and suggested that they might be on more intimate terms than she'd implied.

'Jess. I'm so glad you came.' Elinor took her hand and squeezed it. She seemed slightly drunk and rather overemotional, but her affection was genuine. Clearly, she'd found Jess's presence at the party reassuring.

'It was a pleasure.' Jess spoke with sincerity, but she kept her tone formal, gently removing her hand.

'Let me introduce you.' Elinor turned to her brother-in-law. 'Blake, this is Jessica Mayhew. Jessica, Blake Thomas.'

Blake put out his hand, and gave her a broad smile, showing rows of straight white teeth. Close up, he was remarkably good-looking, with that striking black hair and dark eyes one often sees in Wales. There was a faint trace of Swansea in his accent, à la Richard Burton, which only added to his appeal.

They shook hands. Blake's grasp was firm, confident. It's definitely him, Jess thought. The man on the green. No doubt about it. And now that she saw his handsome face up close, she could see why he had reason to swagger.

'Dr Mayhew, I should say,' Elinor went on. 'She's my therapist.'

As Elinor spoke, Jess felt his hand go limp in hers for a second. She looked up, and saw the colour drain from his face. Then he recovered himself.

'Good to meet you, Dr Mayhew.' He withdrew his hand. She noticed that it was shaking slightly.

'And you. Lovely party.'

'Thanks.' He ran a hand through his hair, as if exhausted by the strain of the evening. Then, rather abruptly, he turned to the next person in the queue, who was waiting to say goodbye.

'See you next week, then.' Elinor spoke in a low voice.

Jess nodded in response. Then she turned and walked quickly to the doorway, where Mari was waiting for her.

8

The following Tuesday, after seeing two clients, Jessica went over to the deli, bought herself a cappuccino, and came back to the consulting rooms. Her next client of the day was Elinor Powell, and she wanted to reflect on the case for a few minutes before she arrived.

She sat down in her armchair and looked up at the white relief on the opposite wall. The circle in the centre of it gauged her mood: if she was upset, it vibrated slightly against the white square behind it; if not, it sat quietly, glowing rather than throbbing. Today it was motionless. She was encouraged by that; she might be struggling to keep up these days, both at work and at home, but at least she was in a reasonably calm frame of mind.

She leaned back in her chair, casting her mind back to when she'd last seen Elinor. It was perhaps unfortunate that they'd met at the party, but Cardiff was a small place, and bumping into clients was par for the course for any psychotherapist practising in the city. Indeed, Jess often reminded herself that, in the early days of psychoanalysis, Freud himself had been very casual about such informal social encounters; he regularly took his patients out to tea, visited their relatives, wrote letters to their friends, and so on. The idea that therapy should – or could – take place entirely within a bubble, hermetically sealed off from the outside world, was a modern invention.

No, Jess mused, there was nothing disastrous about seeing Elinor briefly in her own milieu; indeed, it had been enlightening, in many ways. But it did break into the 'frame' of the therapeutic encounter – the setting of a secure, confidential environment with boundaries and ground rules – so she'd need to bear that in mind during the upcoming session.

Clearly, the twin issue was deeply significant. The fact that, as it turned out, Elinor was a twin made all the difference to her psychological make-up, and might well have been a factor in triggering her claustrophobia. But why hadn't Elinor told her about it? Possibly because she took Isobel so much for granted that she didn't realize the information was significant. As one of Jess's former clients had remarked, 'being a twin is like being in a marriage from the day you are born, without knowing you're in it'. The twins' relationship may have been suffocatingly close, and perhaps the sudden death of their mother had exacerbated the problem, at least for Elinor, pushing her into acute claustrophobia.

Jess moved her gaze from the white relief to the window. It was open just a crack, in readiness for Elinor's session. The weather was still cold, and she could feel a draught coming in from it again.

She furrowed her brow, remembering Freud's dictum that neuroses always have an unconscious purpose. What was the hidden purpose of Elinor's claustrophobia? Perhaps, after the loss of their mother, to express a symbolic need to resume her stifling relationship with her twin; or, more pragmatically, to draw Isobel away from Blake, bring her back by her side, to look after her as a kind of surrogate mother.

Which raised the question of Blake's role in Elinor's life.

Elinor had voiced her doubts about him in the therapy, but initially Jess had been sceptical, reasoning that she was bound to feel some resentment towards him as her sister's husband, especially as she herself wasn't married. Yet Blake's behaviour at the party had, in actual fact, been rather suspicious: when Elinor had introduced her as her therapist, he'd seemed thoroughly rattled. Maybe he did have something to hide, after all.

And what about Blake and Elinor's body language at the party, towards the end, when Isobel had left? While not overtly amorous, it had revealed an intimate, if not necessarily sexual, connection between them. If Elinor was indeed betraying Isobel by having a secret affair with Blake, or at least some kind of complex dalliance, she could well be projecting her guilt about that onto Blake, blaming him for her mother's death, and becoming more and more troubled herself in the process . . .

There was a knock at the door.

Jess realized that she hadn't left it ajar, as she usually did before Elinor's session, and hurried over.

She opened the door. Elinor stood outside, dressed only in a thin T-shirt, jeans and tennis shoes. Her face was milky white, and she was shivering.

'You look frozen. Come in.'

'I can't.' There was a vein throbbing at Elinor's temple, the blue visible beneath her translucent skin. 'I just don't feel too good today.'

'OK.' Jess made a snap decision, disturbed by Elinor's appearance. 'Let's go and do the session in the park. I'll get my coat.'

She went over to the hat stand, grabbed her bag, and put on her coat – the green tweed. Then she picked up the baggy woollen cardigan she'd kept in the office for Frank's session, and a thick, knitted scarf of Rose's that she'd borrowed one chilly morning, and brought them out to Elinor.

Elinor took the cardigan, quite meekly, and donned it,

buttoning it up at the front. It came down to her knees. Then she wrapped the scarf around her neck. She looked like a child, wrapped up by its mother for a winter walk.

Jess got out her keys and locked the door. Then they set off down the stairs.

'What happened to your mac?'

'It got wet.' Elinor didn't offer any further explanation.

Jess was concerned. Elinor's condition seemed to have deteriorated markedly since their last encounter; she was neglectful of her appearance, to the point where she wasn't even bothering to dress properly for the weather, and she seemed unable to stand being indoors for even a moment, let alone a fifty-minute session in the consulting room.

They walked down Cathedral Road, towards the Llandaff Fields. There was a bench by the river there where Jess often went to sit and watch the water birds, and to think. She'd take Elinor there, she decided. It was a calm spot, and few people passed by, except for the odd cyclist or dog walker.

They didn't talk as they walked – Elinor was too tense to make conversation. On the way, she had an attack of nerves and needed to pee, so they had to stop at the public toilets. She was anxious about going, afraid that she might get locked in, and Jess had to reassure her she'd be waiting right outside if anything went wrong. When she emerged, they walked on quickly to the riverside.

They found the bench, and sat down. It was a grey, misty day, and there was little activity in the river, except for a few ducks dabbling in the shallows.

'So.' Jess settled herself on the bench. 'Tell me what's happened.'

Elinor sat beside her, her body inclined slightly towards Jess, with a gap between them. 'It's just the pressure, I think. It's been building up. First there was the private view, which stressed us all out, and then yesterday Blake was taken in for questioning.' She paused. 'This policewoman just won't give up.'

'The same one as before?'

Elinor nodded. 'DS Lauren Bonetti, her name is.'

The name was familiar. Jess had come across DS Bonetti in connection with another of her patients a while back. She'd taken a bit of a shine to her, in fact. She was a bright, inquisitive woman who pursued a case until she found out the truth, Jess knew. She'd respected her for that, and had felt a certain kinship with her.

'As far as I can see, the investigation has been dropped by the rest of the team. They think the thief killed Ursula by accident, in the course of carrying out a robbery. They have no leads, they haven't come up with any evidence, and they've left it at that. But Bonetti isn't satisfied. She seems to suspect that Blake had something to do with it all.' Elinor paused. 'She gave him a pretty hard time, apparently. She'd been to see Mia, Blake's business partner, in London and found that their stories didn't match up. She'd checked their schedules, got hold of all sorts of little details – train times, and so on. In the end, he confessed that he hadn't been with Mia at all. He said he'd been visiting Hefin Morris, and he hadn't told her because Hefin wanted to keep it a secret. She asked where they'd met, and he said at a service station up in the valleys. So now she's checking that out.' Her voice began to tremble. 'They let him go, but I expect they'll want to speak to him again. Isobel's terribly upset.'

'I'm sorry to hear that.'

Elinor nodded. 'She's been in such a state ever since Ma died.' Jess noticed that now Elinor was able to call a spade a spade, without any evasions. 'She had to leave the party early the other night – she just couldn't cope with it all.' Elinor paused. 'I worry about her. She seems very introverted at the moment. She won't talk to me at all about any of it, not properly.'

Jess gazed out at the river. A cormorant landed on a rock, further towards the middle, where the water was deep.

'Perhaps she's not ready yet.'

'We used to talk about everything, though.' There was a note of sadness in Elinor's voice. Then she fell silent, following Jess's gaze.

'You know, I really don't think you ever told me you had a twin,' Jess said, breaking the silence at last.

Elinor frowned. 'Well, I suppose that's because I don't really think of myself as a twin any more. Isobel and I used to be very close, when we were growing up. Inseparable, actually. Even when we left school, we went up to London together, shared a flat, went to Goldsmiths, took the same painting course. She had a very different style from mine. Her paintings were always big and abstract, while mine were small and figurative. The tutors liked her work, and she was seen as an up-and-coming talent. But then when Pa got ill, she dropped out to help him run the gallery. That's how she met Blake . . .' Her voice trailed off.

They watched as the cormorant dipped to catch a fish, but came up with its beak empty.

'After she married him, she stopped taking an interest in me,' Elinor continued. 'Little by little, we began to see less of each other. Blake was nice enough to me, but they never included me in their life together. They never invited me to go on holiday with them or anything.'

Jess couldn't see why a married couple would invite a sibling along on holiday, but she didn't say so.

'And it's been like that ever since. Isobel virtually never gets in touch, unless she needs something. It's all about Blake now. Blake this, Blake that. I get sick of hearing about how bloody marvellous he is sometimes.'

Again, Jess found Elinor's attitude surprising. Obviously a

married woman would be more interested in her husband's doings than her sister's. But Elinor didn't seem to understand that.

'I feel totally excluded from their relationship, to be honest,' Elinor went on. 'It really upsets me.'

Jess was puzzled. She pictured Elinor at the exhibition, after Isobel had left, lolling her head against Blake's shoulder. Elinor's complaint didn't seem to tally with what she'd seen that night.

'He's been good to me, though.' Elinor spoke as if in answer to her thoughts. 'Very supportive of my work.' She paused. 'But I have to say, I don't trust him an inch. He's completely ruthless. Incredibly ambitious. Couldn't you see that, when you met him?'

Jess shrugged non-committally, although she knew what Elinor meant. Blake was an alpha male, no doubt about it: good-looking, confident, and with a general air of entitlement. But that didn't necessarily make him ruthless.

Elinor lowered her voice, although there was no one in the vicinity. 'I think he paid someone to come in and steal my painting. Had my mother not been there, it would have been an easy job. The place wasn't alarmed, he knew that, and the lock on the door was a cinch to pick – the police told me. I expect he thought his hired hand could slip in, nick it, and slip out again without too much trouble.' She paused. 'But then Ma caught the thief red-handed, and he panicked. That's where it all went wrong.'

Jess was taken aback. 'This is quite a serious allegation, Elinor. Don't you think you should talk to DS Bonetti?'

'I don't know.' She paused. 'Isobel would be furious with me if I did. And I can't be sure, of course. But I wouldn't put it past him. After all, it would be easy enough for him to get rid of a Gwen John – he's got connections all over the world. There are lots of collectors who buy stolen work and keep it for private viewing.'

Jess was silent, unsure what to say. She wondered whether

Elinor was slipping into paranoia, or whether she really did have cause to suspect her brother-in-law of setting up the break-in. If the latter were the case, she really ought to persuade her to talk to Bonetti. But for now, it was unclear whether Elinor's suspicions had any basis in reality. She'd have to wait and see what transpired.

'The other thing is, he doesn't like me being in therapy. Not one little bit.' Elinor lowered her voice again. 'He's been trying to stop me coming, actually. I think he's worried about what I might be telling you here. About him.'

Jess remembered the colour draining from Blake's face when they were introduced, and his hand going limp in hers.

'Well, he's not in a position to tell you what to do, is he?'

Elinor didn't reply.

Jess tried again. 'Do you want to continue therapy?'

Elinor nodded. 'Very much so, in the long term.' She gave a sigh. 'But right now, I think I need a break. It's all getting too much for me. I need to get away from Cardiff. From him. From Isobel too, actually. And that bloody policewoman.'

There was a silence. They both looked out at the river again.

'There's this place I know, up in the Black Mountains.' Elinor's voice dropped. She seemed almost to be talking to herself. 'It's right in the middle of nowhere, very wild. I thought I might go up and camp there for a little while.'

Jess was alarmed. Elinor appeared to be in such a fragile state of mind. And the weather was so cold. She seemed barely capable of dressing herself properly for a chilly day in the city, let alone a night outdoors on a windy Welsh mountainside.

'Don't you think it'll be a bit nippy for camping?' Jess did her best not to show her consternation, though inwardly she was beginning to doubt Elinor's sanity.

'I've done it before at this time of year. There are a few farms around, barns I can sleep in. It won't be a problem.'

'But won't you be lonely on your own?'

'Of course not. That's why I'm going there. To be on my own. I like it.'

'So whereabouts do you camp?' Jess didn't want to pry, but she felt genuinely concerned for Elinor's safety.

'Cwm Du.' Elinor's voice was almost a whisper, as if she were giving away a secret. 'It's not far away. It just seems it.'

Jess had heard of Cwm Du. Black Valley, in English. She'd never been there, but she'd heard it was wild, beautiful, and gloriously unspoilt. She'd often thought of visiting – it was only an hour or so's drive away from Cardiff – but she'd never got around to it.

'There's a place there where I go to pray, not that I'm re- ligious in the usual sense. It's a tiny church in a little hamlet. I find it very calming there.' There was a pause, and then an anxious look came over her face. 'Could you keep my session open for me while I'm away? I can pay you, of course.'

'I'm sure we can sort something out.' Jess wondered how she could possibly dissuade Elinor from her camping trip. She couldn't stop her going off, yet she felt most uneasy about it. Especially as Blake seemed to have been pressurizing Elinor to quit therapy.

'I hope this is your own decision?' Jess's tone was tentative. Something else struck her. Could Elinor be placing herself in serious danger here, not just from the elements but from her brother-in-law? If Blake really did have something to hide, then who was to say he wouldn't come after Elinor? It was situations like this that any therapist dreaded. There was no solid evidence that a crime was about to be committed – in that case she could legitimately inform the police – but still, the thought of Elinor alone in Black Valley scared her. She wondered if she shouldn't at the very least consider having a quiet word with Lauren Bonetti, tell her what she knew of Elinor's plans. There again, it was against her professional ethics to interfere in her clients' private lives.

'Yes. Absolutely. I need to clear my head.' Elinor's resolve was firm. 'It won't be for long. Just a few days, I think.'

Evidently, Elinor's mind was made up. She might seem vulnerable, but she could also be very headstrong, like a child. There was a toughness to her, Jess reflected, an imperviousness to discomfort that would perhaps help her survive the elements out at Cwm Du. All the same . . .

Silence descended. They both gazed out at the river. The cormorant dived again, once more to no avail.

'It was good having you there at the party,' Elinor said at last. She hugged the cardigan around her. 'It made me feel better.' She paused. 'What did you think of the paintings, by the way?'

Jess brought to mind the great black canvasses.

'They're not beautiful, are they?' Elinor leaned towards her a little. She seemed anxious to get her opinion.

'No. Not exactly. But they were powerful.' Jess chose her words carefully. 'In the sense that they conjured up a void. I found them compelling.'

Elinor smiled. 'Yes, that's exactly it. You see, art's a language. It can talk about beauty or ugliness. If it's apt, if it does the job, there's a kind of beauty in that, don't you think?'

Jess nodded. Then they both fell silent again.

They went on to discuss the practicalities of Elinor's visit to the retreat. The weather forecast was actually pretty good, and she'd decided to cycle up there, so as to avoid going by car or public transport. She would hire her camping gear from a local youth hostel when she got there. Jess, who knew nothing whatsoever about camping, felt a mixture of horror and admiration as Elinor outlined her plan. She tried not to worry, telling herself that Elinor seemed to have plenty of cash at her disposal, and that, remote as it might seem, Cwm Du was hardly out of the reach of civilization. After all, there were farms dotted all over it, so Elinor told her, and the city itself was not very far away. And if the weather worsened, Elinor reassured her, she could easily find a caravan to rent from one of the farmers; or, if the worst came to the worst, she could always return home.

Their conversation came to a close, and they gazed out at the river again, watching as the cormorant gave up its quest and flew away.

Jess glanced at her watch, realized their time was up, and told Elinor that the session was at an end. On an impulse, before she left she gave Elinor her mobile number, telling her to call if she needed help, which was something she very rarely did with her clients.

'You go back,' Elinor said. 'I'll stay here for a bit.' She gave Jess a timid smile. She seemed altogether calmer than when they'd arrived.

'Good luck, then. I hope it all goes well.' Jess got up to go.

'Bye, then. Oh.' Elinor plucked at the cardigan and the scarf she'd borrowed. 'What shall I do about these?'

'Keep them for now. You can bring them back at our next session.'

'Thanks.' Elinor smiled again. This time, it was a warm, open smile. Jess realized it was the first time she'd seen her look genuinely relaxed and happy. She felt gratified that their encounter had been helpful. It had been a good idea to bring Elinor down here to the riverside.

Jess said goodbye, and walked off towards the street. When she looked back, she saw Elinor hugging the cardigan around her, her head nestled cosily in the scarf, contentedly watching the ducks.

Enactment, she said to herself. Otherwise known as actualization. When your client gets you to play a role for them, drawing you into their drama, so that you stop being the therapist – analysing and interpreting – and become, instead, a docile player in their game, a character in the story of their family dynamic, but entirely under their control. In this case, a nurturing mother. Or perhaps, more confusingly, a protective twin?

Jess gave a sigh. She was somewhat disappointed in herself for not having realized earlier what was going on. Despite her forlorn air, like all neurotics, Elinor had a way of twisting people round her little finger, getting exactly what she wanted. She was quite innocent about it, apparently, but that was what always happened: windows had to be opened, cardigans lent, contact numbers given, rules broken. She'd have to watch out for that in future, Jess told herself.

She gave another sigh, and quickened her pace. When she reached the park gates, she walked out into the street, without looking back at the figure sitting on the bench.

After Elinor's session, Jess saw three more patients, attended a meeting about the service charges in the building, and went home, stopping at the chemist on the way to buy Rose a new washbag. Bearing in mind Rose's new-found disdain for childish things like cuddly animal designs, she chose a rather expensive, sophisticated one, festooned with retro roses, polka dots, zips and pockets. Then she picked up a few items to put in it – lip gloss, hair elastics, a folding toothbrush – paid for them at the till, and headed back to the car.

As she drove down the familiar roads to the house, it began to rain hard. She turned the windscreen wipers on and off to stop them squeaking, cursing herself inwardly for still not having got them fixed, and resolving to do so the next day. Where the road dipped down under the trees, she was overtaken by a smart silver-grey saloon, its wheels swishing in the rain. She nearly drove into a ditch to avoid it, and cursed again, this time out loud. By the time she got home she was feeling tense; Bob was due to drop Rose back any minute, having taken her out again after school, and she was worried that she was going to be late. Then she saw the silver-grey car parked in the driveway.

She parked her own car in the lane outside, got out with her shopping, and locked it, cutting the lights. As she came up the path, Rose jumped out of the stranger's car.

'I'm back.' She had a big grin on her face. Jess noticed that her hair had been curled into ringlets with a curling iron. She was also wearing pale pink lipstick. She looked pretty, and a good deal more grown-up than when Jess had seen her earlier in the day.

The tinted window of the car rolled down.

'Hello,' the person inside called out, so Jess went over.

'Lovely to meet you,' she said, as if expecting Jess to know who she was. And of course, Jess did. This was Tegan, Bob's new squeeze. She looked much as she had on TV, only without so much make-up. She was wearing some kind of padded jacket, beige, with a fake-fur collar and a zip up the front. She was pretty, in a conventional sort of way.

'And you,' said Jess, standing in the rain, feeling it soak into her collar. 'Thanks for dropping her back.'

'No problem. Bob was a bit tied up with work today, so I picked her up from school and had her for the afternoon.'

Jess felt a flush of irritation. So Bob was already palming Rose off on his new girlfriend, was he? Getting her to pick Rose up from school on the days when he was scheduled to do it?

'Well, I hope she behaved herself.'

'She was a dream.'

Rose had skipped up the steps to the house, and was standing by the front door.

Tegan leaned her head out of the window, but only a touch, so that she wouldn't get wet.

'Bye, Rosie,' she called, waving. 'See you soon.'

Rose waved back with enthusiasm.

Tegan gave Jess another wide smile, rolled up the window, and backed out of the drive. Then she was gone.

Jess walked up the path to the house, not bothering to re-park the car in the driveway. When she got to the front door, Rose had already gone in.

'Had a nice time, darling?' In the hallway, Jess put down her things, took off her coat, and went over to hug her daughter.

Rose ignored the question. 'I wish you'd been here when we arrived. We had to wait in the car.'

'Only five minutes, love.'

Rose turned her head away, grumpily, as her mother bent to kiss her. Jess knew why she was moody. She'd made an enormous effort to be nice to Bob's new girlfriend, and now that she was home, the emotional weight of the situation had hit her, and she was coming down with a bump.

'I stopped to buy you something.' Jess took out the washbag, and handed it over.

Rose looked at it, but said nothing.

'I can take it back if you—'

'It's fine, Mum.'

'There are a few little things inside.'

'Right.' Rose nodded but she didn't unzip the bag to have a look. Then she turned and walked up the staircase to her room.

When she was gone, Jess felt tears prick her eyes. It was a trivial thing, and she understood the reasons for it, but the fact that Rose had shown no interest in her small gift had upset her. At times like this, she missed Bob terribly. In the past, when the girls behaved in hurtful ways, she and Bob would have talked it over, he would have comforted her, and then he would have made her laugh about it. That was why she still needed him around. She could look after the girls, but sometimes she needed him to look after her.

A tear rolled down her face, and she wiped it away.

Just at that moment, the front door opened and Nella walked in with Gareth. They were laughing and talking. When Nella saw her mother in the corridor, she made an odd gesture, pulling her baggy cardigan tightly around her. Then she stepped forward and greeted her mother with a smacking kiss on the cheek.

'Hiya Mam.' She seemed oblivious to Jess's mood. 'Me and Gareth are cooking tonight.'

Jess felt her spirits lift. Nella was such a buoyant presence around the house when Gareth was there.

'Lovely. What are we having?'

'We'll have to see, Dr Mayhew.' Gareth spoke in a mock serious voice. 'It depends on what we can hunt and gather.'

Gareth always called Jess Dr Mayhew, as if she were a GP rather than a psychotherapist with a PhD. They were a quirky pair, Nella and Gareth, both sharing the same odd sense of humour – and dress. Today, Gareth was wearing an intentionally hideous sweatshirt with a large horse on the front, while Nella was swathed in the large cardigan of his that reached to her knees.

'Well, I'll leave you to it.' Jess always felt faintly nervous when the two of them cooked a meal. They came up with the oddest combinations of foods, and often left a dreadful mess behind in the kitchen. 'But make something Rose will like.'

She watched them offload their bags and walk down the hall to the kitchen. Nella was putting on weight, she thought. Just a little, round the hips. She was growing up, becoming a woman, rather than a slip of a girl. Or perhaps it was just the jumper that was making her look more curvaceous than usual.

'And don't forget to clear up afterwards,' she called after them.

Good, she thought. I can have a soak in the bath now, and maybe catch up on some paperwork after we've eaten.

She heard a clatter of pots in the kitchen, followed by a burst of laughter. For a moment, she was tempted to go and investigate. Then she thought, what the hell, and walked up the stairs to run her bath.

9

'Sorry I'm late.'

'You're not. I'm early.'

'Well, I should have been here first.'

'Not at all. Drink?'

'I'll get it.'

'No, let me.'

'No, please . . .'

Jessica was nervous. So was Dresler. Their words came out too quickly, in a rush. When she'd seen him sitting at the table, she'd come over, and he'd stood up, and she'd stayed hovering at the table, unsure what to do; and then there'd been a silly 'after you', 'no, after *you*' kind of conversation about where to sit, what to eat, and so on. By the time they'd settled down, their drinks in front of them and their food ordered, Jess was beginning to wish she'd never embarked on this venture. She was too old for dating, out of the habit of it. When after much deliberation, she'd phoned to see if they could meet up, he'd immediately invited her to dinner. Now she wished they'd arranged morning coffee, or afternoon tea, or a walk in the park. Something less formal, less intense.

Not that the place she'd suggested was particularly formal.

It was a welcoming gastropub in Pontcanna, not far from her consulting rooms in Cathedral Road. Pontcanna was the one area of Cardiff that reminded Jessica of the more salubrious parts of London: it was all pretty town houses, chichi florists, gift shops, boutiques and restaurants, with a few rather more workaday establishments – a post office, a butcher's, a chemist – thrown in. Nowadays it was home to Cardiff's small but thriving community of media folk. The gastropub was a lively place, and Jess felt that the relaxed ambience would be helpful in what was bound to be a slightly tense situation – for her, at least, if not for him.

'So. You're looking well.' Dresler gave her a warm smile.

'You too.'

He did look well. He was more handsome than she'd remembered him. Perhaps it was the low light in the pub, or the grey-blue shirt he was wearing, but his eyes looked bluer, his hair thicker and darker than before.

'I like your dress.'

'Thanks.'

After much thought, Jess had chosen a simple black shift with a contrasting cobalt-blue panel down the front. She'd dressed it down with opaque tights and black ankle boots. Around her neck was a pendant, an antique carved mother-of-pearl disc on a silver chain.

'That's unusual.' Dresler leaned forward to take a closer look at the pendant.

She felt her neck heating up. Having him scrutinize her chest, although it was fully covered, made her feel flustered.

She held up the pendant, away from her body, so that he could see it more closely. And her less closely.

'Ah, I see. A button.' He studied it. 'Early nineteenth century, I'd say. Where d'you get it?'

'It was a present from a former client. I'm a psychotherapist, you see.' The heat from her neck began to spread to her face. She hoped it wouldn't show. 'He was scared of buttons. I . . . well, I think I helped him get over it.'

She withdrew the pendant, suddenly feeling shy. This is ridiculous, she thought. I'm behaving like a teenager on her first date.

'That must be a very satisfying job,' he said, leaning back in his chair. He seemed genuinely interested to hear more.

'Well, not always.' She paused. 'But I like my work, actually. Although it can be a little wearing sometimes.'

'I'm sure. But to be able to help people in such a concrete way . . .' He leaned forward again and refilled her glass. 'What's your approach? Dynamic? Gestalt?'

'Existentialist, actually.' She took a sip of her wine. 'We try to work with what you know about yourself, rather than what you don't. And how you can use that to change your behaviour.' She paused, aware that she might be sounding didactic, then added, 'If you want to, that is.'

He looked puzzled. 'But how does that approach tally with the notion of the unconscious? Freud says we're determined by forces we know nothing about, doesn't he?'

'Of course. But we still have a choice, you know. We can choose whether to explore our unconscious wishes, bring them to the fore, or leave them where they are, buried deep, and continuing to confuse us and thwart our progress.'

'So how does one make that choice?'

'Well . . .'

Jess realized, as they talked, that she would never have had this kind of conversation with Bob; he'd been supportive of, but not actually interested in, what she did. And now she thought of it, she realized that the same had been true vice versa. They'd operated in separate spheres, intellectually speaking, as if that was the normal way couples behaved. Perhaps it was; but just half an hour in Dresler's company was giving her an entirely new perspective on a marriage that had lasted twenty years, revealing what had been missing from it. It was a disturbing realization, but an exhilarating one.

When the food came, both of them ate with relish: Jess, a dish of locally caught grey mullet with cockles and laverbread, and Dresler a warming plate of liver, bacon and lentils, both of which married well with the wine they'd ordered, a hearty Tempranillo. Jess asked him about his own work, and he described his life as an art critic and academic, writing and teaching, and occasionally presenting arts features on radio and TV.

'So you're nurturing new talent,' Jess said. 'Helping get artists' careers off the ground.'

'That's the general idea. But it doesn't always work like that.' He paused. 'I don't like the way the art world is going at the moment. It's not good for artists, and it's not good for art.'

'Oh?'

'Don't get me started. I'll be like one of your patients once I get going.'

Jess grinned. 'Try me.'

'Well, if you really want to know.' He put down his knife and fork. 'You see, it's all a bit of a mess at present, in my view. There's been a drift away from independent critics towards the interests of a few rich players. There's a cartel of important people – dealers, collectors, auction houses – who pick a tiny selection of "hot" artists just out of college, usually selected for their shock value, and hype them up, through their friends at the fairs, so their work sells for millions.' He checked himself. 'Sorry, I'm not boring you, am I? I feel rather strongly about this.'

'Not at all.' On the contrary, Jess was fascinated. The world of contemporary art was one she knew nothing about.

'Anyway,' he went on, 'the prices hit the headlines, the artists become celebrities, their work sells for more – it's a self-perpetuating cycle. Everyone's invested in it, so whatever rubbish a so-called hot artist produces, no one's got the guts to criticize it.'

'But isn't that your job?'

'You'd think so. But if you get too out of step with current fashion, you run the risk of being excluded from the game. You see, the critics have no power these days. No one's interested in listening to an independent, objective voice. There's too much money at stake.'

Jess was sceptical. 'But hasn't there always been a hook-up between art and money? I mean, think of the great patrons of the past. The nobility, the Church, and so on.'

Dresler nodded. 'But the thing is, there's so much more money around these days. We're talking billions, not millions. You take these hedge fund guys. Because of the digital revolution, they can buy and sell shares in seconds – and destabilize the economy in the process, I might add. Spending twelve million quid on a stuffed shark represents a few days' work to them. And they don't really care if their investment fails. Art, to them, is just another way to add to their status. And get rid of their cash.'

Jess took a sip of wine. 'Perhaps they're addicted to risk. Not just buying and selling shares, but art, too. Maybe they like the fact that when they buy a contemporary work, they might lose their money.'

'I've never thought about it like that. Buying art as a form of neurosis. But I suppose it is.'

They laughed. She was enjoying herself. Sometimes, after a day in the consulting room, she felt introverted, preoccupied; Dresler made her feel part of a bigger world, one that promised wider horizons.

Dresler reached over for the bottle and refilled his glass. He was drinking faster than her.

'Anyway, the whole thing drives me mad. People don't listen to us critics any more. You've got all these people running round the scene now, telling the collectors what to buy. Take Blake Thomas, for instance. The guy who introduced me at the private view for Hefin Morris.'

At the mention of Blake's name, Jess pricked up her ears.

'He knows his stuff,' Dresler went on. 'I'll give him that. He's got taste. And that's what these bankers want. They're not interested in conspicuous consumption any more; they want to show they're cultured. But what does he actually do? He gets people with money to buy work, and takes a huge cut himself. How does he do that? By cosying up to everyone – the collectors, the dealers, the curators, the auction houses, the artists, you name it. So you get this crazy situation whereby mavericks like Blake are dictating the market. Telling the rich what to buy, because they don't have the time or knowledge to judge for themselves. And everyone's in on the game. It's just so corrupt.'

An angry note had crept into Dresler's voice. Jess wondered whether he was simply impassioned by the situation, or perhaps harboured a personal animosity towards Blake.

'How do you know Blake, then?' Her question was innocent enough.

'Oh, we go back a long way. He was a student of mine at the Courtauld. Very bright. Very able. He's done extremely well for himself, as I knew he would.' Dresler picked up his glass, and took a large swig. 'Unfortunately, he has no moral scruples whatsoever. Which has helped his progress considerably.'

Jess thought for a moment. She wanted to ask Dresler if he thought Blake could have had anything to do with the robbery of the Gwen John, or worse still, covering up the murder, but she decided against it. There would be an opportunity to find out more later on, when she'd got to know him better.

'But surely Blake's not all bad,' she said. 'I mean, he's championed Hefin Morris, hasn't he? And you admire Morris's work.'

'Well, that's the exception that proves the rule.' Dresler frowned. 'I must say, I'm surprised Blake's taken a punt on Morris. He's a complete outsider, someone who didn't go to art school, isn't trained, won't play the game. An artist with a true moral purpose.' He drained his glass. 'It's not like Blake at all to support someone like that. But thank goodness he has.'

'Have you ever met this Hefin Morris?' Jess was curious.

'No. Very few people have. He writes to me occasionally, though.'

'What about?'

'Mostly the paintings. What he's working on. What he's planning. That kind of thing.'

Dresler didn't seem inclined to say more, but Jess persisted.

'How do you reply to him?'

'Through a box number. He's very secretive. He lives and works up in the valleys, but nobody knows where.'

'Not even Blake?'

'No.' Jess thought she detected a tone of satisfaction in Dresler's voice. 'He detests Blake, as it happens. Can't bear the idea that he's trying to sell his work to what he calls those "motherfucking brokers" in the City.'

'Why doesn't he find another agent, then?'

Dresler shrugged. 'They're all the same. It's a case of better the devil you know. There's no way round the system, at the moment, anyway. Though Morris wants to change that. Make an intervention, as he calls it.'

Jess was intrigued. 'What kind of intervention?'

'Ah, that I'm not at liberty to discuss. My lips are sealed.' Dresler was half in jest, half serious.

He changed the subject, picking up the menu. 'Now, what shall we finish with?'

Jess didn't feel hungry. She'd begun to worry about Elinor. Up to now, she'd believed that Elinor's suspicions about Blake were coloured by her emotional state; but Dresler, who seemed perfectly rational, had confirmed that he was a man without moral scruples. What if Blake really had masterminded the stealing of the Gwen John? And covered up Ursula's murder in the course of the bungled operation? What if he was pressurizing Elinor to leave the therapy for fear that she might incriminate him? If that were the case, wouldn't he try to find Elinor, wherever she might be hiding out, and try to silence her? She thought of their body language, Elinor's and Blake's, at the party. Perhaps their intimacy had been one of abuser and victim. Perhaps Elinor had gone on the run because she was secretly in thrall to him, trying to escape . . .

'Just coffee for me.'

Dresler decided against a pudding, ordered coffees for both of them, and they went on talking, this time about their families. He was divorced with a teenage son, and lived in Soho. He'd married young, to a medic who was now a busy consultant in a London hospital. She'd since remarried, but he'd remained single, despite a long-term relationship that had recently come to an end, and about which he understandably said little. Jess spoke of the girls, where she lived, and, in the briefest of terms, her recent separation. When the coffees came, they drank them and carried on talking, until the pub emptied and they were left on their own.

'They're going to close in a minute. We'd better go.'

Dresler paid the bill, Jess promising to treat him next time, and they left. Outside the pub, they stood in the cold air for a moment, facing each other.

'Thanks so much. We must do this again.'

'That would be lovely.'

The nerves had come back, along with the forced small talk.

'Where are you staying?' she asked.

'Just down the road from here. White's.'

Jess knew the place, though she'd never been there. It was a boutique hotel, formerly a B&B, opposite her consulting rooms.

His eyes met hers. 'Did you drive in?'

She nodded, indicating her car on the other side of the road.

'You OK to drive?'

She nodded again.

He grinned. 'I think I must have had most of that bottle of wine.'

There was a pause.

'When are you down next?' she asked.

'I'm not sure. But I'd like to see you again.'

Silence fell between them. Neither of them seemed to know how to leave.

'Well, let's keep in touch, anyway.'

'Let's.'

'Bye then.'

'Bye.'

He leaned forward and kissed her on each cheek, ceremoniously.

There was a moment when he could have pulled her towards him and kissed her. She was hoping that he would, but he didn't.

Part of her wanted to leave it at that, to walk over to the car, get in, and drive home, congratulating herself on how sensible she'd been. The other part asked her what she was waiting for. She was forty-three years old, no longer a teenager. Did she still have to stand there, hoping that a man would take the initiative? Calculating how best to feign modesty, while drawing him into the game of courtship? Of course not. She had nothing to lose by making the first move, except perhaps a bit of dignity, if she'd misread his signals that evening.

She reached up and touched his cheek, looking straight into the pupils of his eyes, which seemed to widen and darken in the half-light. Then she leaned forward and kissed him.

His mouth was warm, his lips soft and welcoming. She knew, as they touched, that she'd done the right thing. This was what he'd wanted. And what she'd wanted, too.

He put his arms around her and hugged her to him tightly. She could feel her breasts pressing against his chest. She buried her face in his neck, breathing in the smell of his skin and hair.

'Let's go back to my hotel,' he said. 'We could have a nightcap in the bar.'

Jess hesitated for a moment. This was their first date. It had been so long since she'd been out with a man, she had no idea what the rules were these days. But had there ever been any rules? In her younger days, there'd been lovers that she'd jumped into bed with immediately; others that had taken weeks, months, years even, to get to that stage. She'd followed her instincts then, just as she was doing now.

'OK'.

They turned and walked down the road towards the hotel, arm in arm. Jess was making some calculations in her head. She'd have to text Mari, who was with the girls, and let her know she was going to be home late, but that wouldn't be a problem. Mari always stayed overnight when she babysat; she liked 'playing mam', as she called it, and she also liked the freedom to down a few glasses of wine during the evening without worrying about driving home.

When they reached the hotel in Cathedral Road, the front door was locked. Dresler produced a key, opened it, and ushered her into the lobby. The lights were on, but when they went into the bar, there was no one there.

'There's a fridge in my room,' he said. 'We'll get something from there.'

Once again, Jess had an opportunity to demur, but she didn't.

As they went up in the tiny lift, they began to kiss again. Dresler slid his hands under her coat, running them up the back of her dress, and her heart began to beat faster. The lift stopped with a sudden judder, followed by a pause. For a moment, they thought they might have got stuck, but then the doors opened and they walked out, both trying to muffle their giggles. Jess had only had two small glasses of wine, but they seemed to have gone to her head.

As he put his card into the door of the room, she felt a mounting sense of excitement, mixed with dread. It had been years, decades, since she'd been in this situation. She was scared, she had to admit. But she was exhilarated, too.

The door opened, and all the lights came blazing on at once. They walked in, and he shut the door, fiddling with the lights.

The lights went dead.

'Oh shit,' he said. He fiddled again, and the room lit up like a Christmas tree.

'Bloody hell.'

Jess reached over and turned them off.

They stood there for a moment, looking at the big bed in the middle of the room, lit only by the lamp in the street outside the window.

'Did you want a drink? I can get you one . . .'

She shook her head. Then she leaned forward and kissed him.

They didn't stop to take off their clothes. Instead, they launched themselves onto the bed, pulling and fumbling at belts and buttons and zips. She kicked off a boot and one leg of her tights and pants; her dress came up, and they began to roll over and over, clinging to each other. He unbuckled his belt and extricated himself from his trousers and then, quite suddenly, he was inside her. There was a moment of surprise, as the relief of arriving so quickly, so easily, at the start of their journey overcame them, and then a frenzy of activity, of pushing, and pressing, and gripping and sweating, until Jess cried out, and he cried out, and both of them lay still.

When she came to, Jess found herself on top of Dresler. She still had one of her boots on, one leg of her tights, and one half of her knickers dangling down from her waist. Her dress had ridden up over her breasts, and her bra was twisted round underneath them.

'God, that was a bit desperate.'

'It was, wasn't it?'

She let out a laugh, and he laughed too. Then he reached out, stroked her cheek, and planted an affectionate kiss on her lips.

She rolled off him, unzipped her remaining boot, took off her dress, and disentangled her underwear.

'You're gorgeous, you know.' He was watching her in admiration.

'Thanks,' she said. She was thankful for the half-light of the street lamp. Her body did look lovely in it, full and rounded, the curve of her hips and breasts outlined in the sodium. So did his. His shirt was unbuttoned and she could see the dark hair across the middle of his chest, around his nipples, a slim line of it reaching down to his navel. He was altogether different from Bob – slighter, more boyish, even though he couldn't be more than a few years younger.

She looked down and saw his penis lying between his legs, shadowed to a delicate bluish grey in the lamplight. It was flaccid, the tip of it just visible under his foreskin. It was crumpled now, but thick and weighty, resting against the wrinkled walnut skin behind. How very strange it looked, she thought. Tender and gelatinous, almost like a deep-sea creature. Yet to her surprise, as she scrutinized it, she felt a subdued urge, almost like a challenge, to raise it up once more.

He moved away from her, pulling off his clothes, until he was only wearing the shirt. As he bent down, she saw the shape of his buttocks, square and hard, jutting out from the top of his thighs. The urge became more clamorous.

'Can you stay? I'd like you to sleep here, for the night.' He leaned forward and kissed her, tucking a strand of hair behind her ear as he did.

'OK. But I'll need to leave really early in the morning. I'll have to get home and get my kids off to school.'

'Whatever you like.' He seemed pleased. 'Can I get you that drink now?'

'Just water for me.'

He got off the bed, went to the fridge, and poured two glasses of water. Jess found her handbag, took out her mobile, set her alarm, and sent Mari a text, telling her she'd be home early in the morning, and that she'd keep the phone on during the night so she could call any time if she needed to.

Dresler came back over and handed her a glass, putting his own down on the bedside table next to him. Then he pulled back the covers, and got in under the duvet.

Jess took off what remained of her underwear and got in beside him.

He gave a sigh of satisfaction as she snuggled into the crook of his arm.

There was a cheerful whistling noise. Jess reached over and picked up the mobile, which was glowing in the dark.

It was a text from Mari.

Holy cow! See you in the morning.

Jess chuckled, and laid the mobile down on the bedside table. 'Everything OK?'

She nodded and resumed her position, cradled in his arms.

They lay there side by side for a moment, looking up at the ceiling. A car drove by and they watched the headlights make patterns on it. Then silence fell.

After a few seconds, another came past. They could hear from the swish of tyres on the road that it had begun to rain.

'I love that sound, don't you?' Jess said. 'It makes me feel secure.'

Dresler chuckled. 'I know what you mean. It's so cosy in here together, isn't it? Safe and warm in bed.'

He leaned down and gave her a long, slow kiss. She looked up at the wall and saw his shadow on it, magnified in the headlights. She pressed her torso against his, and felt his penis flutter. His hands found her breasts, and he sighed happily. She touched his chest, moving her hand along the line of hair on his stomach.

'OK,' she said. 'Let's take it more slowly this time, shall we?'

Jess was by the sea, the sun in her eyes, watching from the jetty as Rose sailed away, her hair sparkling in the sunshine. She was holding a hand-knitted jumper that she wanted to give to her, to keep her warm. The boat was strange, a raft with a flapping tent attached to it. Not seaworthy at all, yet it was speeding along.

On the horizon, she could see the great hulk of the barrage, and she knew that when Rose reached it, she would be swept out to sea. She kept calling to her, telling her to turn the boat round, but Rose couldn't hear her. Then she turned and saw a man standing next to her, a dark-haired man. He was naked and he had a gun in his hand. She tried to run away, but her feet wouldn't carry her. Her whole body was numb, outside her control. He raised the gun and aimed it at her head.

She looked down at his body and saw his penis, nestled against his testicles. He smiled at her. Then she felt the cold muzzle of the gun against her temple.

She looked down again, and saw the penis begin to thicken and rise.

He cocked the trigger . . .

She woke up.

She reached for her mobile, and saw that it was four a.m. Quietly, so as not to wake Dresler, she got up, went to the bathroom, then headed back to bed. The dream had unnerved her. She was obviously more anxious about Rose going to stay with Bob and Tegan than she'd realized. And about this new affair with Dresler.

As she passed the window, she glanced out. It was still dark, except for the glow of the street lamps. On the other side of the street, she noticed a light on in the window of her consulting room. She wondered if she'd left it on before she went home, or whether perhaps one of the cleaners who came in at night had done so.

As she got back into bed Dresler stirred.

'What is it?'

'Nothing.' She lay down next to him, and stared up at the ceiling. She turned to him, put her arms around him, and warmed her body against his back. It was good to have a man in bed beside her once again. His slow, regular breathing recommenced, and with a profound sense of satisfaction, she felt herself drifting off to sleep.

10

When the light came filtering through the window at dawn, Jess woke up. She switched off her alarm before it rang, got up and dressed quietly, leaving Dresler – Jacob – to sleep on. When she was about to leave, he half woke, and kissed her a sleepy goodbye.

She walked quickly down the road, her steps echoing on the silent pavement, got into her car, and drove home down the deserted streets and out on to the country roads. As she neared home, she saw that the sky was turning pink. She pictured 'rosy-fingered Dawn', as the Greek poets had called her, rising from the sea in her chariot, leaving a trail of gold behind her as it scudded through the sky. An early morning mist hung in the air, and when the road dipped down under the trees, she saw that the leaves had unfurled into a pale, translucent green, and that there were tiny, sparkling drops of dew clinging to their crinkled, newborn faces. Watching the dawn break in front of her eyes, she was overcome with wonder. The world was a miracle, and she hadn't noticed the fact for a very long time.

When she got home, she crept up to her bedroom without disturbing Mari and the girls, and readied herself for the day. In the shower, she noticed that her body had seemed to ripen overnight – it was warm and soft, a little sore in places, bruised almost. She treated it carefully, lovingly, picking out her most comfortable underwear, and donning her best work clothes – a wool pencil skirt, a high-necked crêpe blouse and a cashmere cardigan. She put up her hair, pulling it into a loose chignon at the nape of her neck, and adding pearl studs that nestled coyly in the soft flesh of her earlobes. She made up her face with unusual care: just a touch of foundation, lipstick and mascara. She didn't need blusher – there was a healthy bloom to her cheeks that belied the fact she'd only slept for a few hours. In her own private way, she was celebrating the fact that, after months of celibacy, she'd at last broken free from Bob, and made love with a new man.

When she went downstairs to breakfast, the girls remarked how nice she looked, and Mari gave her a knowing grin, which she responded to rather shyly. After breakfast, she drove them all into town, dropping Nella off first, then Mari, then Rose. Mari and she didn't get a chance to talk, which she was glad about; this was her secret, for now, and she wanted to keep it to herself, savour it, for a little longer.

On her way to work, she got stuck in a traffic jam. Normally, she would have been fretting at the wheel, but today she didn't care. She glanced in the rear-view mirror and saw that her eyes were dark and soft, the pupils widened within the iris, making them look almost black. She smiled at herself, and looked away.

Impatient motorists began to bang on their horns, but she ignored them. A neurologist would have told her that she was experiencing the effects of dopamine, serotonin and oxytocin coursing through her system, released by lovemaking after a long period of abstinence. In a paper she'd read recently, there'd been a study on how oxytocin levels – the 'cuddle' hormone – increased over time in a relationship, lessening the impact of the more exciting, sexy hormones (dopamine and serotin).

Perhaps that was what had gone wrong with her and Bob, she reflected: too much oxytocin, not enough of the others.

The traffic cleared, and she drove on.

Nella would have put it more succinctly, of course: she was seriously 'loved up' – not, in her case, through recreational drug use, but through pleasurable human contact. Whatever the explanation, hormonal or emotional, she felt young again, and carefree.

She parked the car at the back of the office and walked round to the front, as if in a dream. She walked up the stairs to her consulting rooms, unlocked the door, and went inside. It was only when she entered the room and saw the light was off that she came back down to earth, remembering that she had seen it turned on the night before. She hadn't just forgotten to switch it off after all. Somebody had been in there in the middle of the night.

She picked up the intercom and called Branwen, the receptionist, to ask whether there'd been a cleaner scheduled to come in during the night. Branwen said that generally the contractors sent staff in during the early evening, but there was nothing to stop them cleaning the offices in the middle of the night if they wanted to. Jess didn't enquire further, not wanting to alarm her, but she wasn't entirely satisfied by this. She looked around the room; there was no obvious sign of any disturbance.

She sat down at her desk, leafed through the correspondence in her in-tray, checked the drawers in her desk, and switched on the computer, which buzzed and flickered as usual. Then she went over to the old wooden filing cabinet where she kept her case notes, opened it, and skimmed through the files. Next, she went over to her bookshelves and ran her eye over the titles on the spines. There were some valuable first editions there that she'd collected over the years, but none were missing.

She turned and cast her eye around the room. The windows

were shut, the door closed. There was a slight tapping at the window, where the branches of the tree outside brushed against the glass, and a play of light on the ceiling from the shadows cast by the leaves. The white relief on the wall sat quietly, the circle among the squares. The cushion on the couch beside the window was in place; the two armchairs by the fireside faced each other. The cushions were plumped up, arranged just so. Nothing had been moved, as far as she could see. A late-night cleaner was doubtless the explanation after all.

She went back to her desk and checked her diary. She had a busy day ahead. Six clients, including Maria, who was coming in for an extra session after missing one the week before. The only gap was between eleven and twelve, when Elinor had been due to come in. Jess was still worried about her being away on this camping trip, but there was nothing she could do about that. She'd use the time, she thought, to catch up on the case. Considering it in depth, and researching some of the aspects she'd neglected so far, might help allay her fears. It would also prepare her for when Elinor came back into therapy – as, sooner or later, she seemed bound to do.

At eleven o'clock, just as Jess had settled down at her desk with a cappuccino from the deli, and was about to log on to the online *Journal of Phenomenological Psychotherapy*, the phone rang.

'Hello?'

Jess immediately recognized the voice on the other end of the line.

'Elinor. Good to hear from you. Are you back in Cardiff?'

There was a pause.

'It's not Elinor, actually. It's her sister, Isobel.'

Jess was nonplussed. The twins' voices sounded exactly alike.

'I hope you don't mind me phoning you like this.'

Jess was unsure how to respond so she said nothing.

'You see, Elinor's disappeared off somewhere. I wondered if you could help me find her. We're . . . I'm . . . worried about her.'

Jess glanced up at the white relief on the wall. Earlier in the day, the circle had been sitting quietly among the squares, but now it seemed to be pulsating.

'I'm sorry but I don't think I can help you.' Jess did her best to be polite. 'Elinor's treatment here is confidential. I can't discuss the details of it with family members.'

There was a brief silence.

'So you say you're worried about your sister.' Jess paused. 'Any particular reason?'

'Well,' Isobel began, 'she's gone off on this camping trip. Did she tell you that?'

'Yes.'

'We're not exactly sure where she is. She didn't tell us where she was going. We're concerned for her.'

'We?'

'Myself and my husband, Blake. Blake Thomas. Elinor must have talked to you about him.' She paused. 'And I believe you met him at the private view for Hefin Morris.'

'Yes, briefly.'

'Well, we wondered . . . I wondered . . . Do you have any idea where Elinor might have gone? Did she say anything to you before she left?'

'Mrs Thomas—'

'Powell. I'm married, but I still use my maiden name. And please call me Isobel.'

Jess didn't respond to her invitation. 'As I said, I'm not at liberty to talk about anything my clients tell me while they're in therapy. I'm sure you can understand that.'

'The thing is, you see, she's in a very fragile state of mind.

114

Before she left, the claustrophobia was getting out of hand – well, I'm sure you know that. She was very upset about the fact that she couldn't go into the studio.' Isobel paused. 'She couldn't paint any more after my mother's . . .' Her voice trailed off for a moment, and Jess realized that, underneath her confident exterior, she, like Elinor, was still recovering from the shock of what had happened. 'I'd hate to think she'd gone off somewhere, by herself, and . . . I don't know.' Isobel paused again. 'Done something silly.' Then she added, rather timidly, as if giving voice to her worst fear would somehow make it real, 'Did she mention anything like that?'

'I'm sorry. I'm afraid I can't tell you what we talked about in our sessions.' Jess spoke more gently, responding to Isobel's evident distress. 'But I can tell you that she didn't mention suicide, if that's what you're worried about.'

Jess decided it was time to end the conversation.

'Well, thank you for calling—'

'Can you help us find her, Dr Mayhew?' Isobel cut in. 'It's urgent. The police will start to suspect her motives if she stays away. I don't want her to get into trouble, you see.' She hesitated. 'She can be a little naive at times. She depends on me, you understand. She needs looking after.'

There was genuine emotion in Isobel's tone, but the way she talked about her sister lacked perspective, Jess thought. Elinor was clearly deeply troubled, yet she had a certain strength of character, too. And Isobel's idea that Elinor was completely reliant on her seemed a little exaggerated, to say the least.

'Tell me.' Jess paused. 'If Elinor was in trouble, why wouldn't she contact you?'

There was a silence.

'Things have been difficult between us for a long time,' Isobel said eventually. 'And since Ma died' – the word came out this time – 'it's been worse. She was completely unhelpful about all the arrangements – the funeral, the will, sorting out the house in Italy, and so on. I had to do it all by myself. She hasn't been supportive at all.'

There was a pause. Jess said nothing, so Isobel filled the silence.

'Look, I need to tell you this. I think my mother's death pushed Elinor over the edge. She lost touch with reality. She became very paranoid. She began to suspect that my husband, Blake, stole a painting from her and caused the death of my mother. Did she tell you that?'

'I'm afraid I can't say.'

'So she did?'

This is why she's called, thought Jess. She wants to find out if Elinor has said anything in the session that might incriminate her husband. Did that mean Blake had something to hide? Had he told Isobel to call, perhaps, to help cover his tracks?

'I've explained my position.' Jess was quiet but firm. 'I can't discuss what Elinor told me in confidence in her therapy sessions.' She paused. 'Is that clear?'

'Yes, of course. Sorry.'

'If Elinor doesn't want to get in touch with you or your husband, for whatever reason,' Jess went on, 'I'm afraid you'll just have to accept that.'

'I know. But I thought perhaps . . . I was hoping, if she told you where she was going, you could just check up on her. See if she's OK.' Isobel's voice trembled.

'Look, I'm not a detective.' Jess spoke gently, responding to the vulnerability in Isobel's tone. 'I'm not in the habit of chasing around after my clients if they decide to take a break. But if Elinor does contact me, I'll ask her to get in touch with you. How's that?'

'Thank you.'

'Now, if you'll excuse me . . .'

'Goodbye. And thank you.' Isobel took the hint and rang off.

Jess put down the receiver, got up from her desk, went over to the window and gazed out, thinking about their conversation. Isobel was upset that Elinor had gone missing, that much was clear. The question was, why? Was she genuinely concerned for her sister's wellbeing? Or had she called, perhaps at Blake's behest, for another reason? Namely, to find out exactly what Elinor had revealed in therapy. If the latter were the case, that made both of them, Isobel and Blake, look guilty of something, didn't it? Perhaps Elinor's suspicions about Blake were not just paranoia, but had a basis in fact – that Blake had actually been involved in the theft of the painting, possibly even Ursula's murder.

Her gaze travelled up to the hotel on the other side of the road where she and Dresler – no, Jacob; she must get used to thinking of him by his Christian name – she and Jacob had spent the night. Their room was on the second floor of the building, a little to the right of the front entrance. She could just make out the white curtains framing the window. They hadn't drawn them together all night. Under the window was the street lamp that had borne witness to their lovemaking; it was unlit and innocent now, as if nothing untoward had ever taken place up there, or in the street below. Yet she distinctly remembered waking from her nightmare, standing at the window, and seeing that the light in her consulting rooms was on. Could Blake have slipped in there, perhaps? Or sent one of his minions to find Elinor's file and check up on her notes?

She turned away from the window and went over to her filing cabinet, where she kept her clients' case notes. She always handwrote the notes and filed them in a cabinet. It seemed more respectful to her clients than storing them on a computer.

She opened the middle drawer, leafed through the hanging

files until she found the one marked *Elinor Powell*, and drew it out.

Inside, there were several sheets of paper, one for each of Elinor's sessions so far. She always took care to keep the notes brief and to the point, referring to disturbing issues in an oblique way, just in case they got into the wrong hands. Also, to tell the truth, she didn't have time to write copious notes; most of what her clients told her was stored in the increasingly crammed filing system of her brain.

She scanned the notes. On the first sheet was a heading, giving Elinor's name, her date of birth, and her contact number. Under this was the day and time of her session: *TUE 11*. There followed a series of initials, mostly using abbreviated technical jargon. There was a checklist for symptoms of PTSD, post-traumatic stress disorder: C (claustrophobia), marked with a tick; FB (flash-backs), SR (startle response) and DP (depersonalization) marked with a cross; and DT (detachment) with a question mark. Elinor's relations were referred to by initial only: M (mother); F (father); TS (twin sister); SH (sister's husband). Beside her mother and father was the initial 'D', signifying 'dead'. Next came various words, rather than sentences, jotted down in a random way that wouldn't have made much sense to a lay person, or even to a therapist who wasn't familiar with the case.

She shuffled through the sheets of paper. She couldn't see anything amiss. There was nothing there that revealed confidential information about Elinor or any of her family – not to the casual observer, anyway. The notes simply served to jog Jess's memory of what they'd discussed in the sessions. She'd have to add a sheet, she thought, detailing the phone call from Isobel she'd just had. She wouldn't normally include such information, but since the twinship between Elinor and Isobel appeared to be so tangled – 'enmeshed' was the technical term – it seemed relevant in this case.

Before she put the notes away, she counted them to check that they were all there. She always wrote one sheet per session, never more, never less. There were three in all.

Surely, there'd been four sessions, she thought. She went over to her desk, bringing the file with her, and looked up Elinor's sessions in her diary. As she'd suspected, there were four sessions booked in, each one ticked off after it had taken place. Four, including the assessment session. Not three. One of the sheets was missing.

Could she have made a mistake? Perhaps so. The last time she'd seen Elinor, they'd gone out to sit by the river, because of the claustrophobia. It was possible that, by the time she'd got back to the office, she'd neglected to write up the notes – left it until the end of the day, perhaps, and then forgotten. However, it was unlikely. She was meticulous about cataloguing all her sessions, if only in the briefest of terms. With such a heavy caseload, having up-to-date information on each of the patients, week by week, was crucial to her practice. Also, it was necessary should any disputes arise.

She cast her mind back to the session, when the two of them had sat by the river. She remembered that Elinor had accused Blake of paying a hired hand to steal the Gwen John painting. Jess wouldn't have written this accusation down in so many words, but it was the type of information Blake would have been looking for. Surely that must be why he'd removed the sheet of paper.

She put the file on her desk, went over to the chair behind it, and sat down. Then she reached for her address book, found a number, and called it.

'DS Lauren Bonetti.'

'Hello.' Jess paused, wondering how to begin. 'It's Jessica Mayhew here. We met a while ago. You gave me your direct line.'

'Oh yes. The Morgan case. Right, I remember. It's been a while. How are you?'

'Fine, thanks. Have you got a moment?' In the background, Jess could hear the sound of people talking.

'Yup. Hang on.' DS Bonetti put the phone down. She must have walked over and shut the door to her office, because the noise ceased.

'Right. How can I help?'

'Well, I've just been going through my case notes on a client I'm rather concerned about, and I've found something missing.'

'Oh yes?' Bonetti was polite.

Jess paused, aware that the problem didn't sound pressing. 'The thing is, I wouldn't normally worry about it, except that this case is quite sensitive. It involves the family of Ursula Powell. My client is her daughter, Elinor Powell.'

'Right.' Bonetti's tone changed.

'Anyway, last night, at four a.m., I noticed that there was a light on in my consulting rooms. The light was turned off again when I arrived here this morning. I think an intruder may have stolen information from my client files. Confidential information.'

'I see.' Bonetti paused. 'Where exactly were you when you saw this?'

Jess hesitated, realizing that what she was going to say next sounded odd. 'Staying in a hotel opposite.'

There was a pause, but Bonetti didn't comment further.

'Did you call the police?'

'No.'

'Was anything else taken?'

'No.'

'And you waited till now to report it?'

'Yes.' This wasn't going well, Jess thought. 'I didn't really think anything of it until I noticed this missing sheet of paper in my files.'

'And you're certain you haven't mislaid it?'

'Positive.'

'Did you check whether anyone in your office came into the building late at night? A cleaner, perhaps?'

'Yes,' said Jess reluctantly, 'that's possible but apparently the cleaners aren't normally there in the middle of the night.'

Bonetti sighed. 'Well, I appreciate your calling, but I'm afraid my hands are tied. You should have reported the break-in, if that's what it was, when you saw it happening last night. It's very difficult for us to follow up a theft hours after the event.'

'I know. I'm sorry about that.'

'I can send an officer round if you like, to check the place over and give you some advice about security in the future.'

'Thank you.' Jess hesitated. She was tempted to report Elinor's suspicions about Blake, but something told her to wait. Elinor was understandably jealous of Blake, given her attachment to her twin, and it wasn't at all clear that her allegation against him had any substance to it.

'Do get in touch, won't you, if there's anything else you're concerned about.' Bonetti seemed to read her thoughts. 'Anything at all.'

'I will. Thanks for your help.'

'No problem.' Bonetti paused. 'D'you want to take my mobile number? Just in case I'm not here when you call. I'm out and about a lot.'

'Oh. Of course.' Jess took the number, feeling somewhat reassured. Bonetti was evidently taking her call seriously, albeit that she hadn't been able to help in this instance.

'Call any time. Day or night. Don't hesitate.'

'OK.'

There was a noise, as if a door had opened, and the chatter resumed again.

'Right, then, Dr Mayhew.' Bonetti raised her voice again, adopting her usual cheerful tone. 'Bye.'

'Bye.'

Jess put the phone down and picked up the notes. Then she got up, went over to the filing cabinet, and stashed them away. She was annoyed with herself. Why hadn't she called the police right away last night, when she saw the light on? Bonetti obviously couldn't do much about the situation now. However, she mused, on the plus side, Bonetti had given the distinct impression that she was still investigating the Ursula Powell murder – perhaps without her superiors' approval, judging by the way she'd lowered her voice when discussing it. So she'd be keeping an eye on Blake's movements, with any luck. And perhaps that would help to provide some protection for Elinor, wherever she might be.

11

That Saturday Jess and Mari met at a fashionable tea house in an elegant residential area on the east side of Cardiff, where Mari lived. The place overlooked a pretty Victorian park with a stream running through it. The cherry trees in the park had recently burst into blossom, and there were daisies and butter-cups in the grass, but the weather was still so cold that the spring scene had a somewhat surreal air, like a film set. The park was deserted, but the tea house was full of people, the windows steaming up as they chatted to each other.

Mari was wearing a tight forties-style dress in a purple pansy print, with a crochet shrug over the top. As ever, she looked stunning. Jess was dressed more soberly, but no less formally, in a grey wool skirt and cardigan, with the collar of a white lace blouse showing underneath. From time to time the pair of them liked to don their best afternoon outfits and sally forth for proper tea and in-depth conversation in town – as, no doubt, their grandmothers had done centuries before them.

They ordered their teas, and while they waited for them to come, discussed Mari's part in the play. Rehearsals were going well, and she'd recently taken up again with an old flame, an actor who was playing the central role. It wasn't a great love affair, but she was enjoying his company, both in the theatre and outside. As ever, she was full of amusing anecdotes about the director and the rest of the cast, poking fun at them with sly observations that were sharp but not unkind.

The teas arrived. Each was served in an individual pot, along with a small bowl for drinking out of, and an egg timer, so that you could brew the tea for exactly the right amount of time, as instructed by the waiter. The ritual was fun, rather than pernickety, and they both enjoyed it. Jess had chosen Jasmine Pearl, her favourite – little buds of green tea that unfurled as they heated up, releasing their scent – while Mari had gone for White Peony.

The waiter left, and they resumed their conversation.

'So how's your new beau?' Mari said. 'Or shouldn't I ask?'

'He's not my beau. He's just . . .'

Mari tilted her head to one side and looked at her quizzically.

'Well, I'm not sure what he is.' Jess nodded at Mari's pot of tea. 'Hadn't you better pour yours out?'

'Don't change the subject.' Mari picked up her pot and began to pour. 'I want to know all about him.'

'Well, there's not much to tell. As you know—'

'You shagged him.'

'Really, Mari.' Jess rolled her eyes. 'That's such a crude expression.'

'All right, then. He did the merengue with your inner goddess. With some salsa moves.'

Jess laughed. She glanced at the egg timer, saw that her tea was ready to pour out, and did so. Then she picked up her cup and inhaled the aroma. It was delicious, perfumed yet with a sour, pungent note. She breathed out again, and felt herself beginning to relax.

'We did make love, yes.' She lowered her cup and took a sip

of tea, feeling slightly embarrassed. 'It was . . . well, thoroughly enjoyable. For both of us, I think.'

'Good. So you like him?'

'Yes, I do.' Jess couldn't help smiling as she spoke. 'He's interested in my work, and I'm interested in his. We had proper discussions about psychotherapy, and art, and stuff. I never did that with Bob. I didn't realize it mattered before, having so much in common. But it does. To me, anyway.'

Mari smiled back. 'And after the discussions?'

'It was great. The sex was easy. Natural. He was very affectionate, too. In fact, I've been feeling high ever since, like a teenage girl having her first romance. Daydreaming about him, whenever I get a moment to myself. I'd completely forgotten how that felt.'

Mari reached out and squeezed her hand. 'Well, I'm really happy for you, Jess. You certainly deserve it, after everything you've been through.' She paused. 'So when are you going to see him again?'

'Soon, I think. He's very keen. He's been texting me two or three times a day.' Jess put down her cup. 'I've never been wooed by text before. When Bob and I were courting it was all windy telephone boxes, or messages on the answerphone, and you couldn't leave anything too passionate on that, in case your flatmate heard it.'

Mari grinned. 'I know, I remember. This is much more fun, isn't it? There's something so erotic about these intimate words of love winging in on the ether, especially when they come in while you're shopping in the supermarket.'

'Or in a meeting.'

'Or in the bath.'

'Or having a conversation with the plumber about drains.'

They laughed.

'I sometimes get cold feet, though.' Jess was serious again.

'I mean, I don't really know him at all. He may not turn out to be suitable.'

'Suitable for what? You're not going to marry him, are you? Just take him as your lover.' Mari pronounced the word 'lover' with a theatrical flourish.

There was a lull in the conversation. They both stirred their teas and looked out through the window at the pink cherry blossom under the leaden grey sky in the park.

'So when's the next date, then?'

'He wants us to go away together next weekend.'

'Well, why not?' Mari waved an airy hand. 'You could go to Paris, or Barcelona. Fly straight from Cardiff, or Bristol.'

'Oh, I don't think so.' Jess was taken aback. 'I wouldn't want to go too far afield, not at this stage.' She thought for a moment. 'Maybe I could take him somewhere in Wales. He'd like that, I think.'

'Make a change from London, even if the weather is dire.'

'Is there anywhere you could recommend?'

'Romantic, you mean?'

'Mmm. Or unusual, historical in some way.'

Mari thought about it. 'Yes, there is, actually. Years ago, I went to this extraordinary place called Twr Tal. The Tall Tower. It's perched up on a windy hillside, overlooking a valley known as Cwm Du.'

Cwm Du. Jess recognized the name. It was the place where Elinor had gone camping.

'Twelfth century. Spectacular views.' Mari sipped her tea, a look of relish on her face as she began her story. 'At one time it became a meeting point for various bohemian artists who lived round there, including Augustus John.'

Jess was intrigued. Perhaps Elinor had gone up there because of the family connection.

'He and his pals, Jacob Epstein and Eric Gill, had this mad

idea. They wanted to make it the headquarters of a religion celebrating sexuality.' Mari raised an eyebrow.

'Wasn't there a biography of Gill a while back, claiming that he was a sexual monster?'

'That's right. It all came out years after he died. No one was safe, apparently. His sister. His children. His dog.' Mari grimaced. 'I often think of that when I go up to the BBC and see his sculptures festooned all over Broadcasting House.' She paused. 'Anyway, nothing ever came of the religion. They all fell out with each other, and went their separate ways, which was probably just as well. But after that, the tower became the headquarters of this tantric sex cult. I went up there once with a boyfriend, Iestyn.' Mari's eyes didn't exactly mist over, but there was a dreamy look in them. 'It was a bit of a disaster, though. The place was shabby, freezing cold, and there were these terrible sessions on body movement, which consisted mostly of horrible old men touching up the women.' She shivered dramatically. 'In the end, the whole thing folded, which was no surprise, and then the place was bought up and converted into a hotel. A friend of mine went up there the other day. He said it was fabulous. Rather old-fashioned, in a quirky kind of way, but very atmospheric.'

Jess thought for a moment. It sounded like the kind of place Dresler would find fascinating. And while they were there, she reflected, she might give Elinor a call, just to see if she was all right.

'Thanks, Mari.' She finished her cup of tea, picked up the teapot, and began to pour another. 'I'll check it out. Sounds as though it might be just the place.'

At that point, the waiter came over with an ornate cake stand loaded with scones and slices of cake. He put it down on the table, along with plates, knives and napkins.

Jess looked surprised. 'Did you order this, Mari?'

Mari nodded a little sheepishly. 'Yes. It's on me. I thought we deserved a bit of a treat.'

'What for?'

'Oh, just getting to the end of the week.' She picked up a hefty slice of Victoria sponge and began to eat.

'Well, thanks.' Jess hesitated, then chose a scone. 'Although I shouldn't really. After all, I've got my new beau to think of.'

'Just work it off in bed.' Mari spoke with her mouth full. 'Ten minutes' foreplay, fifteen for the main event, works off eighty-eight calories. Double that if you do it twice. I read it on the Internet.'

'Really?' Jess added a dollop of cream and a teaspoon of strawberry jam to the scone. She took a bite. It was meltingly smooth in her mouth. 'Well, maybe I don't need to worry, then.'

'I wouldn't, *cariad*.' Mari took another bite of cake. 'Not if I were you.'

Jacob Dresler called on the Sunday evening. Jess told him about the place Mari had mentioned, the Tŵr Tal. He was intrigued, and suggested they go there the following weekend. He needed to come down to a meeting at the museum, which he could easily set up for Friday afternoon. Then they could head off to the countryside together. So that was settled, all with a blessed lack of fuss or game-playing on either side. Jess said she'd book the hotel, and pick him up outside the museum early Friday evening.

When he rang off, she went online and found the hotel's website. It seemed a simple place, rather basic even, but the scenery in the area was breathtaking. There were beautiful walks, cosy pubs and restaurants nearby, and if the weather was bad, they could simply 'cwtch' – snuggle up – by the fireside in the hotel, and watch the rain beat against the windows.

Over the next few days, she and the girls settled the weekend's arrangements. Rose wanted to stay with Bob and Tegan, and they had agreed to have her; Nella would be staying home, with Gareth in attendance. Mari would be close by in case anything went wrong, and Jess herself could get back easily enough, should the need arise. Only Mari knew where Jess was going, and who with – at this stage, Jess thought it best to keep Dresler out of the picture as far as Bob and the girls were concerned. At some point, if all continued to go well, she'd introduce him to the family; but for now, she preferred to keep their affair a secret. It was a sensible decision, she felt – and it also added a certain frisson of excitement to the proceedings.

After work, as promised, Jess picked Dresler up outside the museum. When she saw him standing outside on the steps, waiting for her, she felt a moment's panic, realizing that she hardly knew this man. She'd spent the night with him, of course, but since then they'd only been in touch by phone. Now they had two whole days – and nights – to spend together. What if, after that first night's passion, they found they weren't so keen, after all? What if the weekend dragged, and she had to make up an excuse to get away? What if he did off-putting things in front of her, like flossing his teeth? What if . . .

She needn't have worried. When he got into the car, he leaned over and kissed her on the cheek, immediately establishing a companionable intimacy between them, as if they were old friends. He brought with him a scent of cold air, and rain, and an enthusiasm for adventure that was infectious.

Jess moved the car out into the traffic, heading through the city towards the motorway.

'I'm so looking forward to this,' he said.

She looked sideways at him, and couldn't help but smile. He really was attractive: a man in his late forties, his hair greying slightly at the temples, his chin dark with stubble, lines etched around his eyes. Yet there was an expression on his face that reminded her of a ten-year-old boy.

'I hope you'll like it.'

'Of course I will.' He leaned over and kissed her cheek again. This time she felt passion stir in her, remembering their night together, but she continued to look straight ahead.

'Don't. I'll have an accident.'

He laughed, and moved away. 'I must say, Dr Mayhew, you're looking particularly gorgeous today.'

'Thank you.'

Jessica had dressed with care. It had been a difficult task, trying to combine practicality with glamour, but she felt she'd pulled it off. She was wearing a shortish black sweater dress, thick tights and ankle boots. The button pendant hung round her neck, just to give the whole outfit a bit of a lift.

'You don't look too bad yourself,' she added, as they hit the motorway. It was beginning to get dark, and the rush-hour traffic, which Jess had hoped to avoid, slowed them down, but once they got past Newport and the various junctions, the road cleared. Jess put her foot down and they cruised at speed along the valley roads, leaving the cars behind. When the mountains came into view, silhouetted against the darkening sky, they fell silent, awed by their brooding majesty.

As she drove along, they began to settle into conversation, catching up on what had been happening since they last met. Dresler told her about his son, Seth, who'd been arguing with his mother, Kitty, about smoking weed, as he called it. Jess described Nella's lackadaisical attitude towards her studies, and touched on the fact that Rose was missing her sister, now that Nella was so involved with Gareth. She didn't add that Rose was also missing Bob, or that she'd been singing his new girl-friend's praises ever since she'd met her. She felt instinctively that, at this stage of the game, Dresler wouldn't want to know too much about her emotional dealings with her ex; neither did she enquire too closely about his own. Later, that might change;

but for now, here they were, bowling along a deserted road in Black Valley, as the first stars of the evening came out, and wondering, like two young lovers, what lay before them that night. Their respective families were growing ever more distant as the miles passed; for now, it was best to keep them that way – out of sight and out of mind.

Eventually, the conversation turned to work. As usual, Jess could only talk in the most general of terms about her patients. She couldn't mention what was uppermost in her mind: that Elinor had left therapy, and hadn't yet returned; that she was probably camping somewhere near the tower; and that Isobel had come looking for her, possibly at the behest of Blake. She didn't mention the notes missing from her consulting room, or Elinor's fears that Blake might be behind the theft of the painting. It was frustrating for her to keep silent on these matters, since Dresler knew the family, and could perhaps have shed some light on them. So instead, she listened carefully to what Dresler had to say about his world, fascinated by the internecine conflicts he described regarding the Morris paintings, but also hoping to glean some information.

'The museum is very happy with the Morris purchase. The reviews have been excellent, and it's already drawn in a fair amount of people. But they want Morris to do publicity. Give interviews, and so on. And, of course, he won't.'

'Can't you persuade him?'

'I'm not sure I want to try. You see, I admire his stance. He's explained it in his correspondence with me.' A tone of pride crept into Dresler's voice as he spoke. Hearing it, Jess realized that he was somewhat protective of his special relationship with the reclusive Morris. 'It's a political gesture on his part, you see.'

'How come?'

'Well, his work is about the rape and pillage of an entire

community. The mining community in the South Wales valleys, to be precise.' Dresler sounded as if he was quoting from one of Morris's letters. 'Until that community is properly compensated for the loss of their jobs and homes, he says, he doesn't want anything to do with the museum, the Welsh Assembly, the British government, the media, or anyone at all from the art world.'

Jess thought for a moment. 'But he himself is being paid quite a lot for these paintings, isn't he? How does he square that with his conscience?'

Dresler shrugged. 'Well, he's got to live on something. He needs the money so that he can continue painting. He feels that's an acceptable compromise, and I must say, I agree with him.'

'I see your point.' Jess paused. She could sense this was a touchy subject. 'But Blake Thomas is busy championing Morris's work, isn't he? From what you told me, he's trying to sell the paintings to investment bankers and hedge fund managers, as well as public bodies like museums.' Jess chose her words with care. 'That seems a bit of a paradox, doesn't it?'

'Of course. And Morris is very unhappy about it. He regards the bankers as the dregs of society. Wrecking the economy to fill their own pockets. Buying up contemporary art that they don't like or understand, just to prove they've still got souls.' His voice rose slightly. 'The rich are behaving almost as they did in medieval times, when they bought indulgences to cancel out their sins. Only now the indulgences take the form of art. And the worst thing is, the few serious artists that continue to do proper work either get ignored or lumped in with the charlatans. And no one dares utter a peep.' He paused. 'Morris is thinking of staging a protest about the situation.'

'Really? What sort of protest?'

'He won't say.' Jess glanced over at Dresler. He looked as if he was about to continue, then checked himself. 'But he's definitely got something up his sleeve. We'll find out soon enough what it is.'

By now they had turned off the main road, and were winding their way towards Tyrog Tal, along an unlit lane. The wind had got up, and it had started to rain. As they crawled along, looking for a signpost, Jess began to feel apprehensive. Staying at a secluded hotel among ancient ruins in a remote valley had seemed an exciting proposition by day; now, as night fell, she became aware of just how isolated it was.

They fell silent again as they peered out into the darkness. Dense trees obscured the sides of the road, clustering around them so that it was difficult to tell what lay ahead. Eventually, they saw the signpost and turned into a smaller unmade road, bumping along it until, finally, they reached a clearing. In front of them was a rickety building with a faint light over the door. To the side of that was a high medieval tower made of rough grey stone. Beside it a colonnade of high arches reared up, sections of it gouged out as if a malevolent giant had taken an axe to it that very day.

'My God. Look at that.' Dresler was impressed.

'Amazing, isn't it?' Jess parked the car to one side of the drive. There didn't seem to be a car park. In fact, there was only one other car to be seen anywhere near the hotel, a battered four-wheel drive that probably belonged to the owners.

They got out of the car, took out their bags, and ran towards the hotel, shielding themselves as best they could from the wind and rain. The door to the rickety porch was open. They went in, walked down a few steep steps into the main building, and found themselves in a large, vaulted room with flagstones on the floor, a small bar in one corner, and several oak barrels against the wall. There was no one to be seen.

Jess put her bag down on the floor and looked at her watch.

It was only seven thirty. It wasn't as if they were arriving late. Where was everyone? This wasn't the welcome she'd envisaged.

Dresler didn't seem put out. Instead, he was wandering round the room, inspecting the ceiling and the flagstones on the floor.

Eventually, an elderly man appeared, checked their booking, gave them a key to their room, and pointed out the way to it, up a spiral staircase. There were eight bedrooms in the tower, he told them; theirs was at the very top.

12

They walked up the awkward, narrow staircase, past several heavy wooden doors until they came to the last one. When Jess put the key in the lock, it stuck, and both of them had to fiddle with it until it opened. The door led into a dark, low-ceilinged room with a window that looked out over the monastery. The curtains weren't drawn, and the looming shapes of the ruined arches around the tower were grey against the black of the night sky. There was a four-poster bed with what looked like a rather lumpy mattress on it, and a thick velvet counterpane laid over it, rather worn in places. On a chest of drawers in one corner stood a china jug and washbowl, and Jess noticed that under the bed there was an old-fashioned chamber pot. A necessity, since the bathroom was four floors down.

Despite the romantic setting, she couldn't help feeling a little disappointed. Obviously, in a medieval tower like this, it would have been difficult to add an en suite to every bedroom, but she had at least expected a washbasin and running water in the room. She walked over to the bed and inspected it, prodding the mattress and shaking the curtains, which were covered in dust. As she did, a dead spider fell out on the floor.

She sat down on the bed, suddenly exhausted. She was

annoyed with herself for not thinking the weekend through properly. It would have been nice to go somewhere more luxurious, somewhere they could lie in the bath and chat, or pad about in dressing gowns, or call for room service so they could eat their breakfast in bed. This was all a bit too spartan for her liking. And let alone being modernized, the place didn't appear to have been properly cleaned since the twelfth century.

Dresler, however, seemed to have no such qualms. He walked straight over to the window, peering out at the grounds of the priory, fascinated by the place. Then he walked over to the bed, sat down beside her, and enveloped her in a hug.

'This is perfect, Jess. Absolutely wonderful. Well done.'

'I'm glad you like it. I was hoping for a few more mod cons.'

'Nonsense. We'll manage fine.' He kissed her on the cheek. 'It'll be nice and cosy.'

Jess thought of saying that weeing into a chamber pot in the middle of the night was a bit too cosy for her liking, but she didn't.

They started to kiss, sitting there on the bed side by side, and before long they were lying flat out on it, their bodies pressed together, their hands inside each other's clothing.

'This is going to be great,' Dresler murmured. 'Making love in a tower. In a four-poster bed.'

'With a lumpy mattress,' Jess murmured back.

'And the ghosts of the monks wandering about outside. We'll leave the curtains open, so they can look in on us.'

'You pervert.'

He laughed and they rolled over, still kissing. She put her fingers into the waistband of his jeans, feeling the warmth of his skin against them. Her skirt rode up over her thighs, and his hands followed it.

'I've ordered dinner,' she said, pulling away. 'We'd better go down and eat.'

He brought his hands up to her waist, then ran them over her breasts, feeling the swell of them through her sweater.

'OK. OK.' He sat up suddenly, as if willing himself to do so. 'You're right. Let's eat, and drink, and then have an early night.'

She lay for a moment longer on the bed looking up at him. The light was behind him, silvering the edges of his curly hair like a halo. In his quick movements and slender frame, she saw something of the adolescent that he must once have been. He really is a lovely man, she thought. The lumpy mattress, and the dead spider, didn't matter any more. Soon, she would be tucked up beside him, and they'd have a whole night together, and they'd be able to lie there undisturbed, until the sun peeped through the latticed window . . .

'A very early night,' she said. 'Very early indeed.'

He laughed, and she sat up beside him. Then they got up and began to ready themselves for dinner. Jess unpacked her make-up bag, though there wasn't much she could do with the contents in the half-light, other than apply some lipstick and comb her hair. Dresler took off his jacket and pulled on a thick sweater – it was chilly in the hotel – and then they were ready to go downstairs.

They ate in a large vaulted dining room that led off the bar. There seemed to be no other guests, and only the one old man in attendance. However, a fire had been lit for them, and a table laid beside it, so they were comfortable enough. Their meal was nothing to write home about, but it was good, home-cooked food, and they ate it with relish. The wine list was dull, so instead they drank locally brewed real ale, which proved delicious – a pale golden colour with a bittersweet tang of hops – and surprisingly strong. By the time they had finished their meal, they were both feeling lightheaded and in need of fresh air, so they decided to take a quick stroll before bed.

Outside, the wind had dropped, the rain had ceased, and the

stars had come out. There was a bright sliver of moon above them, hanging like a lantern in the sky. They linked arms and walked together down through the colonnade, the high arches looming up at them from either side. This must have been the aisle, thought Jess, and for a moment, she saw herself and Dresler as the bride and groom walking through the ruined chapel, not to the altar, which had long since vanished, but to the great arched window that gave on to the fields and wooded hills of the valley beyond. It was an image that thrilled and intrigued her; this was no marriage, it seemed to say – all that was finished now, like the crumbling walls around them – but a new rite of passage, towards an unknowable yet tangible kind of freedom that she would taste side by side, as equals, with another human being. It was within her grasp now, for the first time in her life.

When they came to the end of the colonnade, they stood in front of the great arch, and Dresler took her in his arms and kissed her. It was a long, slow kiss, and during it, Jess opened her eyes and looked up at the stars above, framed by the arch. She could see Orion's Belt, the Plough, and the North Star, Polaris. Her father had taught her to recognize them when she was a child. A pale, shimmering band of cloud ran right across the night sky, from one arc of the firmament to the other. Her heart leapt in excitement: the Milky Way. It was hardly ever visible here in Wales, yet here it was, streaking across the sky, more bright, more glorious, than any stained glass window that could have been erected there in the past. It seemed like an omen, a propitious one, that should be heeded right away.

'It's a good omen that we're here together. In this place.'

'I know what you mean.' Dresler paused. 'I was just thinking the same thing. Here we are, the two of us, standing at the altar in the dead of night, looking out on the world outside, instead of being cooped up in a church.'

'Exactly.'

'So this is a kind of ritual.'

'That's right. To bless our . . .'

'Union.'

'Yes. For the future.'

They kissed again. Dresler pushed his hands inside her coat, running them over her breasts. As he did, she imagined that she felt the stirring of her milk glands, letting the fluid down. It was a strange yet familiar feeling, one that she remembered from when she'd fed her babies. She stared up at the sky. She wondered if it really was the Milky Way that she could see above her, or just a streak of cloud. Whichever it was, she lost herself in it, and for a brief moment, her self stopped its clamouring and instead, with a sigh of relief, she became part of the endless infinity of the galaxy above.

'Come on,' he said, hugging her close. 'Let's get back into the warm. It's freezing out here.'

They set off down the aisle again, walking quickly towards the hotel. She felt a little dizzy, after her brief communion with the stars.

They walked past the car park. It was empty. It seemed that, apart from the faithful retainer, they were indeed the only people in the hotel that night.

Once they were inside, it didn't take them long to get to bed. They took turns to go to the bathroom, which was even more dilapidated than their bedroom, and then snuggled down together. Outside, an owl screeched. The moonlight shone through the window, illuminating the bed, just as the streetlight had done on their first tryst together. Jess thought of Dresler holding her tight, the two of them kissing by the altar, under the stars, and couldn't help smiling to herself.

They made love, clutching at the covers to keep warm, and then lay for a moment in each other's arms. The bed felt slightly damp, and the mattress was as uncomfortable as she'd feared, but it didn't seem to matter. Within minutes, she was falling asleep, her head nestled against Dresler's shoulder, listening to the soft beat of his heart, and the gentle rustling of the trees outside the window.

13

Next morning, they slept late, and were woken by the sun peeping in through the ivy-clad window. The rain had cleared, the wind had dropped, and the sky was a bright, clear blue. When Jess saw it, she jumped out of bed, pulled the curtains open, and leaned out of the window. From the eyrie of the tower, she could see a herd of cattle grazing among the ruins of the monastery, wandering up and down the aisle, their heads bowed. Beyond was the green haze of wooded valleys and hills rising up into the mountains. She couldn't wait to be out there.

The room was cold, so they hurried to dress and get downstairs into the warm. The dining room was still deserted, as it had been the night before, but once again the fire was lit. They ate a good, solid breakfast, served by the faithful retainer, and caught a glimpse of the cook, a middle-aged woman, scurrying about in the kitchen, but otherwise there was no sign of anyone. Obviously, the cold weather was keeping people away – not to mention the spartan arrangements in the hotel.

After they'd finished breakfast, Jess stepped outside for a moment of privacy to call the girls on her mobile. Rose sounded happily preoccupied with the prospect of the boat trip, Nella sleepy and not keen to chat, so she kept the calls short.

Just as she was about to go back into the hotel and get ready for the day, a sleek black car pulled up. A man got out. He was dark-haired, and stylishly dressed, in jeans and a navy blue peacoat. As he walked towards her, she recognized him. It was Blake Thomas.

As he approached, she saw, with a shock, that he looked terrible. There was no trace of the confident alpha male Jess had seen at the launch. His hair was dishevelled, his face pale with a waxy texture, and there were beads of sweat on his upper lip.

'Dr Mayhew.' He came up to her and put out his hand. She shook it. The palm was slightly damp, and she could feel that it was trembling. 'I'm sorry to bother you, but I need to talk to you.'

'Blake Thomas, isn't it?'

'That's right. As I said, I'm sorry to bother you. It's just that . . .' A muscle below his eye twitched. 'My sister-in-law, Elinor, has gone missing. We're terribly worried about her. Me and Isobel.'

Jess felt a pang of anxiety. What was Blake Thomas doing here, and why was he looking for Elinor?

'Well, I'm sorry, Mr Thomas, but I don't know where she is, either.'

At that point, Dresler came out of the hotel looking for Jess. When he saw Blake, he did a double take.

'Blake, old man.' He noted Blake's wild appearance. 'Are you OK?'

His tone was remarkably friendly, thought Jess, considering he'd told her how much he detested the man.

'No. I'm not OK at all. I'm having a bloody awful time.' Blake's voice rose. 'The police have been on my back. I told them where I was when it happened, but they wouldn't believe me, because, you see, the CCTV at the service station up there, well, it wasn't working that day, and . . .'

His words came out in a rush. Neither Jess nor Dresler could follow what he was saying.

'. . . So I've got to find Elinor, you see, because she knows I was with her, and if I don't, well, they're going to take me in again and . . .'

So he wasn't terribly worried about Elinor, thought Jess. He was terribly worried about himself.

'Calm down.' Dresler leaned forward and patted Blake's shoulder.

Blake shrank away from his touch. Then he covered his face with his hands. 'I don't know what to do.' His voice was shaking. 'This is a nightmare. I've got to find her, talk to her. That's all I ask. I won't tell anyone what happened. I just need to see her, explain . . .'

He began to sob.

Jess and Dresler looked at each other in consternation.

Jess scrabbled in her bag and brought out a tissue. 'Here,' she said, offering it to him.

'You know where she is, don't you?' He took the tissue, wiped his eyes, and blew his nose. 'Just tell me, please.'

'I honestly don't,' Jess said. In literal terms, that was true. Elinor had said she was going to Cwm Du, but she hadn't specified exactly where.

'You've got to tell me.' He turned his gaze on her. His eyes were a deep brown, the lashes wet with tears. 'Otherwise I don't know what's going to happen.'

Jess was alarmed, but she tried not to show it. 'Look, as I said to your wife, if Elinor gets in touch with me, I'll ask her to contact you.' She paused. 'By the way, how did you know I was here?'

Blake looked at Dresler. 'You told me, didn't you?'

Dresler nodded. He looked faintly embarrassed. 'I think I did mention it, yes.'

Jess was taken aback. From what Dresler had said, he and Blake weren't on good terms. Not good enough to be discussing where he was planning to spend the weekend, anyway, and who with. They were obviously a great deal more tied up together than she'd realized.

'Look.' Dresler did his best to take control of the situation. 'You're upset, Blake. You're not thinking straight. Go home to Isobel. And if you're worried about Elinor, go to the police.'

'That's just what I can't do,' Blake shouted, suddenly losing his temper. He looked as if he was about to lunge at Dresler. 'Don't you understand? I can't! I can't!'

'OK. OK.' Dresler held up his hands. 'Calm down.'

'Blake, I'm sorry, but I don't think we can help you.' Jess tried to lower the emotional temperature. 'I think Jacob's right. You need to go home. If I get news of Elinor, I'll let you know. I have your wife's number.'

Blake took a deep breath, in an attempt to steady himself. 'Yes. Of course.' His voice was still trembling. 'I'm sorry to have disturbed you.'

He gave Jess a searching gaze. She saw that the muscle under his eye was still twitching.

'Goodbye, then. And good luck.'

Blake didn't reply. Instead, he turned on his heel and walked back to his car.

'I hope he's OK to drive,' said Jess, as they watched him go. There was a reckless, manic air to Blake that worried her.

'Oh, he'll be all right.' Dresler's tone was one of relief. He seemed glad to be rid of Blake. 'Though I must say, I've never seen him like this before.'

Blake started the engine and drove off, squealing the tyres as he turned. They watched as he drove down the lane, rather too fast, and disappeared out of sight.

'What was all that about?'

'No idea.'

'I thought you said you couldn't stand the man. But you seemed like old friends.'

'Old enemies, more like.' Dresler's tone was casual, but he looked a little unnerved as he spoke. Jess couldn't help wondering if he was hiding something from her. Perhaps their supposed mutual dislike masked something more complex. But what exactly? Something to do with Hefin Morris?

'It's a small world, this business,' Dresler went on. 'There are a lot of people like Blake in my life – people I don't particularly warm to, but I have to get on with.' He paused. 'Isn't it the same for you?'

'Not really.'

'Well, lucky you.'

There was an awkward pause. Jess changed the subject, not wanting to provoke an argument. Besides, her mind was occupied with another worry – Blake's behaviour had seemed unhinged, and now he was looking for Elinor, who was somewhere nearby. Jess didn't like to think of him catching up with her while she was in such a vulnerable state.

'You don't think . . .' She hesitated. She didn't want to give too much away about what Elinor had told her, in confidence, in the sessions. 'You don't think Blake's the kind of person who would . . . you know, harm anyone?'

'Why d'you ask?'

'Well, actually, as it happens, Elinor Powell is a client of mine.'

'Really?' Dresler was intrigued. 'Why does she come to you?'

'I can't discuss that.' Jess paused. 'But she's expressed some concerns about Blake in the therapy.'

'I see.' Dresler frowned. 'Well, I'd be surprised if he was dangerous. Blake can be a bit of a bastard at times, but I've never seen him resort to physical violence.'

'I hope you're right.'

There was a brief silence.

'Look, you go upstairs and get ready.' Jess was determined not to let the encounter spoil their day. 'I've just got a couple more calls to make out here. Then we'll set off.'

'Fine. See you up there.'

Dresler went back inside. Immediately he'd left, Jess called Elinor's number. She'd listed it on her mobile before she'd left the office. There was no reply, so she left a message. She said that she was staying at the tower, and that Blake had come by looking for her. She asked her to call back to let her know she was all right, or come to the tower and meet her there that evening, when they would have returned. Then she called DS Lauren Bonetti.

'Hiya.' Bonetti picked up immediately.

'Jess Mayhew here. Sorry to disturb you.' Jess paused. 'I've just had a visit from Blake Thomas.'

'Oh yes?' Bonetti was all ears.

'Yes. I'm staying up at Cwm Du at the moment. He followed us up here, I think. He's looking for Elinor Powell.'

'Do you know where she is?'

'Camping, I think. That's what she told me. Somewhere nearby.' Jess paused. 'I'm worried about the situation, to tell the truth. Why d'you think he's looking for her? You don't think he'd harm her, do you?'

There was a pause.

'I don't think so.' She hesitated. 'But I can't be sure. To tell the truth, I have my doubts about him. I've interviewed him several times, and I'm convinced he's lying. But I've got no evidence.' She gave a sigh of frustration. 'And he hasn't committed any crime by going up there and following her around. So unfortunately, there's nothing much I can do at the moment.'

'Oh.' Jess was disappointed. 'Well, I left Elinor a message, asking her to come by if she needs help. I'm at a hotel called Tŵr Tal, the Tall Tower.'

'I know the one.'

There was a pause.

'Look, I really am worried. Blake seemed very disturbed. Unhinged, almost.'

'I'm sorry. But there's simply nothing I can do right now. It's Saturday and three quarters of the force are at the stadium policing the rugby. I've got no one spare and there's no clear evidence that a crime is going to be committed. I'd come myself, but I'm the duty officer.' Jess could hear the frustration in her voice. 'If anything changes, make sure you call me at once.'

Jess sighed. 'OK. Will do.'

She heard Bonetti click off her phone, and did the same.

When she went back up to the room in the tower, she found Dresler leaning halfway out of the window and talking urgently into his phone. As soon as he saw Jessica, he said something quickly, then ended the call.

'Oh, sorry about that,' he said, turning to her. 'Just had to call my editor about a piece I'm writing on the new Peter Doig show. Only way I could get a signal was by practically toppling to my doom.'

He went over to his suitcase, pulled out his camera – a proper old-fashioned one with various different lenses – and started fiddling with it.

Jess went over to the bedside table, picked up her handbag, and began to look through it, checking she had everything she needed for the day. She had the uncomfortable sense that Dresler was keeping something from her, but she couldn't be sure.

'Why did you tell Blake you and I were coming up here?' She did her best to sound casual.

'It just came up in conversation. I told him we were seeing

each other. I saw no reason not to. Mostly we talked about the history of the tower – Augustus John, Gill, and so on.'

'So you see quite a lot of each other, then?'

'In a business context, yes. Not socially.' Dresler looked up at her. 'Why are you quizzing me like this?'

'I'm just concerned about Elinor, that's all. Do you know the family?'

'I've had some dealings with Isobel through the gallery.' Dresler packed his camera into its case. 'She seems nice enough. Devoted to Blake, I get the impression. Elinor I've only met once or twice. She struck me as rather insecure. Bitter about her lack of success. She showed me her work once. She's technically very good, but there's nothing confrontational about her paintings.'

Jess couldn't help feeling irritated by his patronizing tone. Why paintings should have to be confrontational she couldn't imagine. No wonder Elinor was bitter.

She didn't want to provoke an argument, so she didn't pursue the conversation further. Instead, she put on her jacket, an old waxed Barbour, and slung her bag over her shoulder.

'Come on. Let's go.'

They went downstairs, and set off by car. Their plan was to mosey along the winding valley, stopping to see the sights. Dresler had read up on them, and was keen to see everything it had to offer: the crooked church, where landslides had twisted the masonry out of shape, so that the nave was said to be slumped like Christ's body's in death, and the chancel fallen sideways, like his head; the well where an early Celtic saint offered hospitality to travellers but was murdered, and which afterwards became the site of pilgrimages; the tiny church, said to be the smallest in Britain, with carvings by Eric Gill, that Elinor had mentioned as one of her favourite spots; and then on to a small market town, where they planned to eat their evening meal.

The day went well. Dresler was by nature an inquisitive soul, and he liked to record whatever he found, taking photographs, jotting down notes, picking up leaflets and postcards. In the car, he pored over them, evidently fascinated by all that he had encountered. Jess herself was content to absorb the atmosphere of the places they visited: she'd gaze at the face on a statue, turn her head up to a vaulted roof, stand on a hillside and try to imagine what life would have been like there centuries before. It wasn't difficult: in Cwm Du time seemed to stand still, the very air, trapped by the steep hills on each flank, hovered in a corridor of silence, broken only by the lowing of cows, the baaing of sheep, or the distant chug of a tractor. After a while, she began to feel she had entered a different dimension, where only the present existed. A new mood of sensuality, awakened by last night's kiss in the monastery ruins, had come over her, and was continuing to show itself today. As they explored and walked and talked and drove, she experienced the world anew: the smoothness of stone under her fingers; the sigh of the wind as it blew around her ears; the subtle, sharp scents of musk and mould, of warmth and cold, in her nose; the throb of colour, whether the green of the vegetation or the purple of the hills, in her eyes. Little by little, she sensed herself letting go, reluctantly, of all the problems that beset her in her day-to-day life. All except one – that of Elinor. But even that began to recede as the hours passed.

The day was spent exploring the valley, only stopping briefly at lunchtime for a sandwich. By early evening, they were tired out, and it began to rain, so they drove to a small market town, and dived into a cosy pub. They ordered some local ale, and some rather overpriced but superior pub grub. When the food came, they ate hungrily, both famished after the day's outing. Afterwards they sat talking and watching the rain beat at the window, Jess with a coffee, Dresler with another pint. Neither of them wanted to move; so they sat there as the bar filled up, and the air got warmer, the noise level rose, and the drinkers filled their glasses. By closing time the place was positively rowdy.

'We'd better be getting back, I suppose,' said Jess. 'That drive's pretty hair-raising in places. Especially in the dark.'

Dresler nodded, taking another sip of his pint, but he didn't stir.

The barman clanged the bell for the second time, and Jess got up.

'I'll just nip to the loo, and then we'll be off.'

Jess got up and walked over to the ladies', getting a blast of cold air as she opened the door. Inside, it was unheated, so she didn't hang about. She went to the loo, came out, and washed her hands, inspecting her face in the mirror as she did. She wasn't altogether happy with what she saw. Her hair was a disgrace, sticking up in a great frizz around her face, and her nose was red. But there was a sparkle in her eyes and a flush to her cheeks that made her look excited, happy. She scrabbled in her bag for her comb, her powder compact, and some lipsalve, and did what she could to improve matters. As she was returning them to her bag, she caught sight of her mobile. There was a call waiting for her.

Damn, she thought. She hadn't heard it ringing in the pub, what with the noise of the revellers. She was about to check the number, when the phone rang.

'Hello?'

'Jess. It's me, Elinor.'

There was a sound of roaring in the background. Jess couldn't make out what it was.

'Are you OK? Where are you?'

'I'm at the tower. I got your message. I'm waiting for you. But Blake's here.'

As she spoke, Jess felt a pang of anxiety.

'He's angry with me. I'm scared he's going to . . .'

The roaring intensified. Whether it was the sound of trees, or the engine of Elinor's car, or just the signal breaking up, Jess couldn't be sure.

'OK. Wait for me there. I'll come back right away.'

There would be people at the hotel, Jess told herself. The faithful retainer. Maybe some other guests would have arrived.

Elinor went quiet. It was hard to tell whether she'd stopped talking, or whether the signal had died.

The roaring in the background died away, and there was silence.

Jess immediately called back, several times, but she couldn't get through. So she went inside the pub, found Dresler, and told him what had happened. They left straight away.

'I wonder what he's up to,' Dresler said as they left the town and headed out onto the wild country road that led over the moor and down into Cwm Du.

'She sounded terrified.'

'But what does he want from her?'

Jess thought of the missing case notes. It must have been Blake who'd stolen them, slipping in under cover of darkness. Why had he done that? She cast her mind back to the sessions she'd had with Elinor. She'd evidently been withholding something. What could it be? Something connected with the theft of the painting, or her mother's death? Something Blake wanted kept hidden? A secret between the two of them, perhaps?

'I don't know,' she said, in answer to Jacob's question. 'I wish I did.'

14

It was a rainy night as they drove into Cwm Du. The road led over bare moorland, and as they passed, a herd of sheep loomed into view, their long faces ghostly white in the darkness. To her left, she could see the side of the mountain, sloping up towards the summit; to her right, there was a drop. It was a gentle slope most of the way – she remembered it from the drive up, in the daylight – but from time to time it got steep, and there were metal barriers along the edge, so she had to take care.

After what seemed like an age, the road wound down through fields into the valley, and into woodland. They made their way back to the hotel, Jess peering through the silver needles of rain in the headlights, Dresler looking out for the signpost to Twr Tal.

When he saw it, they turned off the road, and found themselves once again on the long, narrow driveway with the trees clustering overhead. On arrival at the tower, the battered four-wheel drive was still in the car park, but there appeared to be no other visitors.

She parked the car and they got out, walking quickly over the gravel to the hotel. There were no lights on inside, except in the hallway. They let themselves in – the retainer had given them a key to the front door – and peered into the sitting room. The dying embers of the fire were still in the grate, but there was no one there.

'I wonder what's going on.' Dresler seemed rattled.

'D'you have a number for Blake?'

He nodded, took out his phone and tried to call, but there was no signal.

Jess also took her mobile out of her pocket, intending to call Elinor's number, registered on the log, but the same thing happened.

'You'd better stay here.' Jess was thinking fast. 'Take a look around the place, see if you can find anyone. I'll go outside and try Elinor again. If the signal's down, I'll drive off a little way, see if that works. Then I'll come back.'

'OK. Don't go too far, though.' There was fear in his voice. The empty tower and these strange shenanigans with Blake and Elinor were spooking them both.

'Don't worry. I'll be back in a minute.'

Jess went outside. It had stopped raining and a wind had blown up. She stood in the porch, but the signal didn't come back. She walked out towards the car park, near to the rustling trees, to no avail. It was odd, she thought. That morning, the phone had been working perfectly well. But she knew these remote valleys in Wales were like that: the signal was always unreliable around these parts, flickering in and out, for no apparent reason. However, if you moved around a little, you could usually catch it in the end.

She went over to the car, her feet crunching on the gravel. She unlocked the door, got in, started the engine, backed out, turned, and drove off a little way. Still no signal. She drove further, until she was halfway down the drive, the trees dark and dense above her. She was scared now, without Dresler beside her, although she told herself there was no reason to be.

She tried the phone again. This time, there was a signal. Only one bar, but it might be enough, she thought. She called Elinor's number. The signal surged in and out, like a defective radio, but it seemed to be functional, up to a point. Once again, there was no reply, so she texted her a message:

Am at tower. Where are you? Please call right away.

She clicked off the message. She wondered for a moment whether she should phone the girls and Mari, just to see if everything was all right at home. But it was late, and besides, she'd spoken to them only that morning. It was only because she was feeling panicky, she reasoned, that she wanted to hear their voices. She'd do better to call them in the morning.

She turned the car round in the driveway, which took a while, as it was narrow, with a shallow ditch either side, and in the darkness she couldn't really see what she was doing. Then she headed back to the tower. As she did, she noticed a car parked off the side of the driveway, almost hidden under the trees. It was Blake's black sedan.

A chill of fear ran up her spine. So Blake was here, at the tower, and he'd tried to hide his traces. She put her foot on the accelerator. What could he be doing there? Might he have encountered Dresler, and, if so, what would be happening? And where was Elinor? Had Blake perhaps caught up with her, brought her here?

She parked the car, slamming on the brakes, cut the lights and got out. The wind was blowing hard, and the trees were moving in the wind, creaking and groaning. She put the mobile in her pocket and hugged her jacket around her, retracing her steps. She wished the bloody phone was working properly. She didn't like the idea of being stranded out here with no communication. Of course, there must be a landline somewhere in the hotel, but the owners appeared to have gone to bed. And there still didn't seem to be any other guests in the place.

The entrance door remained unlocked, so she went in. When she came into the hallway, she saw that there were no lights on in the sitting room, just the glow of the embers in the fireplace. Dresler must have gone up to the bedroom.

The staircase was dark, so she pushed the timer button on the wall, and the narrow stone spiral lit up. She climbed the winding steps up to their room, stopping every now and then to push the timer button again. When she passed the bathroom, she saw that there was no light on in there, either.

As she came to the top floor of the tower, where their bedroom was, she felt a blast of cold air coming down from the staircase. There must be a door up there, she thought, that led to the parapet outside. Someone must have left it open.

She stopped on the landing and opened the door to the bedroom, hoping to find Dresler in there. The light was on, but it was deserted. So she turned and climbed on up the stairs to a narrower spiral that led to a tiny wooden door – the source of the draught. When she reached it, she saw that it was swinging open on its hinges. There seemed to be no lock on it.

She felt her heart thump in her chest. What was going on? Where the hell was Dresler? Where was Elinor? She thought of Blake's car hidden under the trees by the driveway. He must be here somewhere, lying in wait perhaps . . .

She eased herself through the door, taking care to leave it open behind her. When she came out, she was standing on a stone parapet, encircled by a low, turreted wall. The wind whistled in her ears, and above her head, she could see a dazzling array of stars. The tower was so high that she seemed to be walking among them.

For a moment, she felt dizzy, blinded. Then she realized someone was shining a torch at her.

'Careful. Don't go near the edge.' She jumped as she heard Dresler's voice.

Jess put a hand up to her forehead, shielding her eyes from the beam of light. 'What's going on?'

'Stay there.' Dresler lowered the torch and came towards her. In the starlight, she saw that his face was deathly pale.

He stood beside her. She put out her arm, and felt that his whole body was trembling.

'What's the matter?'

He didn't reply. He seemed to be in a state of shock.

'Jacob? What is it?'

'It's Blake.' His voice came out in a hoarse whisper. 'He's . . .'

The whisper faded to nothing.

'What? He's what?'

Dresler indicated the edge of the parapet. Then he turned his head away.

Jess took the torch from him.

'Don't go over there.' He found his voice again. 'You don't want to see it. Please . . .'

She ignored him, marched to the far end of the parapet, and shone the torch over the edge. What she saw made her catch her breath.

Far below, on the ground, lay a dark lump. She ran the beam of the torch over it and saw that it was a body, the limbs splayed out at strange angles. But that was all she could see.

She heard Dresler come up behind her.

She turned towards him. 'What's happened?' Suddenly she had a vision of Blake and Dresler fighting, Dresler punching Blake and Blake falling off the edge of the tower. 'Please,' she said, her voice high-pitched and hysterical, 'tell me what's happened.'

Dresler walked over to her and put his arms around her. She

could feel him shaking. 'No,' he said, 'there was no one here when I arrived. But . . .' He pointed towards the ground below. 'He must have thrown himself over.' His voice was still shaking. 'I came up the stairs and the door was open, so I got a torch and came out here. That's when I found him.' He paused. 'He can't have been there long.'

Jess wondered how Blake had got up to the tower. And whether Dresler was telling her the whole truth about what had happened.

'We'd better get down there.'

'I can't.'

'Course you can. Come on.' Jess grabbed his arm and together they walked over to the door. She eased herself through it, waited for him to do the same, pressed the timer light on the stairs and then ran down them, as quickly as she could. He followed behind her, at a slower pace.

When she got to the bottom, she ran across the hall, out of the entrance, and round to the side of the tower. There was a small gravelled path that led all around it, dotted with garden lamps. She stopped when she came to the dark mass, partially illuminated by one of the lamps. The lamp was smeared with blood, casting an eerie shadow over what lay beside it.

It was the body. Blake's body, or what was left of it. One of the arms was shattered, and one side of the head was a mass of red flesh, where it had hit the ground. Around it was a pool of blood, soaking into the gravel. A little way away was a dismembered piece of flesh that had sheared off from the arm.

Jess turned her head. She felt the urge to vomit, but overcame it, clenching her teeth and swallowing hard. Then she forced herself to look again, this time more closely.

It was definitely Blake. He was wearing the same clothes she'd seen him in that morning – jeans, a dark blue coat and walking boots. She noticed the tufts of black hair on his head. There were streaks of blood in them now, mixed with fatty innards that could have been brains. It was a horrific sight, yet strangely banal. Apart from the collapsed head and the shattered arm, the rest of the body was just as she'd seen him that morning, dressed stylishly for a day out in the country. It seemed utterly surreal that half of him was now a bloody mess, while the other half was intact. It was almost comical, like a bad zombie film.

Dresler came round the corner and stood beside her. She heard his intake of breath.

She closed her eyes and leaned back against him for a moment. He put his arms around her waist, and together they rocked back and forth.

Then she snapped into action.

They went back into the hotel. She told Dresler to go and wake the owners, found a landline on the reception desk, and called the emergency services. She reported that there was a dead man on the ground outside the tower, and that he appeared to have jumped off of his own accord. Her voice was calm as she gave directions to the hotel. She'd dealt with suicide before. There was a procedure to go through, and following it to the letter would help, as she knew from experience.

For the next few hours, Jess continued in professional mode. The emergency services came. Blake's body was removed, the innards carefully placed in a separate bag, and the remains scraped off the gravel. Photos were taken, and tape put up around the area where Blake had fallen. Meanwhile, she, Dresler and the elderly couple who ran the hotel were questioned by the police. The couple, bewildered in their dressing gowns, appeared to have seen nothing, having retired early to bed.

The local police seemed satisfied by the statements, but then a more senior figure, a colleague of Bonetti's from Cardiff, arrived. He took Jess and Dresler to one side and asked them what had happened. They ran through the story again. Occasionally, he stopped to ask for clarification, which the other police officers hadn't done. Jess explained how, shortly before the body was found, she'd had a call from Elinor, who'd said she was at the tower, and that Blake was there too, in an angry mood. She said she was worried about whether Elinor was all right, since she hadn't been able to get hold of her. The DI questioned them closely on the timing of the evening's events, some of which they were unable to be exact about. Then, satisfied that they had told him everything they knew, he went on to talk to the proprietors.

When he'd finished, Jess and Dresler went upstairs to bed. They were both exhausted. After a speedy trip to the bathroom, they undressed quickly and got into bed. The room seemed colder than ever. Their feet and hands were freezing, and every time they touched each other, they gave little gasps of pain.

'I don't know how I'm going to get to sleep. I can't get that awful sight out of my mind.' Dresler reached out and put his hand on her shoulder.

'There are ways of doing that.' She drew in her breath as his icy fingers touched her. 'It's a technique called mindfulness. You have to focus on the immediate sensations around you. Take them in, savour them. Don't try to banish extraneous thoughts or images that come into your mind. Like . . .' She wanted to say, *Blake's dead body*, but she couldn't.

'OK.'

'Just register them, acknowledge their presence, and let them go.'

'I'll try.'

They lay in the dark, side by side, looking up at the ceiling.

He put his arms around her, and she felt that his body was shaking. She tried to calm him, but her heart was thumping in her chest. They hugged each other closer, until they rolled together and began to make love, more to comfort each other than to chase pleasure.

It was a long, slow process, and several times it seemed as though one or other of them would give up, but gradually she felt his trembling subside and her heart begin to beat more quietly. Eventually she climaxed, more in relief than ecstasy. When she did, with the moment of clarity that sometimes comes with orgasm, she saw herself gazing down at the long, lonely Black Valley, as if she were one of the kestrels rising above it. In the far distance, at the horizon, she saw Bob; in the crook of the valley below, Nella, entwined with Gareth; and nearer to her, in the meadows beside the tower, Rose.

Yet to her surprise, Dresler, whose body she was clasping so tightly in her arms, was nowhere to be seen.

15

The following day, they woke up early. After a hurried break-fast, they packed up, paid the bill, and went out to the car. Although neither of them said as much, they couldn't wait to get away.

As if mirroring their mood, the weather had turned even colder. There was frost on the grass outside and a thin, damp fog in the air. As they passed the path that led around the tower, Dresler turned his head away, but Jess peered around the bend. The police tape was still around the area. She noticed that the blood on the gravel had been cleaned away. The garden light had been wiped off, too. Tonight, she thought, when it was illuminated, those sinister streaks would cast their shadows over the place where Blake's body had lain. But there would be no trace of the tragedy that had happened there.

The two of them walked on towards the car, loaded their bags, and got in. Jess started the engine, and turned on the fan. There was a thin layer of ice on the windscreen. While they sat in the car, waiting for the heater to melt it away, Dresler took her hand.

They watched as the clear lines on the windscreen grew wider, until all the ice had melted. Then she started the car and pulled away. As they drove off, neither of them looked back.

Once they got further down the road, away from the tower, they stopped the car on the verge and looked at the map. Their plan had been to stay in the valley that day, visiting an old woollen mill, but instead they decided to have a quick lunch somewhere nearby, then head back through the Brecon Beacons to Cardiff, where Dresler would take the train to London.

They were both traumatized by the previous night's events, and Jess in particular was keen to get home; she wanted to be with her daughters, have them close, and safe, and under her wing again.

They took the road that cut through the valley, this time in silence. It was slippery with ice, and Jess had to take care. The sky was white, the sun invisible except for a faint glow in the sky, and all around them, the landscape was outlined in a sparkled coating of hoar frost. As the woods cleared and they passed fields, they saw sheep huddled together on the hillsides, standing stock still as if to keep out the cold. When they reached the moor, the white of the ground merged with the white of the sky, so that they seemed to be driving into a void, given shape only by the silvered spikes of gorse that lined their path. Neither of them broke the silence, awed by the pitiless beauty of the place.

They drove on, through the narrow Beulah Pass at the top of Cwm Du, and out of the valley. The cold white landscape around them now seemed sinister, and Jess couldn't wait to get away from it. However, she kept her speed steady; there were patches of black ice on the road, and it would have been easy to lose control of the steering had she been going too fast. The road seemed to wind ahead endlessly, up hill and down dale, as if to test her patience; but finally, it dipped into woodland for the last time, and curved its way back into civilization in the shape of the old market town, with its reassuring bustle.

They found a space in the car park and wandered around, not sure what to do with themselves. Neither of them was in the mood for browsing the shops. They weren't hungry, either. So instead, they went into a cafe and ordered some coffees. Jess tried to phone Elinor again, but as ever there was no reply. As they sat there together, waiting for the coffees to arrive, Jess wished she could roll back time to yesterday morning, when they were just two tourists enjoying a weekend break together, away from the cares of the world. Now they had Blake's suicide to try to make sense of.

'Why would he do that?' Dresler shook his head, as if he still couldn't believe what had happened. 'Why choose the tower?'

'Right next to our room. Was he looking for us, do you think?'

'Possibly.'

'But why?'

Dresler shrugged. Once again, Jess had the distinct impression that he knew more than he was telling her.

'Could his business have been in trouble, do you think?'

'It's possible. It's a volatile market at the best of times. He could have made mistakes, lost clients.' He paused. 'And with this recession, the market's down at the moment.'

The waitress brought over a tray with two coffee cups, a cafetière, a jug of milk, and a bowl of sugar. They waited a moment, then Jess pressed the filter down and poured out the coffee.

'But he'd just sold the Morris painting to the museum, hadn't he?' She handed one of the cups to Dresler. 'That must have been quite lucrative.'

'Not necessarily. It depends what the deal was.' Dresler helped himself to milk. 'There's a lot of front in this business. It's possible he may have been having problems with the bank.'

'But in the long term, things were looking good for him, weren't they?'

'Very good. With Morris just about to break into the big time. And anyway, Blake was a pretty tough operator. I don't think a few problems with cash flow would have bothered him too much.' Dresler put his hand up to his forehead, rubbing it as if his head hurt. Watching him, Jess realized that Blake's death was not just a shock to him, as a suicide always is to those acquainted with the victim, but also a personal blow. Whatever the truth about their relationship, they'd clearly been close associates in the art world. Blake had championed Morris, and Dresler, too, had staked his reputation on having discovered this brilliant young outsider. The pair of them, Blake and Dresler, had been inextricably linked, through Morris. Now Dresler had lost an ally, and as a result, his credibility – along with Morris's – would be more difficult to establish.

They sipped their coffees in silence. Jess found it difficult to sit still. She was feeling anxious about Elinor, and beginning to wonder what her role in all this was. She'd been with Blake right before he'd killed himself, hadn't she? Surely she'd be able to tell them more about what had gone on. She needed to talk to her.

She took out her mobile and called Elinor's number. To her surprise, she picked up.

'Jess? Is that you?'

'Where the hell have you been?' Jess got up and walked away from the table. 'I've been trying to call you.'

'OK. Calm down.'

Jess lowered her voice.

'You really could have got in touch. I've been worried sick about you.'

'Sorry.' Elinor was placatory. 'I was going to call you. I just haven't had a minute. It's all been so stressful here . . .'

'So you know about what happened last night, then? After you left?'

'Yes.' Elinor's voice trembled. 'The police came round last night. Isobel's staying with me. Now that Bonetti woman is here, asking questions.'

Jess heard voices in the background.

'Listen, I've got to go now.' Elinor sounded anxious. 'But I promise I'll call you back. OK?'

'OK.'

Jess clicked off the phone, somewhat mollified, and went back to the table.

'So you got hold of her, then?'

Jess nodded and sat down.

'She didn't say much. Bonetti was with her.'

She took a gulp of coffee to steady her nerves.

Dresler picked up his cup. Jess noticed that his hands were shaking slightly.

'What exactly do you think was going on between Elinor and Blake last night?' he asked.

'Well, when she called me for help, she said she was at the tower, and he was there, too.' Jess paused. 'She'd probably gone there to find me. She said he was angry with her. That she was scared of him.'

'Maybe they had a row or something. Maybe that was why he . . . you know . . .'

'Well, I probably shouldn't tell you this. But Elinor told me in therapy that she suspected that Blake had murdered Ursula. I think he may have been angry with her about that.'

Dresler replaced his cup, spilling a little of the coffee into the saucer.

'You don't seriously believe he'd do something like that, do you?'

'I don't know. But the policewoman on the case had taken

him in for questioning. His alibi with Mia, his business partner—'

'Yes, I know Mia.'

'Well, that had collapsed. He was lying about that. And she was investigating further.'

'So that was it. He was being hounded by the police.'

'For a reason.'

Dresler shook his head. 'Jess, I don't think Blake would kill someone, I really don't. I mean, he could be a complete shit. But he wasn't capable of murder.'

'Well, I didn't know him, so I can't say.' Jess did her best to be fair. 'But you'd be surprised what people do when they're cornered. They panic. They lose perspective.'

Dresler didn't respond, but he looked shocked.

They sat in silence for a while, then finished their coffees, got up, and left. Outside, the frost had cleared and the sun was shining. They wandered around the town, but it was hard to relax. Nevertheless, Jess found a second-hand bookshop and managed to come away with a few cheap finds: an old Kate Greenaway birthday book for Rose, a poetry anthology to help Nella with her songwriting, and, for herself, a book of botanical illustrations. Dresler bought nothing; he seemed quite unable to concentrate, shifting impatiently from foot to foot as he gazed into the shop windows, seeing nothing.

After a while, they went into a pub, bought some indifferent sandwiches, drank more coffee, and then headed back to the car park for the journey home. It was a shame that the weekend had been ruined, thought Jess; in normal circumstances, she imagined, Dresler would have liked nothing better than to immerse himself in a bookshop, disappearing among the shelves and emerging with a pile of obscure volumes to take home. Now he was walking along, hands in his pockets, head bowed in thought. Jess, while shaken, had begun to feel calmer; it was part of her training to carry on going through the motions in the wake of disaster. Part of her personality, perhaps, too. She'd been profoundly shocked by the sight of Blake's body, and the knowledge that he'd apparently taken his own life, so suddenly, so unexpectedly. She was still worried, to some degree, about Elinor. But since there was nothing she could do about the situation, at least for the time being, she was able to put the memory out of her mind, and concentrate on the present.

Jess had hoped that as they made their way through the Brecon Beacons, Dresler would be impressed by their majesty, excited by the adventure of passing through them, as she was, even today. Mist hung from the mountain peaks, swirling around them, hovering over the ravines, where waterfalls gushed from the rocks. From time to time, where the road dipped, they could see the fog gather, looking down on it from above, then driving down into it, as if on some great *Lord of the Rings* big dipper. Rather childishly, Jess always imagined herself to be a hobbit, travelling through middle earth back to the shire, when she took this route. She'd planned to tell Dresler of her fantasy, hoping he'd find it amusing, but judging by the look on his face, he was in no mood for playfulness, so she kept quiet and drove on. Besides, the frisson of fear that the mountains provoked in her was too powerful today; when she looked up, she felt genuinely afraid, and wanted to get home to the safety of her burrow, the sooner the better.

When they reached Cardiff, Jess dropped Dresler off at the station. She parked the car and went into the concourse with him, checking the departure board. His train was on time.

'I'll ring you when I get in.'

'OK.'

He drew her towards him and hugged her. For a moment, they clung to each other, both of them experiencing a kind of subdued panic about going their separate ways.

'Or you call me.'

She could feel his heart beating. He was thoroughly shaken, she knew. She wondered if and when her own reaction would set in.

'Thanks for coming down. I'll come up to you next time.' She kissed him on the lips. 'Once things have settled down.'

He nodded, then let her go.

She walked across the concourse, turning to wave as she went, but he didn't see her. She watched him put his ticket into the machine and pass through the barrier. Then he was lost from view, his familiar silhouette obscured by the other passengers.

16

The following evening, Jess was watching TV with Rose. When she'd returned home, all had been well. Rose had enjoyed her stay with Bob and Tegan; Nella and Gareth had spent their time cooking, but had tidied up the house for her. She hadn't mentioned the suicide to the girls; it would have upset them, and there seemed to be no point in doing so. She'd told Mari, but had kept her description brief, knowing what a gossip she was.

As promised, Elinor had phoned, sounding very distressed. On the night of Blake's death, she'd called Isobel and asked her to come up, because she was worried about Blake. While she was waiting for Isobel to arrive, she'd called Jess in a panic. Then Isobel had arrived. Blake had been in a terrible state, threatening to kill himself, but they hadn't believed him and had driven off without him. He'd phoned again while they were on their way home, but Isobel had had enough, and told him to take a sleeping pill and go to bed. The next day, Bonetti had interviewed them, asking them a few more questions about Blake's general state of mind. Isobel had told Bonetti that Blake had been a bit manic, but she'd never expected him to actually kill himself.

Now though – and at this point Elinor began to sound distinctly panicky – something else had happened, something that explained it all, only she couldn't tell Jess what. She added that it would probably be on the news soon. Jess couldn't make much sense of what she was saying, but she was concerned about Elinor's well-being; judging by her tone of voice, she seemed to be very unstable. Jess suggested a session the following week, but Elinor seemed too indecisive to commit to anything and soon rang off.

Jess headed for the living room where Rose was half watching TV and half browsing on the iPad, looking for a new spring coat. Jess was happy to help her, glad to be back in the domestic routine after the horrors of the weekend. Rose was very specific about what she wanted: plain khaki, with fur around the hood, and not too many dangling bits of string around the hem.

'Oh, look.'

For a moment, Jess thought she might have found one she liked. But Rose was staring at the TV, transfixed.

Jess glanced up and saw that Tegan was reading the news. She was seated in front of a photo of the Bay at night. Her hair was expertly coiffed, and she was dressed in a pale grey jacket and a white camisole top. Around her neck was a small heart-shaped pendant.

'Doesn't she look lovely?' Rose sighed in admiration.

If you like industrial-strength hair lacquer and soppy jewel-lery, thought Jess, but she didn't say so.

Tegan's voice was well modulated as she spoke, with just the hint of the Swansea accent that's generally accepted as the Welsh equivalent of RP. 'There has been a sensational new develop-ment in the case of Ursula Powell, killed in October last year in the course of a robbery in which a valuable painting by one of Wales' foremost artists, Gwen John, was stolen . . .'

'Tegan's getting a puppy.' Rose continued to gaze at the screen. 'A chocolate-brown Labrador—'

'Hush a moment,' Jess interrupted her. 'I want to listen to this.'

'Mrs Powell's daughter, Isobel Powell, reported yesterday that the painting has been found among the possessions of Blake Thomas, her late husband,' Tegan continued.

A picture of Blake flashed up on the screen. It had evidently been taken recently, at the private view, since he was standing by one of the Morris paintings. He looked handsome and impeccably dressed, but there was something unconvincing about his brilliant smile.

'Mr Thomas, an art consultant, fell and died last Saturday night, while staying in the remote area of Cwm Du.' Tegan paused, her eyes flickering on the autocue. 'It is now believed that Mr Thomas was responsible for the theft of the painting. It has been suggested that he was in financial trouble at the time. His wife, who runs the well-known Frederick Powell Gallery in Cardiff, refused to make any further comment in response to suggestions that this new revelation might provide the motive for her husband's apparent suicide.'

Jess's mind was racing. So it was Blake who'd stolen the painting, killing Ursula in the process – presumably because she'd got in his way. Elinor's suspicions had been well founded, after all. That was why he'd seemed so nervous at the launch, afraid that what he'd done was about to be discovered. He'd been hiding the theft, and Ursula's murder, from his wife and his sister-in-law. Despite all the bravado at the launch, he'd also been in deep financial trouble. And eventually the lying, and the guilt about what he'd done, had overcome him; he'd gone up to Cwm Du and ended it all. Jess imagined him standing on the parapet, looking down on the ruined arches below, dizzy with fear and remorse, and jumping. It would be easy enough to do. The view there, as she knew, was mesmeric. You could lose yourself in it, become one with the sky, and the deep cut of the valley, fly down to meet it . . .

'She's going to call it Monty.' Jess realized Rose was talking to her. 'And she says I can help her walk it.' Rose paused. 'Mum, are you listening to me?'

The news item finished, and Tegan began to report on local protests against the badger cull.

'Sorry, darling.' Jess turned the TV down, curtailed her private thoughts, and attended to Rose. 'Well, that sounds nice. A little Labrador puppy. Lovely.' There was a brightness to her tone that wasn't altogether natural.

Rose sighed. 'I wish we could get a dog.'

'I don't think so, love, not at the moment.' Jess focussed her mind on what Rose was saying, relieved that the mystery had now, apparently, been resolved. 'It isn't kind to leave a young dog alone for hours on end, stuck in the house. They're like babies. They need company.'

'Tegan says it's OK. She goes out to work every day.'

Jess stifled the urge to contradict Tegan's opinion.

'She's going to fetch the puppy the weekend after next,' Rose went on. She let go of Jess's hand and went back to browsing on the iPad. 'And she wants me to go with her.'

'I'll talk to Dad. I'm sure we can arrange for you to be there.'

The phone rang, interrupting their conversation. Jess picked up.

'Doctor Mayhew?' The voice was familiar, but she couldn't place it.

'DS Lauren Bonetti here.'

For a moment, Jess panicked.

'Hello. Everything all right?'

'You've heard the news, I expect?'

'Just been watching it.' Jess paused. 'I'm absolutely stunned. Explains it all, doesn't it?'

There was a silence. If Bonetti was convinced by this latest turn of affairs, then she wasn't saying so.

'I'd like to talk over a few points with you, as you were on the scene, if you wouldn't mind,' Bonetti continued. 'Perhaps we could meet up for a coffee sometime.'

'When were you thinking of?'

'Tomorrow?

'I'll do my best. I've got a rather busy day—'

'It won't take long, I promise. I just wanted to run over a few details in your statement. You wouldn't have to come down to the station. We could meet somewhere near your office. The coffee bar at the museum, perhaps.'

'What time?'

'Any time that suits you.'

Rose tugged on her sleeve. Jess looked down at the iPad and saw that she was pointing to a khaki parka displayed on it.

Jess thought for a moment. She knew she had a break at twelve on a Tuesday, which she'd taken to spending with Dougie, the therapist in the office opposite, catching up on the latest developments in CBT. But it was an informal arrangement, and she could easily cancel.

'Twelve o'clock?'

Bonetti sounded pleased. 'See you there.'

Jess put down the phone, feeling disappointed. She was loath to go over all this again. She wished Bonetti would let the case go. But, in her heart of hearts, she knew she was right to go through it with a fine-tooth comb. Bonetti's job was like her own: you didn't accept pat explanations, didn't take what people said at face value.

She turned her attention to Rose, who was scrolling through the details on the parka.

'Looks good. Shall we get it?' Jess peered at the image.

'What about these strings dangling down at the bottom?' Rose was a stickler for detail.

'We can cut them off if you like. Or tie them up so they're shorter.'

'I don't know.' Rose frowned. 'I'm not sure I like these pointy bits at the back.'

'It's a fishtail, Rose. Classic parka style.'

Rose looked thoughtful. Jess said nothing, knowing that if she tried to push Rose into the purchase, all would be lost, and they'd have to spend another hour on the iPad, looking for a parka without pointy bits at the back.

'OK.' Rose made her decision. 'Let's get it.' She paused, and a dreamy look came into her eyes. 'I can wear it for walking Monty.'

17

When Jessica arrived at the museum the following day, DS Lauren Bonetti was sitting at the coffee bar in the lobby, waiting for her. She looked much the same as she had the last time they'd met. She was dressed in an asymmetric top, a short skirt, thick tights, and chunky-heeled boots. Her curly brown hair was swept back from her brow, her nose was dotted with freckles, and she had an open, inquisitive expression on her face. There was nothing of the police officer about her, except perhaps her habit of observing people closely, watching their every move. When she saw Jess, she gave a broad grin.

'Good to see you again, Jessica.' She got to her feet. 'What can I get you?'

Jess looked down at the table and saw that Lauren Bonetti was drinking a cappuccino.

'An espresso, please.' Jess didn't want to give the impression she was going to stay long.

Bonetti went off to get the coffee, and Jess sat down at the table. She glanced round the museum. The Morris exhibition was still on, she noted. She'd have to go up and look at the paintings again before it ended. She hadn't really had a chance to take them in at the private view. Jacob rated them so highly, and she wanted to see for herself what she thought about them.

Her faith in Jacob had been restored, she reflected. She'd been so relieved to find that Blake had killed himself. She'd been able to quash an awful unbidden fear that Jacob might have been somehow involved in Blake's fatal fall. Now she could pursue their relationship without that doubt at the back of her mind.

Bonetti came back with the espresso and a packet of Bourbon biscuits, put them down on the table, and sat down. She tore the packet open, offered one to Jess, and when Jess declined, took one herself. As Bonetti munched on the biscuit, they exchanged pleasantries, and then she took out a small reporter's notebook and a pen from her bag. Jess was surprised, as she had been on the previous occasion, that Bonetti wasn't using something more technologically up to date.

'OK.' Bonetti flipped open the notebook. 'Now, I just want to check a few details with you. On the night that Blake Thomas died, you gave a statement to the police, didn't you?'

Jess nodded.

'In it, you said' – Bonetti turned a page on the pad, and read from her notes – 'that you'd seen Thomas earlier that day, and he'd seemed distraught.'

'That's right.'

'Could you fill me in a bit more on that?'

'Of course.' Jess took a sip of her espresso. It was pleasantly bitter. 'He'd come looking for Elinor. Elinor Powell. She was – is – a client of mine.'

'Why did he come to see you?'

'He thought I might know where she was.'

'And did you?'

Jess hesitated. She wasn't prepared to lie, but neither was she keen to divulge too much information. 'She'd told me she was camping up at Cwm Du, but she hadn't said exactly where.'

'So what did you tell him?'

'I said I didn't know. Elinor had told me her whereabouts in confidence. And I didn't altogether trust him. He seemed very agitated. Distressed.'

'In what way, specifically?'

'His hands were shaking, he was sweating, and there was a muscle twitching under his eye.' Through force of habit, Jess described his actual symptoms, rather than using more generalized expressions. 'He was also irritable.'

'What was he anxious about?'

'He didn't explain. He just said he wanted to see Elinor, as a matter of urgency.'

'Why do you think that was?'

'I don't know.'

Jess reached for a biscuit, broke a piece off, and dipped it in her coffee.

Bonetti changed tack.

'According to your statement, on the night that Blake Thomas died, you received a phone call from Ms Powell, who was at the tower.'

'That's right.'

'Could you run through with me again exactly what it was she said?'

'Well, the signal kept cutting in and out.' An image of Cwm Du on that wild, windy night came into Jess's head. 'She said she'd come to see me, and that Blake was there. She said she was scared of him.'

'Why was she coming to see you?'

'I was in the area.' Jess had no reason to feel uncomfortable, but she did. 'Elinor had taken a break from the therapy, and she'd told me that she was going camping up at Cwm Du. I'd been a little concerned about her, so I'd given her my mobile number in case she needed to call me.'

'Do you often do that with clients?'

'No.'

Bonetti made a note in her book.

'And was it a coincidence that you were staying up at Cwm Du, where she was camping?'

'Yes and no. Jacob – Mr Dresler—'

At the mention of Dresler's name, Bonetti looked up.

'Your partner?'

There was a brief pause.

'Yes.'

It was the first time Jess had been asked whether Dresler was her partner, and the first time she'd responded in the affirmative. It felt strange, but not uncomfortably so.

'We were planning a weekend away,' Jess went on, 'so I thought we'd go up there. I'd never been. A friend recommended the hotel.' She paused. 'The fact that Elinor was in the vicinity was in the back of my mind, yes. I thought if I let her know where I was, she could call or drop by. I just wanted to check that she was OK.'

Bonetti nodded. She seemed satisfied by the explanation. She was obviously a person who went the extra distance in her job, and understood that Jess did, too.

'Now, Mr Dresler.'

Jess nodded.

'I'm sorry to ask you this, Dr Mayhew. I don't mean to pry. But it will help with our investigation.'

'Of course. Carry on.'

'Have you known him long?'

Jess was slightly nonplussed. 'No. Not that long.'

'How long?'

'Only a few weeks, actually.'

'And during that time, did you get the impression he was friendly with Mr Thomas?'

'Not particularly.' Jess chose her words with care. There was nothing to hide, but she didn't want to speak for Dresler. Not to a police officer, anyway.

Bonetti made a note in her book and, once more, flipped over to another page.

'Right. According to your statement, it was Mr Dresler who discovered Blake's body. Is that so?'

'Yes.'

'You were elsewhere at the time?'

'I was outside, trying to get a signal. I was trying to get hold of Elinor.'

'She'd left the tower by that time?'

'Yes.'

'Did you manage to contact her?'

'No. I left her a message.'

'So you came back in shortly afterwards?'

Jess nodded.

Bonetti consulted her notes.

'You say you found Mr Dresler up on the parapet alone, with the body on the ground below?'

Jess nodded.

Bonetti checked the notes again. 'According to Mr Thomas's phone record, he spoke to his wife at 11.50. You called the police at 12.05. So Dresler must have discovered him a very short time after he'd jumped. A matter of minutes, in fact.'

Where was this going? Jess wondered.

'How did Mr Dresler seem when you saw him? After he'd made the discovery?'

'He was in shock. Not surprisingly, in the circumstances.'

Jess tried to keep her tone neutral. She was somewhat offended at the policewoman's line of questioning, but she tried not to show it. Bonetti was just being diligent, she reasoned, exploring every avenue. In her position, she would have done exactly the same thing. And however intrusive Bonetti's questions, she told herself, it was up to her to answer them, as fully as she could. After all, they were both professionals.

'He hadn't run down to check the body?' Bonetti went on. 'Called the emergency services?'

'No. It was me who did that.' Jess paused. 'I've dealt with this kind of thing before, you see.'

Jess spoke the words with confidence, but as she did, Blake's head floated into her mind. One side of it was crushed, and there was a mass of soft flesh spilling out of it. She sighed involuntarily. More mindfulness would be needed in the coming days.

'Sorry to make you go through all this again,' Bonetti said, as if reading her thoughts.

'That's OK.'

There was a brief silence.

'Just one more thing. Did Mr Dresler make any phone calls while you were with him that weekend?'

'I don't remember him doing so.'

'Might he have called Hefin Morris?'

'Not that I'm aware.'

Bonetti made a note. Could it be that she suspected Morris of involvement in Blake's death? That was another long shot, Jess thought. Dresler had suggested that there might be some conflict between Blake and Morris, but it certainly wasn't anything of that order. Bonetti was probably just tying up loose ends, as she'd done vis-à-vis Dresler.

Jess finished her coffee, leaving only the dregs in the bottom.

'Thanks, Dr Mayhew. You've been very helpful.' Bonetti's tone signalled that the interview was almost over. 'But before you go, could I ask your professional opinion on something?'

'Of course.'

'When you spoke to Blake Thomas earlier that day, did he seem suicidal?'

Jess frowned. 'I don't think I'm in a position to judge that. I knew very little about him.'

'You see,' Bonetti went on, 'before he died, I interviewed him several times. On each occasion, he seemed very tense. But I wouldn't have had him down as a suicide risk.'

'He was certainly very anxious when I saw him that morning.'

'And could that anxiety have escalated to the point where he'd take his own life, would you say?'

Jess thought for a moment. 'I wouldn't rule it out. There's sometimes a link between acute anxiety and suicide. But it's more common with depression.' She paused. 'However, it's been suggested that he'd committed a murder, and was in deep financial trouble. Both of those are risk factors.'

Bonetti made a final note and closed the pad. Then she leaned forward, broke the last biscuit in half, and offered one piece to Jess.

'I'm on a diet,' Jess said, taking it.

'Sorry.'

As they shared the remaining biscuit, they made small talk. At length, Bonetti stood up to go.

'Thanks again for your time.'

'Not at all.' Jess looked at her watch. 'I've just got time to go upstairs and look at the Morris pictures. Have you seen them?'

Bonetti nodded. 'Before you got here. Can't say I liked them. Load of old bollocks, I thought.'

Jess chuckled. Evidently, Bonetti was not an aesthete.

'OK then.' Jess hesitated. 'Give me a call if you need anything else.'

'I will.' Bonetti turned and walked quickly away. Jess watched as she disappeared into the revolving door of the museum entrance. There was a casual warmth about her that was very Cardiffian, Jess thought, as she watched her go.

Just then something flashed into her mind – an image of Jacob hanging out of the window in the Tŵr Tal, his phone to his ear. He had made a phone call after all, but only to an art magazine. She briefly considered following Bonetti to tell her about it, but decided against it. What use could it possibly be?

When she'd gone, Jess got up, left the cafe, and walked up the grand marble staircase with its polished copper balustrade, past the statue of the Greek god brandishing the Medusa head, and into the gallery where the Morris paintings were housed. It was a large room with other rooms leading off it, and when she walked in, there was nobody there, apart from a uniformed museum employee hovering in the background. In the empty space, the great black canvasses hanging on the walls seemed to reverberate silently, in a way that was almost religious, like a gathering of monolithic dark angels around a tomb. As she approached one of the paintings, it subtly transformed itself, so that it became a dirty pavement, smeared with globules of tar; but when she stood in front of it, she found herself looking at a slab of coal that glittered menacingly in the light, prosaic yet strangely beautiful. Leaning in to scrutinize it, the surface of the coal began to sparkle seductively, then became a deep shaft; she followed it until it seemed to disintegrate into a void, a vortex that threatened to suck her into nothingness . . .

She stepped back, frightened by its malicious intensity yet drawn to it. She knew about black holes. Rose had been studying them in school. They came into being when massive stars collapsed at the end of their life cycle, sucking everything in the vicinity down with them. There was a surface around them called an event horizon, from which there was no return.

Walking away from the painting, Jess became aware that she had been standing on that edge for some time, ever since Bob left, without realizing it. Morris wasn't painting that, of course; he was painting the social collapse of the South Wales valleys, and the communities that had remained there, the gravitational pull of their lives torn away from them, forever balancing on the event horizon of the black hole that threatened, as it grew, to engulf them. But it was still emotional loss, wasn't it, to a greater or lesser degree, and its aftermath of grief and despair . . .

Get a grip, Jessica told herself, as she walked round the rest of the room, merely glancing at the rest of the paintings. You're just overtired. You need some space and time to unwind. She knew it had all been a bit too much, what with finding Blake's body, her new affair, and the split with Bob. Going over the weekend's events just now with Lauren Bonetti hadn't helped, either. You need to slow down.

As if obeying this inner dictum, Jess found herself walking through the other rooms of the gallery, looking for her favourite paintings. She didn't have a client waiting, and although there was work to catch up on, she could afford to linger a while longer in the museum. And she owed it to herself. Looking at paintings, she knew, like observing nature, was therapy for free . . . the seeing cure, if you like.

She stopped in front of the Cézanne, his painting of the Mont Sainte-Victoire that caught exactly the light of Provence, where she'd spent an unforgettable year as a student in her youth – another time, another life. There was the Barbara Hepworth, the 'conker', as the children had called it, that she'd always had to stop them stroking, poking their fingers through the holes, when they were little. Yet another time, another life. Finally she came to the Johns, Gwen and Augustus.

Here they were, Gwen's minute, detailed studies of quiet women sitting in shadowed rooms, their hands neatly folded on their laps. The pale young girl in the blue dress, the nun in her habit, the lifeless Japanese doll sitting by the wooden box. And Jess's favourite, the empty wicker chair by the attic window, a shaft of sunlight falling on an open book beside it. There was a profound, sombre beauty to these paintings, but they were also suffocating. The same small items were painted and repainted over and over again – the chair, a table, a checked tablecloth. You could almost hear the clock ticking away the minutes on the mantelpiece as the artist's life went by.

Jess moved on to Augustus, whose works took up an entire wall of the room. They were the polar opposite, in spirit, to those of his sister. He painted his wives and lovers and socialite friends on big canvasses in bright, bold colours. Never mind that these days, Gwen's paintings were, in many circles, more prized than her brother's, her work spoke of frustration, constraint, the claustrophobia of domesticity, while the record Augustus had left behind was that of a sensual, expansive life lived with vim and gusto.

As she moved between the paintings, Jess couldn't help thinking of Elinor. She could well imagine how Elinor might have felt crushed by the influence of Gwen John's style. She wondered whether the claustrophobia had abated, or whether it had intensified after the traumatic events of the weekend.

It was useless to speculate, she admonished herself. For the time being, Elinor had left therapy, and there was no knowing whether she'd be back. Jess had left her current slot open for her, as she'd promised. But if she didn't come back to her session that week, she'd have to think about filling it. There was always a long queue of people waiting to be seen.

18

The consulting room needed a facelift, Jess was thinking. A change. Nothing too drastic, of course. She wouldn't want to upset her patients. Perhaps a slightly brighter colour on the walls, to make the most of the light filtering through the window. At present, they were a pale, calming grey. Or patterned curtains, instead of the plain cream ones that hung either side of the bay window. She'd seen a fabric she liked at Mari's house: a subtle, contemporary design of bare branches in muted tones that would echo the movement of the tree outside the window.

The white relief on the wall, behind the patient's armchair, would have to stay, of course. That was her emotional compass. Today, as she looked up at it, the circle was throbbing slightly among the squares instead of sitting quietly, telling her to take care, warning her of some potential imbalance in her psyche.

She glanced at the clock on the wall. Elinor had arranged to come in for her session that day, but kept delaying her return. It had been two months now, and each time she'd phoned to postpone, Jess had felt hurt, disappointed. It was a familiar enough feeling – she nearly always became attached to her patients in this way, was sad when they left, however difficult and demanding they'd been. But what surprised her was how intense her relationship with Elinor had become, over such a short period of time. Perhaps, with Bob gone, and this new affair with Dresler on the go, her emotional life had become more intense altogether, and was affecting all her relationships, at work as well as at home.

There was a knock at the door. Jessica's heart leapt. That was odd, too, she thought. This feeling of excitement whenever Elinor deigned to appear.

She walked over to the door, opened it, and Elinor walked in.

'Hello.' Elinor gave her a warm smile, which was unusual. She looked healthy, as if she'd been sleeping and eating properly: there was a tinge of pink to her cheeks, and the lines on her face seemed to have smoothed out a little. 'I'm sorry I haven't been in before. Things have been rather . . . well, you can imagine.'

She was wearing an immaculate linen jacket that didn't accord with her usual style of dress. As she took it off and hung it on the hat stand, Jess realized that it was exactly the kind of thing Isobel would have worn. She'd probably borrowed it.

Elinor went over to the couch. Jess noticed that she didn't even glance at the window, which was open just a crack, in readiness for her session.

'It's been crazy.' Elinor settled herself on the couch. 'We've had so much to do over the past couple of months. Dealing with the police, the post-mortem, the funeral. The gallery, the Morris artworks, Blake's financial affairs . . . it's all so complicated.' She sighed. 'But we're getting through it.'

'You say "we"?'

Elinor looked puzzled. 'Me and Isobel, of course. She's staying with me at the moment. We're thinking of selling Ebenezer.'

'Ebenezer?'

'The converted chapel where they' – she didn't say Isobel and

Blake, but that was what Jess took her to mean – 'both lived. It's about ten miles away, in the Vale.'

'I see.' So now Isobel and Blake had become 'they'. Isobel and Elinor had become 'we'. Clearly, thought Jess, Blake's death had been something of a relief to Elinor. Besides offering closure on the mystery of Ursula's death, it had enabled her to resume her relationship with her sister Isobel; they'd become twins again, living together under one roof, back in the family home. No wonder she seemed unusually cheerful. Isobel had told Jess that Elinor had never been able to come to terms with the fact that Isobel had married and moved away. The sisters had quarrelled; now, with Blake dead, the rift had healed, and Elinor had her sister back to herself again.

'It's been pretty difficult.' A frown came over Elinor's face. 'Isobel's been very up and down. She's been living with a great deal of stress for a long time.'

Jessica didn't respond.

'You see, Blake had been very worried,' Elinor continued. 'People didn't realize, because he was good at keeping up appearances.'

Not that good, thought Jess, recalling Blake's panic-stricken behaviour, both at the private view and at the tower.

'But the fact was, he was in a great deal of financial trouble. He'd overreached himself. He'd got so excited about discovering Morris, he'd been neglecting the business, running into debt.' She paused. 'He made it look like a coup, selling the Morris painting to the National Museum. Mounting the exhibition. But it was all just hype, really. He sold the painting for practically nothing. He was just hoping that by pulling the whole thing off, he'd create a stir in the art world up in London, get Morris noticed.'

'And did it work?' Jess let her curiosity get the better of her.

'It might have. But it all took longer than he'd thought. He began to run out of money. He borrowed from the gallery, from the bank. He began to neglect his clients, his other artists. He stopped paying his bills. It was all getting very precarious. Isobel says it was around the time of Ursula's murder that he started losing his mind. He'd wake up at night and wander round the house, complaining that the walls were closing in. He started coming up with all sorts of ludicrous, short-term plans to make money. She was very worried about him, but of course, at that time she and I . . . well, we weren't on very good terms, so she didn't tell me.'

Jess wondered whether to press her on that point, but decided not to.

'Anyway, he finally decided to steal the Gwen John from my studio. He had a key. He went round while I was out, let himself in, and went down to the studio. It should have been easy.' Elinor paused, frowning. 'But evidently, my mother came in and caught him red-handed. So he panicked. Beat her to death. He was desperate, I think. Out of his mind.' She shivered, clasping her arms around her body, as if trying to warm her limbs. 'And then he ran off with the painting,' Elinor continued. 'He obviously intended to sell it later. It would have been easy enough for him to find buyers for a painting like that. He knew so many collectors.'

'But wouldn't it be difficult for him to sell a well-known painting like that?'

'Not really. There are plenty of collectors in the art world who buy stolen work for private viewing. In fact, it gives them a kind of frisson to own paintings that nobody knows they have.'

'But wouldn't selling the painting immediately mark him out as the murder suspect?'

Elinor shrugged. 'I don't see why. Dodgy art collectors don't go to the police, do they? Not when they're busy buying a stolen painting.'

'But why did Blake hang on to the painting for so long? If he was desperate for money?'

'These things take time, I suppose. Or maybe it wasn't as easy as he'd expected. The whole thing had to be done in secret. So, while he was looking for a buyer, he hid the painting in his wardrobe. And there it remained until Isobel found it.' Elinor paused. 'I suppose, after he'd done it, he must have been overcome with guilt. He couldn't tell anyone. Isobel and I were distraught about Ursula, of course. And the pressure was still mounting up financially. Then there was the stress of the private view, pretending everything was hunky-dory. And after that, the police started closing in, asking questions. So I suppose it got too much for him, and he decided to end it all.'

'Why did he come looking for you that day, then?'

Elinor shrugged. 'I think he wanted me to talk him out of it. Maybe he wanted to confess, and felt it would be easier to tell me than Isobel. I don't know. But when I saw him, he was in such a hysterical state, I was scared of him. He started screaming that he'd killed Ursula, that it was all her fault for interfering. I couldn't handle it. I thought he might attack me. That's why I ran off. I feel terrible about it now.'

Elinor sighed. It was a sigh of remorse, but Jess also detected an element of satisfaction in it.

Jess couldn't help feeling shocked by Elinor's lack of feeling for Blake. She knew that Elinor hadn't had anything directly to do with Blake's death – she and Isobel had been driving away from the tower at the time, and the log on Blake's phone had confirmed that he'd made his last panicky phone call to Isobel before his death. But her apparent indifference was unnerving.

Finally Jess broke the silence.

'So how are you feeling about all this now, Elinor?'

Elinor thought for a moment. 'A mixture of emotions, really.

It's been a relief to find out who killed my mother. A shock, of course, to discover it was Blake. And I miss him. We were . . . close, in some ways. He was always a great supporter of my painting. He thought I was really good.' She paused. 'And I feel sad for Isobel. She's broken-hearted. She loved him, you know.'

Elinor spoke the words as if in surprise. 'But she's back with me now, so she'll be OK. In time.' There was the note of satisfaction in her tone again. 'Everything will be back to normal.'

'Normal?'

Elinor gazed out of the window at the tree outside, an expression of serenity on her face that Jess had never seen before. Her eyes were clear, her brow unfurrowed.

'Isobel and I have always been together, ever since we were children. We need each other. We should never have been parted. She helps me, and I help her.'

Jess was conscious that she felt strangely jealous as Elinor spoke the words, as if Isobel had usurped her own position as Elinor's helpmeet. She was surprised at herself.

'It'll take a long while, of course. Isobel is very fragile at the moment, as you can imagine. She trusted Blake. She feels guilty that he killed Ursula. And then killed himself. She feels it's all her fault. That she should have noticed what was going on, tried to stop it.' Elinor paused. 'It'll be difficult for her to get over this. But I'm sure she will. I'm with her now, by her side. I can help her. We don't need anyone else, as long as we're together.'

Jess noticed the finality in her tone. It was so marked that she wasn't surprised at Elinor's next remark.

'I don't think I need to keep coming here, actually. It's done me good. And I'm grateful to you, Jess, I really am. You helped me through a tough time.' Elinor looked up again. Her eyes seemed to darken with tenderness. 'But I'm all right now, I think. I can go ahead in my life again.'

'And the claustrophobia?'

'Much better. I'm still a bit scared of lifts, but I can cope with everything else. Public transport. Trains. Tunnels.'

'Tunnels?' Jess registered her surprise.

Elinor nodded. 'Odd, isn't it?'

There was a silence. Once again, Jess was taken aback at how upset she felt that Elinor no longer required her services – it felt like a personal rejection.

'Well, if you want to leave, that's fine.' Jess spoke quietly. 'You've only had five sessions, but I'm glad you feel you've benefited from the therapy.'

'I have. Definitely. Although . . .' Elinor's voice trailed off.

Jess waited.

'I still can't paint.' A frown came over Elinor's face, but only briefly. 'The funny thing is, I don't care now. It doesn't seem to matter any more.'

There was a pause.

'Well, if things change and you decide you want to come back, get in touch. I'm sure I can find a space for you, if you'd like that.'

'Thank you. I'll do that.'

Their time was not yet up, but Elinor got up from the couch. Jess got up, too, and walked over to the hat stand with her. She watched as Elinor put on her jacket, fascinated by the change in her client. She seemed confident, assured – nothing like the timid, forlorn creature who had walked into her office only a few months ago.

'Goodbye. And thank you so much, Jess.' On an impulse, Elinor leaned forward and kissed her on the cheek. For an instant, Jess felt the softness of her hair and skin brushing against her face. It was a child's kiss, tender, sweet and innocent.

Jess was moved. She put her arm around Elinor's shoulder, and gave her a hug.

'Good luck. Take care of yourself.'

She turned, opened the door, and let Elinor out. Then she closed it again and went over to the window.

After a minute or so, Elinor appeared in the street below. Jess watched the diminutive figure walk along the pavement, her hair a luminous point of light in the grey street. Even from a distance, she looked small, vulnerable, like Little Red Riding Hood walking through the forest, her wicker basket on her arm.

Jess sighed and turned away from the window. There was no point in wondering what the future held for Elinor. She had signed off. She was now an ex-client, and as such, no longer her concern.

19

That weekend, Jess went up to London to see Jacob Dresler. It was the first time she'd visited him there. She'd made arrangements for Nella and Gareth to look after the house, and for Rose to go over to Bob and Tegan's. Bob had a conference to go to, so Rose would be on her own with Tegan, but she didn't seem to mind. In fact, she was excited and happy at the prospect, especially now they were going to fetch Monty, the six-week-old Labrador puppy Tegan had acquired. As she boarded the train, Jess reflected rather sadly that neither of the girls seemed to make a fuss when she went away these days. In the past, whenever there'd been a parting, even for just a day or so, there'd be whines and sometimes tears. Of course, she told herself, they still need you, at least in the background; it's just that they're growing up, both of them, becoming more independent. But somehow, that didn't seem to help.

She waited at the station, listening to the announcements in Welsh and English. Although it was spring, there was still a chill in the air, but today the sun had come out. The sky was a bright blue, the gulls squawking overhead, one or two of them bold enough to strut down the platform picking up discarded wrappers, looking for food. As the train came in, she saw a gull snatch a crisp out of a young child's hand. The child's mother waved her arms, outraged, and the gull flew away, the crisp still in its beak. For a moment, looking on, Jess wished she was that mother, and the child hers. Those early years with the girls had been hard work, yet in a way, she now realized, it had all been so simple: the aims were clear – you just had to protect your children, care for them, be patient and kind with them. Now that they were older, things were so much more complicated.

The train stopped and the doors opened, disgorging a flood of passengers. The child began to scream. The mother proffered more crisps, but the child would not be placated. The gull had frightened him. She became flustered, as people started to stare. She scolded the child, who responded by screaming louder. When the passengers dispersed, Jess hopped onto the train, thankful that she didn't have a small child in tow, and wondering what on earth had possessed her to envy that poor mother with her bawling offspring, even for a moment. It hadn't been easy at all when the kids were little; at times it had been sheer hell. And now here she was, free as a bird, going to London, on her own, to meet her new lover. This was no time to look back, to mourn what was past, but to savour life as a free agent, and the prospect of what lay ahead.

Jess found her way from Paddington to Soho without difficulty – she'd lived in London as a student, and knew it well. The house was in one of the small paved lanes that cut between Wardour Street and Dean Street. Beside the front door, at street level, was a fashionable men's cobbler's, with a single quirky purple shoe, long and pointed, almost medieval in shape, displayed in the window. Jess pressed the bell, feeling a thrill of anticipation at seeing Dresler again, and at finding herself here, in the heart of Soho, his stamping ground, with its warren

of arcane alleyways bordering up against the great city thor-
oughfares of Shaftesbury Avenue, Regent Street and Oxford
Street.

'Jess.' Dresler opened the door, a broad grin on his face.

They embraced in the doorway, he took her bag, and then
led her up the stairs. On the landing, they passed a room with
an open door. Inside, a young Japanese woman was staring into
a computer. She didn't turn to greet them.

'That's the offices of the art magazine I'm involved with,' he
said. 'They work all weekend. Never seem to take a day off.'

On the landing above was a self-contained flat. Once again,
the door was open.

'Sorry about the mess,' Dresler said, as they walked in. He
showed her through to the living room. 'But it's not as bad as
usual. I tidied up for you.'

It was a large room with high windows overlooking the street.
Everything was painted cream, except for the ancient indoor
shutters, which had been left unpainted and were a pale brown,
knotted oak. Some equally ancient furniture dotted the room
– a wooden table by the window, covered in books and papers,
with an open laptop and a printer winking among them. There
were paintings in dark frames on all of the walls, most of them
abstract. In the corner was a large modern sculpture, and on
the mantelpiece some delicate figurines. Two big leather sofas
bordered a fireplace, in which a coal fire had been lit.

'Sit down and I'll make you a coffee.' He walked into another
room leading off the sitting room. Instead of doing as she was
told, Jess followed him into a spacious kitchen, all done out in
matt black. It was neat and tidy and gleaming, bearing witness
perhaps, Jess thought, to the fact that Dresler didn't use it a
great deal.

While he was making the coffee, Jess went over to the window
and looked out at the view. She could see over the tops of

houses, all the way to Broadcasting House just off Regent Street.

'What a fabulous view.' She noticed a roof garden below, with a metal garden seat, a chiminea, and a few plant pots scattered around it. 'Is that yours?' she asked, pointing to it.

He nodded. 'It's not used much, except by the smokers in the office. In the summer, it comes into its own.' He set the cafetière on a tray, along with two mugs and a bottle of milk. 'Come on.'

They went back into the sitting room. He put the tray on a low coffee table between the sofas, and sat down. She sat beside him, feeling the urge to curl up on the soft leather.

'This place is amazing.'

He laughed. 'It's just a flat above a shop, really. It belonged to my family, and I inherited it. Tailors, they were.' He leaned forward, pushed down the plunger on the cafetière, and poured out the coffees. 'It's worth a fortune now, of course. But only if I sell it.'

'And will you?'

He shook his head. 'No. I like it here. It works well for me. I get a bit of income from the office – I try to keep the rent low for them – and it's security for me if times get hard in future. As they well might, with this financial squeeze on.' He handed her a coffee.

She blew on it, then took a sip. 'This is bliss for me. A taste of the metropolis. I used to live here, you know.'

'D'you miss it?'

'Sometimes.' Jess paused. She did occasionally miss the variety that London had to offer, the different cultures, different lives crushed up against each other, the excitement – and tension – that brought. But since moving away, she'd come to rely on a sense of spaciousness, of ease, of casual trust among strangers, that now seemed quite natural and indispensable to her. 'I suppose I'm a small-town girl at heart.'

He laughed again, and put his arm around her. 'Nonsense. You're a woman of the world, as you well know.'

This time, she laughed. He kissed her, and she kissed him back, feeling the warmth of his body against hers. She began to want him.

'I thought we'd stay here for lunch. I've got some stuff from the deli.' His fingers slid under her sweater. 'Charcuterie, cheese, that sort of thing.' And up to her breast. 'Some focaccia bread. What do you think?'

'Mmm.' Jess looked up at the painting opposite. The sinuous curves of the abstract seemed to take the shape of a white-fleshed woman, held in a pair of huge brown paws, like a bear's.

She lay back on the sofa and closed her eyes. 'Ideal, I'd say.'

'Are you hungry?' Dresler moved with her, nuzzling into her neck, his other hand between her thighs.

'A bit, maybe.' She smiled, bringing her legs up onto the sofa. She put her arms around him, feeling the weight of him on top of her. 'No big rush, though.'

They made love, and afterwards ate their lunch, sitting on the floor and spreading it out like a picnic on the low table by the fireside. Their talk was intimate and affectionate, and Jess was aware that despite their texts and phone calls, they'd lost touch with each other somewhat over the weeks that they'd been parted. Face to face – or was it body to body? – she could gauge his reactions, his moods, and felt she could talk freely, naturally, about what had been going on in her life. But not that freely; although she told him about her meeting with Lauren Bonetti at the museum, she didn't mention Bonetti's questions about him. No need to bother him with all that, she thought. She went on to talk about her visit to the Morris exhibition, and how, for the first time, she'd sensed the depth and complexity of the paintings.

He filled her in on his travels, which had included a spell in

Berlin, advising the Berlinische Galerie on a major exhibition of contemporary British painting that was to open there the following year. He mentioned that Lauren Bonetti had phoned him a couple of times, but didn't go into detail. He also described the moments, waking or sleeping, when Blake's bloodied head, crushed on the gravel, had flashed into his mind; how, during his trip, he'd had some disturbed nights, waking from a dream he couldn't remember clearly, a dream in which he seemed to be packing to go somewhere, but couldn't find his belongings, was late to catch his train, or aeroplane, or ship, or whatever it was that he had to catch. Post-traumatic stress disorder, Jess told him. A mild case of it. It would pass, in time. The mind would heal as the memory faded. As they chatted, her mind was set at ease. Lauren Bonetti's insinuations about him hadn't really worried her. She'd seen him right after he'd discovered Blake's body, and he'd behaved exactly as anybody would have confronted with such a shocking sight. He hadn't shown the slightest sign of guilt then, or since. Even so, during the time they'd been apart, she'd felt the occasional moment of doubt. After all, she hadn't known him for long, and his relationship with Blake seemed to be more tangled than she'd at first realized. Now, however, being with him and watching him talk so openly and honestly, she was reassured.

'I must say, I still find it hard to believe that Blake committed suicide, whatever trouble he was in. He wasn't that kind of guy.' Dresler frowned. 'Even if his debts were huge, I wouldn't have thought he'd panic and steal that painting. Let alone kill for it. He'd have fronted it out. He had nerves of steel when it came to handling large sums of money. All these consultants do.'

Jess thought of what Elinor had told her, about Blake pacing the house in the night, convinced that the walls were closing in on him.

'Well, sometimes people buckle under stress. The mind is like a limb, or any other part of the body, come to that. If you put too much pressure on it, it breaks.'

'I suppose so.' Dresler sighed. 'I must say, this whole thing has really shaken me up. Blake and I weren't close, but I knew him over a very long period of time. And now that he's . . . well, gone . . . I realize how much I relied on him.'

'Relied on him? In what way?'

'Well, mostly regarding Morris. Blake could always get in touch with him. I'm not finding it so easy.'

'But I thought you said Morris wrote to you quite regularly?'

'He used to. But recently, I haven't heard from him. And I've got no way of contacting him.'

'Can't you phone Isobel at the gallery? Isn't she representing him now?'

'She's not returning my calls. Obviously, she's afraid Morris will want to leave the Powell Gallery. Someone like me could easily hook him up with a new dealer, someone with a bit more heft. Isobel's not really a player in this world. She left that side of it to Blake.'

'Well, I wouldn't jump to conclusions. She's obviously rather preoccupied at present.' Jess paused. 'Anyway, is there any pressing need for you to get in touch with Morris right now?'

'Yes, of course. You see, I want him to be part of this group exhibition in Berlin. He'd be perfect for it. He's so much in the tradition of Kiefer. In the past, I could have just phoned Blake, and he'd have sorted it out at once. Now I'm not quite sure what to do.'

'Maybe you should try and contact Morris directly. Find out where he is, and go and see him.'

Dresler nodded. 'I've thought of doing that, many times. He's up in the valleys, I know, but I've no idea where.'

'I'm sure we could trace him.' Jess sat forward. 'How did Blake discover Morris, anyway? Did he ever tell you?'

Dresler nodded, somewhat distractedly, as if tearing himself away from his own thoughts. 'Yes. He often told the story; it was an extraordinary thing. He was at the Cardiff gallery one day with Isobel. They were going over the accounts. The place had been quiet all day, no one much had been in, and then suddenly, this young man appears. A lad from the valleys, with green hair, a pierced eyebrow, and sleeve tattoos. Marches in with a big canvas wrapped in brown paper, dumps it against the wall, and marches out.'

Jess was intrigued, as Dresler warmed to his tale.

'When he left, they unwrapped the canvas and found this marvellous painting. A great expanse of black which, as you experienced, began to mutate before their eyes, into a void, a dirty pavement, a black hole, a lump of coal. Both of them, Blake and Isobel, were stunned by it. But they had no way of contacting the young man. So they waited.

Eventually, two weeks later, he appeared again, with another canvas. It was different from the first, but equally powerful. Blake and Isobel loved it. And they'd sold the first painting very well, considering it was by an unknown artist.

This time, he introduced himself as Nathan Evans, Morris's assistant. Nathan told them that Morris wanted nothing to do with the gallery, or the art world in general. He just wanted to be paid for the first canvas as soon as it sold. When he was, he'd drop off another.' Dresler paused. 'The paintings were extraordinary, and what's more, they were snapped up the minute they were put on show in the gallery. They fetched good prices, for a new artist, and there was always demand for more. So Nathan started dropping off the canvasses more frequently. That's how it always worked. Each time Blake sold a canvas, he'd pay for it, then Nathan would drop off the next.'

'Did they suspect that Nathan was actually Hefin Morris?'

'Yes, of course. Blake asked him directly once, but he flatly denied it. And frankly, if you spent two minutes talking to Nathan, you'd know there was no way on earth he could be producing work of that sophistication. He's a nice lad but not much between the ears, you know. Morris is something else, a proper autodidact. He's always quoting Heidegger or Chomsky in his letters to me. He's no ordinary valleys boy, that's for sure.'

There was a slight note of snobbery in Dresler's remark but Jess chose to ignore it. 'So the only person who's ever been in contact with the mysterious Morris, as far as we know, is Nathan?'

Dresler nodded.

There was a pause.

Jess remembered Bonetti's curiosity about Morris. Perhaps, she thought, Dresler could shed some light on the reason for that.

'You don't think Morris could have had anything to do with Blake's suicide, do you?'

Dresler looked taken aback. 'No. Why?'

'Oh, nothing. It was just something this policewoman was asking me about. She wanted to know if you'd called Morris while we were up at Cwm Du. I told her you hadn't, of course.'

'Why on earth would she ask that?'

'I don't know. I don't think she's convinced that Blake committed suicide, though she didn't say as much. Perhaps she thinks Morris was involved in some way. I remember you saying Morris was thinking of staging a political protest about the current situation in the art world. You know, with the hype, and the money men, and so on.'

'Did I?'

Jess nodded. 'You said he'd got something up his sleeve. And that we'd soon find out what it was.'

'What an amazing memory you have.'

'It's my job. I listen to people for a living. And parrot back to them what they say.'

Dresler chuckled. 'Of course. Well, yes, he did mention to me in one of his letters that he was thinking of staging "an intervention", as he called it.'

'What kind of intervention?'

'He didn't elaborate.' Dresler looked pensive. 'Certainly not killing off the person who championed his work. Morris had his doubts about Blake's dealings in the world of high finance, of course, but . . . no, that's ridiculous. Out of the question.' He thought for a moment. 'You know, we really must get hold of him, so we can put a stop to that kind of speculation right away.' He sighed. 'I just don't know where to start looking for him, though. If only bloody Isobel would answer my calls . . .'

Jess thought for a moment. 'They're taking down the exhibition at the museum in a few days' time,' she said. 'I noticed when I was there. Presumably when it comes to the ones that the museum hasn't bought, Nathan will be taking them back to Morris's studio, wherever that may be.'

Dresler looked intrigued. 'Now that's an idea. Maybe if I followed him – at a distance, of course – I could find out where Morris lives. And then . . . I don't know. Find a way of talking to him about what's going on, now that Blake's out of the picture.'

'I'll come with you, if you like.'

'Why would you want to do that?'

'I know the area. You don't. I should be able to follow Nathan without him noticing us.' Jess wasn't sure why she was offering, but she knew that she was as curious as Dresler to find out the truth behind the Morris story – despite the fact that Elinor was no longer her client.

'OK. Thanks.' Dresler leaned forward and gave her an affectionate hug. 'You know, you're wasted as a shrink. You'd make a good sleuth.'

Jess laughed. 'Well, what I do *is* sleuthing, of a kind.'

She looked out of the window, and saw that the sun had come out. She could hear the bustle of the streets below.

'Come on, let's get going, shall we. I want to look at the fabric shops on Berwick Street. Buy something silly for the girls.'

'And I want to take you to Bond Street.' Dresler began to clear the plates off the table. 'There's a painting I'm thinking of buying in one of the galleries there. I'd like you to see it. Later on, we'll go out to dinner at a nice little Italian place I know. And then home to bed.'

'Of course.' Jess got up. She stretched, savouring the prospect of having Dresler to herself, and the West End as their play-ground, until tomorrow afternoon. 'Whatever you like. I'm all yours.'

20

The weekend had passed all too quickly. After browsing the shops around Berwick Street, they'd gone to the gallery, where in a high, light room they'd seen the paintings, beautiful images of bare-branched olive trees in charcoal, pastel, mud and charred wood. In the evening, they'd eaten in an old-fashioned Italian trattoria, then wandered down to the French House for a nightcap. Afterwards, they'd gone to bed, fallen asleep, then woken up in the night and made love. Next day, after breakfast in bed, they'd wandered around Chinatown, lunched in Dresler's favourite restaurant there, and then it had been time for Jess to catch the train home.

The journey back had been long and tiresome, as was often the case on Sundays, when trains were shunted around via Gloucester while work was carried out in the Severn Tunnel. By the time she got home, Jess was exhausted, but she knew she had an evening's paperwork to catch up on before returning to the office the next day. She also knew that the girls would need her attention, especially Rose, who had spent most of the weekend with Tegan and the puppy, since Bob had been away at a conference.

When she let herself into the house, she heard Bob's voice in the kitchen. She put down her case, took off her coat, and walked down the hallway to find him there with Rose. Rose was sitting on his knee, her arm round his neck. Her nose was red and her eyes were puffy. She looked as if she'd been crying.

'Rosie, darling. What's the matter?' Jess hurried over to her, bent down, and gave her a hug. Rose didn't answer. Instead, she sniffed and turned her head away, towards Bob's chest.

Bob gestured as if to say, Don't worry, we'll talk about this later.

'What's happened?' Jess demanded. 'What's been going on?'

'Things were a bit difficult over the weekend, that's all.' Bob's tone was placatory. 'I think there were problems with the puppy, and . . . well, I should have been there. It was hard for Tegan to cope with it all.'

'Tegan was nasty to me,' Rose piped up. 'She called me a stupid little brat.'

Bob looked embarrassed. 'The puppy kept pissing and shitting everywhere—'

'Weeing and pooing,' Rose corrected him.

'And Tegan got flustered—'

'No, she shouted at me,' Rose interjected.

'Let Rose tell the story.' Jess sat down at the table and took Rose's hand, even though it meant sitting uncomfortably near Bob. 'Now, what happened?'

Rose sniffed. 'Well, Monty kept weeing on the carpet. It's cream, a hundred per cent wool. It's an absolute nightmare to get the stains out.' That was Tegan talking, thought Jess. 'He kept gnawing the legs of the coffee table. Then he nipped at the cover of the sofa. It's suede, it cost three thousand pounds.' Rose paused. 'We took him out for a walk on the lead, but he just sat on his bottom so you had to pull him along. Then he ate a dog poo. And when we gave him his dinner, he just tipped the bowl over with his nose and walked off.'

Rose gave a wobbly smile. Jess squeezed her hand encouragingly.

'Anyway, Tegan got more and more annoyed. So then I had a brainwave. I thought, why don't we bring him over here? You wouldn't mind so much about the sofa and the carpets. It's more scruffy here, isn't it?'

Thanks a bunch, Jess thought.

'And Monty could run around the garden, we wouldn't have to put him on the lead.' Rose paused. 'So I told her my idea, and she just shouted at me. You stupid little brat, she said.'

'She didn't mean it, Rose.' Bob spoke quietly. 'She was just upset about the dog.'

'Yes, she did.' Rose's voice rose in righteous indignation. 'Because when I started crying, she told me to shut up.'

Jess looked up at Bob, wondering whether Rose was telling the truth. From the embarrassed look on his face, it was clear that she was.

'Dad's right, Rose.' Jess squeezed her hand again. 'Everyone gets cross and says things they don't mean.'

'I don't care. I hate her.' There was a finality to Rose's tone. She was a determined child, and once she'd made her mind up about something, it was hard to get her to change it. The crush on Tegan was well and truly over, it seemed.

Jess felt sad for her daughter. To be sure, she'd found Rose's adoration of Tegan somewhat trying, but it was painful to see Rose let down by her idol, and Jess wished it hadn't happened. By the look on his face, so did Bob.

There was a noise in the hall, and then Nella and Gareth walked into the kitchen. Rose immediately got off Bob's knee. When she saw Bob, Nella nodded her head in greeting, but she didn't go over to kiss him. Gareth, on the other hand, came over and shook his hand. They began to talk about rugby.

Jess busied herself in the kitchen making tea. Nella came over and lolled her head on her shoulder. She seemed to do a lot of lolling these days. Jess wondered whether it was because she was in love or, God forbid, she'd been taking drugs.

'What's the matter with Rose?' Nella stepped back, and began pulling at her T-shirt. That was another peculiar habit she was developing, Jess thought. She prayed she wasn't pregnant. She realized she must find a moment to talk to her about it, and soon. Of course, it might simply be that she was putting on weight with all this cooking, and was feeling self-conscious about it.

'She just got a bit homesick, that's all.' Jess saw no need to fan the flames of Nella's resentment towards her father. 'Is Gareth staying tonight?'

'No. He's off in a minute.'

'Well, maybe you could watch telly with Rose while I make supper. Keep her company. She misses her big sis, you know. Especially now that . . .' Jess moved her head in the direction of Bob, who was talking animatedly to Gareth.

'Of course.' Nella stopped lolling, adopting a serious, responsible look instead.

The kettle boiled, and Jess poured it into the teapot. She'd used loose tea that she'd bought in Soho instead of bags. She felt in need of a proper brew.

Nella did as she was asked, and took Rose off into the sitting room to watch TV. Once the topic of rugby was exhausted, Gareth followed suit, leaving Jess and Bob alone together.

'I'm really sorry about all this, Jess.' Bob sounded genuinely remorseful.

Jess poured out two cups of tea, added milk and sugar for Bob, and brought them over to the table.

'Tegan's not used to having kids around,' he went on. 'Or a bloody puppy, come to that. She just couldn't cope.'

'It's understandable.' Jess sat down opposite him. 'Although

I'm surprised she was quite so bad-tempered. I mean, Rose is a very cooperative child. And she hero-worships her. Or did.'

'I know.' Bob looked down at the table. 'The thing is, it's not altogether her fault. There's a certain amount of tension in our relationship at the moment.'

Jess wasn't sure if she wanted to hear more.

'She wants children herself,' Bob went on. 'In the long term, of course,' he added hastily, seeing the look on Jess's face. 'But I'm not sure if I . . .' He came to a halt. 'I mean, I've already got the girls.'

Again, Jess didn't respond. Listening, as she knew from long experience, was the best policy in such situations.

'And to be honest . . .' Bob hesitated. Jess wondered what was coming next. 'Tegan doesn't seem all that keen to have Rose over at the weekends. Not quite so much, anyway.'

Bob lifted his eyes from the table, looking into hers. For a moment, they both shared the pain of their child's rejection by another adult.

'She's never shown any interest in meeting Nella, either.' There was more than a hint of resentment in Bob's voice.

'I think that's mutual.'

'I know. But . . .' Bob sighed. 'To be honest, I don't really think there's a great deal of mileage in this relationship, if that's her attitude. If she doesn't want to take on my kids, I can't see much future for us.'

Jess felt relieved that she'd kept quiet. Bob had taken the words out of her mouth. They would have led to a row if she'd spoken them.

'How did your weekend go?' Bob changed the subject.

'Fine. I had a lovely time.' Jess picked up her tea and blew on it. 'Though, in retrospect, perhaps I shouldn't have gone.'

'Nonsense.' Bob paused. 'So who is this . . . friend of yours? Anyone I know?'

'No.'

'Is it . . .' He seemed flustered. 'Is there . . . I mean, how's it going?'

'Fine.' Jess was determined not to get into a discussion with Bob about Dresler. The less he knew about her private life at present, the better.

Bob took a swig of tea. 'You make a lovely cup, Jess.'

'Thanks.'

They'd begun to speak as if they were strangers.

'Well.' He put his mug back down on the table. 'I suppose I'd better be heading off.'

There was a silence.

'You know, I miss all this,' he said suddenly, gesturing round the room. 'The house. The girls. You.'

Jess nodded in the non-committal way she'd perfected over the years.

'I sometimes dream about it. I dream that I'm still living here with you, that we're back together, a family again, just as it was before. Then I wake up, and I find you're not beside me and . . . well . . .' He shrugged, and looked away. Jess could see that there were tears in his eyes.

She couldn't help feeling touched. She missed the familiarity of their life together, too. They had been happy, the two of them, the three of them, the four of them, for a very long time. But she was also irritated that he was saying this now that he was considering a split from Tegan.

'Things move on, Bob.' Jess spoke in a soft, low tone.

'Yes, but I wish they didn't.' His voice had dropped, too. 'I wish they hadn't. Between us.'

He was waiting for a reply, but it didn't come. Jess remained silent, looking down at the table. Then he drained his mug, and got up. Jess got up, too.

'Thanks for being so understanding.' He moved forward to

kiss her. She offered him her cheek, stiffening slightly at his touch.

He sensed her reserve. 'You stay here and finish your tea. I'll say goodbye to the kids on the way out.'

'OK.' Jess sat down again. 'We'll speak on the phone.'

'See you.' He hesitated briefly, as if struggling to find something to say that would prolong the intimacy of their moment together. Then, failing to do so, he headed for the door.

21

Jess and Dresler were waiting in the car. They hadn't seen each other since the previous weekend, up in London. They were parked in the street, at the back of the museum. They could see a white van in a loading bay. There was no logo on the side of it. The wheels, Jess noticed, were splattered with reddish mud. It looked promising, she thought; it could be Nathan's. On the other hand, they could be wasting their time.

It was a rainy Saturday and a wind was blowing up. Shoppers were scurrying down the streets, battling with their umbrellas. It was a day for going into town, for sitting in a cafe with a cappuccino, watching the windows steam up, not for hanging around in a dismal car park. But Dresler was in a determined mood. He'd decided that he didn't just want to contact Morris about the Berlin exhibition, but to offer him his services as an agent, now that Blake was out of the running. So he was hell-bent on tracking Morris down, starting by finding out where his studio was.

Dresler craned his neck forward, peering through the glass of the windscreen. 'I'm not sure about this,' he said. 'They may be using some other exit, for all we know.'

'I don't think there is another exit.'

'Well, we can't sit here all day. We've already been here for two hours.'

Jess was beginning to realize that Dresler wasn't a patient man.

'Look, the exhibition comes down today. They definitely haven't all been bought by the museum. You checked that, didn't you?'

Dresler nodded.

'And this is the only way they can come out. So let's just wait till they do, shall we?'

Dresler sighed. 'You're right. I'm just not really cut out for this sort of thing—'

'Hey,' Jess interrupted him. 'Look at that.'

Two men appeared from the back entrance. One of them was wearing a peaked cap and a hoodie, the other was dressed in overalls. They were carrying what looked like a large wooden crate. The man with the cap opened the back doors of the van and then they put the crate inside. Once it was safely stowed away, they went back to the entrance, disappeared inside, and reappeared again a moment later with another crate. This happened twice more, and then the man with the cap locked the back door of the van and went round to the front.

'OK.' Dresler was whispering. 'Don't follow him too closely. Leave a gap. Make sure he doesn't see us.'

'Jacob, he can't hear us. You don't need to whisper.'

'OK. OK.' Dresler didn't laugh. He was obviously tense. Jess felt less so. After all, they weren't committing any crime, following a van to see where the owner stored his paintings.

The van pulled out of the car park, stopping at the barrier to slot in a ticket, then moved off slowly into the traffic. Jess waited for a moment and pulled out behind it. It would be easy to follow, she thought; even if other cars cut in between, the van was high sided, and she'd be able to see it from a distance.

They drove through the city centre, heading north, over the flyover. Immediately after the junction with the M4, the van turned left, towards the valleys. They came to a roundabout, and this time the van turned right. Jess followed, keeping at a reasonable distance, occasionally letting another car come between them. As they drove along, Dresler kept up a steady stream of instructions. He was beginning to irritate her. She was a good driver, careful yet not overcautious, and she knew this patch well. She was also feeling quite calm and controlled, which was more than she could say for him.

The road wound up a hill, past a warren of industrial estates. It was the kind of bastard sprawl that is never honoured with the name of countryside: a half urban, half rural no-man's-land of factories, warehouses, garages and small businesses. Further up the road, the estates gave way to a series of ramshackle smallholdings, and then there was a turning to the right, to an old mining village, now a pretty dormitory town. The van went past it, climbing on up the hill until they came to a wide gravel path that led off up into the woods, with a sign beside it advertising aggregates, whatever they might be. The van turned off onto it. Instead of following it, Jess drove on.

'What did you do that for?' Dresler burst out.

'I'm hardly going to follow him up that hill, am I?' Jess slowed down, looking for a place to park the car. 'We'll park the car down here and go up by foot, through the woods.'

'Fine.' He seemed to calm down. 'Sorry.'

Jess didn't reply. She found a lay-by and parked the car. Then she went round to the back, opened the boot, and put on her walking boots. Dresler hadn't thought to bring any, but his shoes looked fairly sturdy.

'OK.' She fished out an old padded coat from the boot, and put it on. It wasn't far up the hill, she knew, but they might be hanging around in the woods for a while. Dresler was wearing a dark blue wool coat. It looked a little too good for forest wear, but it would be serviceable enough if it started to rain.

They set off, up a marked footpath through the trees. It was strange, this place, Jess thought. She'd never been here before, but she'd heard of it: Bryn Cau, the Hollow Hill, so called because since the nineteenth century, as much as a million tons of iron had been hacked out of the bowels of the hill. There were holes all over it, so that if you left the path, you could fall into the tunnels below. The beech wood was one of the most ancient in the country, yet it was just a stone's throw away from the industrial estates. The air was still, the trees arching above them like a great cathedral. There was a carpet of ramsons and wood anemones below their feet, the flowers bowing their heads in the shade, their petals closed, and opening them again where a shaft of sunlight penetrated the canopy above. The earth was soft and springy, the rich mulch of rotted leaves silencing their steps.

They walked on, savouring the deep quiet of the woods that was almost religious in its intensity, despite the fact that only a few yards below them, cars sped along the main road, while above, the odd car travelled up the gravel path. Yet the roar was somehow stifled by the damp sponge of the earth and the panoply of beech trees above their heads. The climb wasn't steep, but it needed effort and concentration to keep going, so they didn't talk. Besides, they were both now beginning to feel keyed up; Dresler's nerves were catching, and by the time they reached the top, Jess's heart was thumping in her chest.

At the top of the wood, they came out onto the gravel path. Opposite were the gates to the gravel pit, and a sign warning that the premises were controlled by security guards. Inside the gates was a warehouse building, the same kind of identikit structure they'd seen below, in the industrial estates. Like the van they'd been following, it was unmarked.

'Is there anyone around, d'you think?'

'Doesn't look like it.' Jess looked down the road. There was no sign of the van. 'He must have come up, unloaded quickly, and gone.' She paused. 'Shall we take a look?'

Dresler nodded, and together they stepped out of the woods. They walked over to the open gates, which were surrounded by plastic bottles and Coke cans. In among them, Jess noticed, an orchid was growing. She wanted to go over and look at it, but this wasn't the time or the place.

'If anyone sees us, we'll just say we were walking in the woods,' Dresler said.

'Good idea.' Jess was doing her best to be polite, but she couldn't help feeling irritated at Dresler's obvious suggestion.

They walked through the gates towards the building. On the way, they peered down at the quarry. It looked as if some massive crater had dropped on it from on high. All around it were ledges, like windowsills, where the rock had been hewn away. On the flat surface of the bottom were triangular piles of gravel, together with tractors, machinery, and pipes running all around it. Yet there was no activity. The place was completely still, an echoing, empty canyon.

Jess heard a cry and looked up. Above their heads, a falcon wheeled in the sky. It flew off towards the far side of the crater. She was fascinated, wondering if the falcon was returning to its nest. The ledges on the sides of the quarry were said to be home to falcons, goshawks, tawny owls. She'd read about it in the *Western Mail*. These bird-friendly ledges had been an unexpected benefit of new technology, arising out of the way rock was now blasted out of the quarry.

'Come on.' Dresler was impatient. 'We don't want to be seen. Let's get this over with.'

They walked over to the warehouse. They tried the front door, but it was locked. They went round to a side window and peered in.

Inside, the building was empty. It was one great room, like a vast garage. The lights were off, so it was hard to see, but they could just make out the crates stashed against the far wall. Further down in the room were some tins of paint. The floor and walls at that end were smeared with paint, mostly black, but with other, lighter colours glinting in the darkness – red and white, a glittering yellow, and a kind of silvery black. Jess squinted, trying to see more. She could see the outlines of a great heap of something. Cubes of rock. Coal, perhaps?

Something moved in the darkness. A flash of fur. Of teeth. A face sprang to the window, the face of a dog, angry and barking, the roof of its mouth ridged and red, its tongue salivating.

Jess and Dresler shrank back. The dog went on barking, working itself up into a paroxysm.

'I hope that bloody thing's locked in there.' Dresler's voice shook with fear as he spoke.

They were just about to turn tail and run when a man appeared from the back of the building.

'Oi. What you doin' down by yer?' He was squat, thickset, middle-aged. A long, wispy beard curled down from his chin, and there was a large black plug in one of his earlobes. An ancient woolly hat was jammed on his head.

'Nothing. Sorry . . . Sorry to trouble you.' Dresler was flustered.

'Just seeing if we could find someone who could tell us about those falcons,' Jess said. Her tone was friendly but respectful. 'We noticed them nesting over there.'

The man looked relieved. 'Oh. The birds, is it? Well now, I'm not a bird man myself.' He approached them. He smelled of damp, of earth, of musty, unwashed clothing. 'But we've got a nesting pair over there. Peregrine falcons, they are.'

The dog saw the man speaking to them, stopped barking, and left the window.

Jess got into conversation with the guard. They talked about the falcons for a while, and then, eyeing Dresler, he checked himself and remembered his role.

'Anyway,' the man checked himself. 'This is private property, mind, so you'd better be on your way.'

'Of course. Thanks for your help.' Dresler began to walk quickly towards the gate. Jess followed him, in the hope that he'd slow down. He was altogether too jumpy.

The man went round the side of the building, away from them, and disappeared into a side door.

'What did you make of that?' Dresler asked, when they were out of earshot.

'You mean, the warehouse?'

He nodded.

'It's obviously where Morris works, isn't it? All those pots of paint. And the piles of coal.' Jess paused. 'Though no sign of any canvasses or brushes. That was odd, wasn't it? I wonder where he actually does the paintings.'

'He must live somewhere around here.' Dresler sounded excited. 'If only we could find out where.'

'Unless that guy we just met is Morris?'

Dresler frowned. 'I doubt it somehow. But it's a possibility, I suppose.'

'Perhaps if we come back sometime, we'll see him.'

'I'm not chancing it.' Dresler's tone was final. 'I don't want to annoy him. And that dog looked vicious. Come on, let's get back to the car.'

'No rush,' said Jess. 'We're perfectly entitled to walk here, you know.' She paused. 'There are some rare orchids around here, I've heard. The red helleborine and the coral root. I just saw one, I think, at the entrance to the gate. I'd like to see if I can find another.'

Dresler laughed. Now he was out of danger, he seemed to

relax. 'We're supposed to be on the trail of a reclusive genius, not looking for wild flowers.'

'I don't see why we can't do both.'

'Fine. But let's not be hours, eh?'

'It'll take ten minutes.'

They crossed the gravel road, and headed up the hill on the other side. All around them, there were fields dotted with mole-hills, as if the moles had redoubled their tunnelling efforts to compete with their human counterparts. They stopped at another view of the quarry. From this angle, they could see great blue and yellow lakes surrounding it, the flooded remains of the iron and ochre mines that wound under the earth.

'Wow. It looks like the Mines of Moria from up here,' Jess murmured, gazing on the spectacle below. The abandoned quarries were sinister and silent, the vivid blues and yellows almost surreal, a testament to humanity's ability to wreak havoc upon nature. Yet, apparently, nature had struck back: this place, like so much of the pillaged valleys of South Wales, was teeming with wildlife. Part of the reason being that few people ever saw fit to visit the area: its raddled post-industrial beauty simply didn't appeal to most people's idea of a rural idyll.

'Yes, and I think we just met one of the Longbeards,' Dresler said.

She laughed, and he leaned forward and kissed her. Their good humour with each other seemed to have returned.

She looked for the orchids, but found none. Instead she found other treasures – wood barley, sanicles, rare ferns. The wood anemones were closing their petals for the night. For a mad moment, elated by the majestic beauty of the landscape, she imagined what it must be like to be one of them, dimly aware of the heat and the cold, the light and the dark, for a few glorious days of life in the dappled shade of the beech trees before withering away. Then she put such fanciful thoughts out of her mind, took Dresler's hand, and led him down the hillside, through the woods and back to the safety of the car.

22

Dresler left for London that evening. He'd wanted Jess to come with him, but she'd decided to spend the rest of the weekend at home. She'd been away too often of late, and she needed some 'downtime', as her colleagues called it, lounging around on the sofa, cooking the odd meal, and pottering about in the garden. Rose had a number of activities planned, and Nella would probably be spending most of her time with Gareth, but she hoped that at some point, they'd have the chance to regroup. She'd always found that the only way to catch up with what was going on in her children's lives was to be around the house for a while, in the background, picking up discarded socks and tidying away bowls of cornflakes, until at some point, one of them started up a conversation with her.

She dropped Dresler off at the station and drove home, tired and a little dispirited. She wasn't sure why she'd gone off on this wild goose chase with him. She'd been curious about Morris, of course, and the mystery of his true identity still intrigued her, but she was aware that the issue really didn't concern her. After all, with the girls and her clients to attend to, she had more than enough on her plate already. Not only that, but Dresler had irritated her somewhat on the trip. She couldn't help feeling that for all his evident love of Morris's work, what he really wanted was . . . not money exactly . . . but power, power over Morris's career, power in the art world. She would have done better, she thought, to stay at home, catch up on the housework, the laundry, and a million other tasks that needed doing.

When she got in, she had a surprise waiting for her. Nella and Rose had cooked supper – just a simple pasta with a ready-made sauce and a salad, but it was a sweet, thoughtful gesture. Mari was there too, having just dropped in to visit on the off chance that Jess was at home, and having stayed to chat with the girls. Jess suspected it was she who'd suggested that they cook for her, but even so, it was good to be looked after for once. In the past, Bob would have had dinner waiting for her when she got home late after a day out; she wondered, some-times, if that was what she missed most about having him around.

As she, Mari and the girls sat down together to eat, Jess sensed that a calm had descended on the house, one that had been largely absent since Bob's departure. Nella and Rose served the meal in a rhythm of domestic order that she'd established since they were little, copying the touches that made it hers: heated dinner plates, ice in the jug of water, paper napkins – in this case, kitchen roll – and, in the centre of the table, some small flowers or a simple bit of greenery picked from the garden – today, a few primroses in a tiny cut-glass vase her mother had given her years ago. The girls were growing up, she real-ized, learning her way of running a household.

Rose was affectionate and chatty, almost back to her old self. She seemed to have relaxed a little since the debacle with Tegan, secure in her father's affections once more. Bob had made a special effort with her that day, taking her out to play tennis and afterwards to lunch. Nella, on the other hand, seemed slightly preoccupied; she was tugging at the hem of her T-shirt again, trying to cover her navel. She'd never been self-conscious about it before – indeed, there'd always been a rather large expanse of it, proudly displayed in low-cut jeans and skimpy tops. She'd have to have a talk with her, Jess thought. Surely if she was pregnant, she'd have come to her. Or perhaps there was some trouble with Gareth; this was the first time she'd seen her on her own, without him, for ages. Then again, maybe Nella was simply being Nella: head in the clouds, either plotting world domination or worrying away at some minor problem that had reached epic proportions in her mind.

The food was good, and their conversation full of warmth and humour. Mari had known the girls since they were babies, and they'd come to treat her as one of the family. They behaved naturally in her presence, so much so that when it was time for their favourite programme, *Come Dine with Me*, they asked if they could finish their meal in front of the television. Mari didn't mind, so they picked up their plates and went off.

'So what were you up to today?' Mari asked, as soon as they were out of earshot. 'Were you with Dresler?'

Jess nodded. 'It was rather exciting, actually. We went off looking for this reclusive artist, Hefin Morris. You know, the one who did those black paintings we saw at the party.'

'Oh God, those. So Dresler's a fan, is he?'

Mari hadn't listened to a word of Dresler's speech at the private view, Jess realized.

'Absolutely. Thinks he's a genius.' She paused. She was going to add that she, too, thought the paintings were impressive, but she decided not to. She didn't want to get into one of those tedious 'call that art, you must be joking, I could do that standing on my head with my eyes closed' kind of conversations. Not that she dismissed such views – indeed, she herself had often had the sense, standing in front of some baffling installation, that much contemporary art was really a case of the emperor's new clothes – it was just that the arguments against it tended to be so repetitive.

'He must be off his rocker.' Mari took another helping of tagliatelle, sprinkling a handful of pine nuts over it. 'Why was he looking for this guy?'

'Well, Blake Thomas was more or less acting as Morris's agent. He sold that picture to the museum, and was hoping to sell a lot more, as a consultant to all these international hedge fund managers and so on. And then . . . well, you know.'

Mari nodded. Jess had told her about Blake's suicide at the tower, but had warned her not to mention it to the girls. There was no reason to frighten them with the details of a horrific event that didn't concern them. They were in the sitting room now, out of earshot, but there was no telling when one of them might wander in and overhear their conversation.

'Anyway,' Jess went on, 'Morris needs a new agent. Dresler seems to fit the bill. So that's why he wants to meet him. To offer his services.'

'Did you find him?'

'We found a warehouse where he keeps his stuff. Nearly got attacked by a dog. It was quite exciting, actually.'

Mari laughed. 'He sounds rather intrepid.'

'Not really. It was more the other way round.' Jess put down her fork. 'To be honest, I found him a bit irritating. He kept bossing me around, and then getting flustered when anything went wrong.'

Mari laughed again. 'Doesn't take long, does it?'

'I suppose he was out of his comfort zone. I can't blame him for that.' Jess hesitated, about to voice a thought that had troubled her all day. 'It's just that he seems slightly wrapped up in himself, that's all. In his career, his rarefied little world. I sometimes feel he doesn't really listen to what I say.'

'How unusual.' Mari reached for the grater and the parmesan, helping herself to a generous portion. 'But there must be compensations?'

Jess nodded, but didn't reply.

Mari stopped eating, and gave her a quizzical look. 'You know, considering you're a psychotherapist, you're very prudish about some things.'

'What things?'

'Sex.'

Jess laughed. 'Well, talking about it, anyway.'

'I see. So there *are* compensations.'

'I suppose so.' Jess was serious for a moment. 'I mean, of course it's wonderful to have sex again, especially after so long without it. And I do really like him. Sometimes I think I've fallen in love with him.' She sighed. 'But even so, I miss that feeling of being . . .' She searched for a word. '. . . I don't know, bonded with him. Like I was with Bob.'

'Well, Bob's the father of your children. You are bonded to him, literally, whether you like it or not.' Mari twiddled her tagliatelle around her fork, and popped it in her mouth.

'You're rather good at that,' Jess said.

'Mmm.' Mari spoke with her mouth full. 'Learned it from an Italian boyfriend of mine. His family ran a cafe in the valleys.'

She did another expert twiddle. Jess watched her, following suit.

'The thing is, at this stage of the game, you don't really know what you're looking for.' Mari swallowed her mouthful and went on. 'You want a suitable man. But suitable for what? You don't need a father for your children. You don't need someone to live with. You just need a bit of companionship from time to time.'

'I think I want more than that.' The tagliatelle didn't seem to be behaving itself so well for Jess. There were bits of it dangling down from her fork, instead of being wrapped around it. 'I want someone I feel close to all the time. Spiritually. Emotionally.'

'Well, good luck with that, as they say.' Mari finished eating, and dabbed her lips with her napkin. 'By the way, have you got any wine in the fridge?'

'Help yourself. I'm not drinking. I've got some reading to catch up on after this.'

'OK, you carry on.' Mari got up, went over to the fridge and opened it. 'I think I'll go and watch telly with the kids. And don't worry about clearing up, we'll see to it.'

'Thanks, Mari.' Jess paused. 'And thanks for coming over. The girls really like you being here. And so do I. We need another adult in the house sometimes, the three of us. It feels more like a family, somehow.'

'It is a family, of sorts, *cariad*.' Mari found a bottle and unscrewed it. Then she went over to the wall cupboard to find a glass.

Just then, Jess's mobile went off. It was on the sideboard, and she went over to pick it up.

'Hello?'

Mari left the kitchen, carrying her glass of wine.

'It's Elinor.'

'Oh, hello.' Jess wasn't overjoyed that Elinor was phoning her at the weekend. Especially since she'd recently signed off as a client.

'I'd like to see you. Soon, if possible.'

It was her own fault, Jess told herself, for giving Elinor her mobile number. Even so, she thought, she might have waited until Monday.

'Things aren't going well with Isobel,' Elinor continued. 'I . . . I need to talk to you.'

Jess sighed. She'd taken on a new client to fill Elinor's session.

The only way she'd be able to see her would be to offer her an after-hours appointment.

'OK,' she said. As ever, she found herself unable to refuse Elinor's request. 'I could see you one evening this coming week. When would you like to come in?'

23

Elinor arrived for her emergency session the following Tuesday. It was early evening, when Jess had finished seeing her patients, and the staff in the building had left. The place was quiet, and when she heard Elinor press the bell, Jess went down to the front door to let her in.

'Hello.' Elinor stood on the doorstep. She looked different. She was wearing a leather jacket, and she'd had her hair cut in a fashionable asymmetric style.

'Hi. Come up.'

As they went up, she noticed that Elinor moved differently, more like a woman, swaying her hips slightly, and running her hand up the banisters as she took the stairs.

When they reached the landing, Jess ushered her into the consulting room and closed the door.

'It's nice here in the evening.' Elinor looked around the room. It was lit only by a Japanese floor lamp and the picture light that hung over the white relief on the wall. 'Nice and calm.'

'Thank you.' Jess paused. 'Take a seat.'

She didn't offer her the couch, as this was a one-off session.

Elinor went over to the armchair and sat down. Jess took the chair opposite.

There was a silence. Elinor fiddled with her hair.

'So, what brings you here?'

'I don't know, really.' Elinor sighed. 'Things aren't going as well as I expected.'

'Oh? Is it the claustrophobia?'

'No. That's much better. In fact, it's more or less gone.' She paused. 'It's Isobel. I thought everything would be all right, now I've got her back. But it isn't.'

Now I've got her back, Jess thought. That's an odd way of putting it.

'I can't understand why,' Elinor went on. 'I mean, everything's back to normal, but somehow we're not as close.'

'Elinor, the situation is hardly normal.' Jess's tone was gentle. 'You've recently had two bereavements. One was your mother, the other Isobel's husband. It's not surprising that she's grieving for them. And that your relationship should have changed.'

Elinor looked puzzled. She really could be obtuse, Jess thought, then wondered why she felt so impatient. She realized that she was tired after her day's work, and wished she hadn't acceded to Elinor's sudden request for a session.

'You're right,' Elinor said. 'Isobel's missing Blake. She misses him a lot. I wake up at night and hear her crying.'

'You hear her?'

'Yes.'

'Does she sleep next door to you?'

'Yes. She leaves the door of her room open, and so do I.' She sighed. 'I'm so happy to have her back, and she's so miserable. I didn't realize Blake meant so much to her.'

Elinor's tone was sad, but there was resentment there, too.

'Elinor, the situation has changed.' Since this was a one-off session, as far as Jess knew, she felt she could speak her mind. 'You've both moved on. Isobel was married to a man she loved for many years. You can't pretend it never happened.'

Elinor didn't respond. Then she covered her face with her hands, and burst into tears.

Jess felt an urge to go over and hug her, but she resisted it. Instead, she pushed over the box of tissues that was sitting on the table between them.

'I miss you, Jess.' Elinor's sobs were coming from her chest. She was crying as if she'd never stop. 'I miss you so much. Not really the therapy. Just being with you, here, in this room. It's the only place I feel safe.'

Jess was taken aback. She wondered what was going on in Elinor's mind. Elinor had often been so distant, so distracted, in their sessions. In many ways, she'd never really engaged with the therapy. But now she'd left, it was clear that Jess had meant a great deal to her; indeed, she seemed to have become essential to her wellbeing. Twin behaviour, Jess reflected. With twins, there was never any in between. Either Jess meant nothing to Elinor, or she filled in as her twin, and meant everything.

'You could come back into therapy if you wish. You've had a long break.' Jess cast her mind back. 'Four weeks, isn't it?'

'I'd like that.' Elinor took a tissue and blew her nose. Her sobs were becoming quieter now, though they still came up from her chest, making her shudder. 'Just so I can see you. But I don't think you can help me.'

She began to sob again. Jess looked at her small frame wracked with grief, and felt tears prick her eyes. She wished she could go over and comfort her. But she remained where she was.

'Well, there is clearly still quite a lot of work for us to do here.' Jess spoke in a low tone. 'You've never really talked about your relationship with your mother—'

'I don't want to talk about my mother,' Elinor interrupted. 'I don't feel anything about her. I never did. She was irrelevant to me. The only person that ever mattered to me was Isobel. And my father, I suppose. But then he went and died.'

There was anger in her voice.

'Ursula was hopeless as a parent,' she continued. 'She liked us to call her by her Christian name, said it made her feel boring to be called Ma. To be honest, I didn't think of her as my mother at all. She was completely self-obsessed. There was always some drama going on, some secret affair or mysterious illness, something that meant she was always out, or lying on the sofa in a darkened room. My father coped with her as best he could – we all did. It was really a case of us mothering her, rather than the other way round.' Elinor paused. 'I suppose I ought not to say this, but I couldn't care less that she's dead. She was a bloody nuisance, and I'm glad to be rid of her.'

Glad to be rid of her. It was chilling the way Elinor spoke about Ursula. She was resentful towards her, of course, but even so, it seemed very harsh to discuss her in such terms, especially after she'd met such a horrible end. Not for the first time, Jess realized that beneath Elinor's air of timid vulnerability there was a cold, unforgiving side to her nature. Or perhaps it was simply that Elinor found it easier, at this stage, to be angry with her mother than to mourn her loss. At any rate, Elinor seemed more positive in general, and her claustrophobia appeared to have gone.

'I'm more upset about Blake, to tell the truth. He was always so supportive of my work. Believed in me as an artist.' She sniffed. 'And he was a good husband to Isobel. Helped her run the gallery, expand it. They were happy together, I think. She loved him.' A forlorn tone crept into her voice. 'I often felt rather excluded.'

'Excluded?'

She nodded. 'I was terribly lonely when Isobel went off with Blake, leaving me alone. Then my father got ill, and my parents went off to Italy. When he died, it was completely traumatic for all of us. He was the one who'd held the family together.

My mother became more neurotic than ever. She couldn't decide whether to sell up in Italy and come home, or to stay there. She was forever flitting back and forth, turning up unexpectedly, interfering in our lives, offloading all her misery onto us, then disappearing again. I remember thinking at the time, I wish it had been her rather than Pa who'd died. It would all have been so much easier.'

Jess couldn't help feeling sorry for Ursula. However difficult she'd been, by the sound of it, Elinor seemed to have been unable to offer her mother any comfort in her time of bereavement.

'Blake was pretty good with her, I must say,' Elinor went on. 'He and Isobel used to have her to stay for weeks on end. I couldn't cope with her.' She furrowed her brow. 'I think that's when things really changed between me and Isobel, come to think of it. She grew closer to Blake when our father died. I think she came to depend on him a lot.' Elinor hesitated. 'More, even, than me.'

'Well, that's natural, isn't it? To lean on your husband, first and foremost, at such a time?'

'Yes.' Elinor seemed puzzled. 'I suppose so.'

There was a silence. Once again, Jess was struck by the strange dynamic of the twin relationship. Frederick's death had strengthened the bond between Isobel and Blake, yet Elinor appeared to be having trouble understanding how that could be. For Elinor, the relationship between her and her twin sister seemed always to take precedence over any other.

'I must admit, I felt jealous of Blake.' Elinor was getting into her stride now, talking more freely than she'd ever done in her regular sessions. 'I felt he'd taken my sister away from me. Isobel didn't come over to the house much any more. And when she did, we didn't really talk.'

'So you missed her?'

Elinor nodded. 'Very much. I didn't have a man in my life, never have had, really. There's been the odd one here and there, over the years, but none of them ever lasted. I didn't mind.' She shrugged. 'I always felt I could manage without all that. As long as I had my painting. And . . .' Her voice trailed off.

'And?' Jess prompted.

'And Isobel.' She paused. 'I'd always taken it for granted that we'd be together. I can remember when I was a child thinking, I don't care what happens to my parents, as long as I've got Isobel. So of course, when she came back to the family house, after Blake died, I felt so happy.' She paused, as if checking herself. 'No, not happy exactly. Relieved. Because things were back to normal. It was just like old times. Me and Isobel, together again.'

There was a brief silence.

'Of course, Isobel was devastated about Blake. She couldn't understand why he'd committed suicide. And when it all came out, that the business was in trouble, that he'd killed Ursula and stolen the painting, she said she didn't care, that she still loved him.' She paused. 'I thought, over time, she'd start to feel better. But she hasn't.' A look of anguish came over Elinor's face. 'It's not the same now. She wants him, not me. It's almost as if . . .' She broke off.

Jess didn't prompt her.

Elinor began to sob again. 'As if she blames me for everything.'

Jess thought for a moment. Psychically speaking, Elinor had wanted Blake out of the picture. After all, he had supplanted her in her sister's affections. And psychically speaking, Isobel must have sensed Elinor's hostility, so that a part of her blamed Elinor for Blake's death. In terms of the twin dynamic, Isobel's reaction had an emotional logic, however irrational it might be in reality.

Elinor changed the subject. They began to discuss the many practical issues that needed to be resolved in the wake of Blake's death, including whether to sell the chapel or the family house at Llandaff Green. Elinor seemed to take it for granted that she and Isobel would be living together in future, despite the tensions between them. Finally, as the session came to a close, Jess asked her if she wanted to continue with the therapy.

'I don't know. I can't be sure about that.'

'Well, I think you need to make up your mind.' Jess was firm. 'I can't keep arranging one-off sessions for you like this.'

'I know.'

There was a silence.

'You've talked more freely in this session than usual, haven't you?'

Elinor nodded.

'I wonder whether that's because it's a one-off, and you feel you don't have to commit?'

'Perhaps.' Elinor hesitated. 'It's weird, but in the past I felt guilty if I told you too much. As if I was being disloyal to Isobel. But now that things are changing between me and her, I think that might change, too.' She looked pensive. 'Can I think about it and let you know?'

'Of course. But I'll need an answer soon.'

Jess glanced at the clock.

'Now, Elinor, I'm afraid our time is up.'

24

After Elinor left, Jess stayed on in the consulting room. During the session, she'd begun to feel that there was something going on between Elinor and Isobel that she didn't fully understand; some kind of secret pact that they were engaged in together, which Elinor only hinted at from time to time. She wondered what it was, and how, if Elinor did come back into therapy, she could help her to unburden herself of it, since it seemed to be troubling her so deeply.

She walked over to the couch under the window, and lay down. She'd made it a rule not to, but she was breaking it now, because she was using it for its proper purpose: to allow her mind to wander, to free associate, until it showed her what she wanted to know. This was a feature of the psyche that was so often forgotten in the hectic pace of life, and which, she told herself, she ought always to remember – the way that, given time and space, fleeting thoughts could, as if by their own accord, assemble themselves into a pattern without being directed to do so. And a pattern was what she needed at the moment, as the first step in coming to some understanding of what was happening in Elinor's life, and why she was so disturbed.

The tree outside the window was coming into leaf, the bark

black against the bright green of the foliage. If she listened intently, she could hear the crackle of its leaves unfurling, or so she fancied. Probably, it was just the sigh of the branches as they moved in the wind. She focussed her eyes on a twig that tapped the window: two leaves curled on either side, soft as gristly babies; the twig between them brown and stiff and knobbly, a grandmother's arm. She thought of Elinor and Isobel, and their grandmother Ariadne, Augustus John's lover. Their mother, Ursula, didn't come into the picture. Jess thought she knew why that was. As a neglectful mother, Ursula had, to all intents and purposes, been absent to her daughters. In death, she seemed to loom larger over them than she had done in life. And because they were twins, perhaps more dependent on each other than they had been on their mother, they had been protected, to some degree, from grief over her passing.

A painting by Gwen John jumped into her mind. It was of a Japanese doll, sitting by a small, open wooden box. The colours were muted. The slanting attic window, with its weak shaft of light, spoke of dim, dark days shut away from the bustle of the street below. Then another image came before her eyes: Dorelia, Augustus's wife. Her hair was like the doll's: square cut, black as coal. But the paint was bright, the face forceful, strong. Too strong, perhaps. Too definite.

Augustus and Gwen. Somewhere she'd read that the two of them had shared rooms together when they were struggling artists, surviving, like a couple of monkeys, on a diet of fruit and nuts. They'd been affectionate towards each other, protective, united in their hatred of their cold, unbending father, their mother having died when they were young. They'd loved one another. Despite the fact that Augustus was the more successful of the pair, there had been little competition between them; he had admired Gwen's talent, and predicted that in time, she would be seen as the greater artist.

Monkeys. Twins. Castor and Pollux. When Castor, a mortal, died, Pollux pleaded with his father to let him into heaven. Inseparable, they reigned there as Gemini, the twin stars.

Isobel and Elinor, living together. No more painting, just running the art gallery, Isobel the practical one, Elinor the dreamer. Jess thought of the doll, blank-faced. The wooden box. What did Elinor have in her box? Perhaps an artist's box, full of paints, pencils, brushes. More paintings to come? But the doll couldn't paint. She was inanimate. Lifeless. Gwen, stuck, a woman alone, with no lover, walled up in her attic. It would take a man, a man like Augustus, with muscle and vigour, to breathe life into the doll, paint her big and strong and full of life, six foot tall, as he had Dorelia, his muse . . .

Jess sat up suddenly on the couch. A man, she thought. Morris. If Elinor painted like a modern-day Gwen, with her brooding, feminine domestic world, then could it be that Isobel painted like Augustus – bold, angry, masculine? And could it be that, rather than own up to the fact, Isobel had invented a male persona for herself, as the ex-miner and recluse Hefin Morris?

Outside, the branches of the tree continued to sigh, but Jess didn't hear them now. She sat up in excitement. It was obvious now she thought of it. Elinor had mentioned that Isobel had painted big abstracts when they were at art school, that she'd been seen as a talent to watch until she'd dropped out. That story about Nathan marching into the gallery with a mystery painting, plonking it down in front of Blake and Isobel, then coming back with another one once it sold. It was so unlikely. No, it must have been Isobel who was painting the Morris canvasses in secret, in that warehouse up on Bryn Cau. Most probably, it had been Blake's idea, to pretend that 'Morris' was an ex-miner and a recluse, so as to get the right kind of publicity, cause a stir in the art world. It was a clever scam, and one that

Elinor and Isobel seemed to be continuing with, now that Blake was dead.

Jess got up off the couch, and went over to her desk. She felt a sense of satisfaction, as she often did when she understood a profound truth about one of her clients for the first time. Only now, it was mixed with foreboding.

She picked up the phone and called Dresler, eager to share her discovery with him.

When he answered, he sounded distracted.

'I'm just finishing off this piece. Can I call you back?'

'It won't take a minute.' Jess could barely contain her excitement. 'I've got something to tell you about Morris.'

'Oh yes?'

'There is no such person.' Jess paused for dramatic effect. 'I've worked it out, I think. Isobel Powell is painting as Hefin Morris. She and Blake cooked up this story together, that they'd discovered this genius painter in the valleys, a recluse, an ex-miner who loathed the art world. That way they could—'

'Hang on a minute,' Dresler interrupted. 'I think you're getting ahead of yourself here.'

'No, listen.' In her excitement, Jess didn't catch the irritation in his tone. 'It explains everything. The way nobody ever sees Morris, nobody knows where he lives, or anything about him. The way he always communicates by letter. The way the only person who'd ever met him, apparently, was Blake.' Jess paused for a moment. 'That story about Nathan coming into the gallery, dropping off the paintings each time they sold one. It just doesn't ring true. Isobel's been churning out the paintings, up in that place in the valleys. That's why the guard is there, so no one can find out what's going on.'

'You're way off course here, Jess.' To her surprise, Dresler was beginning to sound angry. 'This is just pure speculation—'

'I don't think so. It makes perfect sense. How would Isobel

sell her paintings as Isobel Powell? She hasn't got the credibility. You told me yourself, the quality of the work is never enough; the art world needs a story, a myth behind the artist, too.' Jess was thinking out loud now. 'What if Blake and Isobel just decided to make one up, about a reclusive ex-miner from the valleys, painting the devastation wreaked by the collapse of the mining industry there? Pretend he was a recluse, a politico, opposed to the whole circus? That way, they could create a stir in the art world, make a splash—'

'That's just not possible.' There was anger in Dresler's voice. 'A person like Isobel Powell could never paint the way Morris does. You can see it in his style. The whole of his life is there on the canvas. He's an outsider; it's in the whole composition of the paintings, in every stroke of his brush. You can see it all in the paintings: growing up in the valleys, the brutality of going down the mines, the crumbling of the infrastructure, the moral and spiritual vacuum created in the wake of that implosion . . .'

It was Jess's turn to be angry. Dresler sounded as if he was giving one of his lectures.

'I'm a critic,' he went on. 'I know what I'm talking about. Morris is unique. Untrained, but a massive talent.' He paused. 'And besides, it's such a masculine style.'

'So you don't believe a woman could paint like that?'

'I'd be very surprised.'

There was a short silence.

'Look, I'm going to have to get back to this piece.' Dresler was doing his best to be polite, but Jess could hear the tension in his voice. 'I'll call you later.'

She was stung. She'd hoped to talk further with him, convince him that her theory was worth pursuing, but he wasn't interested.

'Fine.' She tried not to sound hurt. 'OK, then.'

She put down the phone. She was disappointed by Dresler's reaction. She'd expected him to be intrigued, at least to listen to what she had to say. Then, as her excitement ebbed away, she began to think more clearly about what her theory had meant to him. Dresler had championed Hefin Morris's work from the beginning. He was convinced that Morris was the greatest painter to come out of Britain in years. He loved the idea that Morris hadn't emerged from an art school but was a kind of noble savage, untainted by the corruption of the art world. He'd staked his reputation on him, and now here she was, questioning the whole myth. Obviously, if her theory was correct and Isobel was shown to be behind the Morris paintings, Dresler's entire career would be ruined. He'd be a laughing stock. He'd be revealed as being conned by the same nonsense that he complained of in the art world – building a myth round an artist, rather than simply judging the work for itself.

Jess gave a sigh of frustration. How could she have been so insensitive? she wondered. Clearly Dresler would be thoroughly rattled by the idea that Isobel Powell was painting the Morris works. Why had she told him her theory? Why hadn't she thought about how he'd feel, what it would mean to him?

She stared at the screensaver on her computer, Rose's child-hood drawing of their family home. It seemed anachronistic now, she thought, rather sadly, in passing; she must change it some time. She typed in a search for Hefin Morris, then pressed 'images'. A set of paintings by Morris came up on the screen, and she scrolled through them absent-mindedly. Strangely, on the screen, the complexity of them didn't come over at all. They were lifeless, dull expanses of black.

She began to wonder if she'd imagined what she'd seen in them – scenes of destruction, of a vortex, a black hole, drawing her in.

Perhaps she'd been wrong about Isobel, too, she thought. No

doubt Dresler was right, and Hefin Morris really was who he claimed to be, an ex-miner from the valleys.

She glanced up at the darkening sky outside the window. She'd stayed in the consulting rooms too late, worrying away at a problem until she'd lost all perspective. It was time to go home.

25

The following day, Jess went over to the deli at lunchtime, bought herself a sandwich and a cup of coffee, and came back to the consulting rooms. She'd been wrong about Isobel being behind the Hefin Morris paintings, she realized. Free association – letting thoughts come into the mind with no conscious direction or censorship – was a technique in psychoanalysis that sometimes yielded profound insights; but in this case, it seemed to have led only to wild conjecture. Even so, she instinctively felt that Elinor and Isobel were keeping some kind of secret, colluding together in a way that was oppressing and frustrating both of them. If Elinor were to come back into therapy, Jess would need to reflect more deeply on what it might be. Besides, as a therapist, she was naturally curious. The twin relationship fascinated her, and she was certain that exploring it further would help to explain Elinor's anguished psychological condition.

When she'd finished eating, she went over to the shelf in the corner of the consulting room, where she kept her reference books. There was a small section on twins – it was an under-researched area in psychoanalysis, with most studies focussing on twins separated at birth, rather than on the actual

241

relationship of twins brought up together within a family.

She took down a book, *The Twin in the Transference* by the Kleinian psychotherapist Vivienne Lewin, and began to leaf through it:

> *Our fascination with twins is linked with the universal urge towards twinning. The phantasy of having a twin is ubiquitous and is based on developmental factors linked with essential loneliness, a longing to be known, and the creation of a sense of self . . .*
>
> *The specialness with which we regard twins stems in part from our narcissistic wish to be totally understood and merged with an object, as well as from a sense of the uncanniness of the double.*

The uncanniness of the double. It had been uncanny, Jess thought, the way she'd mistaken Isobel for Elinor at the party. And the way both twins constantly appeared to make the same mistake, psychically speaking. Both twins seemed fundamentally unaware that for most people, there are firm boundaries between selves – not shifting, unmanned borders that can be slipped across at any time, at a whim.

The book wasn't an easy read, but she felt excited and inspired by the ideas Lewin put forward. The theory she advanced was that from birth, twin babies inevitably experience a certain amount of maternal deprivation, simply from having to share their mother in a 'triadic' relationship. Depending on how overwhelmed the mother is by this situation, the babies may begin a lifelong habit of seeking comfort from each other, rather than from her; and as they grow up, their relationship may become so close that they begin to exclude their parents altogether. When this happens an 'enmeshed' twinship develops: the twins become entirely dependent on each other, but there is also an extreme rivalry, such that, when they become adults they will be tempted to use partners and children as substitute twins.

Jess looked up for a moment, considering all this in relation to Elinor. It made perfect sense where she was concerned, she realized. Elinor's dependence on Isobel had been compounded by Ursula's inability to mother the twins. But over the years, the twinship had become enmeshed, holding her back:

> . . . it is not uncommon to find twins who are locked into an enmeshed relationship with each other in a rigid structure that results in the impairment of individual development of each twin. Even where there has been a greater degree of personality development in each twin, and a sense of separate identity in each, there is always a shadow of the other . . .

A *shadow of the other.* Jess thought back to her theory that Isobel had been painting as Hefin Morris. Perhaps it wasn't so stupid after all. Such a dynamic would have made it easy for Isobel to take on the identity of Hefin Morris; as a twin, she was used to merging her personality with another's, and experiencing no sense of guilt or discomfort when doing so. For 'enmeshed' twins, it didn't seem inappropriate to adopt other people's identities at the drop of a hat; after all, it was what they'd been doing all their lives.

She read on:

> The twins feel bound to each other and extremely anxious when apart. But they also feel trapped in the twinship and unable to escape from it, as if they have been sucked in by the other twin.

That helped to explain the claustrophobia, she thought. Ursula's death, after Isobel's departure, had caused Elinor's already fragile sense of self to collapse. Meanwhile, Isobel had managed the situation better, by transferring the 'internal twin-ship' onto her marriage with Blake, in quite a healthy way. Perhaps, also, by expressing her sense of loss by continuing to paint, in secret, as Hefin Morris?

Separation from the twin may be experienced as extremely threatening, even catastrophic, as it exposes the patient to a loss of known boundaries, with the consequent fear of dropping into a void or 'nameless dread'.

There it was, the void that Hefin Morris always painted. Surely, she thought, looking up for a moment at the white relief on the wall opposite, there must be something in her theory that the real Hefin Morris was Isobel Powell.

The circle within the squares began to pulsate. Jess looked away. What she read next made her afraid for Elinor:

Where the mother has not been able to create a space in her mind for each child separately, the rivalry between the twins will . . . result in violent hatred towards each other . . .

What would happen now? she wondered. Now that Isobel had lost Blake? Would the anger between the twins finally erupt? Evidently the relationship was already showing signs of strain.

Jess sighed. She sometimes found the Kleinian view of the world a little too grim for her liking. She walked over to the corner of the room, and put the book back on the shelf, prom-ising herself that she'd return to it later.

The phone rang. The answerphone came on.

'Jess.' It was Dresler on the end of the line.

Jess walked over to the desk, and waited beside it.

'Just wanted to tell you. There's been an extraordinary new development.'

She picked up the phone. 'Sorry, I'm here. What's happened?'

'Well, it's about Morris.'

Jess felt a thrill of excitement. 'You mean, I was right? About Isobel?'

'What d'you mean, Isobel?'

Jess was irritated. And hurt. Not only had he discounted her theory that Isobel was painting as Morris, he'd completely forgotten it.

'Nothing,' she said.

'Oh that.' He caught her slightly frosty tone of voice. 'No, no. This is something quite amazing. Morris has asked me to be his agent.'

'Really? You mean, you met him?'

'Not yet, no, but I'm sure I shall. He's written to me, telling me that he's broken with the Powell Gallery. He didn't have any faith in Isobel. She's not at her best at the moment, by all accounts.' There was a pause. 'Anyway, he's come to me. I'm going to be looking after him.'

'Oh.' Jess wasn't quite sure what to say.

'We're calling a press conference—'

'We?'

'Well, I am. Under Hefin's instructions.'

Jess noticed that Morris had now become 'Hefin'. 'Is he going to be there?'

'It's possible.' Dresler paused. 'Anyway, he's decided to hold it up at Ferndale.'

Jess knew of Ferndale, but she'd never been there. It was a small town in the Rhondda, one of many blighted by post-industrial decline.

'It was where the first coal mine was sunk in the nineteenth century, apparently. Hefin wants to draw attention to what's happened to the place since.'

'Well, I hope you're going to be able to get people to go up there. It's not exactly a cultural hub, you know.'

'That's the whole point, Jess. This isn't a smug gallery opening. It's an intervention.'

'Right.' Might as well call it a happening, Jess thought, rather sourly, but she didn't voice her opinion.

'Anyway, it doesn't matter if we don't get a good turnout,' Dresler went on. 'It'll be reported in the papers just because it's something different. I think it's a brilliant idea.'

He paused, waiting for her to agree. When she didn't, he continued, 'We've called it for next Tuesday evening, seven o'clock. At the town hall. We haven't got long to plan it. We're organizing transport from London. I'll be coming down in a charabanc' – he laughed – 'with a bunch of critics, buyers and the like. Will you be able to drive up from Cardiff?'

'Let's see. Tuesday.' Jess thought for a moment. Her last session on a Tuesday was at five. 'Should be all right.' She paused. 'Can I help in any way? Bring anything?'

'No, just yourself.'

'OK.' Jess adopted a bright, breezy tone. 'I'll see you up there. Don't worry if I'm a bit late, the traffic can be bad getting out of Cardiff at that time of day.'

'Fine. Oh, by the way, can you stay overnight? I've booked a load of us into a hotel nearby.'

'I don't know. Depends on what I can arrange for Rose. Can I let you know?'

'Of course.'

There was a short silence.

'Bye then, darling.'

Jess found she couldn't respond in kind.

'Bye, Jacob. And good luck.'

26

The evening she drove up to Ferndale, Jess was running late. She'd had a stressful day, particularly in her last session with her long-standing client Maria, who was suffering from depression, and whose children had now been sent to stay with a relative. She'd let the session go over length, and had had to stop for petrol on the way. While she was filling up, she'd noticed that one of the tyres on the car was down, so she'd faffed about in the rain with the garage pressure pump, smearing grease over her dress in the process. It was a linen shift, worn with a short, unlined jacket, and as she grappled with the air hose she realized it was the wrong outfit for the weather: it had turned wet and cold, and she'd have done better to wear a winter coat. By the time she started the car and pulled out of the garage, she felt thoroughly irritable.

The traffic slowed to a crawl as she came out of Cardiff, but cleared as she hit the road up to the valleys. It wasn't a particularly scenic journey at the best of times, she reflected, as she left the city behind: residential sprawl gave way to industrial estates, then to a landscape that bore silent witness to the ravages created by two centuries of coalmining – the 'heritage' of the Rhondda, as it was now called. Rusting iron wheels and ruined red-brick chimneys rose up from abandoned pit heads; quarried mountains and grassed-over slagheaps, dotted with spindly shrubs, created an unnatural horizon; and crouching in their shadow, long, neat rows of terraced houses jutted out into the hillside and came to an abrupt, arbitrary stop, as if, when they reached the middle of nowhere, they'd given up hope.

As Jess drove along, she began to relax. A calm came over her as the city, the consulting rooms, and her thronging clients with their neuroses, grew further and further away. She wondered whether Isobel and Elinor would be at the launch; probably not, she concluded, since Morris had taken the opportunity of Blake's death to break with the Powell Gallery, and asked Dresler to be his agent.

The deeper Jess penetrated the Rhondda, the more compelling she found it. Along the old road, the towns were like a corridor, running into each other, perched alongside the wide, shallow valleys. The squat Victorian chapels and stone terraces weren't beautiful, but with the ruined mountains behind them, there was a mystery to the place. This was a world where the aftermath of an epic struggle between humanity and nature was on show for all to see. She could see why Morris had decided to call his press conference – intervention, whatever it was – up here in the Rhondda. It was one of the most depressed areas in the country, yet the ravaged landscape had a kind of sombre dignity about it, and the people who still remained here a tenacious way of adjusting to hardship that really did add up to a 'heritage', one that the average mollycoddled city visitor couldn't help but find sobering.

Towns succeeded towns, one after the other, huddled on the hillsides, until eventually she came to Ferndale. The venue was not hard to find. The centre of Ferndale consisted of only a few streets, and she soon found a space. She parked the car, and walked the short distance to the venue, a community arts centre that had once been a municipal building of some kind. When she got there, the meeting was already in progress, so she slipped in at the back.

Contrary to her expectation, there were quite a few people in attendance, including a small film crew. Most of them were Londoners from the art world, soberly dressed but sporting the odd, carefully chosen quirky item to demonstrate their membership of the tribe. To her surprise, she noticed Mia, Blake's former business partner – dressed from head to toe in black, and still wearing the bicycle chain – standing next to Dresler; given the animosity between Dresler and Blake, and her questionable part as Blake's alibi in the police investigation of Ursula's death, she would have thought Mia would have stayed away.

As she'd predicted, Elinor and Isobel were nowhere to be seen. She wondered for a moment if Elinor was all right; since their last session, when she'd been dithering about whether to come back into therapy or not, she hadn't been in touch.

Dresler was running over more or less the same speech about Morris that he'd given at the museum when Jess had first met him. He delivered it with confidence, his eyes shining with enthusiasm, and once again – although she'd heard most of what he had to say before – she was impressed. He was dressed casually, in a cord jacket with a Nehru collar, a chambray shirt and jeans, but he looked distinguished, and she couldn't help feeling proud of him. There was a future to this relationship, she thought, as he talked on; whatever minor problems they had at present would be ironed out in time. She was looking forward to introducing him to the girls; they'd like him, she thought. Nella would find his world interesting, and she could imagine that he would be sensitive and kind to Rose. She wondered what his son, Seth, was like, and whether he'd get on with her daughters; they might find him rather glamorous, as a London boy. He might even, in time, become something of a brother to them . . .

She brought her mind back to the present, realizing that she'd wandered off into a bit of a daydream. She looked around her. The staff working at the centre were standing by the tea urn they'd set up at the back of the hall. They were listening attentively, some of them with a perplexed look on their faces, others evidently trying to fight off boredom. She turned her attention back to Dresler, and found herself feeling a little uncomfortable. Ostensibly, he was singing the praises of the mining communities of the Welsh valleys; yet in reality, there was a subtle air of entitlement about him that contrasted strikingly with the deferential demeanour of the staff. For Dresler and his crew, Jess realized, as he talked on, the actual people of Ferndale were entirely invisible.

'And now I come to why we're gathered here today.' Dresler put down his notes and addressed the assembled company directly. 'I've received a communication from Hefin to say that he cannot be with us this evening.'

There were cries of dismay. Angry voices were raised, and people began to complain to each other.

Dresler held up his hands in an effort to mollify them, pausing to let the fuss die down, then continued, raising his voice slightly. 'My sincere apologies. However, what I can tell you is that he is planning a number of new large-scale works. These will be site-specific, and will be shown at different locations in the valleys. The first of them is to be unveiled in a few weeks' time, not far from where we're standing today.'

The crowd were not impressed, but Dresler hid his embarrassment and soldiered on, discussing the virtues of these 'site-specific' works, until he brought the speech to a close. There was a feeble round of applause, and some booing. At the back, the urns started to hiss in readiness for the refreshments to be served. Then people got up from their chairs and began to move around the hall.

Dresler stowed away his notes, came over, and gave Jess a kiss on the cheek.

'God, what a fiasco,' he said.

'What happened?'

'He just didn't show.' Dresler gave a sigh of frustration. 'Still, we'll have to try and make the best of it.'

He took Jess over to his party and introduced her. There was Mia, the gallery owner, a young man named Jake who worked for her, a journalist called Giles, and Akiko, the Japanese woman she'd seen at the computer in the magazine office below his London flat. Mia was friendly, but evidently completely obsessed with her work; she talked animatedly about Morris and a number of her other artists, all of them 'politically engaged', as she called it, without ever asking Jess a single question about her. Giles, Jake and Akiko were less intense, but no less immersed in their own worlds; they, too, talked shop, and took little interest in their surroundings.

The community workers served up the refreshments, along with a selection of biscuits ranging from bourbon to rich tea. One of them, Rhys, a dreadlocked outreach worker with boundless enthusiasm, came up and chatted to Jess. He was excited about the project, and had been hoping to meet Morris so that he could get local people to visit the site-specific work, and perhaps get them involved. She took him over to talk to Dresler, but he was preoccupied with the film crew, who were about to leave. They stood around waiting for a while, but then the staff began to clear up, and Rhys had to go off and supervise the washing-up.

'Right. Let's go.' Dresler gathered together his things. 'I've booked us all into a hotel just off the M4. It's on a golf course, I believe.'

Jess knew the one. It was where all the football teams stayed when they came to Cardiff. Not Dresler's cup of tea at all, she'd have thought.

'We should be able to get a decent meal there, anyway,' he said, as if reading her thoughts. 'There's nowhere else around here.'

They made arrangements to leave. Jess would drive over to the hotel, since she knew the way, and Dresler would follow with the others in his car. Mia didn't offer to accompany Jess, and neither did any of the others. Jess couldn't help feeling slightly miffed, but at the same time she was somewhat relieved. The thought of talking to Mia about her newest artist's coruscating work with Palestinian refugees as they drove down the country lanes to a four-star hotel for a slap-up dinner wearied her more than a little.

They set off, Jess leading the way, the others behind. She drove slowly, so that they wouldn't lose her. On the way, she put on Radio 3, hoping it would calm her growing impatience with Dresler and his crowd. She liked practically everything that the station played, apart from a certain type of modern orchestral music featuring flurries of woodwind, stabbing horns and rolling timpani. What came on was exactly that, so she switched off again, and drove on in silence.

By the time they got to the hotel, it was beginning to get dark, but it was ablaze with lights. Coaches were lined up outside it, and the place was full of handsome young men in tight-fitting shirts and jeans, brandishing mobile phones. Beside the entrance was a huge gym, lit up to display rows and rows of enormous weights. Jess was immediately cheered by the sight: after the squat, dark chapels and terraces of the Rhondda, this shining pink palace told another story. Here was where the young lions of the valleys, the footballers and rugby players and rock singers, celebrated their victories; where people came for a taste of luxury, of glamour; where they got married, played golf, sat about in dressing gowns, ordered themselves massages, champagne breakfasts and 'sumptuous banquets'. As she got out of the car, Jess was excited: she had no responsibilities for the evening, except to have fun. Nella was over at Gareth's place for the night; Rose was with Bob at his flat in the Bay, and happy to be there. When the wine began to flow over dinner, the Londoners would warm up, and they'd all have a good time.

She parked the car, picked up her overnight case, and walked over to the entrance, where Dresler and the others were waiting.

'God, this place is awful,' he said in a loud voice as they went in. 'I don't know what I was thinking of.'

Mia laughed, and Jess realized that his comment had been directed at her, to somehow impress her with his good taste. She wondered for a moment if anything was going on between them, but put the thought out of her mind.

They went over to the reception desk, got their room numbers, and went up. They were all on the same floor, just one storey up. Dresler had booked a table for dinner and they were slightly late, so they didn't hang around in the rooms, simply parking their suitcases, nipping to the loo, and reassembling downstairs.

The meal was a disappointment. The food was good, if not spectacular, but no one seemed to have any appetite for it. Morris's non-appearance had cast a damper over the proceedings. Nobody except Jess and Dresler seemed to be drinking. Mia ordered sparkling water and picked at a salad, Jake spent most of his time texting on his mobile phone, and Akiko remained polite but silent. Only Giles made an effort, engaging Dresler and Mia in conversation about an artist Jess had never heard of; yet he too eschewed the wine, saying that he had an early start in the morning. Don't we all? thought Jess, but she didn't comment.

As the evening wore on, she began to feel tense. She wasn't used to this kind of social occasion. Nobody laughed; nobody told funny stories; nobody got tipsy; nobody got to know each other. It was all serious discussion, or silence. By the end of the meal, with the peppermint teas ordered, Jess was half minded to go and sit at the bar, where a raucous crowd had convened; within minutes, she knew, this being Wales, she would have got into conversation with someone – preferably one of those modern-day Greek gods in their tight pink shirts and fitted jeans and pointed shoes.

'Well, I'm going up to bed.' Mia dabbed her lips with her napkin, and got up. 'Jacob, I'll meet you in the lobby at eight. OK?'

She didn't offer to pay her share of the bill, or thank him for the meal, Jess noticed.

'Me, too.' Akiko rose from her seat.

Jake looked up momentarily from his phone. 'Oh. Right. OK.' He stood up, too. 'Goodnight all. See you in the morning.'

They went off upstairs.

Jess glanced at her watch. It was only half past ten. What was the matter with these people?

The waiter brought over the bill. Dresler gave it a cursory glance, then produced his credit card. Evidently, he was picking up the tab for the whole shebang.

Jess got out her credit card too, but Dresler waved it away, as he and Giles continued their conversation.

'Shall we go over to the bar for a nightcap?' Jess ventured.

'I don't think so. I'm whacked, to tell the truth. Let's go on up.' Dresler smiled at her and took her hand. It was the first time he'd acknowledged their relationship that evening, she realized.

Giles excused himself and left. They waited a few moments, finishing their teas, and then followed suit.

In the lift, they stood side by side, waiting for it to reach their floor. When they got out, Dresler opened the door of their room, and turned on the lights. Jess went into the bathroom, shut the door, and went to the loo. Then she cleaned her teeth, took off her make-up, squirted some scent on her neck, and went back out to the bedroom. Dresler then took her place in the bathroom, while she undressed.

Just as she was about to get into bed, his phone went off. She looked around for it, and saw that it was on the bedside table on the far side of the bed. She leaned over and picked it up, but it stopped ringing. When she peered at the screen, she was surprised to see that the caller was named as Isobel.

She put the phone back down on the table. She was perplexed. Dresler had told her that Morris had 'broken with' Isobel and the gallery after Blake's death, and that he himself had taken over as Morris's agent. Those were the exact words he'd used, she was sure of that – paying attention to such details was part of her training as a therapist. So if that were the case, why would Isobel be phoning Dresler at this hour of the night? Surely they wouldn't be on friendly terms after he'd poached her most successful artist? Something odd was going on, and whatever it was, Dresler hadn't filled her in on it.

He came in wearing only his boxer shorts, and got in beside her. He glanced at the phone, registered the call, and put it back on the side table, without a flicker of surprise. Then he leaned over and switched off the light.

For a few moments, they lay staring up into the dark. There was a faint noise coming from the bar – the sound of people laughing.

'What's the matter?' There was no note of concern in his voice, only irritation.

'Nothing.' Jess was determined not to respond in kind.

'It's not really a problem. This will all be OK.' For a moment, Jess thought he was talking about their relationship, but then realized that he was still preoccupied with the event. 'The film can be edited. Giles is going to write it up for the magazine. The important thing is, we've announced the exhibition. Mia's also very enthusiastic . . .'

He began to burble on about Mia. That's odd, too, thought Jess. Mia was an associate of Blake's. If Morris had parted company with the Powell Gallery, what was she doing here? Most probably she'd switched sides, loath to give up her stake in Morris's career.

It was when Dresler came to eulogizing Mia's commitment to radical politics in contemporary art that Jess's impatience finally got the better of her.

'Oh, stuff Mia,' she said. 'And her fizzy water. And her bloody salad.'

The minute Jess said the words, she regretted them. Mia had been getting on her nerves all evening, but it was only now that she realized how deeply she'd been irritated by her.

There was a pause.

'You're jealous, aren't you?' There was a note of amusement in Dresler's voice.

Jess thought for a moment. 'No. I really don't think so.'

'Don't worry, there's nothing going on between us.' Dresler's tone was placatory. 'It's strictly business.'

'I'm sorry.' Jess paused. The conversation seemed to be going awry. 'I didn't mean to be rude about her. I think perhaps I've drunk a bit too much.'

Dresler didn't reply.

'But I don't know,' she went on, doing her best to make amends. 'Here we are in this swanky hotel, with a bunch of your friends. I just thought we'd have more fun this evening. More of a laugh.'

'We're all busy people, Jess. And it's not exactly the right kind of place, is it?'

Jess was annoyed by the snobbery of his remark.

'You know, there's something I don't understand about you left-wing intellectuals.' She could feel the wine going to her head. 'You're all so worried about the fate of the working classes, the unemployed, and so on, but when it comes to actually meeting one of them, you're not the slightest bit interested.'

There was a silence.

'I mean, take that guy Rhys at the centre.' Jess decided it was time to speak her mind. If they had a row, she reasoned, it might help clear the air. 'He was dying to meet you. He runs an art workshop for young people in the area. He really wanted to get involved. An artist like Morris could be so inspirational up here. But you totally blanked him.'

'That's not fair.' Dresler's tone was measured. 'I was extremely busy. I had to get the film crew off, sort out all manner of details. I simply didn't have time.'

'Well, OK. If you say so.'

They relapsed into silence. It was a warm night, and the window of the room was open. There was a gale of laughter from the bar below, which only served to emphasize the tension in the room.

'Right. Now, if you don't mind, I think we should get some sleep.'

'Well, before we do, there's something else I want to ask you.'

Dresler gave a deep sigh.

'I don't think you're telling me the whole truth about what's going on with Morris. You said he'd decided to leave Isobel and the Powell Gallery and come to you, didn't you?'

'Yes.'

'Well, how come she just phoned you, then?'

'You mean to say you've been monitoring my calls?' Dresler was outraged.

'No, of course I haven't. Your phone rang when you were in the bathroom so I just checked it, that's all.'

'Well, please don't do that again.' Dresler's tone was cold. 'As it happens, there are some negotiations between us—'

'That take place in the middle of the night?'

Dresler sat up in bed. 'Look, Jessica, this is my business. What the fuck's it got to do with you?'

Jess sat up too, keeping a firm distance between them. 'Quite a lot, actually. Elinor is – was – my client, and I've also had dealings with Isobel. I told you my theory that Isobel is painting as Morris. You dismissed that idea out of hand, and I went along with that. But now I'm beginning to wonder what's really going on. And whether you're telling me the truth.'

'Are you saying I'm lying?' Dresler raised his voice in anger.

'I'm asking you to be straight with me. I think you know there's something funny going on here, but you're turning a blind eye.'

'Of course I'm not.' Dresler was furious now. 'You're imagining all this. The idea that Isobel Powell could be painting the Morris works is utterly preposterous.'

'But you've never met him, have you?'

'No, but—'

'And nor has anyone else, have they?'

'Oh, for God's sake.'

'I think you know very well there's something wrong here, Jacob.' Jess tried to temper her own anger. She knew how important Morris was to Dresler, understood that he was in a dilemma. 'All I'm asking is that you discuss this with me, and tell me the truth.'

'I am telling you the truth.'

'Well, I don't believe you.'

'Listen, Jess.' Dresler looked her in the eye. 'I'm not having you meddling in my business affairs. You know nothing about what I do. So keep out of it. Please stop this. Now.'

'No.' She returned his gaze. 'I won't stop. Because it involves a client of mine. I think you're afraid if the truth comes out about Morris, that'll be the end of your career. I think Blake and Isobel were involved in a scam together, and when he died, she asked you to take over.' She paused. 'As it happened, his death turned out to be quite convenient for you, didn't it?'

'That's enough!' Dresler shouted. Then he steadied himself. 'I'm not going to argue with you any more. And I'm afraid if you keep this up, that's the end of it between us.'

There was a silence.

'I'm going to sleep. If you decide to drop this, we can talk in the morning, when you're sober.'

She was stung by his remark. The wine had loosened her inhibitions, but she certainly wasn't drunk. He was trying to patronize her, but it was clear that he was rattled by what she'd been saying.

He turned his back to her and lay down. After a few minutes, she heard the sound of his breathing slow. Then he started to snore.

She lay awake beside him, her heart pounding, wondering how he could sleep so soon, and so easily, after their argument.

She tried to calm herself, but her whole body was trembling with anger. Christ, she thought. How do I pick them? Another self-centred, lying, cheating bastard, just like Bob. How could I have thought he was any different?

She took a deep breath, let it out slowly, and repeated the action. After a while, the trembling stopped and she felt herself begin to calm down.

Dresler was lying to her, she was sure of it. And possibly lying to himself, which, as she knew all too well, most people find it very easy to do – especially when their livelihoods are threatened. There was no future in the relationship, she realized, unless she was prepared to collude in his self-deception, which was out of the question.

She glanced at the bedside clock. Eleven fifteen. Not late at all. She could easily get up and drive home, she thought. She tried to remember how many glasses of wine she'd had over dinner. Two or three perhaps – but they were large ones.

There was a blast of noise from the bar, as a door opened and closed, and then she heard voices outside. People were gathering on the courtyard to smoke and talk and laugh. Smirting, they called it: smoking and flirting. Apparently, it had become a popular way for people to meet partners: standing outside in the cold, they felt a bond with each other as members of an 'exiled community'. She felt a sudden urge to go downstairs and join them.

Tears pricked her eyes, but they were tears of anger, not sadness. She was damned if she was going to cry for Dresler. It wasn't a tragedy, after all. In fact, it was probably a blessing that it had worked out this way. Better that she'd found out what he was really like before she'd introduced him to the girls, before he'd become part of her life . . .

Dresler shifted in his sleep, still snoring. She felt like smacking him over the head. There was something so repulsively smug, so self-satisfied, about the way he'd ended their argument. He'd given her an ultimatum, with no room for discussion or compromise. She'd thought they were equals, but she'd entirely misread the level of his self-regard. All that nonsense about being interested in her work, wanting her to be interested in his; it was all a complete sham. What he really wanted was a plucky little woman by his side, cheering him on, never for a moment doubting his moral and intellectual superiority, whatever nefarious activity he might be engaged in.

A drift of laughter wafted in from the terrace below. She lay staring up at the ceiling listening to it. There was no possibility of her getting to sleep, she knew. Her anger with him was mounting, and unless she woke him up and continued their argument, which she wasn't going to do, she'd lie there awake all night.

She made a decision. She'd get up, get dressed, and slip out of the room, without waking him. She'd go downstairs and have a strong black coffee in the bar, possibly two. Maybe go outside for a smoke on the terrace if she felt like it. Then she'd get in the car and drive home.

27

Driving out of the car park of the hotel, Jess felt a burden lift from her. All this while she'd been a spectator in Dresler's life, she realized, a person whose role and function was indeterminate. Now she was herself again, back in her own sphere, one that she understood and controlled – at least to some degree, anyway. As she passed the executive suites lining the driveway, she was glad not to be a part of this leisured, international world, but a person with a job to do, two girls to mother, a home to make – with or without a man at the centre of it – and a life to get on with.

It was a clear night as she bowled down the motorway, the moon hanging like a great yellow lantern in the sky. Jess put her foot down. The house would be empty, she knew, as Rose had gone over to Bob's for the night, and Nella was at Gareth's.

There was little traffic at that time of night, so it took her under an hour to get home. Even so, by the time she went up to bed, it was half past one. As she turned out the light, she realized she was utterly exhausted. As soon as her head hit the pillow, she fell fast asleep, and didn't wake up until morning.

* * *

Next day, she had a full schedule. There were three patients to attend to in the morning, and then she had a meeting with Maria's social worker regarding the arrangements for the children. Afterwards, she felt the need to get out of the office, so she went over the road and got herself a sandwich and a coffee from the deli before heading over to the park nearby. Her plan was to go down to the river, sit on a bench, eat her lunch, watch the ducks, and think about what had happened the night before.

The row with Dresler was playing on her mind. She knew from experience that she could lay her personal problems to one side and continue to work effectively with her patients, whatever her mood – and that being able to do that was, in itself, a boost to her confidence and a source of comfort. In that sense, at times she needed her patients just as much as they needed her. However, she also knew that the kind of turbulent emotions she was experiencing that day could, despite her best efforts, affect her judgement – not consciously, but unconsciously. That was one of the pitfalls of her chosen profession: one always had to be one step ahead of one's own unconscious, which to some degree was a contradiction in terms.

Jess walked quickly over to the park, found her favourite bench in a solitary spot by the river, and sat down. She watched a family of ducks swimming in the shallows at the edge. The ducklings swam behind their mother, all of them poking their beaks in and out of the rocks, looking for food. From time to time, one of the ducklings would lag behind, and she would turn back and chivvy it along. The drake was nowhere to be seen.

She unwrapped her sandwich and took a bite. Hummus and a salad of tomato, cucumber and lettuce. Nutritious, but not all that delicious.

One of the chicks drifted off in the swirling eddies, dangerously close to the mainstream of the river. Mother duck was pecking at some algae on a stone. On the river bank, a large black crow, silent and motionless, watched its passage.

What happened to us? she wondered. It started out so well. When we first met at the museum, and discussed the Morris painting, he seemed so cultured, civilized. He was so knowledgeable, without being snobbish about it. And distinguished-looking. Those blue-grey eyes. That chambray shirt. She sighed involuntarily. That first night we spent together, in the hotel, making love in the lamplight. It all seemed to happen so easily. He seemed so delighted by me, by everything, when we were at Cwm Du, before . . .

The crow opened its wings and took off, heading for the river. Crows don't eat ducks, Jess told herself, and took another bite of her sandwich.

That was it, most probably, she thought. Blake's suicide. It had been too soon in their courtship for them to weather such a storm. The cracks in the relationship had taken a while to show. At first, they'd clung together for support, both of them shocked by finding the body at the tower; then there'd been the trip to London. She'd loved his flat, the galleries, the restaurants, Soho – his whole world. The lovemaking had deepened and intensified. But then there'd been the attempt to track down Morris. She'd found Dresler irritating on that occasion: on the one hand, bossy; on the other, easily flustered. And ever since then, a certain distrust had crept into their dealings with each other. When she'd phoned him with her idea about Isobel and Morris, he'd dismissed it out of hand, rattled by the notion that anyone might question his judgement. And now, as far as she could see, he'd started lying to her. Morris, whoever he was, hadn't broken with Isobel and the Powell Gallery after Blake's death, and asked him to be his agent instead. It wasn't as simple as that. There was some kind of scam going on, whether it involved Isobel painting as Morris or not. Dresler was covering it up, or at least turning a blind eye to it. Obviously, he was enjoying his new-found status as Morris's agent, showing off to his pretentious, boring friends.

She finished the sandwich, opened the lid of her paper coffee cup, and took a sip.

He'd seemed so different from Bob at the start, she mused. And yet, when it came down to it, he hadn't been; clearly, despite his relaxed, urbane manner, he was extremely self-involved, ruthlessly ambitious. His career was far more important to him than his relationship with her. He'd lied to her, expected her to go along with whatever he told her, whatever he did, no questions asked. That was the deal he'd offered her, and he'd given her no choice but to accept it, if she wanted them to stay together. But she couldn't accept it. She wanted to know the truth, and she wanted to be with a man whose dealings were honest, not just with her, but with other people, too. Clearly, he wasn't that man.

So why, she asked herself, had she been attracted to him in the first place? Perhaps there was some docile, quiescent, feminine aspect to her nature that always impelled her towards the alpha male. Perhaps, in future, she'd need to be aware of that, so she wouldn't keep making the same mistakes . . .

There was a sudden squawking, as the mother duck turned and saw the crow descending from on high towards her offspring.

Her mobile phone went off, but she let it ring.

Where's the bloody drake? thought Jess. Then she remembered she'd read somewhere, probably in one of Rose's nature books, that drakes play no part whatsoever in raising their families.

All thoughts of Dresler left her mind as she watched the drama of the riverbank unfold. The mother duck paddled frantically towards the duckling, which was by now drifting away.

The crow swooped down and pecked at the duckling. The duckling, finally realizing the danger, tried to scurry towards its mother, but it was caught in the undercurrent of the river. Suddenly, the mother duck stood erect in the water, flapping her wings, her squawking reaching a crescendo. The crow swooped again, but this time the mother duck took flight, landing smoothly on the water and edging the duckling back into the shallows, along with the rest of her brood, where they continued to poke about in the rocks. Defeated, the crow gave up, and flew away.

Jess gave a sigh of relief, and scrabbled in her bag for her mobile phone. She checked the log, found that the caller was registered as 'unknown' and called back, just in case it was something to do with one of the girls.

A female voice answered.

'Hello? Did you call me just now?'

'Is that Dr Mayhew?'

It sounded like Elinor, yet the number was registered as unknown. And the caller had addressed her rather formally, as Isobel might do. Jess hazarded a guess.

'Isobel. Is that you?'

'No, it's Elinor.'

'Elinor. Sorry. You sounded like Isobel.'

'That's OK. People always get us mixed up on the phone.' Elinor paused. 'There's something I need to talk to you about.'

'OK. Carry on.' Jess glanced at her watch. She didn't have much time to talk. Her next patient was due in fifteen minutes' time and she needed to check her notes before she came in.

'I really just wanted to ask you a favour.'

Jess sighed inwardly. 'Oh yes?'

'Well, I've started painting again.' Elinor sounded excited. 'And I'd like to show you some of my new work.'

'Oh.' Jess was surprised, and somewhat relieved. 'OK. That would be very nice, Elinor.'

'I thought maybe this Sunday, if you're not too busy.' There was a certain timidity in Elinor's tone.

Jess thought about it. She had nothing particular planned for Sunday. She'd envisaged staying home, cooking lunch, and pottering about the garden as the girls came and went. She could spare an hour or two of her time for Elinor – indeed, it would be a pleasure to see her getting back to work again. And she was curious to see these paintings she'd heard so much about.

'How about Sunday afternoon at four? But I'd need to be home by six. Is that OK?'

'Fine.' Elinor sounded pleased. 'I can come to your house and pick you up, if you like.'

'No, don't worry. I'll drive in. Where are the paintings – at your house?'

'Actually, no.' Elinor paused. 'They're in rather a special place.'

'Meaning?'

'They're not hung in a studio. They're exhibited somewhere rather exciting, outside the city. It's a bit difficult to find.'

Jess thought for a moment. 'Tell you what, pick me up outside the consulting rooms. I'll be there at four.'

'Great.'

'See you then.' Jess brought the conversation to a close.

'See you. Bye.' Elinor rang off, sounding pleased.

Jess got up, gathered her belongings, and walked back through the park the way she'd come. On the way, she threw the sandwich packaging and her coffee cup, still half full, into the bin. She'd had enough coffee for one day, she thought. She needed to be calm, cool and collected for the afternoon sessions.

She came out onto Cathedral Road. The trees lining the street were now in full leaf, and they rustled above her in the wind, casting dappled shadows on the pavement. She'd always liked this street, ever since she'd set up the practice here, all those years ago. The grand Victorian gothic houses had a sombre, respectable air, softened by the murmuring trees that stood sentinel before them. Most of the houses in the street were professional rather than residential, and had always been so – doctors, dentists, insurance consultants, and the like. It made her feel proud that, with her own practice, she had become part of that sedate history that stretched back to the nineteenth century.

She walked up the steps to the consulting rooms. If Jacob texted her, she'd text him back, she thought. Just to be friendly. But the relationship was over. There was no doubt in her mind about that.

28

When Sunday came, Jess began to regret her offer to view Elinor's new work. She was enjoying being at home, in the peace and quiet. Nella and Gareth were staying over at his place, and Rose was at Bob's. The rain was drumming on the window outside, and it was cosy in the sitting room, where she was lying on the sofa, her head propped up on a cushion, reading.

Separation from the twin may be experienced as extremely threatening, even catastrophic, as it exposes the patient to a loss of known boundaries with the consequent fear of dropping into a void or 'nameless dread'. This may result in a narcissistic collusion between analyst and patient, echoing the narcissistic twinship, and designed to maintain the 'special relationship' between them and to cover up the painful and difficult developmental matters that are being avoided by the patient . . .

She was making good progress with *The Twin in the Transference*. Not only had the book helped her to understand Elinor's behaviour, it had also explained her own, to some degree.

Lewin argued that when a twin undergoes therapy, the therapist herself is drawn into this dual psychic world, unknowingly playing the role of the 'other twin':

> *The analyst is treated as part of the patient, as a twin part who knows all about the patient . . . The emergence of the transference twin in psychoanalytic work leads to an intense and tenacious relationship between analyst and patient, echoing the internal twinship.*

No wonder she'd found it so difficult to maintain the boundaries between herself and Elinor, she thought. She'd granted her all sorts of special privileges – changing the time and place of the sessions, allowing her to phone whenever she wanted – that she denied her other clients. Elinor had treated her as a twin, transferring her feelings for Isobel onto her therapist, but she hadn't been fully aware of that. She'd also failed to realize that she herself had responded to Elinor as a twin, enjoying that feeling of having a 'special' relationship with her, one that broke all the normal rules.

She looked up from her book, aware of the silence in the room. Perhaps her eagerness to indulge Elinor was also to do with what was going on in her personal life. The girls were less dependent on her these days, often out of the house, engaged in their own activities. Perhaps unconsciously, as a mother, she'd been feeling that loss – while also, of course, enjoying the freedom it brought – and using Elinor to fill the gap, as a kind of substitute daughter.

She glanced at her watch. She'd have to leave in fifteen minutes. She didn't want to go, now that she was deep in thought. Reading Lewin's book, she'd begun to realize that she, too, had become 'enmeshed' – with Elinor. Elinor had treated her, Jess, as a twin, a confidante, seeking to replace Isobel, who'd gone off and married Blake. Isobel had, in effect, moved on from the twinship to her relationship with Blake, which was a healthy, adult development. Significantly, Elinor had given up the therapy when Isobel had come back to her, after Blake's death. Later on, Elinor had realized that things wouldn't be the same with Isobel, not after what had happened, and had come back to see Jess.

Given Elinor's 'twin' dynamic, Jess reflected, it wasn't surprising that she herself, as the therapist, should have been drawn into enacting the role of the 'other twin'. There was no need to blame herself unduly for that. However, now that she'd begun to understand the situation better, she realized that there was a limit, and that she'd now reached it. After this trip to see Elinor's new work – which she had to admit she was extremely curious about – the boundaries would have to be redrawn, and in future maintained much more firmly.

She read one final sentence:

The internal twinship is a fundamental and powerful factor in twins. It will be an active force in the transference relationship with an analyst, and is ignored at our peril.

Then she closed the book and got up off the sofa.

There were few cars on the road as she drove into Cardiff. The trees were heavy with blossom, and cow parsley lined the verges of the road. Spring was giving way to summer, but it was still cold outside. She'd dressed warmly for the outing, in a padded mac and boots, grabbing a knitted beanie of Nella's, and putting it in her pocket. The studio or gallery or exhibition space or whatever it was she was going to see would probably be freezing, she reasoned – Elinor didn't seem to feel the cold at all, or to make any allowances for those who did.

When she got to the consulting rooms, it was easy to find a space on the street outside. It was Sunday afternoon, and everyone seemed to be indoors – as she should be, she reflected. She waited in the car, looking out for Elinor. Then she saw her, pulling up in a battered old Volvo a little way further down.

She picked up her handbag, checking that she had her mobile phone and her keys, and got out of the car, locking the door. She crossed the road. When Elinor saw her, she wound down the window and waved, a wide smile on her face. She seemed pleased and excited, and as Jess got into the car and they exchanged greetings, she found herself caught up in the general air of anticipation.

'Well, this is fun.' Jess settled herself in the passenger seat. 'Where are you taking me?'

'It's a secret.' Elinor gave a mischievous grin. 'Here.' She reached over and took a silk scarf out of the glovebox. 'I know this is silly, but before we start, I'd like you to put this on.'

'How d'you mean?'

'Over your eyes. So you don't know where we're going. It's all part of the concept.'

'What concept?' Jess began to feel uneasy.

'Of this new work.' She paused. 'Would you mind?'

Jess hesitated a moment. Then she nodded assent. It seemed like an odd request, but harmless enough.

Elinor leaned over and tied the scarf on, not too tightly but it completely covered her eyes, leaving no more than a tiny gap at the bridge of her nose, where only a small crack of light came in. Then she heard her start the car, and they began to drive off.

'So this is all in the name of art, is it?' Now that she couldn't see, Jess felt slightly uncomfortable. But, she reasoned with herself, she could easily take the blindfold off if she wished. She wouldn't for the moment, though – it would be spoiling the game.

''Fraid so.' Elinor laughed. She seemed happy, Jess thought. Happier than she'd ever seen her before, in fact.

'How are things, anyway?' It felt odd having a conversation with a blindfold on, but Jess did her best.

'Much better.' The car turned a corner. 'I feel like a new person now I've started painting again.'

'And the claustrophobia?' Jess had noticed that the car windows were closed.

'That's what these new paintings are about, actually. But you'll see. I don't want to spoil the surprise.'

From the stopping and starting at traffic lights, Jess guessed that they were driving out of Cardiff, but she couldn't say where to. She was enjoying the mystery ride to a degree but she was also slightly afraid. As a child, games of blind man's buff had excited her, but there had been an element of fear in the thrill: that feeling of utter dependence, of having to surrender one's trust completely; the way that the world suddenly became strange and hostile, familiar objects mutating into dangerous obstacles to be tripped over, and banged against; and the laughing voices of the other children, innocent and playful, yet with a harsh, spiteful edge to them as the blunders increased.

'Is it far?' Jess didn't want to be rude, but she'd stipulated that she'd need to be back in Cardiff in a couple of hours' time.

'Not at all. Should take us about twenty minutes.'

By Jess's calculation, it only ever took a maximum of fifteen minutes to get from one place to another within Cardiff. Any more and you would have left the city. So the studio, she reasoned, must be somewhere on the outskirts of town.

As they drove on, Elinor chatted away. She was uncharacteristically relaxed. She talked about the sale of Ebenezer, Blake and Isobel's former home, and the plans she and Isobel had for refurbishing the house at Llandaff Green. They were also thinking of changing the direction of the gallery, selling cheaper work by less well-known artists, rather than trying to make a splash with big new names, as Blake had. She didn't mention the fact that Morris had left the gallery and gone to Dresler, and Jess didn't question her on the matter. Neither did she ask questions about Elinor and Isobel's rapprochement, or about how Isobel was faring after Blake's death. This wasn't a therapy session, and for the time being at least, Elinor was no longer her client; so she kept the tone light, and Elinor responded in kind.

After a while, the conversation stalled, and they drove on in silence. The stops and starts had ceased, so they were probably out of town now, heading out on a clear road somewhere. They seemed to be going uphill, judging by the sound of the engine and the gear changes. Then Elinor turned off the main road onto a bumpy gravel path. After a couple of minutes driving up it, she drew in to the side of the road and parked the car.

'OK. Don't get out, you might bump into something. I'll come round to your side and help you.'

Elinor got out of the car, went round to the passenger door, and opened it. Jess got out, holding on to Isobel's arm.

'Now can I take this off?' Jess pulled at the blindfold.

'Oh please,' Elinor giggled. 'Keep it on. It'll be so much more fun.'

'Sorry, but no.' Jess fiddled with the knot at the back of the scarf, untied it, and took it off.

As the light hit her eyes, Jess realized that even though she'd only been blindfolded for less than half an hour, her senses were heightened. They were standing in a wood where the trees were a bright, almost luminous green. Above her, she could hear their branches blowing in the wind, not just one or two of them, but seemingly a whole forest; below her feet, as they left the path, the ground was soft with a carpet of rotting leaves. She could smell their pungent decay, and there was another powerful scent in the air. She sniffed. Wild garlic.

'Where are we going?' Jess asked, as Elinor began to walk downhill.

'We're just coming up to the site now.'

They walked down the hill, onto a path of beaten earth. Then Elinor asked Jess to wait a moment, and left her side. In that moment, standing alone in the wood, Jess listened intently to the sounds around her. She heard the rustle of the trees, the muffled crackling of fallen leaves, the drip of rainwater soaking through them. In the distance, she could make out the hum of traffic.

She put her hand down and felt the soft ground they'd just been walking on. It was hollow yet buoyant, like a pocket-sprung mattress. Her fingers found a small plant. She traced its fleshy leaves, its slender stem, its paper-thin petals. A wood anemone.

In that moment, she knew exactly where she was. She remembered the wood anemones from her walk with Dresler, when they'd tried to track down Hefin Morris. She looked up above her, at the cathedral of beech trees, shafts of sunlight penetrating the leaves. She was standing on Bryn Cau, the Hollow Hill.

29

Elinor called over to her. Jess stepped forward and looked down. Elinor was standing next to a pair of heavy iron doors set into the hillside. She'd opened them wide, and was heaving up a boulder to keep them open.

'Come on.'

Jess walked down the bank of leaves and stood next to Elinor. This was obviously the place where Elinor was going to show her the paintings. And evidently, the real Morris was about to be revealed, as either Elinor or Isobel – perhaps even both of them.

'Be careful now. You might get your feet wet.'

They peered into the tunnel. Water was dripping from the ceiling, the sound magnified by the echo from the walls.

'So your work is in here, is it?'

Elinor nodded. 'It's dry further in. There's an open space which was originally a blacksmith's forge. That's where the paintings are.'

Jess was slightly unnerved. To tell the truth, she didn't like enclosed spaces. She never went into caves, or mines, or long underground tunnels, if she could help it. She didn't even like tube trains, although she forced herself onto them, knowing that to avoid them would exacerbate her fear. But she didn't want to tell Elinor that. If Elinor's paintings were hung in some sort of underground cave in the hill, that meant she'd overcome her claustrophobia. It wouldn't do to undermine her new-found confidence by admitting to her own mild claustrophobic tendencies.

There was a small machine by the entrance to the tunnel, mounted on a trailer. Elinor went over to it and flicked a switch. Immediately, it began to emit a low, chugging noise. Up ahead, a bank of lights came on, illuminating the tunnel.

'I hired this from a film company,' said Elinor. 'Underground lighting. And it powers the film show that runs alongside the artworks.' She sounded excited as she spoke.

They walked into the tunnel, Jess rather less enthusiastically than Elinor. The lights lit up the walls of brown rock streaked with ochre. As they went on, the tunnel narrowed, and the air around them became dank and cold. Their steps echoed around the walls, which seemed to be closing in on them.

'Are we nearly there?' Jess asked, trying to quell the nervousness in her voice.

'Not far now.' Elinor spoke to her as if she were a bored child on a car journey.

They walked on. From time to time, the lights above them flickered. Jess wondered, if they gave out, whether they'd be able to make their way back.

The tunnel wound on. The further they went, the more restless Jess became. She'd never liked magical mystery tours. Her view was that they always turned out to be a complete pain in the neck, one way or another. She chided herself for having agreed to take part. But now that she had, she felt she really ought to play along, just for the moment. Elinor was such a child. But a harmless enough child, she reasoned. Artists were like that, after all, she supposed; people who hadn't lost their sense of wonder at the world but who hadn't really grown up, either. That was their strength, and their weakness.

They walked on into the tunnel, a lot further than Jess had anticipated, or perhaps it was her mounting fear that made it seem that way. Then the tunnel widened and they came to a halt.

Jess looked around her. She was standing in a small recess, hewed out of the rock. Propped up against the walls were three large canvasses. On a video screen a loop of abstract film, showing the inside of the tunnel, was playing.

Jess stepped forward to take a closer look.

The paintings were all views of the tunnel they were standing in, but abstracted, so that the colours and textures of the rock were foregrounded. There was a strange, eerie hue to them that mimicked the artificial light of the floodlamps, making the colours sing out. They were joyous, vibrant works, but there was a sense of foreboding in them, too, as if such intense saturation of colour could not be a part of the natural world above ground – of light, and air, and freedom to move – but belonged to a deep, subterranean existence inimical to human life.

'These are yours, are they, Elinor?'

Elinor gave a proud smile.

Jess looked back at them. She couldn't say she liked them, or disliked them. It was almost as if they were requiring one to enter a new level of experience, one in which one's likes and dislikes were irrelevant.

'They're extraordinary.'

'I know.' Elinor was matter-of-fact. 'They're my best work yet.'

She stepped forward and stood in front of the central painting. 'You see, when Isobel came back, the claustrophobia lifted.' She turned back to Jess. 'I was able to come down here again.' She walked over to the rock wall and ran her hand over a reddish yellow streak. 'I've always been fascinated by the colour and texture of this rock. They used to mine ochre here as well as iron, you see.'

Jess looked up at the central painting, flanked by the two

others. The more she gazed at it, the more it seemed to draw her in, to a mass of pulsating reddish yellow flesh, almost as if she were travelling up the inside of a vagina, into the cervix, back into the womb, the egg, and thence into nothingness, the state before conception. As far as she could understand it, Elinor was painting annihilation, but not that of death and destruction; this was another kind of nothingness, that which exists before life, rather than after it.

A loss of known boundaries . . . the fear of dropping into a void, or 'nameless dread' . . .

The void, she thought. The event horizon. Death, at the end of life. Whatever there is before life begins.

'You're Hefin Morris, aren't you?'

Elinor flashed her a brilliant smile.

'Of course. Hefin is me. Not Isobel.' She looked up at Jess, her eyes suddenly ablaze with anger. 'How could you have thought Isobel did those paintings?'

'Who told you I said that?'

'Isobel.' A petulant tone came into Elinor's voice. 'I was really upset about it.'

Jess wondered how Isobel knew what she'd told Dresler. Then she remembered the missed call at the hotel. Dresler was in on all this, as she'd suspected. He'd been lying to her, and to everyone else. Dresler had obviously told Isobel what Jess had said, and she'd passed it on to Elinor.

'How could you think that?' Elinor narrowed her eyes. 'Obviously, it was me doing the paintings. Isobel could never do work as good as that.'

'Elinor, I know nothing about your work. You told me your paintings were like Gwen John's. Small, meticulous. You told me Isobel painted in a bolder style. Perhaps more like Augustus—'

'Well, you were wrong.' Elinor came over and stood in front of Jess. 'I thought you understood me.'

Elinor's whole demeanour had changed. Down here, in the tunnel, she seemed like a completely different person – threatening, aggressive, and not a little unhinged.

'Calm down. I'm trying to understand you. That's why I'm here, isn't it?' Jess tried to humour her. 'I'm very impressed by your paintings. And the fact that you've been able to come into the tunnel, overcome your claustrophobia. It's a great achievement.'

'Thank you.' Elinor was somewhat mollified. 'You're right. I have done well, haven't I?'

'Very well.'

'I'm so pleased with these, Jess.' Elinor adopted a conspiratorial tone. 'Actually, to tell you the truth, I think there's a spirit of genius running through me now.' She paused. 'I'm just a vessel. A mere vessel.'

By now, Jess was thoroughly alarmed. Evidently, Elinor had overcome her claustrophobia, but she seemed to be displaying a more worrying condition: psychosis, presenting with the classic symptoms of loss of contact with reality and delusions of grandeur. She should have recognized the signs earlier – all that nonsense with the blindfold, and so on – instead of taking them as part of a harmless game.

She wondered what to do. The best course of action, she decided, was to play along, admire the paintings, and then lead Elinor gently out of the tunnel. After that, she could think about getting help for her. Elinor's condition clearly needed psychiatric care. With any luck, she'd respond well; the condition appeared to be type one, a brief psychotic disorder with a stressor such as a trauma or death in the family – in Elinor's case, two such stressors.

There were footsteps in the tunnel. Elinor's rapt expression changed, in an instant, to that of a guilty child, caught in the act of perpetrating some minor domestic crime.

The footsteps came nearer, and then Isobel came into view. She was carrying a large torch in one hand, and a rolled-up projector screen in the other.

When she saw Jess, she gave a sharp intake of breath. Then she looked accusingly at Elinor.

'I just brought her here to see the paintings.' There was a childish whine in Elinor's voice. She was obviously afraid of her sister, and keen to placate her.

Isobel's expression turned from astonishment to rage.

'What the fuck did you do that for?' she burst out.

'She thought you were doing them.' Elinor was petulant. 'I wanted to show her it was me.'

'You idiot.' Isobel was incandescent. 'You little idiot. You've really done it this time, haven't you? Screwed everything up.'

'You don't understand, Iz. She won't tell. She won't tell anyone. She's on my side. Aren't you?' Elinor looked pleadingly at Jess, who stood rooted to the spot, speechless.

The twins turned away from her and began to talk in low voices. Jess strained to hear them, and realized they were speaking Welsh. She could barely understand what they were saying – her grasp of the language was very limited – and they were gabbling very fast. On top of that, both their voices sounded exactly the same. When one spoke and the other interrupted, it was hard to make out which was which.

She listened in, trying to follow what they were saying.

. . . *Something something Morris something something . . .*

'. . . *cael gwybod . . .*' . . . *find out . . .*

'. . . *fydda'i ddim yn gwend wrth neb . . .*' . . . *won't tell anyone . . .*

'. . . *ar fy ochr . . .*' . . . *on my side . . .*

'. . . *os ei di o flaen dy well, a'i yno hefyd . . .*' . . . *if you go down, I'll go down . . .*

'. . . *bydd rhaid ei llad hi hefyd nawr . . .*' . . . *we'll have to kill her too, now . . .*

Jess felt a cold fear grip her chest. It was her they were discussing.

Their voices rose as they argued, and then they went back into English.

'Don't, Iz. I'll explain it to her. She'll understand.'

'Understand? After what you've done, you bloody psycho. No one's ever going to understand, except me.'

'You're just jealous.'

'No, I'm not. I couldn't give a shit about you. But if you go down, I go down.'

'That's not true.' That was Elinor, beginning to whine. 'You love me, I know you do.'

'No, I don't. I hate you.'

'Maybe.' The whine turned to a taunt. 'But you're stuck with me now, aren't you?'

By now, the twins' conversation was becoming more heated. Jess realized that, for the moment, they'd forgotten about her. So, very tentatively, she began to tiptoe out towards the tunnel, heading for the entrance.

'Stop there.' She heard Isobel's voice, and turned round.

Isobel was facing her, holding up a small aerosol canister.

At that moment, Jess could have made a run for it. But she hesitated for a split second, and then Isobel lunged forward, pressing down on the spray can's nozzle. Jess felt a stinging pain in her eyes and nose. She couldn't breathe. Her head began to spin, and she staggered forward, trying to keep upright. She felt herself trip over a rock.

Then her legs gave way.

30

Crouching on the ground, Jess felt a wave of nausea come over her. Her head swam, and she retched. Nothing came up, except sour-smelling bile. She wiped it away with her sleeve, and retched again. This time, there was only a thin trail of saliva. She felt a painful spasm in her stomach. Then she heard the sound of retreating footsteps. The twins were running away, down the tunnel. She scrambled to her feet, stumbling blindly about.

'Help me!' she cried. 'Elinor, come back. Don't leave me here.'

Her words echoed back to her, reverberating around the tunnel walls. The footsteps died away and she knew that there was no one there.

Her eyes were burning, and all she could see in front of her was a white fog. She felt her way around the recess, knocking into the table, and tripping over one of the buckets on the ground. Then she sat down against a wall, afraid of hurting herself.

Mace, she thought. One of those sprays they use in America. She didn't know much about them, except that they weren't lethal. The thought calmed her a little. The effects of the spray would wear off, sooner or later. Then she'd be able to make her way back to the entrance of the tunnel. It was just a question of sitting it out and waiting until her sight came back.

She fumbled in her pocket and pulled out her mobile phone, hoping that by some miracle, she might get a signal. Then she remembered that even if she did, it was a smart phone, rather than one with buttons, and she wouldn't be able to see to make the call. Nevertheless, she tried her best, making a swiping motion with her hand to unlock the phone, touching the screen here and there, attempting to memorize the routine for making a call. But the phone remained silent in her hands.

Her lungs tightened in her chest, and she struggled for breath. The effects of the spray, she told herself. But she knew that it was panic, too.

OK, let's take this step by step, she reasoned, trying to calm herself. I know exactly where I am – at Bryn Cau, the Hollow Hill. I'm not far into the tunnel, and I know where the entrance is. I've got light in here – the floodlight, powered by the generator. There's a torch on my phone, too. I'll be able to use it in the tunnel, to help me get to the entrance. This is really not a disaster.

She thought of the clanging door she'd heard Elinor open when they'd arrived. What if the twins had locked it? What if they'd turned off the generator, and plunged her into darkness. What if they meant to kill her, to leave her here to die?

Panic rose in her chest again, and she became light-headed. She heard a voice inside her head. Breathe slowly, it told her. In through the nose. Hold for a moment. Out through the mouth. And again.

She did as the voice commanded, and after a while, the panic subsided. If the entrance was locked, she reasoned, she'd stand by the door and yell. Sooner or later, someone would pass by and hear her. And if no one came, she'd find another way out. She'd seen the opening of the mineshaft from the other side of the quarry, when she and Dresler had gone looking for Morris. It came out beside a pair of lagoons, one blue, one yellow. And there must be other shafts down here, too. Bryn Cau was called the Hollow Hill because it was a warren of underground tunnels. She'd find one of them, get out somehow.

She leaned her head back against the wall. The searing pain in her eyes had subsided, but now they'd begun to itch. She had an urge to rub them, but she knew instinctively that she shouldn't. She breathed in again, and out. She could hear the water dripping in the tunnel. It was probably clean, she thought, coming from an underground spring. When her sight came back, she'd be able go out there and splash her eyes, cool the burn.

Time passed. Her head was aching, and her limbs felt shaky. She kept up the breathing, in the hope that the effects would wear off. She kept one hand inside her pocket, clutching her mobile phone as if it were some kind of talisman. And, as she waited, she cast her mind back over what had happened.

What the hell were the twins up to? she wondered. She tried to remember what they'd said when they were arguing. It had been hard to follow what was going on, but she'd caught a few words: one of them had said 'If you go down, I go down', implying perhaps that Isobel was covering for Elinor. Then the chilling words she'd heard in Welsh came back to her, their meaning as clear and sharp as the echoing drops of water in the tunnel: 'We'll have to kill her too, now.'

Did that mean they'd killed before? The words 'bloody psycho' had been used, hadn't they? Elinor had killed, and might very well kill again.

The panic rose once more, cramping her gut and tightening her throat so that she retched again, but she fought it down. The twins were insane, she told herself. Insane and incompetent. There was no plan, no rationale to what they'd done. They hadn't thought it through. They were bound to have made some stupid mistake, such as forgetting to lock the entrance as they fled. And it was also possible that Elinor, in her deluded state, would return to save her. Even if she didn't, sooner or later someone would raise the alarm. Bob would be bringing Rose back to the house soon, and when she didn't return, he'd raise the alarm and start looking for her.

She cast her mind back. She hadn't told Bob where she was going that afternoon. She hadn't told Nella, either. No one knew where she was.

She shivered. The air was cold and damp. She put her hand in her pocket and pulled out Nella's beanie. The wool under her fingers felt soft and warm. She sat with it in her lap for a moment. Just touching it brought her a sense of comfort. Then she reached up and put it on her head. Thank God she'd brought it, she thought, and worn sensible clothing. She was already getting cold, but without them, she'd have been frozen stiff by now.

There was silence all around her, except for the crystal clear sound of the water dripping in the tunnel.

She waited. And waited. All her thoughts frightened her, so she tried not to think of anything, but simply to focus on the sound of the dripping water. The mindfulness technique. But it didn't seem to be doing the trick. After a while, she began to hear a hissing in her left ear. Gas, she thought, and the panic rose in her throat again. No, tinnitus, she told herself. Probably brought on by shock.

Slowly, the white fog in front of her eyes began to lift. She waited for the shapes of the objects around her to come into view – the generator, the lamps, the table, the buckets, the paintings propped against the wall. But the white was replaced by black. Fear gripped her as she began to realize that her vision had come back, but that all she could see around her was total darkness. The twins had switched the generator off.

She brought the mobile out of her pocket, her fingers still clasped around it, and now that she could see, turned it on. A bright light shone out from the screen. The screensaver showed a photograph of her, Nella and Rose standing in front of the mirror in the hallway of the house. She, Jess, was in the middle, taking the photo. Nella was grinning, her head lolling on her mother's shoulder, and Rose was pulling a face.

She looked to the edge of the screen at the top, to see if she had a signal, but the icon was tiny, and her vision was still too blurry to make it out properly. So she called up the keyboard, dialled 999, and put the phone to her ear. Silence.

There was no signal.

She gazed down at the screensaver and began to cry. That cooled her eyes, like some miraculous balm, so she went on crying. The tears rolled down her face and plopped onto the screen, onto the faces of Nella and Rose, the two people she loved most in the world. She cried for them, and for that moment when they'd stood in front of the mirror in the hall, fooling around and laughing; and she cried for her home, and her life, and her years with Bob, and her mother, and her father, and everything and everyone that she'd known and loved until she found herself here, alone, abandoned in the darkness, left to die.

Then she wiped the tears away, got up off her feet, and got on with the business of saving her life, and getting back to them all.

The torch on the phone worked, emitting a surprisingly powerful beam of light. She shone it around the recess, until she saw the tunnel. She walked over to it, then shone the beam to the right. The tunnel stretched into the distance, the rock hewn into a low curve overhead. She shone it to the left. The same.

She thought back to when she'd come into the tunnel with

Elinor, but it was hard to work out which direction they'd arrived from. She remembered that they'd turned a corner, just before they came to the recess. The entrance would probably be visible once she'd got round that.

She edged out into the tunnel, holding the torch in front of her. She knew the battery wouldn't last long – she'd tried it once before, for map-reading in the car while Bob drove, and it had given out after less than twenty minutes. She'd go along the tunnel a little way, she decided, and if she couldn't see the light from the entrance, she'd turn back and go the other way.

She walked carefully, keeping well away from the walls, and trying to ignore the fact that the curve of rock above her head was narrowing, until it became perilously low. The dripping of the water around her became louder, echoing in her ears, and there was a sound of rushing water ahead.

What if the place has flooded, she thought, and I'm walking right into it?

Unlikely, the calm, sensible voice inside her head told her. Why would the twins set up a studio in a mine that regularly flooded?

Wouldn't put it past them, a fearful, doubting whisper replied.

She quieted the voices, and walked on. The tunnel veered off around a corner and narrowed still further, until she had to bend her legs and her head, and the walls were close around her. She kept going, her heart in her mouth. The rock was not supported; she couldn't see any wooden struts, as one might expect in a mine. This part of it obviously hadn't been used for many years; it could well be unstable. There could be a fall at any time, burying her in rubble.

She hesitated, and stopped in her tracks. She was going the wrong way, she thought. And it would be foolish to move too far away from the recess. At least there was air to breathe there, and room to move around.

She shone the torch up ahead, this time scanning the walls of the mine. The rock was yellow, pitted and streaked with red and black. It had been hewn by hand, squared off in places, and left to curve in others, where the stone was too hard to break. Parts of it hung down like great blunt stalactites. On the ground beneath her feet was a series of ridges, as if a small railway track had once been laid there, and later pulled up. There was no sign of light anywhere.

She gave a sigh of frustration, and turned round, pointing the torch in the other direction, so she could see what lay there. Just as she did, it gave out. Once more, she was plunged into darkness.

'Fuck,' she said out loud. 'Fuck, fuck, fuck.' Her words echoed around her, mocking her impotent fury.

The panic came back, but this time it was mixed with rage. It didn't help. She was stranded here in the dark, in fear of her life. It didn't matter whose fault it was. It was up to her to deal with the situation, and she'd managed to blow her only chance, taking the wrong route. And now the torch had given out, and she couldn't see a thing.

She banged her foot on the ground and screamed – a wordless scream of frustration, of panic. When she stopped, all that came back was a ghostly echo. And then silence.

Right. OK. That's enough of that. The sensible voice took on a scolding tone. Now for Plan B. Stand here for a while, let your eyes accustom to the dark. You might be able to see enough to guide yourself out. You need to go the other way. The entrance must be in the other direction.

Yes, but the fucking entrance is fucking locked, isn't it? the panicky voice screamed back. The bloody twins have locked me in here. They want to kill me. And nobody knows I'm here. And there may be gas in here, and floods, and rockfalls, and—

That's enough of that, Jessica Mayhew. Call yourself a

psychotherapist? You're just indulging in catastrophic thinking. Imagining the worst-case scenario. You've warned your clients against it often enough, haven't you? Now pull yourself together, and get on with finding a way out of here.

But I can't. I can't . . .

Jess began to sob. Great panicky gasps that escaped from her chest and up into her throat. Her body started to shake. Her legs felt weak, as if they were about to give way under her.

Stop that pathetic blubbing, the voice commanded, sounding like a sergeant major. You should be thoroughly ashamed of yourself.

Jess did as she was told, took a deep breath in, and let it out slowly, trying to steady herself.

That's better. Now, can you see anything?

Of course I can't.

Anything at all?

Jess looked around her. Her eyes were adjusting to the darkness. Around her she could see the shapes of the walls, and the rocks above her head, looming over her. She peered ahead, into the gloom. At the very end of the tunnel, she thought she could see a tiny pinprick of light.

Her heart leapt.

It could just be a chink in the rock, letting in a bit of sunlight, said the whiner. You might get there and find there's no way out.

Oh, shut up. The sergeant major was impatient. Now, just move towards it. Come on. At the double.

Jess was making progress. Slowly, but surely. The pinprick of light was still far away, but it was getting bigger. She walked carefully towards it, feeling her way along the walls. Her fear was still there, but now that she'd found a way out, or so she hoped, it was tempered by excitement.

On her left-hand side, she passed a cavern. She peered into it, but the inside of it was inky black. Then she heard a rustling, and a squeaking. A tiny creature flitted by her head.

Just a bat, the sergeant major remarked. Nothing to worry about.

Sars, murmured the whiner. Ebola.

We're not in Africa, are we?

Bats are quite sweet, actually, thought Jess. Her own voice intervened. As long as you don't disturb them, they won't harm you.

Vampire bats. Rabies.

The voices in her head were beginning to worry Jess a little. Hearing voices was one of the first signs of psychosis. On the other hand, the sergeant major had been quite helpful.

She carried on and the chink of light began to get bigger. Then she turned a corner and it was lost to view.

Oh my God. It's gone.

Keep going. Just keep walking forward.

I'll never get out.

You will. Have faith.

She walked on. There was no light, only a soft, black darkness. The walls of the tunnel seemed to close in around her.

The voices ceased.

Have faith, Jess. Have faith. She heard her voice break the silence. She was talking to herself. Come on. Keep going.

She turned a corner, and the light came back into view. She breathed a sigh of relief, and looked around her.

The tunnel had opened out into a chamber, hung with stalactites of ochre rock. In front of her was a great lake, about fifty metres across, filled with water of an intense turquoise blue. Around it was a path, and above it a shaft of light, shining down from a gap in the rocks above.

She caught her breath. It was beautiful. The most beautiful

sight she'd ever seen. She closed her eyes in relief, and she offered up a prayer. 'Thank you, God,' she whispered. She remembered it was Sunday, and she thought of the bells ringing out for evensong in the church beside her house. She'd hear them again, next Sunday, and the one after that. She thought of the bell-ringers pulling them, hanging on to the ropes for dear life, jumping up and down, and the bells pealing out, all over the world, and she understood why they did it, and why people listened, and why their hearts were uplifted, and why they found strength in themselves to carry on. It was to give thanks to God for the simple fact of being alive. Whether or not he heard them, or gave a damn.

She took the path that led around the lake to the hole in the rock face above, where the light was coming through. When she got there, she looked up at the shaft. It had obviously been used as an escape route before. A series of metal handholds had been set into the rock, leading all the way up to the top. It didn't look easy to get up there, but neither did it seem impossible.

She peered up at the shaft, and, at the top, saw clouds scudding across a blue sky. The sight thrilled her. She imagined herself climbing out, hearing the soft rustle of the trees. She could almost feel the breeze against her skin. It was just a matter of time. Time, and effort.

She put her hands on the first hold, and tried to haul herself up to the second. The metal felt hard and cold against the flesh of her palms. Her arms hurt, but she persevered, willing herself on, inching her way up the shaft. She was breathing heavily. She wished that she were fitter, and the holds closer together.

She was just congratulating herself on reaching halfway up the shaft when she heard a low rumbling noise. The walls around her began to shake. She looked up at the sky again, and saw a few small rocks tumbling towards her. She dodged her head. The quarry, she thought. The shaft must be right beside it. And they're blasting.

She edged herself up, an inch at a time, until she reached a small ledge hewn into the rock. It was big enough to squat down on, so she stopped there for a moment, pausing for breath. She reached out for the next hold, but it came away in her hand. It was damp and rusted. She threw it down the shaft, onto the rock below.

The next hold was too far away for her to reach, so she had to remain where she was. She looked up at the shaft and saw the sky and the trees above, so near and yet so far. Damn, she thought. Now what the hell do I do? On an impulse, she took Nella's neon beanie out of her pocket and threw it, as high as she could, up out of the shaft. It disappeared from sight. She hoped it would attract attention, tell someone she was down here, and in danger.

There was another explosion, this time closer, and louder. More rocks came tumbling down, and there was a ringing in her ears.

Then there was a deafening blast, and the sky went black. She felt the darkness close around her, like a blanket. It had come back for her, reached up out of the mine to claim her once again.

She fell like a lover into its soft, silent embrace.

When she opened her eyes, she saw a halo of light above her head.

I'm dead, she thought.

There was a loud chugging sound all around her. She wondered whether she was going to be run over.

She gave a scream. Her voice sounded as if it belonged to someone else, high and piercing.

Nothing happened.

A few minutes later, a face appeared in the halo. The face of a man with long, tangled hair and a beard.

That must be God, she told herself.

Her eyes adjusted to the light. He was wearing a filthy knitted cap. He had a plug in one ear.

Maybe not.

There was a look of horror on his face.

It was the Longbeard.

'You all right?'

She croaked out an answer. 'I think so.'

So she wasn't dead.

He held up his hand and she saw that he was holding Nella's neon pink beanie. He gave it a shake, as if in triumph. He must have seen it fly up out of the shaft when she'd thrown it, and come to investigate.

'Stay there. I'll get help.'

The Longbeard vanished. Jess lay there, looking up at the sky. Her head was throbbing, her hands were burning, and there was a deafening noise in her ears. But the sky was still blue, and there were still clouds scudding across it. And she was here to see it.

The chugging stopped.

In the silence, she could hear the trees rustling above her head. They sounded religious, she thought. A living cathedral.

The deafening sound stopped. There was shouting.

The man would come back for her, she knew. He'd lay a blanket over her, and then other men would come. They'd wait for an ambulance, and she'd be taken to hospital. Doctors would look at her head, and maybe put a bandage on it, and tell her to be careful, she had concussion, but it wasn't serious, and she'd be all right in a few days' time. They'd clean up her cuts and bruises, and send her home. Nella and Rose would be there, and she'd tell them she'd had a stupid accident, fallen over on a hillside. They'd be nice to her, get her a cup of tea. Fuss over her, till she told them to stop.

And then, after a while, everything would go back to normal. The bells would ring out again on Sundays, and she'd be there to hear them. Every Sunday, for now, and for years to come. It was a miracle, but that was what was going to happen.

Yes. That was how it was going to be. She'd known it all along.

Everything was going to be all right.

31

Jess was in hospital, in a room on her own. She'd been there four days. Bob and the girls had visited her, but she'd heard nothing from Dresler. And now she was beginning to get bored. There was no reason for her to stay any longer, as far as she could see. She hadn't fallen very far in the shaft, but had been hit on the head by some falling rocks. She'd suffered mild traumatic brain injury, what used to be called concussion, and a series of tests had been done. She'd seen the report. The scans had shown no gross structural changes to the brain, and there was no cellular damage. However, they were keeping her in for observation, since she had shown signs of 'post-traumatic confusional state': cognitive impairment, behavioural changes, irritability, sleep disturbance.

What they didn't seem to realize was that there was actually nothing wrong with her. All these so-called symptoms were the result of no one believing what she'd told them about her experience in the mine, and of being kept in hospital against her will. At first she'd found it profoundly disturbing that not only the medical staff but her own family had doubted her account of what had happened that day; now, however, the shock had worn off and she merely felt frustrated, and desperate to get out of hospital and go home.

The door opened, and a woman came in. It took Jess a moment to realize who she was – Barbara Brown, a colleague who worked at Whitchurch, the local psychiatric hospital. In the past, she'd referred a number of her clients to Barbara, sometimes for treatment, sometimes when they needed to be sectioned.

'Jess.' Barbara took a chair by the bed. 'How are you doing?'

Jess had always liked Barbara. She was a woman in her fifties with a mass of unruly dark hair, now streaked with grey, who dressed rather soberly, as if trying to compensate for the hair. They'd known each other for more than twenty years, and Jess trusted her implicitly; she'd always shown common sense and compassion, as well as a gentle good humour, when dealing with her clients.

'Fine. I'm hoping to be out of here soon, actually.'

'Well, I wouldn't rush it. You've had a nasty shock. You could probably do with a bit more rest.'

It was nice of Barbara to visit, Jess thought, but she couldn't help feeling irritated by her advice.

'How did you know I was in here?'

'Bob gave me a call. He thought it would be a good idea if I could pop by and have a chat.'

Jess's irritation increased. What was Bob doing poking his nose into this? He hardly knew Barbara. They'd met at various social functions to do with work, but that was all.

'The thing is,' Barbara went on, 'you do seem to be a little confused at the moment. That's completely consistent with the nature of your injury. MTBI – concussion – can be caused by nearby explosions, as well as a blow to the head.'

'There's nothing wrong with me. The scans have shown that.'

'Scans don't pick up everything. With diffuse injury—'

'Look, as I keep saying, my memory of what happened in the mine is perfectly clear. One of my patients, Elinor Powell, took me into the tunnel at Bryn Cau to see her paintings. While we were in the mine, her sister Isobel turned up. They argued, Isobel sprayed mace into my eyes, and then they ran off, leaving me there. I wandered around down there for hours. I could have died.'

'Yes, we know.' Barbara adopted the patient, understanding voice that Jess had heard her use so many times with her clients. 'You told the police that. And they told you they'd sent a search team down the mine but there was no evidence of any paintings, anywhere. Neither was there any sign of mace in or on your body when you were tested.'

'Well, the test must have been wrong.'

Barbara looked sceptical. 'Whatever the explanation, the fact is you were found alone in a shaft by the quarry. You had no business to be there. I know it was a Sunday, but blasting sometimes goes on there at the weekends. You were taking a huge risk.'

'You haven't been listening.' Jess tried to control her irritation. 'I had no intention of doing anything dangerous. I was abandoned in the mine. And that shaft was the only way out.'

'OK.' Barbara nodded her head in agreement, in that way psychiatrists do when they realize their patient has completely lost contact with reality. 'I understand.'

Jess stopped talking. There was no point in continuing the discussion.

Silence fell. Barbara fiddled with her glasses, which hung on a string around her neck.

'I expect you're bored stiff in here,' she remarked after a while.

'I am. They don't like you to read too much, or watch the box. Taxes the brain too much, apparently. Even daytime TV.'

Barbara laughed.

'Listen, Jess. Take advantage of the situation. Get some rest.' She paused. 'You've been under a lot of stress lately. Bob told me you and he had parted. I was sorry to hear that.'

Jess shrugged, but she was annoyed. Why Bob had to go around telling anyone and everyone about their separation, she didn't know.

'This has nothing to do with that. I'm coping fine.'

'Of course you are.' Barbara was tactful. 'But it must be a lot of work looking after the girls on your own. And then there's this client, Elinor Powell, isn't there? The twin. It sounds as if she's been quite demanding. Getting you down to the tunnel to come and look at her paintings . . . and, what was it, running off and leaving you there?'

Jess knew that technique, as well. Going along with your patients' deluded stories, so as to gain more insights into their mental condition.

'I've dealt with a number of twins myself,' Barbara went on. 'They're quite complex individuals to deal with, in my experience. In fact, it's frustrating that there are so few clinical studies on the subject. Heaps of stuff about genetics, as if twins are just there to be used as guinea pigs to tell us about "normal" people. But nothing about the twin relationship as such.'

Jess thought of mentioning *The Twin in the Transference* but decided instead to rest her brain, as she'd been ordered to.

'I had one patient who had a breakdown after his twin brother married and moved away.' Barbara fiddled with her glasses again. 'He used to look in the mirror and see no one there. It was very strange. And what was also strange was how quickly I became drawn into his world. He treated me as if I were his twin, and I found myself responding to that.' She hesitated. 'You have to be very careful, don't you? Not to get too close.'

Jess didn't reply. She was trying not to get angry. She didn't want to be told how to handle her client. And she didn't like the implication that she'd lost control of the situation, either.

299

Barbara sighed and stopped fiddling with her glasses. Then she changed the subject.

They made small talk for a while, and at last she shifted on her chair, as if getting ready to leave.

'Listen,' she said, 'when you get out of here, don't go straight back to work. Take a few weeks off. Your patients can wait. You need time to get well yourself. You're a good therapist, Jess. We don't want to lose you.'

Was that a veiled threat? Jess wondered.

'If you want some proper R & R, I could have a word with the people at The Grange, if you like. It might be better than going home, where you'll have the girls to deal with.'

The Grange was a private mental hospital – mental health rehabilitation centre, as it called itself – where Barbara often sent patients to recuperate. Some of Jess's own clients had come from there, continuing their therapy with her after their stay at the hospital. It was a pleasant enough place, a country mansion on the outskirts of Cardiff, overlooking the Bristol Channel. But the fact that Barbara was recommending it as a place for her to recuperate offended her greatly.

'No thanks. I'll sort myself out.'

'I'm sure you will.' Barbara got up to go. 'But whatever you do, don't rush back into action, will you.'

Jess didn't respond.

'Promise me.'

Jess gave a vague nod.

'OK.' Barbara sighed. 'Well, let me know how you get on.'

'I will.'

'Bye, then.' Barbara gave her an encouraging smile. 'Good luck.'

Jess did her best to smile back, but failed.

Barbara walked over to the door. Before she opened it, she turned to Jess, a look of concern on her face.

Jess gave her an airy wave. 'Thanks for dropping by.'

Barbara sighed again, opened the door, and left, shutting it quietly behind her.

When she was gone, Jess leaned over and picked up the remote control on the bedside table. She'd been told not to read, text, or watch television, but none of the nurses were looking. In fact, they never came near her, except to serve her meals. There was a small glass panel in the door, and from time to time, a face would peer in, but it happened less and less often as the days passed.

She flicked through the channels: news, pop, chat. A panel of middle-aged women discussed the contents of their knicker drawer. One of them kept theirs in a mess, the knickers all jumbled up; another made sure that each pair was neatly folded and ranged by colour. Chat, pop, news. As she switched back to the news, she was confronted by Tegan Davies, sitting in front of the Pierhead building in the Bay.

Tegan was looking immaculate, as usual. The cream outfit was spotless, her hair was carefully sprayed into place, and her make-up was perfect.

'A press conference was called today at Blackwood Miners' Institute to announce a new site-specific work by local painter Hefin Morris.' There was a smug lilt to her voice that irritated Jess. 'Mr Morris, an ex-miner from the Rhondda, is making a name for himself nationally with a series of paintings based on his former work in the mines. A self-taught artist, Mr Morris has in the past declined to appear in public, and his identity has remained something of a mystery, but today, he surprised onlookers by making an unscheduled appearance, as Betsan Evans reports.'

Jess turned up the volume, as the scene switched from the studio to the museum. There, sitting behind a battery of microphones, was Dresler. He looked much the same as ever, dressed in a dusky blue cord jacket that matched his eyes, a striped scarf round his neck, and a self-satisfied smile playing on his lips. Beside him was a man in a peaked cap and a T-shirt. There was a streak of green in his hair, his nose was pierced, and both his arms were covered in tattoos.

For a moment, Jess didn't recognize him. Then she realized he was Nathan, the man she and Dresler had followed in the van the day they'd gone up to Bryn Cau to find Morris.

The reporter burbled on, but Jess wasn't listening. So that was the latest scam Dresler and Isobel had cooked up together, was it? To present Nathan, the guy who'd supposedly first brought the paintings in to the Powell Gallery, as Hefin Morris. Evidently, in reality, Nathan was Elinor and Isobel's factotum; and now he'd got the job of actually pretending to be Hefin. His was a rather limited approach to the role, Jess thought, consisting mostly of grunting his agreement to whatever art world verbiage Dresler came out with. On the other hand, his tattoos did give him the air of an authentic radical.

Jess watched as Dresler continued to do the talking. The phrases tripped off his tongue – political engagement, cultural philistinism, savage cutbacks, social deprivation – but she didn't follow what he was saying. There was no need to. Because he was lying through his teeth. He knew full well that Elinor was the real Hefin Morris; he was simply going along with the twins' scam, using Nathan to pose as Morris in a last-ditch attempt to save his reputation.

As he chuntered on, Jess felt a surge of fury rise up into her chest. Fury, and humiliation. Dresler had blatantly lied to her, lied to himself. How could she have trusted such a man, believed for a moment that she could make a life with him? He'd called her several times since they'd last met, but she hadn't responded; she never wanted to see him again. Perhaps, she mused, in the wake of the separation from Bob, she really was losing her judgement. Even now, watching him speak, she found she couldn't tell what kind of a person he really was. Vain, ambitious, deceitful, yes; willing to put his career before his relationship with her, yes. But a party to attempted murder? She wasn't sure. Did he know that the twins had tried to kill her, lured her down to the mine and left her there to die? And if he did, was he turning a blind eye to that, as well?

Surely not, but the thought frightened her. She wouldn't put it past him to collude with the twins, now that she knew how many other lies he'd told on their behalf, and his own. While she doubted he'd known what Elinor was planning, he was certainly playing with fire. The twins were dangerous. They had to be stopped.

Nathan began to mumble a few words, the lights of the cameras popping. Once again, Jess wasn't listening. She was looking at his face, trying to work out whether he, too, was involved in perpetrating the scam, or just doing his bosses' bidding. She suspected the latter.

As the questions continued, Dresler took over again, and Nathan relapsed into silence, a look of mute hostility on his face, as befitted the new *enfant terrible* of the contemporary art world. Then the scene switched back to Tegan in the studio.

A face appeared in the glass panel of the door. It was one of the nurses, peering in at her. Jess leaned her head back on her pillow and closed her eyes. When she opened them again, the face was gone.

She picked up the remote control, and switched the television off. Then she reached for her mobile phone and keyed in a number.

'Dragon Taxis.'

'Yes, I'd like a taxi to St Fagan's, please.' Jess paused. 'I'm at the Heath. I'll be waiting outside the main entrance in ten minutes.'

32

The taxi dropped Jess off outside her house. She stood for a moment looking at the front door, holding her overnight bag, feeling like a visitor, a stranger, come to spend the night. Such odd thoughts seemed to flit across her mind quite often since the incident in the mine. Maybe there really was something wrong with her brain. Or perhaps it was just the emotional aftershock of what had happened, still shuddering through her, destabilizing the foundations of her life, just as the explosions in the quarry had rumbled through the tunnel, causing the rock to crack.

She let herself in, dumped her stuff in the hallway, and walked down to the kitchen. She needed to call Lauren Bonetti and tell her she had a plan. It was a simple one, but she was convinced she could make it work. She'd need help, but if Bonetti couldn't give it, she'd be able to carry it out on her own – though it would be more dangerous. Brain fog or not, she could see quite clearly what she had to do, and she was determined to do it.

To her surprise, Nella was in the kitchen. She was sitting at the table among a pile of books, her laptop open, deep in concentration.

'Mum.' She looked up, confused. 'What are you doing here? I was going to come in and visit you today.'

'I checked myself out. There's nothing wrong with me, so I decided to come home.'

Jess walked over to the kettle, filled it up from the tap, and switched it on to boil.

Nella jumped up from her chair. 'I'll do that. You sit down.'

She came over and enveloped her mother in a hug. Then she led her to a chair, as if she were an invalid, sat her down, and busied herself with making the tea.

Damn, thought Jess. She was pleased to see her daughter, but she needed to get on and phone Bonetti.

'I thought they were keeping you in for observation. I thought—'

'They were fine about it.' In actual fact, she'd slipped out without anyone noticing she was leaving, but she wasn't going to tell Nella that. The hospital had left a message on the mobile asking for her whereabouts, but she hadn't replied to it.

'Are you hungry? I could make some toast? Scrambled eggs?'

'No, no. I had breakfast ages ago.'

'Biscuit, then?'

Nella brought over the tea and sat down. She looked different, Jess thought. She'd tied her hair back, and her clothes were dark and neat. Her figure was filling out, and she moved around the kitchen quietly and gracefully, like a young woman, rather than a girl.

'Nothing for me, thanks.'

'Are you sure you're OK?' Nella reached over and took her arm, a look of concern on her face.

'Fine, love. Don't worry about me. Honestly, I'm OK. There's absolutely nothing wrong with me.'

'Well, I'm glad you're back.' Nella gave a sigh. 'It's been awful without you and Rose here. I've really missed you both.'

Rose had gone to stay with Bob while Jess was in hospital.

'Hasn't Gareth been here?'

'Not so much. I've been trying to get some work done. I find he distracts me.'

Jess smiled. This was a side of Nella she hadn't seen before. Perhaps her sojourn in hospital had helped her daughter to take responsibility for herself at last.

Nella took a sip of her tea. 'Actually, Mum, there's something I have to tell you. I should have done it before. But I never seemed to find the right moment.'

Jess stopped smiling. Her heart sank. The words *she's pregnant* flashed through her mind.

'What is it?'

Nella hesitated. She looked anxious, ashamed.

There was a silence.

I should have stopped her sleeping with Gareth, Jess thought. It's my fault this has happened. I must have been mad . . . Jess stopped herself. There was nothing to reproach herself for. When Nella had met Gareth, she'd come to her and told her she wanted to sleep with him. It was her first time, she'd said, and she didn't know how to go about it all. They'd discussed the various methods of contraception, looked through some information online, and decided that the Pill, combined with condoms, was the method best suited to her. Nella had gone to the doctor, got herself kitted out, and hadn't mentioned the matter since. As far as Jess knew, it had all been going smoothly. At the same time, Nella was only seventeen. And she was, by nature, a forgetful person. She could have forgotten to take her pills. The condom could have broken. They were too young, perhaps, to . . .

Nella stood up and lifted up her T-shirt. On her navel, near her hip, was a tattoo.

'I'm sorry, Mum. I know you said I couldn't until I was eighteen, but I went off and got it done anyway. I feel really bad about it.'

Jess closed her eyes, sat back in her chair, and gave a sigh of relief. Then she opened them again, and realized Nella was waiting for her to say something.

'Well, you really shouldn't have done that without my permission.'

'I know. I'm sorry.' Nella hung her head. 'I wish I hadn't now. It made me feel so guilty keeping it a secret from you all this time.'

Jess peered at the tattoo. It was an image of an old-fashioned gramophone with a pair of wings on either side.

'What do you think?'

In truth, Jess thought it was rather sweet. But she wasn't going to say so.

'It's not too bad, I suppose. At least it's quite small. And hidden away.' Jess paused. 'But you're not to get any more done.'

'Of course I won't.'

'Well, as long as that's clear.'

Nella nodded, let the shirt drop, and sat down again. She looked relieved, as if a tremendous burden had been lifted from her.

Jess changed the subject.

'So what's been going on while I've been away?' It had only been a few days, but it felt like a lifetime.

'Nothing much. I've been working, mostly. Cooked a few meals with Gareth. Mari came over to see me before she went off on tour with Sexual Perversity, did a bit of watering in the garden. Oh yes, and a friend of yours dropped by yesterday. Someone I hadn't met before.'

'A friend?'

'Elinor, her name was. Elinor Powell. An artist. She seemed really nice.'

Jess froze.

'We talked about painting and stuff. She was interested in my music. Said she'd like to hear it some time.' Nella paused. 'She didn't seem like your usual friends. How do you know her?'

'She's an ex-client.' Jess kept her tone steady, but her heart was thumping in her chest.

'She wanted to know how you were,' Nella went on. 'I told her you were still in hospital. I said you were getting better. I didn't know you were coming out today. Anyway, she sent her love. Actually, she said she was going to pray for you, although she wasn't religious. She was quite intense about it.' Nella looked pensive. 'She was a funny person, but I kind of liked her. I told her I'd let you know she'd called by.'

'Thanks.' Jess tried to speak normally, but her voice came out in a whisper. She was frightened. She wondered how Elinor had found out her address, but she didn't want to worry Nella, so she didn't quiz her about it. Instead, she changed the subject.

'How's the work going?' She picked up one of Nella's books and flicked through it, not taking in a word.

'Fine. It's easy if you put in the hours.'

'I told you it wasn't that hard, didn't I?'

Nella grinned. 'Actually, some of it's quite interesting. This business about social exclusion—'

'Well, you carry on.' Jess interrupted her. 'I've got a few calls to make.'

Nella looked up, surprised.

Jess finished her tea and got up, doing her best to hide the fact that she couldn't wait to get away. 'What are your plans for the day?'

'I'm going in to college this afternoon. I'll come back and make you supper tonight, if you like. Will Rose be coming back from Dad's?'

'Not right away. I think I'll leave her with him for a while longer.' Jess paused. 'And don't worry about cooking for me. I'm not sure when I'll be in.'

'Oh. OK.' Nella was disappointed. 'I'll cook something nice on Sunday, then. For all of us. I'll do a nice roast, celebrate your homecoming.'

'Lovely, darling.' Jess leaned over and squeezed her arm. 'Now, I must be getting on. See you later.'

Jess registered the perplexed look on her daughter's face. She didn't try to explain herself. Instead, she went into her study to make her call.

'DS Bonetti?'

'Dr Mayhew.' Bonetti was polite, but there was an unmistakeably frosty tone to her voice. 'How can I help?'

'I want to ask you a favour.'

'Oh yes?' The frost turned to ice, but Jess persevered.

'I'm going to see Elinor Powell. There's something I need to talk to her about. And I'd like you to accompany me, please. Just in case there's any trouble.'

There was a silence.

'I don't think it'll take up too much of your time.'

'Dr Mayhew.' Jess noticed Bonetti didn't use her Christian name. 'I'm afraid I really can't help you. I'm sorry, but I've been taken off this case.'

'Oh really. Why's that?'

'Because, as you know, acting on your allegations against Ms Powell, I sent a search party down into the mine. It took a great deal of police time, and cost a lot of money. And we found nothing.' Bonetti paused. 'My boss wasn't impressed. In fact, I got into a lot of trouble over it.'

There was a brief silence.

'Well, I'm sorry about that.' Jess was apologetic. 'The twins must have come back and cleared everything away before you got down there. But it doesn't matter now. You see, I've come up with a plan. I think I can nail this once and for all. I'll explain what I've got in mind, if you want—'

'No thanks.' Bonetti was firm. 'I couldn't find the time if I wanted to, anyway. I've got a lot on here at the moment.'

'I see.' Jess was disappointed. She'd expected more support from Bonetti. 'Well, I'll just have to pursue this matter myself then, won't I?'

'Sounds like it.'

Jess was angered by Bonetti's offhand tone, but she didn't rise to the bait.

Silence fell. Bonetti didn't break it.

'OK, then.' Jess took the hint, ending the conversation. 'I'll be back in touch. And this time I'll have the evidence you need, I promise you. Hard evidence.'

'I'll look forward to that.' Bonetti spoke in an even tone. She wasn't being sarcastic, Jess told herself. She was just doing her job.

'Bye, then.'

'Goodbye.'

Jess rang off, her hand shaking as she replaced the receiver. It was partly anger, but also fear. It was foolhardy to set off by herself to look for Elinor, she was aware of that. She knew only too well what the twins were capable of. They'd tried to kill her once, and they would do so again, to protect their secret.

But with Bonetti out of the picture, she had no other choice.

33

That afternoon, Jess drove into Cardiff looking for Elinor. Now that she knew Elinor had been snooping around her house, talking to Nella, she was more determined than ever to find her, and put her plan into action.

When she got to the city, she drove past the museum, into a small crescent, and parked the car. She took a pair of sunglasses from her bag and put them on. They were expensive-looking and rather large – a present from Bob that she'd never worn. She'd also brought a scarf with her, a silk horsey number with snaffles all over it that she'd bought in an airport once, years ago, her judgement clouded after a long delay and a couple of stiff gin and tonics.

She arranged the scarf on her head, knotting it under her chin like the Queen, and inspected herself in the rear-view mirror. She was pleased with the general effect. She looked like a well-heeled, middle-aged Italian tourist, someone with money whose fashion sense was designed to advertise the fact. From the neck up, at least. The rest of her clothes were rather dull in comparison, she had to admit, but smart enough not to give the game away: a neat pair of navy chinos, a beige sweater with a crisp white shirt showing underneath, and a pair of tasselled loafers.

She got out of the car and walked quickly down the street to the Frederick Powell Gallery. It was an elegant red-brick building with a large window at the front, in which a painting was displayed. As Jess got closer, she saw that it was a picture of a young woman, painted in muted tones of grey, cream and black. She stopped in front of it for a moment to take a look.

This must be one of Elinor's, she thought, as she scanned it. The style was very much that of Gwen John. And the subject could have been Isobel or, indeed, Elinor herself. It was the work of a talented painter – the modelling of the head was sensitive, the light falling on the girl's bony shoulder blades skilfully done – but it was somewhat derivative. No wonder, thought Jess, that Elinor hadn't got very far doing this kind of stuff.

She peered round the painting to look inside the gallery.

Immediately, she saw Isobel sitting at a desk to the right of the door. There was no mistaking her pale, translucent bob.

Isobel looked up.

Jess backed away from the window. Her disguise was serviceable enough from a distance, but close scrutiny would reveal her identity.

She walked quickly back to the car, hoping that she hadn't roused Isobel's suspicions. Probably not, she thought; at this time of year, there were lots of foreign tourists in the city, popping in and out of the museum and the galleries around it, wandering around aimlessly with no intention to buy. She'd be unlikely to stand out from the crowd. Even so, she told herself, she'd do well to get a move on, just in case Isobel's suspicions had been alerted.

She got into the car and drove up to Llandaff. Isobel was safely in the gallery, so there was a good chance that Elinor would be at home on her own, perhaps painting in the studio.

The traffic was light, it being mid-afternoon, and when she got to Llandaff Green she found it easy enough to park the car, next to the statue of the gaitered cleric. As she got out, she looked up at him. He was gazing out towards the cathedral, as if surveying all that was happening on the green. He must have seen what happened on the evening of Ursula's murder, Jess thought. If only he could speak, tell her what had happened.

There was no one around as she walked up to the Powells' house; this corner of the city was always quiet, except on Sundays when the services at the cathedral were in progress. All to the good, she thought. The fewer witnesses the better.

When she got to the black iron gate, she looked up at the house. It was neat and tidy, the porch freshly swept, the curtains drawn back from the arched white windows. But there was no sign of life within.

She opened the gate, which creaked a little as it swung on its hinges, and walked up the path, past the rowan tree in the middle of the front garden. She noticed that the lawn had been recently mowed. When she arrived at the front door, she saw that there was a leaflet stuck in the letterbox – junk mail.

She pressed the old-fashioned bell beside the door, and heard it chime through the house. She waited, but no one came. She wondered whether perhaps Elinor was at the back of the house, in the studio, and couldn't hear the bell. And whether, if no one answered, she'd have the nerve to creep down the side entrance and investigate further.

She rang again. Once again, there was no reply, so she pushed the leaflet through the letterbox and bent down to peer through the slit into the hall. There was no sign of life.

She stood up, turned, and walked back down the path, deep in thought. It probably wasn't worth trying to get into the studio. Elinor evidently wasn't at home, otherwise she'd have picked up her letters. Moreover, since the break-in, she might have fixed up an alarm. Better to work out where she was, and track her down.

She made her way back to the car. As she walked past the

cathedral, Nella's words came back to her: *She said she would pray for you.* On an impulse, she walked down the steps, and went inside.

There was no service in progress. There was no one there, not even one of the old people who manned the postcard stall. The place was completely empty.

She walked down the aisle, her footsteps echoing on the flag-stones, and took a pew. She sat down and gazed up at the figure of Christ suspended over the concrete arch, arms outstretched in a gesture of forgiveness.

Strange religion, she thought. At the centre of it, a mutilated man on a cross. A crown of thorns round his head. Whacking great holes in his hands and feet, bits of his skeleton showing through his skin, like a zombie.

She knelt down. As her knees touched the hassock, she felt the sore skin on them where her cuts were still healing.

Father, forgive them, for they know not what they do.

She looked up again. There he was, Jesus Christ, forgiving the people who'd nailed him up there. *Forgive and forget.* As if you could pretend, when someone tried to kill you, that it had never happened. It was stupid to expect that of anyone. In fact, it was wrong.

Vengeance is mine. I will repay.

The Old Testament approach. That was more like it.

Jess bowed her head and closed her eyes, bringing her hands up to her face, as if deep in prayer. But she wasn't praying. She was thinking.

If Elinor had flown the coop, where would she go? To Black Valley, most probably. That was her bolt-hole. Exactly where she'd be camping, it was hard to say. But there were a few places up there she'd be bound to visit. The old haunts of Augustus John and Eric Gill and Jacob Epstein, whose figure of Christ she was kneeling before.

I'll pray for her.

The little church at Capel-y-ffin, she remembered. The one she and Dresler had visited, with the inscription by Eric Gill etched into the window. Elinor had said she liked to go there and sit quietly inside, when she was feeling troubled.

She opened her eyes. Christ looked down at her, arms outstretched. She noticed that his face was impassive, not forgiving at all. Perhaps Epstein had meant to convey that he was standing in judgement. Perhaps she'd got it wrong, after all.

It was worth a try, she thought. She'd go to Capel-y-ffin, and wait there for Elinor, however long it took. Sooner or later, she was bound to come by.

And then Elinor would have to start praying for herself.

It was getting dark as Jess drove into Capel-y-ffin. She parked the car by the side of the road, got out, and made her way to the tiny chapel that gave the hamlet its name. She stopped beside the church gate, noting from the wooden board next to it that services were still held there. Then she peered through the shadows at the church itself.

It was a tiny whitewashed stone building with a wonky wooden turret at one end of the roof. Jess remembered Dresler reading out a quote about it, the day they'd toured around the valley in the car. The Victorian diarist Francis Kilvert had noted that it squatted 'like a stout grey owl among its seven great yews'. It was an apt description; the tilt of the turret gave it a homely, comical air, yet there was also something a little sinister about the way it glimmered in the dusk, shaded by the ancient yews, as if watching and waiting, in the silence, for night to descend.

She walked up the path. As she neared the porch, she heard music. Someone inside was playing the organ.

She wondered for a moment whether to turn around and come back later. Then she decided to go in. Whoever it was might be able to tell her about the people who came and went here. And throw some light on Elinor's movements, perhaps.

She walked into the porch and lifted the latch on the heavy wooden door. As she did, a blast of music hit her ears, cascades of Bach tumbling out of the church like water out of a floodgate.

She looked around. There was an old organ at the back of the chapel, jammed up against the wall. The pipes in front of it were tall, obscuring the person who was playing it. The rest of the church was very simple. There were a few rickety pews lined up in front of the altar, a tiny table covered in a white cloth. A staircase led up to a wooden gallery, only wide enough to accommodate one row of seats. The place smelled musty and damp.

She walked down the aisle, sat in a pew, and waited. In another mood, she would have relaxed into this wholly unexpected pleasure: hearing this bright, nimble music played with such vigour, in a pretty little church in the Black Valley, with the night coming down.

Not now, though.

She looked up at the arched window above the altar. There was an inscription engraved into the glass: *I will lift up mine eyes unto the hills, from whence cometh my help*. The lettering was beautiful, unmistakeably Gill's handiwork. Behind it, in the fading light, she could see the great purple mass of the mountain, rising up from the valley to the sky.

She gazed up at it and couldn't help letting out a sigh. She could see why Elinor liked this place. There was something magical about it, a kind of modesty that you didn't often see in a British church. More like a Greek chapel, Mediterranean . . .

The Bach piece ended. There was a pause, and another began. A different one, with more bass chords, more pomp and circumstance. She waited patiently through it. And then she heard the player get up.

She got up, too, and stood in the aisle, turning towards the organ. A man appeared from behind it, dressed in a full-length black Anglican cassock, a dog collar at his neck. By his side was an enormous black poodle, who'd evidently been sitting with him while he played.

'That was very nice.' She greeted him with a smile.

'Thank you.' The man didn't seem surprised to see her there. 'Just keeping my hand in. The organ needs to be played from time to time.'

The dog bounded through the open door of the church, and out into the churchyard.

'So you still have services here, do you?'

'Evensong once every two weeks. That's all I can manage at the moment, I'm afraid.'

Jess nodded. 'D'you get much of a congregation?'

'Oh yes.' The cleric looked over her head, out at the church-yard, rather distractedly.

'I suppose you know them all.'

'Hmm.' He wasn't listening. Probably wondering where his dog had got to.

'I'm looking for a friend, actually.' Jess tried to sound casual. 'I believe she comes here sometimes.' She paused. 'Her name's Elinor Powell.'

'Elinor? Of course. I know all the Powells. Ursula was a dear friend, at one time. Such a terrible loss.' He paused. 'I saw Elinor here yesterday, as it happens. She often drops by when she's up in the valley. She'll probably be in later on.'

'Really? You mean, you keep it open all the time?'

'Oh yes. We allow people to come and go as they please. We've never had any trouble.' He turned to look at her. 'I believe it's because this is a very special place.'

'It is.'

'You see . . .' He looked away again, up at the window. 'In this place, the skin between this world and the next is very thin.'

There was a silence. Jess didn't break it, and neither did he.

The dog started to bark, and the priest hurried out after it without saying goodbye, his black skirts flying in the breeze.

Jess waited until he'd gone, and then she climbed behind the organ and sat down. She wasn't visible from this position, she knew. If Elinor came in to pray, she wouldn't be able to see her. She could sit there and observe her, undisturbed.

It was just a question of waiting.

34

Jess was getting cold. The wooden bench she was sitting on was hard and uncomfortable. There were hymn books piled on top of the organ in front of her, and she could see how the damp had rotted and curled their spines. She could feel the damp seeping into her bones, too.

She shifted her position, rubbing her hands together. It was useless, she thought. Elinor wasn't coming. The chances of her dropping in the same night she herself happened to be there were slim. Perhaps she'd already come by, earlier that evening. Perhaps she'd gone back to Cardiff. Perhaps . . .

The wooden door to the church creaked open. Jess caught her breath. From the position she was sitting in, she couldn't see who had entered. That would only become clear once he or she walked down the aisle to the altar.

She heard the sound of footsteps on the flagstones. The steps were soft, those of a person light on their feet. She held her breath, though there was no need to do so.

Elinor's familiar figure came into view. She was wearing her old navy blue mac. Above it, her hair shone pale and translucent in the gloomy light of the chapel.

She watched as Elinor went up to the step in front of the

altar and kneeled down on it. She bowed her head and began to mumble. Jess strained to hear what she was saying, but she couldn't make out a word.

The whispering rose and fell, swelled and slowed. Evidently, she was passionate in her prayers, whatever they were about. As she prayed, Jess felt a crescendo of emotion rise in her, too. But it was emotion of a different kind. She was experiencing an intense urge to creep down the aisle behind Elinor, grasp her round the neck, and throttle her. Squeeze the breath out of her, until she lay lifeless on the flagstone floor.

Jess glanced around her. Beside the organ, leaning against the wall, she saw a long iron candlesnuffer. That would do it, too, she thought. A sharp blow on the head while she was kneeling there – the temple was supposed to be a good place, wasn't it? A good beating once she was down, just to make sure. With the snuffer, there wouldn't be a struggle. She could catch Elinor by surprise and be sure of doing a proper job of it.

Elinor went on mumbling.

It would be quicker too, Jess thought. Although, of course, strangling her with her bare hands would be altogether more satisfying.

She shivered. She was shocked at herself. She'd never in her life before fantasized about killing someone. She wondered whether it was sheer anger and the desire for revenge that was making her feel this way, or whether the concussion had changed her personality. She'd had a few clients like that, people who'd been trundling through their lives quite happily, until a blow to the head had changed everything: cheerful people who'd become morose, good-natured souls who'd become raging bulls, conventional types who'd morphed into flamboyant extroverts . . . Come to think of it, Augustus John, Elinor's putative grandfather, was reputed to be one of those . . .

That was another thing. Her mind seemed to wander, constantly, these days. It sometimes felt as if there was a clot in there, a damp patch shuffling about.

She checked herself. Whatever was wrong with her mind, if her plan was to work, she'd have to keep focussed, keep calm. She needed to think straight. However murderous she might feel towards Elinor, she needed to control herself.

Elinor continued to pray, head bowed, whispering. Then she came to the end of her prayer and raised her head, gazing out through the arched window above the altar.

I will lift up mine eyes unto the hills, from whence cometh my help.

No help from up there, thought Jess. Sorry about that. Not tonight.

'Elinor.' She stood up, and said the name loudly and clearly, her voice breaking the silence.

Elinor turned her head, a look of terror on her face.

'Who's that?'

Jess came out from behind the organ.

'Jess.' There was relief in Elinor's voice, but it was mixed with fear. 'You scared me. What are you doing here?'

'I've been looking for you.' Jess spoke in a low, gentle tone.

Elinor stayed on her knees as Jess walked down the aisle towards her, crouching like a cornered animal.

'Don't worry.' Jess kept her tone calm. 'I'm not angry with you. I just wanted to talk.'

Elinor glanced towards the door.

'I'm not going to harm you,' Jess came to a halt, standing in front of Elinor. 'I know you're innocent. It was Isobel, not you, who left me in the mine, wasn't it? You tried to protect me.'

Elinor got up off her knees. They were face to face now, Elinor's back to the altar.

'Let's sit down for a minute, shall we?' Jess extended her hand.

There was a moment's silence. Jess wondered whether Elinor would make a run for it, and if she did, whether she'd be able to stop her. But Elinor didn't move. Instead, she hung her head, ashamed to look her in the eye.

'Come. Sit down.' Jess led her to the front pew by the altar, and they sat down side by side.

Elinor began to cry, letting her hair fall over her face so that it was hidden from view.

Jess felt her hands grow warm, the blood rushing to the fingertips. I could do it now, she thought. While she's weak and defenceless.

She dismissed the thought, and instead, fished in her pocket for a tissue. Her long years of training had taught her always to have one handy. She was beginning to wonder if that was the only thing she'd ever learned.

She handed the tissue to Elinor and patted her knee.

Elinor blew her nose, still hiding her face. 'I'm sorry, Jess. I should have stopped Isobel. I wanted to come back for you, but Isobel wouldn't let me.' She paused. 'Can you ever forgive me?'

'Of course I can. It wasn't your fault, was it?'

Elinor looked up, her blue eyes glittering in the fading light.

'No, it wasn't.' She paused. 'Are you hurt? You were in hospital, weren't you?'

'A bump on the head, that's all. A few cuts and bruises. I'm fine now.'

'Thank God.' Elinor began to twist the tissue in her fingers.

'Listen.' Jess lowered her voice. 'I'm not going to tell anyone you're Hefin Morris. I'll keep your secret for you. You don't need to worry about that.'

'Well, I don't know what's going to happen about that.' Elinor gave a sigh. 'I'm having trouble painting now. Isobel's furious. All this effort she's gone to, and then I let her down. That's why I've come up here. To clear my mind.'

'I can help you to paint again.' Jess took her hand. 'I can help you sort all of this out. Come back to therapy.'

Elinor looked wary. 'You mean, you're not angry with me?'

Jess shook her head. 'I was. But not now. Now I realize you're just confused. Confused, and in thrall to Isobel. I can help you break free of her.' She paused. 'But this time, you must be honest with me. You must tell me everything. From the start.'

Elinor turned her head away. 'I can't do that. I've done some terrible things, you see. Things I can never tell anyone.'

Jessica leaned over and took her hand. 'It doesn't matter what you've done. I'm not here to judge you. I'm here to help you.'

'But if I told you, you'd have to report me.'

Jess shook her head. 'No. I'm a psychotherapist. Anything you say to me is in complete confidence. It's part of my job.' She paused. 'People tell me their secrets all the time. I never divulge them.'

'But if it was something against the law?'

'Happens all the time.'

'So you wouldn't go to the police?' Elinor withdrew her hand.

'Not in a million years.'

There was a long silence. They both looked up out of the window and watched the mountain slowly fade from view in the evening light. When it had gone, Elinor spoke.

'All right, then.'

Jess turned to her and saw that she was smiling. She smiled back.

'But there's just one thing.' Jess was serious once more. 'You mustn't breathe a word of this to Isobel. She mustn't know.'

Elinor nodded assent, her eyes round like a child's.

'It's a secret between the two of us.'

'So.' Elinor was smiling at her. 'When can we start?'

Jessica thought back to the first time Elinor had asked her that question. So much had happened since then. So much that had shaken her faith, not only in her client, but in herself, too.

'Any time you like. Tomorrow, if that suits.' Jess tried not to sound too eager. 'I can see you in my consulting rooms at eleven o'clock. Can you get down to Cardiff by then?'

'I've got the car. I'll drive down tonight.'

'Fine.'

Jess got up to go. Elinor got up with her. For a moment, they stood facing one another in front of the altar.

'Are you coming, then?' Jess hoped she could escort Elinor to her car. She wanted to make sure she didn't change her mind.

'I think I'll stay here for a bit longer. I like being on my own in here.'

Jess felt a pang of fear run through her. What if Elinor had something else up her sleeve? What if she'd just been playing along? However, she didn't try to persuade her to leave. She didn't want to arouse her suspicions.

'See you tomorrow, then.' On an impulse, Elinor leaned forward and gave her a hug.

Jess let herself be drawn in, willing herself not to stiffen as Elinor squeezed her tightly in her arms, laying her head affectionately on her chest for a moment.

'Till tomorrow, then.' She forced herself to be gentle. 'Take care.'

She extricated herself from Elinor's embrace and walked down the aisle towards the door. When she got there, she stopped for a moment and turned to look back. Elinor was kneeling in front of the altar once more, her head bowed in prayer.

Jess let herself out of the church, lifting the heavy iron latch of the door and shutting it quietly behind her.

Her plan was working. As far as she could see, Elinor didn't suspect a thing. So far, so good.

35

Jess was wandering in the mine. She'd been in there for a long time, but her eyes hadn't adjusted to the dark. She was feeling her way along, but the tunnel was getting narrower, so that she had to bend her knees and incline her head to move forward. The walls were closing in tight around her. The darkness seemed to grasp her round the throat, choking her so that she couldn't breathe.

She raised her hand and felt a sharp point of rock above her head. She kneeled on the ground and shuffled forward on her knees.

Stalactites cling to the ceiling. Stalagmites grow from the ground.

Someone was talking to her. She looked down and saw a tiny furry animal the size of a mouse. It had pointed ears, beady eyes, and a squashed-in nose the shape of a horseshoe.

A bat is talking to me. That means I'm dreaming, she thought.

She shuffled on, leaving the bat behind. The tunnel became smaller and smaller until it was just a hole in a wall of rock. She put her head through the hole, hunched her shoulders and squeezed them in, then wriggled her hips this way and that, until her body was through it.

On the other side of the hole, the tunnel opened into a cave, lit by a single shaft of sunlight beaming through a crack in the rock above. Under the shaft was an altar. Sitting on the altar was Nella. She was naked, and reading a book. The light was falling on her shoulders. A few feet away was Elinor, standing by an easel. She was painting Nella.

Jess stood up and dusted herself off. Neither of them noticed her.

She felt an itching in her hands. They grew hot, the blood rushing to her fingertips.

She walked forward, clenching and unclenching her fists. When she reached Elinor, she put her hands around her neck.

Elinor looked surprised, but she didn't resist.

Jess placed her thumbs on Elinor's throat. Her fingers touched round the back, at the nape of her neck. The neck was just the right size for her hands. She could feel the arteries jumping under her fingertips. Big, soft carotid arteries. She began to squeeze.

A strength came into her hands she didn't know she possessed. She squeezed harder. Elinor began to choke. She struggled, trying to pull Jess's hands away. But Jess tightened her grip. Elinor reached up and scratched at her face, making her cry out in pain, but she still wouldn't let go.

She heard Nella's voice. 'Mum! Stop!'

She looked up, remembering Nella was there, sitting on the altar.

There was an explosion, and a shower of rocks began to fall from the hole in the rock above Nella's head, where the shaft of light came through. Jess tried to scream at her to get out of the way, but her voice wouldn't come through.

The rocks tumbled down. She screamed again.

Look out, Nella, look out!

This time, her voice came out loud and clear.

She woke up. She was lying in bed.

Nella was leaning over her, shaking her by the shoulders. 'Mum, stop. Stop.'

Jess blinked. 'What's going on?'

'You were having a nightmare. You were screaming my name.'

Nella was half dressed, her hair on end, wearing a T-shirt of Gareth's. She looked frightened, like a little girl.

Jess sat up in bed. She glanced at the clock. It was half past four in the morning.

'It's just the after-effects of the concussion, I think.' Jess tried to sound calm, but she heard her voice shake. 'I keep having nightmares.' She reached forward and squeezed Nella's hand. 'Thanks for coming in, but it's nothing, darling. Go back to bed. I'm sorry I woke you.'

Nella didn't budge. 'Are you sure you're OK? Shall I get you a glass of water or something?'

'I'm fine. Now, come on, we've both got a busy day tomorrow, so let's go back to sleep, shall we?'

Nella looked dubious. 'Well, if you're sure you're all right.' She leaned down and kissed Jess on the cheek. 'Call me if you need anything.'

She went out of the room, looking worried.

Damn, thought Jess. If there was one thing she hated, it was having her children worry about her. She was the parent; it ought always to be the other way round. She was glad that Rose was with her father, just for the time being, until she got this situation with Elinor out of the way.

She lay back down again, and closed her eyes. She needed to sleep, but her heart was still thumping. She began to worry. What if she was too tired to carry out the plan? What if it didn't work? What if she'd forgotten something? What if . . .

No more 'what ifs', she told herself. Half past four in the morning was no time to think about anything. That was what she always advised her clients.

She went over to the window, opened it wide, and got back into bed. The sound of the trees outside, rustling in the wind, soothed her.

There was nothing wrong with the plan, she told herself. The plan was fine. It was just a question of keeping calm and putting it into operation.

She began to practise the mindfulness technique. Concentrate on the here and now.

She focussed her attention on the whispering trees. She heard the patter of rain on the leaves. Trees, rain, leaves. It wasn't that complicated. Life was simple, really.

Or it would be again, after tomorrow.

At seven o'clock the next morning, Jess woke up. She switched off her alarm and looked out of the window. The rain had dried, and the sun had come out. It was sparkling on the leaves, and the sky was a clear blue, without a cloud in sight. It was going to be a beautiful day.

She got up, showered, and dressed, picking out her clothes with care: a sleeveless shirt dress – sober, yet summery – and flat shoes. She applied her make-up: sunscreen, foundation, and just a sliver of lipstick. She checked that her mobile was fully charged and put it in her handbag, a tan leather satchel-type affair. Then she was ready to go.

She went downstairs to the kitchen and was surprised to find Nella there. She was in her dressing gown, eating a bowl of cornflakes and gazing into her laptop.

'You're up early.'

Nella looked up as she came in. 'I thought I'd make you breakfast before you went to work.'

'Oh. That was kind of you.' Jess paused. 'I'm not actually very hungry today, though. You could make me a cup of tea if you like.'

Nella frowned, got up, went over to the kettle, and put it on.

'But you always have breakfast, Mum.' She busied herself with making the tea.

'I know. I'm just a bit tense at the moment. I've got a rather difficult client to see this morning.'

'I thought you weren't supposed to be back at work yet.'

'I'm not. This is just a one-off session.' Jess paused. 'As a favour.'

Nella brought over a cup of tea and handed it to her. Jess didn't sit down to drink it.

'Well, I don't think you should be doing anybody any favours. You should be staying at home looking after yourself.' There was a patient yet frustrated tone to Nella's voice that reminded Jess of herself. 'This screaming in the night. What's all that about?'

'I told you. Sometimes you have nightmares when you get a bump on the head. It's nothing. It'll go soon.'

Nella sighed. 'Well, I hope so.' She nodded at Jess's cup. 'Drink your tea. It'll get cold.'

Jess sipped her tea obediently.

Silence fell.

'Right.' Jess put the cup down, still half full, on the counter. 'I'm going to have to get going, Nella. I've got a bit of paper-work to catch up on before this client gets in.'

Nella looked perplexed. 'But it's still so early. I thought we could go in together. I was hoping you could drop me off.'

'You'll have to take the bus.' Jess came over and kissed her on the cheek. 'Have a good day. I'll see you later.'

'What time?'

Jess shrugged.

'And when is Rose coming back?'

'Soon. This evening. Probably. I don't know.'

'What on earth is the matter with you, Mum?' Nella was half angry, half frustrated. 'Just tell me what's going on.'

'Nothing's going on.' Jess picked up her bag, ready to go. 'I've got a lot on my mind at the moment, that's all. I really can't discuss it right now.'

She paused, realizing she'd just spoken Nella's usual lines.

Nella sighed. 'Well, just take care, that's all. Don't overdo it. I'll be back from college at six, and I'll hope to see you then.'

'Fine. Whatever.'

Jess gave her a quick wave, walked out into the hall, grabbed a jacket, and slung it over her bag. Then she left, without a backward glance.

36

It was good to be back, Jess thought, as she let herself into her consulting rooms. On the way in, she'd had a brief conversation with Branwen, the receptionist, who'd been surprised to see her since she was supposed to be off sick. She'd explained that she'd arranged an emergency session with a client, Elinor Powell, just for today, and told Branwen to show her up when she arrived. Branwen began to ask after her health. Jess responded politely to her enquiries, but cut her off as soon as she could, and went upstairs.

She went over to her desk and switched on her computer. She scrolled through a list of clients, checking that Branwen had contacted each one of them to cancel for that week. She answered a few emails and sorted through some post, throwing the junk mail in the bin. Then she opened a drawer in her desk and took out a Dictaphone that she'd bought some while ago, but had hardly used.

She tested it, checking the batteries, speaking into it, and playing it back. When she was satisfied that it was working properly, she went over to the mantelpiece, placed it inside a small pot, and switched it on. The battery life was seventy-two hours – she'd checked when she'd bought it. That should be plenty, she thought.

She went back to her desk, picked up her handbag, took out her mobile phone, and called DS Lauren Bonetti.

Bonetti picked up immediately, as was her wont.

'Hello. It's Jessica Mayhew here.'

'Dr Mayhew. How can I help you?' Bonetti's tone was stiff.

'At a quarter to eleven, I'm going to phone you on this number. I want you to pick up the phone, leave it on, and listen carefully. OK?'

'Can you tell me what this is all about, please?'

'You'll find out. But please make sure you do this. It's extremely important.' There was a sharpness in Jess's tone that was quite uncharacteristic.

Bonetti sighed. 'OK. As it happens, I'm in the office this morning. But if I get called away—'

'Just follow my instructions, please.' Jess paused. 'Goodbye.'

She put the phone down.

She got up from her desk and walked around the room, tidying as she went. The cleaners had been in, so there wasn't much to do. She adjusted the cushions on the couch and on the armchairs, made sure that the pictures on the walls were straight, pulled back the curtains so that they draped nicely either side of the bay window. She opened the window just a crack, so that a slight breeze wafted in. Then she sat down in one of the armchairs and looked up at the white-on-white relief on the wall. The circle was sitting nicely in the squares. She was pleased to see that it wasn't moving even slightly.

At a quarter to eleven, she got up, went over to her desk, switched off her computer, picked up her bag, and took out her mobile phone. She called Bonetti's number, checked that she'd got through, and laid the phone on her desk, under the screen, out of sight.

Then she went back to the armchair and waited.

At eleven o'clock there was no knock at the door.

She gazed up at the relief. The circle didn't move.

She glanced at the clock on the coffee table. She could hear it ticking in the silence.

A minute went by.

Then another.

At 11.02, the knock came.

She got up and opened the door. Elinor was standing there, an eager look on her face.

'Come in.' Jess gave her an encouraging smile.

She watched as Elinor went over to the couch. She was wearing her usual scruffy black clothes, but her hair was freshly washed and shining in the sunlight.

Elinor lay down on the couch, settling her head on the cushion. Jess sat down on the armchair behind her, out of her line of sight.

There was a silence.

'I don't know where to start, really.' Elinor gave a deep sigh. 'It's all such a mess.'

'Why not try the beginning?' Jess's voice was gentle.

'OK.'

Another silence. Jess could feel her heart thumping in her chest but she tried to ignore it.

'Right.' Elinor seemed to make a decision. 'Well, I suppose I've got to tell you. I mean, as you said, this is all in confidence, isn't it?'

'Absolutely.'

'Whatever I tell you?'

'Yes.'

'Even if it's . . . a criminal offence?'

'Elinor, I'm your therapist. You know you can tell me anything.'

'Well, then.' Elinor took a deep breath, then let it out. 'It was me who killed Ursula.'

Jess thought of the Dictaphone on the mantelpiece, and the phone on the desk. She hoped to God they were both working. And that Bonetti was receiving the message loud and clear.

'It was her fault. She came round to my studio while I was out, started rooting around, and found a phial of ochre that I'd been using. She put two and two together and realized it was me doing the Hefin Morris paintings. She'd obviously suspected something all along.' Elinor paused. 'When I came home and found her there, she started waving the phial about and threatening to tell everyone what was going on. She kept saying people need to know the truth, but I knew it wasn't that. She was just jealous of my talent, you see.' A bitter note crept into Elinor's voice. 'I tried to talk her out of spilling the beans, but she wasn't having any of it. She was determined to go ahead. We started to argue, and then I decided I'd had enough. So I picked up a canvas stretcher bar, a great big metal thing, and hit her with it.'

There was a long silence.

'Go on.'

'It only took one blow. She went down.' Elinor gave a smile, almost a smirk. 'I couldn't believe how easy it was, actually. There was hardly any blood. Just a big bruise on the side of her head.' She paused. 'I didn't feel sorry, not at all. I felt relieved. I hated her, and I was glad she was dead.'

'Well, that's understandable.' Jess spoke in a low voice, hoping her words wouldn't be audible except to Elinor. 'I suppose you must have felt she betrayed you.'

Elinor nodded.

'What happened next?'

'Well, while I was there with her, wondering what to do, Blake appeared. He had a key to the place, too; just let himself in whenever he felt like it. He'd come to talk to me about a new painting I was working on. You see, he and I were in on the Hefin Morris project together. In fact, it had been his idea. It was a secret between the two of us. Nobody else knew about it. Not even Isobel.'

Elinor smiled. Once again, the smile was almost a smirk.

'Anyway, of course, when he saw the body, he panicked. Told me to call the police, say it was an accident. But I had a better idea. I told him to remove the Gwen John painting that was hanging on the wall, take it home, and hide it. We'd pretend Ursula had been killed in a robbery at the studio. I'd clean off the stretcher bar and use it for a canvas, so there wouldn't be a murder weapon.' She paused. 'Blake went off and did what I told him. It all went to plan. But later on, he began to crack. He couldn't cope with the guilt, he said. That was where it started to go wrong.'

'Go wrong?' Jess echoed Elinor's words, just to let her know she was following them.

'I don't know if I should be telling you this.' Elinor shifted her head on the cushion.

'You can trust me, Elinor. I've told you that. Carry on.'

'It just makes me so sound horrible, though. You won't like me any more if I tell you.'

Elinor was truly insane, thought Jess. She was talking as if she'd stolen a bag of sweets, not murdered her own mother.

'I'm not here to judge you. This is a safe space.' Once again, Jess lowered her voice as she spoke, ashamed of trotting out the clichés.

'OK. Well, that was when I realized Blake would have to go. He was running round behaving like an idiot. Kept coming to see me, telling me I had to go to the police and confess. Threatening to tell Isobel. He was frightened that I'd tell you everything, so he'd be incriminated, as an accomplice. That's why he broke into your office and looked through your file on me. He didn't find anything, except the time of my appointment, so he got Isobel to call you to see if she could find out more.'

'So Isobel was in on all this?'

'Not at that stage, no. She just did what he told her. You see, the policewoman was closing in on him – she was convinced he was involved with Ursula's death.' Elinor sighed. 'I suppose I tried to take advantage of the situation. Make him look guilty, so they wouldn't come after me. I started telling people I suspected him. Including you.'

There was a brief silence.

'I'm sorry about that, Jess. I shouldn't have done that. Lied to you. I feel bad about that.'

'I understand.'

'You see, I was disappointed in him,' she went on. 'It was just weakness on his part. He couldn't cope with the situation. And of course, I realized that if he cracked, I'd be done for. So I decided something had to be done.'

'And what was that?'

'When he came to find me at the tower, I ran up to the top.'

Elinor came to a halt. Keep it rolling, Jess thought. Nearly there.

'He came after me. We were arguing. He was telling me that if I didn't confess, he would. He was waving his arms about, shouting at me, like Ursula had. I was scared. I thought he was going to push me over the edge. So I got in first. I pushed him. Gave him a shove, and he went over.'

Good, thought Jess. Got that in the bag.

'That wasn't hard, either.' Elinor paused. 'It's funny, it's actually quite easy killing people. I always thought it would be difficult.'

I'm doing the right thing here, thought Jess. Even if it doesn't feel like it.

'After that, I ran off, of course. I was in a bit of a state, to be honest. I liked Blake, I didn't want to kill him. But, you see,

I had to.' She put her hand up to forehead, rubbing her eyes. 'It was a mistake, really. I shouldn't have done that.'

Once again, there was a silence. Jess knew better than to break it.

'I'd made a complete mess of things,' she went on, 'so I called Isobel and she came and got me. I called you too, of course, but Isobel got there first. And once we got home I told her everything. She was appalled, of course, and absolutely furious with me. But she didn't turn me in. She couldn't, you see.'

'Couldn't?'

'No. That's the kind of relationship we have. We stick together, whatever happens.' Elinor shrugged. 'She covered for me. And she's very practical, you see, which I'm not. She came up with a good plan. She took the painting to the police, said she'd found it in the house, that Blake had killed Ursula and committed suicide. The police were happy with the story. And for a while, it looked as if everything would be OK. Isobel came to live with me. I was thrilled that she was back. But, of course, it didn't work. She was heartbroken about Blake. Couldn't forgive me. I don't think she ever will.'

For the first time, there was genuine remorse in Elinor's voice.

'We decided to keep the Morris project going,' she went on, after a pause. 'It seemed a shame to let it drop. So Isobel got in touch with Jacob Dresler and told him the truth.'

Jess put her hand up to her mouth in horror. Surely Dresler hadn't . . .

'Only about me painting as Morris,' Elinor continued. 'Not about the other stuff, of course.'

Jess took her hand away.

'He was happy to front up the operation. He would have looked a bit of a fool if the truth had come out, after all.'

'I suppose so.'

'But then he mentioned to Isobel that you were getting suspicious about the Morris paintings. He said you thought Isobel was behind them. I was upset about that.' Elinor frowned. 'Isobel could never have done them. She just hasn't got the technique.'

'Well, I don't know much about painting, you see.'

'I should have realized that.' Once again, Elinor seemed remorseful. 'But anyway, that's why I asked you to come down to the mine and see my work. I wanted to show you it was me who was doing the Morris paintings. And I wanted to show you that the claustrophobia had lifted, that I was painting in the mine again.' She paused. 'Then Isobel came into the mine while we were there. I'd forgotten that she was coming in that day, to set up some stuff for the exhibition.' Elinor frowned. 'She got scared, I suppose, thought you would tell everyone what you'd seen, and the whole project would be ruined. That's why she maced you and left you there.'

Jess wondered whether Bonetti was listening, and, if she was, whether she'd decided to act.

'Isobel made me run off with her,' Elinor continued. 'I told her we could trust you, that you were my therapist, and that everything you witnessed was confidential.' She paused. 'She didn't believe me. She thought you'd find out about what had happened to Ursula and Blake and report us to the police. But I told her she was wrong.'

Jess remained silent.

'Later on, I persuaded her that we should come back and look for you.'

Oh yes, thought Jess. I'm sure you did.

'You weren't there so we assumed you'd got out. I was so relieved about that, Jess.' She hesitated, perhaps sensing Jess's disbelief. 'So we just got on and cleared everything away. That's why the police couldn't find anything.'

Elinor came to a halt. Once again, Jess waited for her to go on. Eventually, she did.

'I felt really bad about it all. That's why I came round to your house to see you. To tell you I was sorry. I met your daughter. She told me you were in hospital. She was so nice. She reminded me so much of you.'

'She liked you, too.'

There was a long silence. Where are you, Bonetti? Jess thought. Get down here, for God's sake.

Elinor gazed out of the window, a dreamy look on her face.

'You've got another daughter, too, haven't you?'

'That's right.'

'Rose.'

'Yes. Rose.'

'How old is she?'

'Eleven. Coming up to twelve.'

'I'd like to meet her, too.'

As she spoke, the door to the consulting room opened.

Elinor sat up on the couch, as if a bolt of electricity had gone through her, and swivelled round towards the door.

Lauren Bonetti marched into the room. Behind her were two uniformed male police officers.

Elinor stared at Jess, a look of incomprehension on her face. 'What's going on? Tell them to go away.'

One of the policemen stepped forward.

Bonetti began to speak. 'Elinor Powell, you are under arrest for the murders of Ursula Powell and Blake Thomas.'

Elinor looked stunned. She jumped up off the couch and tried to dodge round the policeman. He moved towards her and grasped her round the shoulders, holding her as she struggled. The other policeman came forward and handcuffed her.

'You do not have to say anything.' Bonetti was still talking. 'But it may harm your defence if you do not mention, when questioned, something which you later rely on in court . . .'

340

Elinor wasn't listening. Instead, she'd fixed her gaze on Jess. There were tears in her eyes.

'How could you?'

Jess looked away.

'You lied to me. I trusted you. You told me I could tell you anything.'

The policeman pushed Elinor towards the door.

'You said . . .'

The policeman gripped Elinor's body more firmly, leading her away.

'Call yourself a therapist?' Elinor began to shout, her voice shaking with rage. 'You lured me in here. You laid me down on that couch. You got me to talk. And then you turned me in!'

They led Elinor through the door. In the corridor, she began to kick and scream.

'You bitch! You fucking liar!'

The screams echoed down the hallway.

'Don't listen.' Bonetti went over and closed the door. Elinor's muffled screams were still audible as she was led down the staircase.

Bonetti came up and stood beside Jess. 'Look, you don't have anything to reproach yourself for. You did the right thing.'

Jess didn't respond.

'I'm going to have to go now. But I'll be in touch as soon as I can.' She paused.

'Try to put this out of your mind. Get some rest.'

Bonetti reached forward and laid a hand on her arm. Jess shrugged it off and walked over to the window, her back to the policewoman.

She heard Bonetti walk away, opening and closing the door to let herself out. She didn't turn round.

She looked out of the window, her mind a blank. After a

while, she saw Elinor in the street below. She'd stopped screaming. She wasn't struggling. There was an officer either side of her. Bonetti had caught up with them, and was walking behind her.

Some words that Jess remembered ran through her head.

Being trustworthy is regarded as fundamental to understanding and resolving ethical issues. Practitioners who adopt this principle act in accordance with the trust placed in them; regard confidentiality as an obligation arising from the client's trust; restrict any disclosure of confidential information about clients . . .

The Ethical Framework for Good Practice in Counselling and Psychotherapy. She'd learned it off by heart.

As Elinor got into the police car, she looked up for a moment at the window where Jess was standing. Jess put her hand up in a gesture of farewell. Elinor ignored the gesture, and continued to stare up at her, as if in a trance, until the policeman pushed her into the car.

Both the policemen got into the front of the car, one in the driving seat, one in the passenger seat. Bonetti got into the back, next to Elinor. Jess watched as the car pulled out into the road and drove away.

She stood there for a long time. The tree outside the window began to rustle in the wind, its branches casting a play of light over the walls of the room.

She turned and walked away from the window. She went over to the hat stand, picked up her bag, and slung her jacket over it. Just before she left, she looked around her.

She didn't want to be here in her consulting rooms any more. She didn't want to see the couch by the window, or the chair positioned behind it, or the two armchairs by the fireplace, either side of the low coffee table. Or the white relief on the wall, the circle sitting quietly among the squares, or the small pot on the mantelpiece. Or her desk, or her books, or her papers.

Or any of it, ever again.

All she wanted was to be outside, walking in the sun, with her daughters.